JACK SIMMONDS

Alfie Brown: The Boy With Purple Eyes

(Who Discovered He Could Do Magic)

Contents

Prologue

They say we go through our lives only using 10% of our brain. Most often we tread the same streets, go to the same school, same shops, with the same friends, in the same town, city or country, our whole lives and rarely venture further. I mean, have you ever been down that alley, near the back of those houses the other side of town? No. Exactly.

You could say we barely *see* more than 1% of the world throughout our lifetimes. This isn't meant to depress you, merely to make a point; how would you know if those *strange things* you were always told were nonsense, did actually exist? How would you know that other lands, made unseeable to you, with people living in them existed? How would you know that they can do things that you would call impossible?

You wouldn't.

So please, no arguments about this.

There are things in this world you will never know about, things that if you found out would make you wish you had never known, and things that will excite and scare you silly in equal measure.

Let me cut to the chase and tell you this… *magick* is real. It exists like the air you breath, like the blood than runs through your veins, like the inevitability of death. And now, let me excite you… I can do magick and so can you!

We spell magick with a K at the end to differentiate it from modern trickery magic, the useless entertainment and foolery kind.

I am talking about *real* magick.

If you can accept this, then I suppose your next thought is: 'This is all as well, but theres no magick around here. It's probably far away from here hidden in some hidden, special lands...' — or so your arguments will go.

Not so.

It can and does occur in the most ordinary of places of which I am about to share with you. I will tell you this story as best as my memory will allow and I hope you can keep an open mind. You don't have to believe me, all I ask is that you listen and enjoy the story...

The night air was cool and dry. Like it would always be in a perfect world. There was an odd but beautiful purple hue across the underlay of fluffy clouds above and a tuft of tall grass on the curbside was tussled by the wind. The country road, surrounded by two fields of mud recently turned over, led directly on to a small town. There was no sign of life, especially not at this time of night.

And then, something amazing happened.

In a spot between the lamppost and a tall oak the air seemed to flicker like a bad television signal. There was a crackle of noise and light like spitting electricity before shapes started to whirl amongst the flicker. All of a sudden, without batting an eyelid, the form of a full grown man, six feet tall or more, came spiralling out of the crackling flicker. For a moment, he stood totally still. This was Nikolas Wiseman, a most respected and honoured Wizard. Yes, you heard me correctly, a real Wizard. Being a person of magick, he wore the clothes you would kind of expect; long black overcoat slightly too big, shiny black boots reflecting the one orange lamp above. He had shoulder length black hair and could have been mistaken for a woman from behind, for it was shiny and well cared for. On top of his head, oddly, was a rather battered brown cowboy hat. It looked out of place in the rural countryside of England. Or more specifically, Cornwall.

For all intents and purposes Nikolas Wiseman looked to be in his early thirties, yet carried himself like a man full of weighty wisdom, the world on his shoulders you could say, which gave the impression of a man twenty years older.

Wiseman sniffed the air like a dog, his nose high as if catching a scent on the passing gust. Then, he moved away from the spot he had just appeared from and began to trudge along the road towards the small town. Walking with a slight boyish bounce and a casual pace, you could be forgiven for thinking that his appearance was not that urgent, or presence essential. But it was. It absolutely was. And he knew it.

Wiseman was alert, although he strolled casually, he used his near perfect eye sight to scan the darkness. He knew what he was looking for, there had to be some about, he just knew it. His right hand was in his pocket and tensed into a tight fist.

The town was small and pretty. But he had no time to take in the beauty of the surroundings. He had a job to do. The road stretched right up ahead into the town, and was lit by orange lamp lights dotted all the way along. Marching a little quicker, Wiseman passed a cemetery on his right, then a tall church, as well as several twee cottages with mullioned windows and thatched roofs. Fifty yards ahead the road split in two, in the middle of the fork was, not a park exactly, but a small square with a one bench, surrounded by black iron railings. Wiseman tensed, but carried on walking as nonchalantly as he could. The sound of small muffled conspiratorial voices reached his ears causing them to twitch and train towards the almost imperceptible noise. Wiseman had a sinking feeling in his stomach, he should have been more careful, being this brazen could just attract more attention. And that would not be good. But has to be dealt with. Approaching the iron gate to the small square, he stopped and lay a hand upon the cold metal. Almost at once, *they* became visible; three men were now sat on the bench muttering madly to each other and cackling. Their long coats battered, worn, and dirty. Their voices scratchy and hoarse. But their faces were the worst part; blotchy, pockmarked and with scabs all over. They looked like a corpse that had risen from its grave.

These, as Wiseman knew full well, were called Scabs.

Scabs used to be Wizards, but somehow or another, lost their magic. But now, they were in an endless struggle to try and get it back. This involved some very dark, horrible practices which I won't go into. Suffice to say, they were not nice individuals.

When they finally looked up and saw Nikolas Wiseman leaning casually on the railings watching them like you might an animal at the zoo, they stood sharply causing the bench to tip backwards. "Who are you?!" the middle one demanded.

"Yeah, tell us or we will do magick on ya' and kill ya'!"

"Is that so?" said Wiseman picking his teeth.

"Oi! We asked you *who* you was!?"

Wiseman took off his hat and did a small, sarcastic curtsy. "I am Nikolas Wiseman."

The three Scabs froze like statues. An uncomfortable few

seconds later, the middle one pointed a long scabby finger at him. "You are *the* Nikolas Wiseman?"

"Indeed I am. Unless I am an imposter pretending to be him." Wiseman chuckled. "But last thing I checked, I wasn't."

The Scabs looked perplexed, they were not the brightest.

"Anyway, it don't matter," said a brave one. "Cos we was here first you old basket case!" With that the Scab threw his hands out like he was pitching a baseball. With an almighty rush of air, a stream of yellow light blitzed through the night at the speed of light, straight towards Wiseman's face!

He hardly moved, only to pull his hat down as the spell, as it was, deflected upwards off the hat and into the sky, before dissipating like a firework.

Wiseman tutted and wagged his finger as if telling off a group of particularly naughty children.

Red chains bound the Scabs arms, legs and mouths as they struggled on the grass. These red chains were magical of course, and were almost impossible to get out of. "Why are you here?" said Wiseman with a snarl.

"Mmmm—mm..." said the middle one into the red light masking his mouth. Wiseman raised a finger, the light peeled away. "Why should we tell you?!"

Wiseman gave them a long look as if it hardly needed mentioning, before reaching into his jacket pocket and pulling out a small black crystal, upon sight of it they began to scream.

"I'll tell ya! I will! I will!"

Wiseman put the crystal back in his pocket.

The Scab was breathing hard, his black eyes darting around the empty town before leaning forwards. "We can smell the magick. It's thick here. It's coming from one of these houses..."

Wiseman sniffed before he picked up another sound up ahead, someone nearby just kicked an empty can over. Anyone else would have assumed it was a fox or cat, but not Wiseman, this he knew, was caused by a human. Wiseman followed the noise, at the same time lifting a finger—the red mask covered the Scabs face again—before he took out the black crystal and dropped it at their feet causing them to scream with fright. Except they made no noise.

Wiseman left the square in search of the human. He soon realised there were more Scabs in the vicinity than he cared for, or could handle alone. Up ahead, were several lolling up the street together. Wiseman had never seen so many together. He slid into a nearby alley, pulled up his sleeve and started to speak softly into a bracelet on his arm. "Calling for backup, three Scabs detained, more than expected in the vicinity."

There was a crackle from the bracelet. "Understood," came a voice. "Sending backup now."

"Tell them to protect the perimeter of the Brown's cottage."

Crackle.

"Understood."

Wiseman moved out of the alleyway and up the street, the Scabs couldn't see him. They would only see him if he wanted them to. He also knew where he was going. They didn't.

A second later, what looked like twelve white twinkling stars, in a full circle around the town, lit up the sky. They fell to earth in perfect synchronicity, falling like shooting stars, silent and graceful, a nonintrusive light, like a snowflake.

Wiseman grinned continuing on to the Brown's cottage as the Scabs scattered at the sight of the falling white lights.

The cottage was atop the hill, small and down a country lane with a small wooden fence and no lamplight. Orange firelight burned bright from inside. Wiseman checked around him once more, before knocking upon the door. He could hear the buzz and nervous energy of people inside. Footsteps rung across creaky floorboards, before the door was wrenched open. A small man with a gaunt, tired face stared up at Wiseman, worry lining every space of his face.

"Nikolas, you're here at last!" the man blustered, all but dragging Wiseman into the house, before peering outside and closing the door. The man barely gave Wiseman room to move in the tiny hallway, leaning so close Wiseman could feel his breath. "Have you called the council members?" he whispered at a fast pace.

"Yes. Twelve. Around the perimeter."

The man nodded, his small bloodshot eyes twinkling as he rubbed them. "I saw Scabs, earlier, at the top of the street. It's just like you said."

Wiseman, remaining modest, nodded. "You must remain calm Bernard." He said, laying a hand on his shoulder. "Magick flows better when you are calm."

"Calm? How can I be calm!" he spat as quietly as he could, before a ladies voice called from the next room.

"Who is it darling?" she sounded tired and hoarse.

"It's Nikolas."

"Oh good!"

Bernard led Wiseman through the tight hallway into the first room on the right. Four people stood when they saw Wiseman. "You came," said a woman sitting in a rocking chair next to the fire. She looked as tired as she sounded. In her arms was a tiny baby wrapped in a bundle of sheets. Even though she was young, she looked worn out, her hair astray, but she was still very beautiful.

Bernard rushed to the woman and sat her back down in her chair next to the fire. A tall container full of coal tipped itself into the orange flames, before a poker jabbed the embers. A large cauldron bubbled away atop the fire sending a strange concoction of smells through the room.

Standing before the kitchen table were three people. Dressed similarly to Wiseman, as if they lived a hundred years ago. Wiseman docked his hat to them. "Penwood. Dray. McCarthy."

Each looked inclined to speak, but Penwood stepped forwards first. He was a tall man with sharp features and messy black hair, and a good family friend to the Browns. "It happened just like you said it would—"

"Just like the prophesy read," said Dray, a woman with long bright red hair.

McCarthy, an older grey-haired gentleman wearing a khaki coloured overcoat had more scars on his face than a Scab, wrapped his knuckled on the table and said in a thick Irish accent. "He's got the eyes too. He's got the purple eyes."

Wiseman ignored them and looked towards the baby, wrapped up so tightly in his mothers arms. "You can hold him, if you like?" she said.

"Oh Maggie," said Bernard with a short snort. "Wiseman won't want to—" But he trailed off as Wiseman put his arms out. Maggie smiled, placing the bundle of sheets into Wiseman's outstretches arms. It's fair to say Wiseman was more nervous about this than anything else he had done in the past few years, and that's saying something. He had not felt his heart beating so hard since the time he came face to face with a demon.

The baby was lighter than he expected and he was surprised how easily he could hold him. It almost came naturally. Now, peering through the soft sheets, the baby opened his eyes at the man. Wiseman's heart almost gave in as he saw them for himself. The sight of them sent a shiver down his spine at the miraculousness of it. The baby's eyes were such a bright purple, they almost shone through the gloom of the Brown's cottage kitchen. For a long moment Wiseman just stared, too embarrassed to say anything. Bernard and Maggie smiled at their mentors speechlessness.

"What—what have you called him?" he managed.

Maggie gave Bernard a glance as if to confirm it. "Alfie," she said.

"Alfie Brown," said Wiseman sounding it out. "And... no middle name?"

"We haven't decided yet," said Bernard.

Wiseman raised his eyebrow slyly. "Hmm... well Nikolas is a good name," he winked, causing a small nervous titter to skate around the room. "He's perfect, just... perfect."

"He is," said Bernard coming around the chair. "But you know as well as I do that he won't be unless we put some protection around him fast," he said jabbing a hand at the window. "I don't want him to be found."

"Quite right," said Penwood.

McCarthy waved a hand making the curtains draw themselves shut. "Then we gotta' do strong magic ta' make sure *they* don't find him."

Maggie frowned and pulled Alfie closer. "I don't want magic done to him."

"My dear," said Bernard taking her shoulders softly. "We've spoken about this, it must be done. His life depends on it."

Maggie looked to Dray for a second opinion, and she nodded. "Okay, but you know I don't understand magic, I am not magical like you lot so forgive me for being anxious."

"Perfectly understandable," said Wiseman. "But honestly, there is nothing to worry about," he smiled, almost convincing himself.

"Will this room be big enough?" said Bernard, opening the door and flicking the light on. The room was small, dim and empty.

Wiseman strolled in, giving it a cursory sniff, before nodding. "It will do."

Penwood and McCarthy followed in behind and stood at the side of the room against the wall. Maggie, clutching Alfie in her arms, with a resentful scowl on her face stood in the doorway, with Dray at her shoulders.

"It must be done," whispered Dray. "We have little choice. This will protect him."

"If you say so," said Maggie, as Bernard flicked his hand at a small fireplace that burst to life.

"Switch the electric light out," said Wiseman, putting his hands together and rubbing. "No one move." With a grimace and a grunt he said a spell. There was a sucking sound and a pop as a room full of all different kinds of boxes popped into existence; mostly they were black leather boxes of many different varieties, housing lots of magical items, no doubt. Wiseman instantly began to rummage around after things in leather bags and cardboard boxes next to him.

"Which one are you doing?" said McCarthy opening the lid of a box next to him, peering inside and then recoiling at the terrible smell. Wiseman didn't answer, he didn't want to.

"Make yourselves useful," he said, calling over McCarthy and Penwood. "I need frankincense, my three iron candlesticks, silver dagger—"

"Dagger!?" Maggie cried. "Why do you need that?"

"It's ok dear," Bernard took her by the shoulders as reassuringly as he could. "It's just ceremonial."

"Perhaps we should leave the room?" said Dray sensing this *ritual* may upset Maggie.

But she bit back. "I am not leaving him!"

Soon enough, Wiseman had arranged the room. A circle of salt with seventy-seven magical rune markings surrounded Alfie's small cot in the middle of the room. Three dangling golden spheres burned an acrid incense, that got in their throats. As well as the walls being coated in sprays of essential oils, made the environment quite pungent. But necessary. The fire burned sea green. Four silver goblets popped into the air. Wiseman made the potion hanging above the fire in the other room, sail into the room and pour itself into the goblets. One by one they drifted across to each persons outstretched hand.

"Around the circle," said Wiseman as Penwood, McCarthy and Bernard took their places. "And now for Alfie to be placed in the middle."

Maggie had tears streaming down her face. Dray reached out and took Alfie from her hands, walked to the middle of the room and put the sleeping baby inside the cot. Maggie burst out crying and ran from the room.

"Carry on," said Bernard fixedly with sweat dripping from his brow.

Wiseman pulled out his notebook and read the correct passages. He had never done anything so important and difficult as this. Penwood looked from Alfie to Wiseman. "Are you sure this is the right thing to do?"

Wiseman fixed Penwood with a stare. "I am certain." He lied. Penwood nodded, appeased.

A translucent lectern appeared before Wiseman to prop his book open. He took a deep breath, before diving headfirst into the most complicated ritual he had ever done. Waving his right arm, and repeating the incantation in his head, caused the salt circle to take flame. The next second, the seventy-seven runes burst to life, burning an acrid red colour. Bernard went to open the window. "No!" said Wiseman.

Despite feeling giddy already, Wiseman knew he must finish the ritual. The potion took hold of their senses. It must have looked frightening as Dray shut the door and went to see to Maggie. Wiseman felt the potion make him feel otherworldly, or drunk, like he was sailing a ship through the fifth dimension.

But it had the intended effect; he could see strange shapes, the floor vibrated, the walls seemed to be breathing in and out and the window was like a kaleidoscope. Wiseman peered down at the words in his notebook which looked odd and archaic. Knowing he must remain disciplined, he carried on speaking the words aloud.

The potion took hold of the others too, Bernard was inspecting his hand with intent before pulling himself back to reality. Penwood was staring at the runes with a terrified expression but remained standing. Only McCarthy didn't seem to be effected and was repeating Wiseman's chant.

The noise in the room seemed to be rising like a cacophony, strange wailing noises from the walls rung out agonisingly loud as if the walls between the realm of the living and the dead were closing in. A whipping wind came, seemingly, from nowhere and burst around the room like a tornado. The pitch reached a crescendo before... silence.

Thud.

Wiseman hit the floor and blacked out.

"Oh god, they're here!" called McCarthy coming running up the hallway.

Wiseman swallowed, taken by surprise and sat up. Dray was leaning over him with a wet flannel and patting his head. Bernard was being comforted by Maggie, Alfie back in her arms, while Penwood sat on the floor looking dazed.

"What?" said Wiseman, whose head was now pounding.

"They're here!" McCarthy shouted back looking as animated as he had ever seen him.

"How many?"

McCarthy swallowed. "Lots."

Wiseman rolled up his sleeves. "Then we must disappear."

༄

I ask you to zap forwards in time with me just a few months. We go to Number Ten, Downing Street, London where Nikolas Wiseman is having a meeting with the new Prime Minister of the U.K, about magick.

"And I do also regret to inform you," said the Prime Minister sternly. "That you cannot just climb through my mirror into my private office like that. You gave me quite the shock! What will my staff say if they come in and see you here, knowing they have not let you in?"

"Apologies Prime Minister."

"I know we had a meeting booked, but I expected you to—"

"Knock on the front door?" said Wiseman with a sly grin.

"Well no," she said rubbing her chin. "I don't know, I

expected..." she trailed off, not knowing how she expected the Wizard to arrive. She also didn't know how to talk to him, did she lay down her marker early and be stern? Or perhaps she was to be civil? That had gone out the window now, as the fright of seeing him clamber over the mantelpiece had brought out her former stern headmistress days.

The last Prime Minister, who resigned in the summer, gave her no warning that she was to have meetings with Wizards about magick, and who would unannounced, walk straight into her room through the big mirror atop the fireplace. She was new to the job and quite unprepared for all this 'weird stuff', as her advisor called it earlier that morning.

Wiseman reclined backwards in the chair, comfortably at home. "Aren't you going to offer me a drink or something?"

"Oh, yes of course. Tea?"

"Grand. Would you like me to fetch it up?" said Wiseman wiggling his fingers.

The Prime Minister's eyes bulged. "No!" she said rather too quickly. "I mean, no thank you. I'd rather we left all that sort of stuff for now. It would be a PR disaster if it were to cause any... undue complications." She picked her words carefully, so as not to offend. "I can have it sent up." She pressed a button on her desk which beeped. "Sharon, can you bring up a pot of tea."

She was curious, she had never seen *real magick* performed, and now she regretted being so hasty, he may now think she was a prude and be unwilling to demonstrate.

"You've changed the painting..." said Wiseman who had been busy inspecting the room. "There was a portrait up there," he pointed to a place behind her desk. "But now there is a landscape."

"Correct," said the Prime Minister turning to look, he was

either introspective, or he had been to this office more times than she would have assumed. "I painted it myself."

"Did you really?" said Wiseman leaning forwards with genuine interest. "It's very good."

"Oh, thank you," she blushed. "Just an old university project."

Wiseman leaned back in the chair and yawned. "The President is late."

"The President is *always* late."

Wiseman checked his watch, and she noticed it did not look like other watches. There were, in fact, no numbers on it. But odd signs and shapes.

The silence was making her uncomfortable and felt the need to fill it until the President of the United States arrived.

"Have you come far?" she said finally, after toying with a few questions.

Wiseman looked up at her with an amused look. "Nothing is very far when you know the right magic."

She cleared her throat. "How did you... you know, come through the mirror? What sort of... *magick* would you need to do..." she cleared her throat. "I am sorry, I don't even know how to ask you. I've not been briefed about this meeting at all."

"No apology necessary," said Wiseman undoing his jacket and straightening it out. "There is a place beyond each mirror in the world through which one can travel. I can walk through the mirror in my bedroom and ten minutes later be in your office. We call it the MirrorWays."

"My goodness."

The amazement was wiped off her face the next second as there was a knock at the door and she resumed her best neutral expression. "Tea Prime Minister," said a burly woman, coming into the room with a large tea pot on a tray, laying it down on her desk.

"Thank you Sharon," she said pouring two cups as Sharon left the room with an uninterested glance at Wiseman. The Prime Minister slid the cup and saucer towards Wiseman who took it and sipped. Wiseman checked his watch again, before sitting up straight and seemingly deciding that the meeting would start now, regardless of the other missing attendee.

"So, you now know that real magick exists," said Wiseman putting his saucer on the edge of her desk. "That's magick spelt with a K, to differentiate it from modern trickery *magic*. You may or may not have been briefed that we Wizards perform magick on a daily basis. We live in your world amongst your people, but we also have our own separate lands. These lands were negotiated with the Monarchy of England at the time. These lands were taken off the maps and hidden from the vengeful masses. As part of the deal, we agreed to live in secrecy, never to reveal our talents. In exchange for this the War was ended and peace has sustained, give or take, for the remaining years. These magical lands are governed by our own Magickal Council and WMP's—"

"WMP's?"

"Wizarding Members of Parliament."

"Of course."

"Questions?" said Wiseman downing his tea.

The Prime Minister felt a thousand such questions bubbling to the forefront of her mind as it whirred with this incredible information. Was this man a loony? Was this some test? Perhaps he was a journalist trying to make her look stupid and gullible.

"Do you use... *wands*?" she regretted it as soon it left her mouth, but it was too late now.

Wiseman grinned encouragingly, he didn't seem to mind.

"Not anymore. They are quite unfashionable these days."

"These lands you have hidden from ordinary folk…" she stopped as she realised what she just said. "I didn't mean… I only meant…" Wiseman chuckled and waved her on. "These lands, how big are they?"

"Our population is around sixty-thousand. Our lands are small, but enough."

The Prime Minister sat back in her chair and inspected this apparent Wizard. "So, what is the real meaning of todays meeting? It's surely not just to update me on the existence of Wizards and magick? Everyone has a want… more land, money, gold…"

Wiseman looked blankly back at her. If he did want something, he wasn't giving it away.

"My advisor mentioned something to me, that she retained from the previous Prime Minister. It was about some… *prophesy*? It seemed to be a big deal that he talked about quite often. Or so I am told."

Wiseman looked up at the painting behind her head and seemed to be trying to make a decision. Tell her, or not. "You are quite right," he said finally standing up, as if to leave which caused the Prime Minister to stand too, but then he went to the window and looked out. "I find it strange that they are going about their business, working hard, and none of them know that the course of history can be changed in an instant by one person. Not one of them knows that magick exists, that their relatives are living just the other side of an invisible wall. That they are so hopelessly dependant on the system that they will fight to protect it. They are not ready to learn the truth, nor have they been primed to learn the truth. Even though it will make the world a greater place if they should learn their innate talents..." Wiseman sighed. "Yes there is a prophesy and a quite important one, but the details of it I cannot tell you — the timelines can dictate who I can tell and who I cannot. It's not personal." He grinned before turning back and looking across the rooftops. "It will come to pass in the next twenty years."

"What will?"

"The saviour of magick and the reintroduction of it to the masses," he pointed out the window. "But there are many obstacles and enemies to overcome before we reach that utopia."

The Prime Minister was staring so intently at Wiseman, using all her skills to work out if he was telling the truth or not, that she did not notice another figure climbing through the mirror above her fireplace. He was a young good looking man in his twenties, dressed in buckskin breeches, tailcoat and riding boots.

"Nikolas," called the man, clambering down quickly, the urgency in his assistants voice caused him to turn with a whip.

"What is it Theodore? Can't you see I'm..."

Theodore was breathing heavily. "It's the Browns... they've gone."

Wiseman stared. "No, it can't be."

"Maggie disappeared, most likely just how you said she might. Not a whiff of her anywhere, I've checked using all the instruments. Bernard is consumed with finding her."

Wiseman took a deep breath, prepared for the worst. "And the boy?"

"He's fine. Bernard took him to his Grandparents."

The Prime Minister felt the need to offer her condolences, but knowing nothing of the situation, stood awkwardly in the silence while Wiseman thought. "You will excuse us?" he said finally, taking the Prime Ministers hand. "But I must attend to this situation urgently. I will arrange another meeting soon, if you are able."

"Of course," she said as the Wizard and his assistant jumped clean through the mirror, disappearing beneath the pane of glass. For a fraction of a second, she thought she saw something behind it, then again, it could have been a trick of the light. But no, she was certain she had just seen a long stone bridge and a starry night sky. She blinked and slumped down in her chair, her mind whirring like a spinning wheel. That was, quite possibly, the most incredible meeting she had ever had.

The next second, knocking her out of her daze, her office door opened. It was her chief advisor. "PM, the President is here."

🕮

Wiseman sat toasting his sore feet over the fire and reclining back into his comfy high backed leather chair. It had been a long day. Some of his clothes hung on a dryer, dripping into the hearth. This front room was big, the house was victorian in its design and decoration. The floorboards were worn and rickety, the rugs were greying and frayed and tall windows were accompanied by long dusty maroon curtains. Above the fireplace, past the collection of several antique clocks which ticked in unison, was a very large ornate mirror about the size of door. A mountain of books lay about the room in a messy fashion, some open at specific places and frozen in place. In one corner was a large drawing bureau littered with papers, letters with wax stamps, a three piece candlestick and a large bowl of sand.

A door suddenly appeared in the wall where there was no door before, fading up into the room and taking place as if it had always been there. It opened, and in walked Theadore, Wiseman's assistant. His boots clapped across the wooden boards importantly. Wiseman didn't look up or acknowledge his appearance, but merely pointed to the seat opposite.

"Fill me in dear Theadore," Wiseman exited his stare and reached for a glass next to him and took a big slurp.

Theadore paused before sitting down. He took his hat off and lay it upon his lap. Wiseman could tell he was not happy with him — he didn't want to be reporting back on the boy, especially as Wiseman was making a mess of the house. Theadore could not resist a moment longer, his nose wrinkled at the smell in the room before he said it.

"How can I do my best job reporting back to you, undercover, in my disguises, if I have the state of the house on my mind?"

Wiseman slurped his drink and watched the fire. "Your job description has changed, you're no longer my assistant. You are my confidant. I can trust you."

Theadore sighed. "Oh you know just what to say to make me feel dis-warranted in my resentfulness."

"It serves no one." Wiseman sat up straighter. "Enough of this. Please, tell me what you have."

Theadore knew he would get nowhere in his protests and must settle for a messy house — he supposed he could get used to it, and then when he moved back in and became the servant again he would employ a team to clean it from top to bottom. "Well, he is midway through his second year at school. He seems to have settled as well as can be expected and is, as far as I can tell, happy."

Wiseman gave a short nod of appreciation.

"But…" Theadore started.

"A but?"

"Yes, a but."

"Well go on and tell me this very important *but*."

"I will, if you'll let me." Theadore straightened his jacket. "He is very naughty." This caused Wiseman to chuckle. "What is so funny?"

"I thought you were going to tell me something like he has been openly performing magick, having realised his innate skills."

"No," said Theadore blankly.

Wiseman shrugged. "Go on. How does this mis-behaviour present itself?"

"He has a friend he made on the first day of school. Tommy his name is. The other teachers call them *the terrible twosome.*"

"Do they indeed!" Wiseman laughed.

"It's no laughing matter Nikolas," said Theadore sternly. "He has nearly been exspelled three times. Anyway, apart from the misbehaviour, he seems to be clever, adventurous and good-natured."

"Has anyone been curious of your involvement in the school?"

"Not at all — I am just a young teaching assistant," said Theadore, whose face started to change and morph, like a melting waxwork until a young, unassuming, plump blonde woman sat in the chair opposite Wiseman, before changing back to his normal self.

"Strange things still happening around him?"

"Yes," said Theadore with a deep sigh. "During times of extreme emotions, it has caused problems."

"It's to be expected," Wiseman grinned. "Tell me specifics."

"He was in a mood about not being able to feed the fish some of his sandwich, and for the rest of the day the lights throughout the school flickered, as if someone was tapping the wires."

"What else?"

"Where the terrible twosome are, strange things always seem to occur."

"Entertain me," said Wiseman stretching his legs out across the hearth.

Theadore sighed, clicked his fingers and a glass appeared in his hand and filled with wine. "If I had to guess, I would say you are enjoying this, more than you should be."

"Your guess would be spot on as usual."

Theadore pulled out a notebook to jog his memory, he kept an account of most things. "How long do you have?"

"All night."

Theadore would report back to Wiseman weekly with updates, news and stories about Alfie and Tommy's time at school over the next ten years. Theadore never thought he would have to do so, and certainly not for ten years. But do as his master asked he did, faithfully. In various disguises as teaching assistants, caretakers and even other children, Theadore would keep a close, but careful eye on Alfie — but never intervening. His worries about Wiseman's reclusive habits played on his nerves, but what with everything that had happened over the last decade and a half, it was to be expected.

Ten years later

Wiseman sat in the same chair, in the same position on the same day as he had ten years previously. I don't want you to think he never moved from that spot. He does and had of course.

But there is some newfound sadness in his eyes that permits him to stay indoors more, as older Wizards tend to. Except for the fact that he looked not a day older.

Soon came the familiar whir of the door fading into the wall and the heavy boots of Theadore, reporting back the weeks findings. Theadore had come to ignore the musky smell that came with little ventilation and unwashed dinner plates.

"Tell me the weeks news," Wiseman called with a flurry, comfortable to try out some quirkiness around Theadore.

Theadore sighed at the crumpled clothes Wiseman had himself dressed in and sat down. It was not his place to comment anymore. "You must get yourself another assistant." Wiseman frowned and waved at him to speak of the weeks news. "They have a problem with Tommy's older brother, bit of a vagabond by all accounts. I watched him and his six friends on the school field try to accost Alfie and Tommy and steal their football. There was a heated debate, before a chase and... well, the next second the six older boys chasing Alfie and Tommy ended halfway up a willow, dangling like fruit and wondering how they got there."

Wiseman burst out laughing. It sounded like he had not laughed for months for it was almost maniacal.

"It's not funny. Even he is starting to realise that there might just be something different about him. What with the *strange goings on.*"

"It's his magick expressing itself."

"Yes, but around people who know no better! It's like a madman in a nursery. People will twig that he is not one of them and then scared, they will turn." Theadore leaned back in the chair and inspected his nails. "I mean, it's surprising he hasn't been ostracised already for having purple eyes. But his friend Tommy is very protective of him. The spells you put on him and around his house seem to be working. So far only three reporters and two television documentary crews have arrived on the doorstep wanting to make a programme about *the purple-eyed boy…*"

"My magick is not as full-proof as it could have been then." Wiseman grumbled annoyed.

"The Grandparents were quick to turn them away. They are good people. Turning down a rather large cheque too." Theadore said it in such a way to make Wiseman look up and take note — it was something he hadn't considered — what if the Grandparents accepted a lot of money for access to the boy, that would break a protection charm and then anyone could get access to him. People who would do him harm and ruin the prophesy. Then everything would be ruined.

"As I said, they are good people," said Theadore knowing what Wiseman was thinking. "You are too immersed in magick. It will rot your brain. It can't help going out and trying to understand how the unawakened ones live."

"Hmm," Wiseman hummed, returning to his stare.

"Could you answer me a question?"

All this time, Theadore had been a loyal servant to Wiseman and dare not want to know the significance of the colour of Alfie's eyes. However, secretly spying on Alfie for those ten years had led him to *almost* care for the boy, not least the amount of time and work that had gone into this operation — he wanted to know that it was all at least worth it.

"What is the significance of the purple eyes?"

Wiseman almost didn't answer the question straight away, he felt strangely hurt by it. "You question my judgement?"

"Not at all! I am curious. Don't be cross with me. You ask me to trust you, yet do not trust me yourself."

Wiseman scratched his beard. "True enough. Well to be honest with you, I don't completely know.The only thing I know is what the prophesy said."

"That magick will flow through the saviour like blood?"

"Yes."

"Purple is the colour of magic, correct?"

"Correct."

Wiseman stood up from his chair, as if this would stop the questioning. But maybe it would be good to talk about it. He needed a sounding board sometimes, to make sure his ideas and plans were not completely crazy. Wiseman walked around the chair and slid his finger along the fireplace, knowing he must confide, but the weight of time seemed to press down upon his vocal chords.

"He is the key to the whole thing. To getting them both back. But it could re-start the ancient magickal war."

Theadore felt a grin slide up his face — he knew it was all about the girl. His reply came out low and hissy. "And you are willing to risk war… the annihilation of our people… for her?"

Wiseman's eyes looked pained for a second. They gave him away. Theadore looked away and into his glass, before both their eyes lifted upwards to a small golden picture frame. Inside was a beautiful woman draped across Wiseman's lap, both laughing in high spirits.

Wiseman stared at the picture for a long moment, before pulling it away. "You know war between us is inevitable anyway. It's all part of the plan. I'd prefer no war, to defeat them peacefully but they've taken over everything. They have infiltrated us almost completely. They couldn't take us over by force, so they used stealth. We, and this prophesy, are the last hope of saving Wizard and Humankind.

"A third magickal war," Theadore tutted. "Two were enough."

"How should you know? They were hundreds of years ago. And we won them. Now we are losing."

"I just wish I could charm you into understanding that she is never coming back."

Wiseman looked at Theadore like he was a foreign species. "How dare you." This seemed to cause something inside Wiseman to snap. He slammed a fist into his chair and pointed threateningly. "I never give up!" he cried. "I know I am right, even if my closest confidant does not. This is all part of the prophesy—"

"The prophesy that only you saw."

"And you call me a liar. Any more insults while we're on the subject?"

"How long do you have? I'll get my notebook out."

"God-dammit Theadore!" Wiseman stormed around his chair and kicked out at the fire, in favour of the man in the chair. "I am trying to save the world!"

"At the expense of yourself."

Wiseman shook his head into the fire and felt the burden rest heavily upon him. "They have seized control of both the human and now wizarding worlds, so quietly it was imperceptible — only the enlightened ones such as I saw, warned against it and are now a laughing stock for having said anything. They control the media, they control education, they control the supply of food, the taxes, governments, they own the judges and the justice system and even the bloody air we breath!"

"You can control the air you breath in here by opening a window."

Wiseman ignored him. "They have poisoned the food supply.

They are indoctrinating people with their own unhealthy beliefs. You see it everywhere. They've made people confused about their own minds. But don't you see, that's how they want you. Confused and dazed, easier to defeat. And glorifying the lesser parts of the human soul; hedonism, nihilism, these things that are intrinsically part of *them* — but will be the death of us, and they get what they think is theirs back again. It's my life's work to change this, if it kills me. They will not win. And that boy is the key to it all." Wiseman turned. "That's why we might have to start earlier than planned."

"You can't!" said Theadore. "It's too early. It will mess him up. At least wait until he's finished school."

Wiseman shook his head, he had thought long and hard about it. There was no other way. To prove his point, he flicked a hand upwards at the mirror, which flashed on like a television. "I recorded this earlier."

A news jingle echoed out of the television-mirror, before a stern voice began to speak. "A conspiracy theory that the red-jacketed Scarlett Council, a theory originally attested to by recluse-wizard Nikolas Wiseman, was given fresh focus today as witnesses in Magicity say they accidentally burst in on a secret meeting of around twelve Scarlett Council members. The Scarlett Council is believed, by some, to be..." the newscaster put a funny, jovial voice on. "... A secret society that is intent on killing the entirety of humanity." Then he chuckled softly. "Unfortunately, the witnesses cannot be interviewed, as this morning it was found out that the three people aged 17 to 23, all died of natural causes. A government official has calmed any conspiracy theories about their death and cited, after a quick investigation that the cabinet in the second hand furniture store they went through into this alleged 'secret room', was laced with noxious poison which caused the hallucinations and their subsequent death. The owner of the store has been arrested and will be tried on charges of negligence later this week."

"The Scarlett Council are active," said Wiseman flashing a hand at the mirror causing the screen to vanish. "They are back in action and are pushing their plans forward as we speak. We need to counter it."

"You do know how dangerous this is?" said Theadore. "If you go near the boy, the ritual, the magick protecting him will all vanish — then he will be left completely exposed."

"It makes me think that this is part of the prophesy, that its meant to happen this way."

"Sometimes I start to wonder if they are not right about you."

1

The Exploding Television

A thin ray of light streaked through a gap in the curtains across a messy boys bedroom. At first, all was quiet, in the distance a milkman did his morning round. It was so peaceful and quiet, you could almost hear the mice snoring beneath the floorboards. A moment later however, all the peace was unceremoniously shattered as across the morning—startling all, even itself as it toppled to the floor, was a loud, ringing alarm clock. The boy in bed jumped up and scrambled around the floor for it, eyes still closed. He slammed the snooze button and lay back, letting his hammering heart rest. Realising it was the first day back at school he pulled the duvet closer. He lay dozing for a while, then he sat up and looked around, his dark, matted hair falling everywhere, eyes barely open—but just about revealing the thing that people found most strange about him—his purple eyes.

Alfie Brown, like most teenagers, didn't like early mornings and he especially didn't like early school mornings. They were the worst. Getting up, he pulled the curtains wide and instantly regretted it as he was almost blinded by a dazzling morning sun.

He rubbed his eyes and looked up the street, it was your bog standard suburban street—pavements, houses, a few trees and lots of cars in neat rows. He stumbled across to the wardrobe where he clambered into his school uniform and looked at himself in a full length mirror next to his bedroom door. This felt horrible, it was too early, his clothes felt uncomfortable and even worse—it was the start of a new school year—his last, in fact.

His room was quite big enough, bed in the corner with it's sheets hanging off and crumpled, looked like it had been slept in by a werewolf, not a fifteen year old boy. A large antique wardrobe sat disused as most of Alfie's clothes lay crumpled up on the floor, along with several dinner plates with a collection of dated mould, old school books, toys, two footballs and well, you get the picture.

His Grandma was out, so after a round of burnt toast, (his Granddad had never mastered the toaster) and a cup of sweet tea—"Five sugars! That will get you off to good start today… all that *learning*," said his Granddad winking and Alfie was off, into the sunny fresh morning to school, still half-asleep.

Five minutes walk along Mulberry Drive then Thistle Street and he was outside his best friend Tommy's house. Alfie crunched up the long gravel drive to Tommy's front door and tapped the silver Eagle knocker—*dun dun, dun dun dun*.

As he waited, he looked aimlessly up the street. Alfie had to blink and look properly, for several houses along the road, leaning nonchalantly against a lamppost and watching Alfie intently, was a small upright, white rabbit.

The front door opened and Tommy's mother stood, tall and fierce with her short black hair and grey, knowing eyes, reminding Alfie of a badger—you would not want to get on the wrong side of her. Alfie glanced back at the lamppost, but the upright white rabbit had vanished. Perhaps he was still dreaming.

"Thomas has promised me that you will both be good this year," she said. "It's your last year of school and I don't want him or you messing up these exams. They are rather important, you do know that?"

"Yes Mrs Eagles. I promise," Alfie said, doing his best charming smile. She eyed him for a second, chewed her tongue, then went to fetch Tommy.

A second later, a boy with bright blonde hair, blue eyes and a wide toothy smile came bounding to the door. "First day of school!" Tommy shrieked, flailing his arms around in the air in mock celebration. Alfie laughed even though he tried not to and stepped out the way as Tommy slammed his front door. "BYE MOTHER!" Tommy screamed, before grinning at Alfie. Tommy was Alfie's best friend in the whole world and had been best friends since the very first day of school. They were like chalk and cheese. Wherever Alfie was, Tommy was too.

To get to school they had a fifteen minute walk through town. A shortcut took them through the park and over a bridge that crossed the railway, past the newsagents which usually had children pouring out with bags of sweets. Then up Black Street, passing the large, looming Church that housed many old moss covered grave stones, the path through which the younger years refused to walk as it was *too scary*. Alfie and Tommy always went that way, it was quicker.

"It feels so weird to be back in these horrible school clothes again," said Tommy, in the relative silence of the graveyard. "Mother had to stop me burning them at the end of last year."

Alfie frowned as if to say—*don't tell lies.*

"Well not really, but I wanted to. Anyway it's the last year of school and then we're *FREEEE!*" he cried swinging his bag round his head.

"Watch it!" cried Alfie as it nearly hit him.

"Anyway, what are you unusually quiet about?"

Alfie chuckled. "Okay, see if you can explain this one... I just saw a white rabbit, standing upright leaning against a lamppost, staring at me."

"What?" said Tommy stopping to look at him, obviously wondering if this was a joke or not. "Your not ill are you?" he said feeling Alfie's forehead.

Alfie slapped his hand away. "When I knocked for you, there *was* a white rabbit, it was looking at me then it was gone. I mean, I could have still been dreaming I suppose."

Tommy told Alfie that it was probably someones pet rabbit that escaped. *Yeah,* thought Alfie, that was probably it.

"Cheer up, it's the first day of school!" Tommy said with a side-ways smile.

"Time to have some fun?" said Alfie grinning.

"Don't you mean cause trouble?"

"Same thing."

They both stood under a tall tree by the school's main entrance and watched people arriving. Buses and coaches pulled into the main courtyard and began jostling for position. Teachers arrived in their cars carrying large stacks of books whilst huge swathes of children piled into the courtyard leading to the school entrance.

The smell of freshly cut grass, the sound of the caretaker on his tiny tractor, the hubbub of excited chatter as friends welcomed each other back after a long, lazy summer hit the boys senses all at once. It was kind of good to be back.

"Never changes this place…" said Tommy as a squawk of high pitched noise made him jump.

A gaggle of girls had all spotted each other and ran forward hugging and making a racket. They were a pretty bunch of girls in Tommy and Alfie's year—all in the top classes—they were very pretty and received a lot of attention from the boys, of which they quite enjoyed. Sarah Ashdown with her friends Lacey something, Eliza something, and Lisa something.

Alfie didn't think he had ever spoken to any of them, he would be too nervous anyway.

A large lumbering collection of boys charged through the playground, each about three times the size of a normal person, most of the children parted, not wanting to get in the way—these boys were affectionally known as *thebullies*. Frank, Curtis, Titan and Bruce were all as thick as they were wide.

The next second they threw a ball. Poor Henry Goofham, with his thick glasses, bad luck and accident proneness, got hit in the face and promptly started crying.

A car pulled up past the buses and fought its way through the crowds who all stopped to have a look amid exclamations about how nice and posh the car was. It was a big black car with black windows. The passenger door opened and a girl got out, a few more boys turned to look this time, including Alfie whose attention was caught. She was very beautiful with long, dark curly hair, golden skin and rosy red lips.

"Did you see *her*?" said Tommy nudging him hard in the ribs.

Alfie certainly had seen her. "She must be new, never seen her before."

The school bell rang high and shrill, knocking Alfie out of his daze.

"Right, better go get our timetables for the year," said Tommy.

"Oh, goody, goody gum drops!" Alfie pretended to squeal with excitement.

First class of the day, according to their time tables, was History. Upon entering the classroom Alfie gazed around at the very familiar faces that he supposed he had missed over the summer, but would never tell them that.

Alfie shooed Henry Goofham from a table at the back of the room so he and Tommy could sit together.

Then, when all of the class were inside, sitting down and awaiting the teachers presence, someone else made an entrance. A rather large boy poked his large head round the door, then back at his piece of paper. Alfie thought he must have the wrong room and was just about to tell the dozy idiot, but then he waddled in sideways through the door, as he was rather large and began looking around at the full room with big saucer shaped eyes, taking towards a free chair in front of Alfie and Tommy's table.

"Erm…" snorted Alfie loudly. "Did you want something?"

The boy stopped, hand half reached out for the empty chair, opened his mouth to speak but shut it again and glanced round the room. "You want to sit on *my* chair?" said Alfie deliberately.

The poor boy was obviously new and went bright red.

"Y-y-yes please," he stammered.

"Well you can't… it's *reserved*."

"Who for?" said Jessica Curdle, she thought she was IT and had always held a grudge against Alfie, he couldn't remember why.

"The Queen actually," he said. "She's making a rare appearance

6

to knight me Sir Alfie Brown of Westbury-rubbish-school. *I knight you for putting up with the shoddy place for more than five years…"*

Tommy and some other boys laughed.

"Really?" she said in a sarcastic tone that suited her.

"No," said Alfie, who preceded to tell them that his black belt Karate brother was on his way to take the seat.

"Really?" said the new boy looking terrified and backing away from the empty chair.

Alfie sighed, this boy was obviously one matchstick short of a fire.

"No of course not. Here you can have the ruddy chair, I don't care."

The boy sat down and muttered thank you. A second later the History teacher Mr Ward made a rather flustered entrance. "Sorry I am late everyone," he said hurriedly handing out workbooks. "And welcome back to the first lesson in the new school year. I am sure you're all glad to be here. I certainly am," he smiled unconvincingly.

There was a short knock at the door from a girl Alfie knew to be Sarah Ashdown.

"Sorry I'm late," she smiled, flashing her brilliant white teeth. "Guess I am in this set now." She fluttered her timetable and walked slowly through the class. As she passed they smelt her sweet floral perfume, which danced under the boys noses. Sarah Ashdown was the prettiest girl in school, everyone was in agreement—Alfie and Tommy, nor any of the boys could help their eyes follow her. Eventually she took up a seat next to Jessica Curdle, who went bright red. Tommy poked Alfie in the ribs. "Stop looking at her," he whispered. "She'll think you're weird."

"Like I have to worry about that," said Alfie pointing at his eyes.

Tommy grinned. "I can't believe we've got Sarah Ashdown in our class."

A snotty nosed boy a few tables ahead looked round and clocked Alfie getting his pens out of his bag. "Oh dear," he announced in a snobby voice, glancing across at Sarah Ashdown, obviously trying to impress her. "Most people get new bags for the start of the year, but look at yours, looks like an animal you'd find dead in the road!"

The class laughed.

Alfie hated Joel Pope—he was such a smarmy git who loved to take the mick out of him at every opportunity, just because Joel had money and Alfie didn't. The two boys hated each other and had been nemesis for as long as Alfie could remember.

Instead of dignifying Joel with a response, Alfie leaned under the table and kicked Joel's chair legs—as Joel was swinging back on it and laughing at the time, he went flying backwards and landed in a heap, before sitting up, bottom lip quivering.

The class laughed harder this time, and Alfie grinned as Tommy clapped him on the back.

"Right!" cried Mr Ward. "I saw that, go straight to the Headmaster this instant!"

"That's not fair sir!" cried Tommy standing. "Did you not hear what slime-ball said? You deaf or something?"

Alfie and Tommy were both being marched to the Headmasters office. The new boy had been charged with escorting them there. He had tried to tell Mr Ward that he didn't know the way, for he was new. But Mr Ward (who was a bit deaf) didn't hear him.

"W-w-where is the Headmasters office?" said the new boy. Alfie and Tommy looked at each other and grinned, ready to lie to the new boy and get out of having to visit the Headmaster. But then, and it was just their luck, that the Headmaster happened to be passing and asked what they were doing out of lessons.

"Are you the Headmaster?" said the new boy.

"Yes of course I am!" he blustered.

"Oh, right, sorry sir. I'm n-n-new you see. And well, I've been asked to escort these two to your office sir," he said.

"Ok off you go, back to lessons." The new boy left and immediately went down the wrong corridor.

"You two," said the Headmaster shaking his head and looking at his watch. "This must be a new record for you both, it's not even nine o'clock yet!"

Alfie and Tommy looked down at the ground, feigning penance.

"Sorry sir," they mumbled.

"Ok, be off with you. I've got more important things to worry about than your recent antics."

Alfie and Tommy solemnly walked back until they were out of the Headmasters sight, then high-fived.

"Ha!" cried Tommy. "Easy, peasy!"

***

The lesson before lunch was French, Alfie and Tommy's least favourite lesson. They did plan a whole host of pranks and tricks they could play on the new teacher (the last one left with stress). But, in actuality, their planning turned out to be in vain.

Alfie's attention was caught firstly by the addition to their class of the new girl, who had arrived that morning in the big black car. She sat next to Ashley Di Franco, a rich daddy's girl who made everyone aware of just how much more important she was than them.

"Tommy look," Alfie whispered. "It's the new girl."

"Yeah I know, fancy her do you?" he said nudging Alfie in the ribs, Alfie said that no of course not, he hardly knew the girl.

Alfie and Tommy nudged each other in excitement as the new teacher swept inside, closed the door, took off his long black jacket and looked around. He had a very handsome face, with dark stubble and golden olive skin.

"Bonjour class, I am Mr Sapiens, your new French teacher."

Girls silently swooned.

"I 'ave 'ere your new books, so come to 'de front and get them." The girls rushed up out of their seats, Alfie didn't bother moving just yet. "That includes you Alfie," said Mr Sapiens not looking up. How did he know Alfie's name? Perhaps he had been warned about Alfie in the staff room.

Alfie grumbled and collected his book, somehow he didn't fancy doing any of the pranks anymore.

Geography was the second to last lesson of the day and was one of Alfie and Tommy's worst. The teacher—Mrs Crawford hated them, so they made a habit of being late for it.

"Come in!" called a scruffy, straggly haired woman with an evil grin, as if she were a wicked wolf sizing up her prey. "Take a seat," she all-but cackled.

Alfie and Tommy scrambled to the back, to claim their usual table—the only table in the room that was next to a window. The new boy who had taken them to the Headmaster earlier appeared at the door, still holding his timetable and looking confused.

"Yes?" snapped Mrs Crawford, gorping at him.

"I'm n-new," said the boy trembling. "I was wondering if this was the right classroom."

"Oh, well—name?" she asked snatching up the register, he told her his name was *Daniel Sparker*, some people in the room sniggered.

"Yes, *whatever* take a seat… anywhere, anywhere." She waved at him and Daniel who was very red in the face took a seat at the front on his own, where he got out some books to hide his face.

To Alfie's left was his least favourite person in the world—Joel Pope, sitting next to his best friend Christian, who all the girls loved for some unknown reason, they would often comment on how tall and handsome Christian was and how luscious his golden curls were. Alfie thought he looked like a gormless scarecrow.

"Oi," hissed Alfie as Joel's sulky face slowly turned. "Same class again Joel, anyone would think we're becoming good friends. But it's ok, I just remind them that I could never be your friend because I'm allergic to slime… and a slime-ball like you would send me into a fever."

Alfie sat back as Tommy grinned. Joel scowled, glanced around before leaning a little closer.

"Did you work over the holidays?" he said. "I'd have thought your *Grandparents* would need all the money they could get, if the state of your house is anything to go by."

"Took you all of the summer holidays to think of that didn't it?" said Alfie.

Joel mouthed that there was plenty more where they came from.

11

Tommy nudged Alfie in the ribs, which he had a habit of doing lately, and pointed to where the new boy Daniel sat. He was having balls of paper and ink cartridges thrown at him by Curtis, Titan, Bruce and Frank, the school bullies—Mrs Crawford seemed to be ignoring it. Poor Daniel was trying to hide behind his book as the perpetrators gleeful with their new game.

Curtis was the unofficial leader because he was slightly bigger than the other three and had a modicum of intelligence. Frank longed to be the leader, whereas Titan and Bruce would do anything you told them and were as daft as a brush. They were all large and stupid and the prize asset to the rugby team.

Tommy shifted uncomfortably in his seat, he didn't like bullying.

"We're going to watch a video about how important these upcoming exams are," said Mrs Crawford as if she couldn't care less, popping the video into the recorder.

"*Passing exams is very important*," began the video at an annoyingly slow pace. "*Very important indeed. In fact, if you don't have any, you can't get a job, which means life will be very, very hard.*" It droned on in this fashion for at least ten minutes.

"I wonder," Alfie whispered. "If Mrs Crawford—the old bag—has ever passed her exams? Everyone reckons she's just a old fraud."

"I know," whispered Tommy. "Look at her, she's almost asleep!"

"And all this *pass your exams or you'll die rubbish*—Granddad told me that the schools aren't supposed to be teaching us good stuff that we'll find useful, just stuff that we need to pass an exam and the better we do, the better grade the school gets—so it's not even about us!"

"I think it's all a big scam really —"

"YOU TWO!" half the class jumped as Mrs Crawford was on her feet (for once) looking angry. She stopped the video and turned on them. "Why were you talking?" a large green, bristly moustache on her top lip quivered.

"We weren't," said Alfie at once.

"Liar, pointless liar. I was watching you," she spat.

Alfie thought what a sly old person she was, sitting there with half an eye open like a crocodile.

"You might charm your way with all the other teachers, but not me. *After school detention* for you both tonight!" she smiled at them menacingly as Joel chuckled.

Alfie couldn't believe it, he hated this teacher almost as much as Joel.

"That's not fair," said Alfie standing up.

"Life isn't fair Alfie Brown," she called, sitting down and smiling like an old witch. "And if your not careful, it'll be a weeks worth."

Alfie gritted his teeth, he could hear Joel sniggering loudly. As Alfie stared at her sunken eyes, she flashed her horrible teeth at him, she had the power and could use it however she liked. Alfie wanted nothing better than to throw a chair at her.

The television in the corner gave a sudden crackle. The video stopped. There was a short silence as the screen flashed grey, before the lights inside the room flickered.

BOOM! The television exploded! Everybody screamed as glass rained down and people ducked for cover. There was a thud as Mrs Crawford fell off her chair backwards.

After a few seconds of silence they looked up. Mrs Crawford peeped up over her desk, hair everywhere.

"Must have been faulty..." she said as the television gave a crackle.

***

When the bell went for the end of the day Alfie and Tommy had to hang around so they could attend their after school detention. They were sat on a bench glumly watching everyone else going home. Tommy started nudging him in the ribs looking off into the distance.

"What?" said Alfie, about to tell Tommy to stop poking him in the ribs because it was getting annoying now.

"The new boy," said Tommy pointing and looking concerned. Daniel, the new boy was being pushed around between the bullies. "We should help."

"This is new," said Alfie. "A caring side."

Tommy told Alfie quite plainly not to take the mick, then muttered that they should go and do something about it.

"And say what?" said Alfie. "Oh excuse me bullies, can you stop bullying him. I know he's fat and weird looking and probably thick as this concrete playground but if you could just find it in your hearts—"

"Don't be nasty," said Tommy. "He looks ok, I think I feel sorry for him."

Tommy shot him a look when Alfie suggested that Tommy was getting soft in his old age. Nevertheless, Alfie somehow found himself walking across the playground on an impassioned rescue operation.

Alfie and Tommy did a rocks, papers, scissors as to who would actually be the one to speak to the bullies, it was likely they would receive a swift punch to the gut—Alfie lost, he knew he should have gone for scissors.

"Oi Titan," called Alfie, all four looked round at him, not unlike a chimp would in a zoo. "Leave him alone."

Titan, who was holding Daniel's collar frowned. "Why?" he said in a dopy voice.

"Because if you don't I'll..." Alfie looked around for inspiration and saw a small gaggle of girls. "I'll tell Joanna Hurst that you fancy her."

Titan's eyes bulged and he let Daniel's collar go and slumped away scowling, muttering to his hefty friends that he did *not* fancy her.

Daniel picked up his school bag and hurriedly put the contents back in, then stood up and muttered thank you whilst still looking at the ground. Alfie told him not to worry.

Someone rushed up and tapped Daniel on the back.

"Are you ok?" It was the new girl with the wavy hair and golden skin from their French class.

"Oh yeah, I'm fine, t-thanks *er*... G-Gracie."

"If you need me I'm here for you," she said wondering back off to where Ashley DiMarco stood waiting. Alfie and Tommy just watched, mouths a little open.

"She was in my school induction," said Daniel. Alfie and Tommy nodded still watching her walk off.

Eventually they turned back around to face Daniel. "So, what's your name?" said Tommy.

"Daniel, but everyone just calls me fatty, except my Mum who just calls me Daniel, or Dan."

Daniel was zipping his bag up very slowly, trying to avoid eye contact. Alfie thought that *fatty* was not a very good nickname.

"What's your last name again?" said Alfie. "Sparkly or something."

"Sparker," said Daniel, undoing the zip again.

Alfie and Tommy looked at each other and smiled. Daniel looked worried.

"Sparky!" They chorused and looked at Daniel who thought about it, then smiled and nodded.

So Sparky it was, Alfie and Tommy pretended to christen him, showering Sparky with fake holy water.

"Hey, stick with us and you'll be fine mate. Those bullies will leave you alone now," said Tommy joining Alfie as they went off to their detention, waving him goodbye. "Bye *Sparky*!" they called.

Sparky smiled to himself, this was a better first day than he'd imagined and he was pleased that for once, his nickname was something other than *fatty*.

.

2

Ghost Corridor

Alfie and Tommy sat next to a window at the back of a stuffy classroom in after school detention, watching everyone walking home. Alfie was pretty sure they made them sit up here on purpose, to make them jealous about not leaving early.

Alfie saw Gracie say goodbye to Ashley DiMarco before getting into the large black car.

He watched Joel and Christian, with a few other posh friends standing around by the entrance, one of them said something and they all laughed—Alfie loathed them more than a kick in the stomach.

They were not the only ones in after school detention however. Curtis, Bruce and Frank were in there too for throwing a ball at Henry Goofham.

"Hey," said Tommy nudging him in the ribs, *again*. "I really hope my mother doesn't find out that I've had an after school detention on the first day!" he grimaced.

"I know," said Alfie sharing Tommy's pain, even for him the first day back this was a record. "Tell you what, you tell your mother you came round mine, and I'll tell my Grandma I went round yours." They both laughed.

"That old trick eh?"

The teacher at the front looked up. "Quiet please, you two," he said, then glancing up at the clock behind him shrugged. "Right, we can all—I mean… you can all go now."

Alfie and Tommy left slowly, descending the stairs and dodging the bullies who were arguing and pushing each other around. As they approached reception, which was bland and always smelt like toffee mints and dust, Alfie saw through the library window—his next door neighbour Nigel, two years below him, was working at a computer. Clearly Nigel was taking his new role as *editor of the school newsletter* very seriously. Alfie agreed with Tommy, *they* wouldn't be caught dead *working* in school after hours.

Alfie suddenly had a devilish idea for a prank on Joel. "Follow me, I've got an idea."

Alfie pushed open the doors to the nearest toilets, which smelt like fresh disinfectant and in the distance several vacuum cleaners could be heard blaring away. Alfie had the strange idea of stuffing Joel's locker with toilet paper and he began pulling reams of the stuff away from the wall.

When they got to the locker room, both boys giggling with armfuls of toilet paper, they began scanning the numbers.

"What number locker is his?" said Alfie looking around at the hundreds of small blue locker doors.

"That one," said Tommy pointing. "I remember always seeing him near this one."

Looking closer it was obvious, as on the front of the locker Joel had scratched his name. After a few minutes of trying to force tissue in through the cracks, they decided that it would be a lot easier to just try and open the locker and stuff all the tissue inside.

"How do we open it?" said Alfie who fiddled with the lock for a minute.

"Stand back," said Tommy rolling up his sleeves, before elbowing the locker directly beneath the lock. It gave a short clunk and fell open. Alfie asked Tommy why he hadn't just done that earlier, but he was too busy rooting around at all the things in Joel's locker. Alfie had a peep too, inside was a muddy sports kit, some old school books and two thick bronze bracelets.

"Why's he got a couple of girly bracelets?" said Alfie poking them as if they held a disease.

"Come on," said Tommy. "Let's stuff this locker and get out of here."

They picked up the piles of toilet paper and stuffed it as hard as they could into the locker, then leaned against the door until it clinked shut. Alfie and Tommy high-fived.

But then as they turned back to leave Alfie saw something. Across reception, and far along the corridor was an upright white rabbit, the same one he had seen earlier that morning, standing up, bold as brass and staring at him.

"We should set fire to that paper, no, no that's a bad idea... *what*?" said Tommy seeing Alfie's shocked expression. Tommy followed his gaze, then he saw it too.

"What the hec's a rabbit doing—" he said.

"The same one I saw earlier," Alfie mumbled.

For a moment, they both just stood, unsure what to do. Then it turned and started to hop back up the corridor.

"Come on," said Alfie as the rabbit scampered off. They had to run to keep up with it. Finally, after a short chase, it stopped in one of the oldest corridors in the school, no one really came down here anymore as there were no useable classrooms and the old library hadn't been used in years.

The white rabbit was stood up very casually waiting for them in the corner but then began to jump up and down. Alfie and Tommy exchanged confused looks, was it scared of them? Or was it trying to tell them something?

"It's a clever rabbit I'll give it that," said Tommy. "Be better if it could speak though."

Alfie suggested that they copy it and jump up and down.

The rabbit suddenly stopped, and shook its head!

Tommy grabbed Alfie's arm out of fright—"I think it's a person trapped inside a rabbits body!"

The rabbit put one of its tiny paws to the wall then looked back at them.

"Touch... the... wall?" said Alfie, the rabbit jumped up and down manically.

Together they moved towards the wall and lay a hand on the cold, dusty stone. Alfie didn't know what he was expecting to happen, but the white rabbit seemed to brace, watching the wall expectantly. After a few, long seconds Tommy glanced at him.

Nothing happened and Alfie had to admit he was glad the school was empty.

But then, the amazing happened. The wall in front of them rippled as if it were a mirage. Seeing it together they both stepped back in amazement, taking their hands from the wall. The outline of a door faded into the stone. Dark outlines swimming across the stonework and solidifying. A wooden frame, translucent and golden swam into a rectangular shape before becoming solid wood. Then with a loud pop, a bright purple door with silver knocker appeared in the middle of the frame.

"Is that... is that real?" said Alfie.

Tommy mumbled that it looked pretty real as the rabbit nudged the door open and disappeared inside.

"Where do you suppose it goes?" Tommy whispered.

Alfie walked forwards and pushed the door a little further. It definitely felt real and it swung open to reveal a long dark corridor. Silver shapes crawled through the cracks in the stonework and shaped themselves slowly into fire brackets with dancing blue flames. This revealed a long, shadowy corridor with grey stone walls and a dusty, dank smell. More purple doors grew and popped into place along the length of the mysterious corridor, all with a shiny silver knockers.

"This is so, so,so, so... weird!" said Tommy eyes wider than saucers.

A new corridor had appeared in front of them, out of nowhere. Behind them came footsteps and the sound of a vacuum cleaner—one of the school cleaners was coming round the corner!

"Quick," said Alfie. "Before she sees us!" he pulled Tommy towards the corridor.

"I am not going in there!" he said pointing and digging in his heals.

"She's gonna see us!"

The white rabbit was jumping up and down inside the dark corridor.

Alfie walked forward through the purple door and felt a freezing cold breeze run straight down his back. Tommy glanced around once, sighed and then crossed the threshold too, recoiling as he felt the freezing cold air slide down his back.

"That's cold!" he said.

As soon as they were both inside the door closed itself with a click. All sound from the school disappeared. Flickering blue light cast eerie coloured shadows, which bounced across the walls.

"What is this place?" said Alfie walking slowly along the corridor, inspecting the purple doors—there must have been ten on each side all the way to the end.

The rabbit moved towards the last door on the left and nudged it open. Instantly sound flooded into the corridor. Calls and shouts from what sounded like a market and the hum of hundreds of people pierced the air along with a slither of bright light.

"Where's it gone?" said Alfie moving cautiously, it sounded oddly like a London market, but how on earth would that be possible?

"Have a look…" said Tommy not sounding convinced.

Alfie looked through the small gap and saw, to his astonishment—a town square! It was bright and sunny with lots of people. In the middle was a large rock, surrounding that was an old cobble-stone square. It looked warm and inviting and there was a buzz to the air. There was a click behind them, Alfie and Tommy turned round quickly as one of the other purple doors opened.

A man dressed all in red with a hood covering his face clicked the door shut behind him. Another cold shiver ran down Alfie's spine, this time his gut was telling him to run. The man was covered head to toe in one long red garment. His hands pressed together as if in prayer, he lifted a hand and the door behind them closed with a click. The corridor became dim and silent again.

Alfie could hear Tommy breathing loudly as they backed up against the wall.

"You are Alfie Brown?" came a quiet slow voice, the person did not look up from its hood.

"Err, *err...* yes I am," said Alfie edging back towards the exit, getting ready to tell Tommy to run.

"And your friends name?" it said even slower.

"No-one, I'm no-one..." said Tommy backing away a little faster than Alfie.

"I like your eyes," said the man, a tiny rasping laugh echoed inside it. "You can both come with me now."

"No, I think there's been some mistake," said Alfie walking a little quicker. "We came here by accident. Sorry."

"You never find a place like this by *accident*," it mumbled as it walked—or rather glided—towards them.

It started to lift its hands. Alfie felt himself being pulled towards it, his feet sliding over the stone.

"*Ahhh!*" he struggled against the invisible pull—what on earth was happening?

"Leave us alone!" Tommy called, trying to grab hold of the ledge of a door.

At the end of the hallway another door opened. The silhouette of a man stood in the doorway, face hidden by the bright light behind him, oddly, atop his head was a cowboys hat.

"Don't do what it says," called the silhouette.

Alfie was about to say that they were trying—Tommy was even clawing at the cracks in the stone work, but still they slid ominously towards the thing in red, which now sounded furious.

"Be off with you *Nick!*" it spat.

The man named Nick was chewing a toothpick. He flicked it away. "Not until you leave them be."

"You cannot save him now, he belongs to me."

23

"Do you really think so?" said Nick casually.

The thing in red began to swish his hands through the air. Little sparks and whooshes of air went whizzing off around the place. In mid air a long transparent red chain shot towards Alfie and Tommy.

"I asked you a QUESTION!" called Nick jumping into the corridor and clapping his hands.

A bright green flash erupted inside the hallway, followed by an enormous deafening flash of thunder. With the force of a tidal wave, it launched them all off their feet. Alfie felt himself sail through the air, out of the purple corridor before skidding on the rough dusty school carpet. Red and green flashes and crashes shook the school. With a small pop the purple door vanished completely. Only dusty school stone remaining.

Tommy coughed loudly next to him. "What... the... *hell just happened*?" he said before getting up.

Alfie just lay where he was, his bum was sore. "Did that actually just happen?"

Tommy mumbled something about it must have because "It must have because my butt's got friction burn."

"How *did* that happen?"

"How did what happen?" said Tommy. "Which bit?" he said standing and glancing at the wall where the door had been. "What were those flashes of thunder?"

"I have no idea mate," said Alfie dusting himself down and walking smartly back towards reception.

"But, seriously there is something so, so, *so* weird going on. Those people, I think they wanted to kill us mate!"

Alfie wasn't sure, it was hard to think straight, his heart still hammering against his chest. Alfie reasoned that the man called *Nick* who had the cowboy hat appeared to be trying to save them.

"It's that man in red that scared me," said Alfie shuddering. "I got bad vibes from him."

Tommy nodded as if he were remembering a particularly nasty spider.

"He had a gold badge on his red coat thing... did you see it?" Alfie said he hadn't seen it. "Yeah it was just two letters... *S* and *C*... what do you reckon that stands for?"

Alfie shook his head, he hadn't a clue.

"Where do you think the rabbit went?" said Tommy.

"I don't know. It went into that *market thing* through the door." And it didn't return, Alfie hoped it was ok.

All the way home Tommy asked Alfie what he thought the corridor was, who the man in red was and if *Nick* was a good guy, or bad. Alfie became increasingly frustrated and had to shout at Tommy in the middle of the park that he had no flipping idea! He knew as much as Tommy did, so could they just walk home without talking about it. Tommy muttered something about it being bad to keep problems inside and its better to talk about them. Alfie disagreed, he had a thumping headache, and found talking made it thump more.

3

The Shadow Thief

That evening Alfie was lying on his bed staring at the ceiling, trying to make sense of everything that had happened and yet it made no sense whatsoever. Someone tapped his door, Alfie looked up as his Granddad came into the room holding a steaming cup of tea.

"Hello mate," he said putting the tea on Alfie's desk and sitting down on the end of the bed. "Good day at school today?"

"Well…" Alfie sat up. "It's certainly been… interesting," he said, more to himself.

"Oh, why's that?" said Granddad, taking a loud sip of tea. "You haven't been getting into trouble again have you? I told you about that Joel, he's not worth it —"

"I know," said Alfie trying to quell any lecture.

His Granddad took another loud sip. He looked a lot like Alfie but with shorter receding silver hair and a kind, rounded face with clever brown eyes—which began to inspect Alfie's room.

"Might need a lick of paint this room. When we've got some spare cash," he said hopefully.

"Yeah, I've been meaning to ask you about that," said Alfie. "Could I perhaps dip into my savings, what there is of it, and get my room done up really nice?" Joel's voice was replaying inside Alfie's head: *if the state of your house is anything to go by.*

"We'll see what we can do. Let's see if you can't keep this one tidy and in good condition first. Then we'll see." Alfie nodded solemnly, whenever his Grandad said *we'll see*, it meant *no*. "You know we're out tonight?" said his Granddad getting up slowly. "There's some fresh lasagne in the oven, so you might just need to heat it up."

Alfie smiled, he loved lasagne and he was particularly hungry. "So, just what did you get up to at school today?" said his Granddad turning.

"Well, me and Tommy we…" Alfie wanted to tell his Granddad everything, but somehow the words got stuck in his throat. "We… we stuffed Joel's locker full of toilet paper."

His Granddad looked solemn for a moment. Alfie thought he might get an ear bashing. "Did you leave trails of paper coming out of the sides of the locker?" he said straight mouthed.

"Yeah I think so…" said Alfie as his Granddad shook his head.

"No, no, no…" he began. "You want to stuff it all in, so they don't suspect a thing until they open it and get a face full of the stuff!" he cried, laughing.

"Oh yeah!" laughed Alfie. "I hadn't thought of that."

"Ok you two," called his Grandma from outside his door, before walking in putting her gloves on. "That's quite enough, and Alfie that's very naughty of you, encouraging your Granddad for thinking mischievously. You know how he gets."

"Sorry Grandma," said Alfie trying not to laugh at his Granddad who had his head hung in shame trying not to laugh. As they left his Granddad closed the door and winked at him.

Alfie stretched out and lay back on the bed and stared up at his ceiling as the front door slammed shut. Alfie wondered how the person dressed all in red had known his name. What was that place through the gap in the door? And who was the man in the cowboy hat? Did they know each other? Then, the thunder flashes—they *were* weird. Alfie felt sure that it had been caused by Nick. But how? And what was it? Perhaps it was some kind of electric gun? But the person in red had made things move without touching them, and made a chain just by waving his hands around.

It was all too much for one day, Alfie's eyelids began to droop. None of it made sense. He dozed until the sun began to drop, the light becoming dim outside his window as street lamps began to pop on—bringing an orange glow in through his room.

In the late evening Alfie awoke from his slumber by a loud grumble from his stomach. He sat up sharply, feeling groggy. Going downstairs he popped the leftover lasagne in the oven and yawned. It was bin day tomorrow, he should be kind and put them out now ready for the morning - his Granddad often forgot. Alfie wrenched the bag out of the bin, tied it and dragged it to the front of the house. The wheelie bin smelt funny, opening the lid he tossed it in quickly for it was nippy out here now. Before he shut the lid he could suddenly hear running and shouting. Alfie's road was a relatively quiet suburban one so Alfie was curious as to what was going on.

A stone dropped in Alfie's stomach. Nigel Scampton, his next door neighbour, was being chased by a gang of about ten people. Poor Nigel was running for his life, a huge aggressive dog barking on the end of a chain.

"Help! Help!"

Alfie was caught in two minds. What could *he* do? But there was no time to think. Alfie ran into the road after Nigel.

Suddenly, for some unknown reason Nigel ran down an alleyway to the adjacent street - away from his own house! Alfie took the street parallel to it, bursting along the road as fast as his feet would take him. Alfie didn't know what he was going to do. Nigel turned into the street and saw Alfie, at first he paused, unsure if Alfie was another one of the gang come to block him off or not—but then he realised and waved frantically with the gang closing in on him.

"Run to your house Nigel!" Alfie cried, his voice echoing along the brick walls.

Nigel was twenty feet away, but then—Nigel who looked exhausted, tripped and fell into Alfie—who stumbled and sprawled across the tarmac in the street—scraping his hands and knees. Nigel yelped with pain, as the gang slowed to a jog behind them. Their long, looming shadow eclipsed them.

The gang encircled them, blocking any way out. Alfie's knees were grazed and he had a hole in his trousers, but right now that was the least of his problems. Nigel glanced across at him frantically.

"Please Alfie, please Alfie don't let them hurt me!" he pleaded, clinging onto Alfie as tightly as he could. Alfie stood lifting Nigel too. "Please Alfie, please…"

"Let the kid go," said one of the gang in a deep voice, he stepped forward. He had a shaven head, several tattoos and was at least a foot taller than Alfie.

"I can't," said Alfie, he was scared and his voice betrayed him. "I can't let you hurt him."

Why was he doing this? He shouldn't have got involved he

knew it.

"We aint' gonna hurt him. We just wanna," the man looked around at his compatriots. "*Talk* to him." Some of them laughed. "Let the kid go and *you* won't get hurt." he said, leaning a little closer to Alfie—Nigel gripped him even harder.

Alfie thought his heart might pop out of his chest. One of the gang made a movement and darted forwards seizing Nigel who screamed as he was wrenched away, a large hand covered his mouth muffling his cries. The dog barked at the commotion, its sharp teeth aimed at Alfie.

"Who are *you*?" said one of the girls in the crowd, sneering at him.

"I'm not telling *you*," said Alfie.

The crowd jeered.

The leader of the gang leaned forwards and put his face directly in front of Alfie's, so that was all he could see—his breath smelt nasty. "Tell us who you are."

"His name's Alfie Brown," said one of the gang. "He lives over there!"

Alfie knew that voice—Tommy's brother Kevin was looking excited that he could be of use. So this is what he does with his time, thought Alfie. "Gaz, he's my brothers best friend," said Kevin looking at the man with squinty eyes. Gaz looked like he didn't much like Kevin either, but looked back at Alfie and smiled.

"You have two choices, join us or run away."

"Did you realise you only have one eyebrow, or was it intentional?" said Alfie, showing more confidence than he felt, people had always said his cheek would get him into trouble one day. They were right.

"You do not interfere in our business and get away with it,

you understand?" spat Gaz.

Alfie stepped back but was blocked by a large chest.

"You're not going anywhere sunshine," whispered Kevin's cold voice in his ear.

Gaz swiped a large fist straight at Alfie who instinctively lifted his hands in some vain attempt to block it. But then—Gaz's fist froze in mid air. Alfie squinted through his fingers at Gaz's puzzled expression, face contorted with effort. The gang stared at him wondering what on earth he was doing with his fist hanging in mid air. His face growing purple with effort. as Alfie dropped his hands Gaz suddenly toppled to the floor, hitting the tarmac with a thud and scraped back along the tarmac like a magnetic force was propelling him away from Alfie.

There was what felt like hours of silence as their eyes, one by one, came to rest upon Alfie. Gaz looked around at the gang, who slowly pulled him up and gazed at Alfie as if he were a giant slimy insect.

"You're a *freak*!" he mouthed viciously.

"Look!" said one of them, pointing up at a street lamp behind Alfie, which began flickering on and off. Orange lamp light sparking green. Then in a flash, one long streak of green electricity flashed from the lamp across the road. They all jumped, sprawling into the road out of the way of it.

"AHH!" they all cried and three more streaks of green thunder scorched the air, blitzing the road as the gang danced out of the way looking terrified. The gang took one short breathless look up at him, once at each other, then scattered. They ran without turning back and disappeared.

Alfie couldn't believe what had just happened—surely he was dreaming? He caught his breath, heart threatening to pop out of his chest.

Nigel tugged Alfie's arm, his small face a comical mix of terror and greedy, jealous envy.

"What?" said Alfie feeling uncomfortable with Nigel standing with his mouth hanging open.

"How-how-how *did* you do that?" said Nigel pointing at his hands.

Alfie glanced up the street to see if anyone else had seen what had happened, he was struggling to compute it all himself—his head thumping even harder. "You pushed that person away *without* touching him! Then you made green *electric* come out of the lamppost!" Nigel looked like he was about to explode and Alfie started to walk back to his house, checking as he did that no curtains were twitching.

"I didn't! He just *fell*. And I did not make green electricity come out the lamppost!" Alfie chuckled.

"No, no, you made him!" cried Nigel. "I saw you, I saw you! You did superpowers Alfie! Alfie you did super —"

"*Shhhh*! It's pretty late you better get inside. Go on! And Nigel, don't tell anyone." Alfie had to practically push Nigel into his own house to avoid any more questions.

"Can I write about this in the school newsletter?" said Nigel through his letter box.

"No! Definitely not. Nigel, please, let this be *our* secret." Alfie pleaded. "What were you doing getting chased by them anyway?"

"I was at the park," said Nigel who was still in his school uniform. "Walking back from school, looking over some notes for the newsletter, when I saw them up to something, so I went to *investigate* and well," Nigel looked down. "They saw me and chased me." Alfie sighed and told Nigel to be careful and pleaded again for him to not say anything.

As Alfie went back to his own house, he saw something out of the corner of his eye. He was sure as he turned back that he had seen a tall man in a cowboy hat standing in the bushes fifty yards away. Then, racing back inside he sprinted upstairs and straight to his window, peering out of the window. But the man in the cowboy hat was not standing in the bushes anymore.

What Alfie didn't see, as he sighed and went downstairs, was a small white rabbit making its way up his drain pipe and into Nigel's room.

After dinner Alfie collapsed on his bed. He didn't want to assume but he could have sworn he *had* moved the boy Gaz away from him—*without* touching him and he could have also sworn that a green electrical current had shot out of the lamppost. That's what made the gang run away, they were petrified of *him*.

Was he a superhero? Did he have powers?

Alfie had a sudden image of himself in a tight latex suit, running around Westbury fighting crime with Tommy as his sidekick. Alfie wondered who he could possibly tell who wouldn't laugh at him—Tommy for sure, but who official—the police? What on earth would they do about it? Say that he had needed to see a doctor probably.

Alfie got up and started to pace his room. He'd never paced his room before, because he had never had to think so much in his life. The last time he'd thought about something this much was the time he had to come up with an explanation as to why he had let off a fire extinguisher in the headmasters office.

The man in red in the corridor had closed a door without touching it, but the problem was Alfie had absolutely no idea who or what the man was. If indeed he was a man.

And now Alfie had assumably, done the same. His brain started to itch with unanswered questions—would the gang come back?

A cold breeze ran down his back, like he had been touched with freezing cold hands. Alfie jumped and looked around. The cold tea on his desk began to ripple. Then his bedroom began to shake! A thin, black mist tickled the air and Alfie felt his heart hammer hard against his rib cage. Terror gripped him and he jumped for the door, but pulling it he realised it wouldn't budge! He wrenched it but it was stuck, as if it were made of solid stone. His room started to fill with an eerie whistle. Horrible visions entered Alfie's mind—screaming people, melting faces and dismembered beings climbing up his walls. Alfie sunk back into the wall and closed his eyes.

Wind burst from nowhere throwing his bed covers into the air, as his desk scrapped across the floor, the whistle reaching fever pitch. His books, papers and clothes were pulled into a swirling tornado. Alfie backed against the wall shielding his eyes and ears as best he could from the awful wails and stinging winds. In an instant, the wind dropped. Alfie left standing in a trashed room, his hair stood on end. The horrible wails had ceased but he could sense … he wasn't alone. It was quiet, too quiet.

Cautiously, he scanned his room without daring to move a muscle. A vile smell almost choked him half to death, he clasped his hands to his mouth and nose, it smelt like nothing else he'd ever smelt before, hundred year old rotting flesh and burning, acrid smoke. It burnt his nostrils making him feel dizzy. A large transparent shape in the middle of his room materialised, a thin outline of a giant slug type creature. One giant tentacle flew across his sight swiping the air and catching him across the face. Alfie hit the back of the wall banging his head. Dazed and with stars swimming across his vision he heard the invisible thing move, floorboards creaking under the apparent weight.

He managed to look up just in time, the thing wasn't invisible anymore. Alfie wished it was for a full bodied faceless green-brown entity with thirty or more swinging, slimy, sucking tentacles with eye balls at the end and tiny razor sharp teeth and a large gaping black mouth greeted him. Alfie couldn't even scream, for all the air and sound had been sucked from the room.

To Alfie's utter disbelief the tentacle had grabbed his something... his shadow. Alfie's shadow cast long against the wall, began hitting and swiping at the tentacle as if it had a life of it's own, but the long, slimy tentacle wrapped slowly around the shadows waist and in one quick movement, pulled.

Pain burst from nowhere! Invisible flames licked Alfie's whole body and he fell to the floor, head hitting the wood with a thud as his shadow was dragged away. The large beast with Alfie's flailing shadow started to swirl round like a tornado, getting faster and faster, the two shapes forming to become one. Green tentacles and transparent shadow merging—razor sharp teeth forming at the shadows mouth, eyes popping into place and the shadow becoming dense and dark until there was no green tentacled monster left.

Standing before Alfie was a dark, dense mass in the shape of a person, head bowed. A pair of transparent purple eyes began to look up at him, a thin mouth with razor sharp pointy teeth began to smile devilishly.

It clambered through the crack in the window, glanced back at Alfie, then jumped, there was no thud, or sound. Alfie clambered up as fast as he could and looked out of the window. His shadow was running away up the street descending into the darkness of the night. Alfie felt his head where a large lump was forming and twinged at the slightest touch.

To make things worse he just heard the back door open, his Grandparents were back—how on earth was he going to explain this?

4

Spellbound Cats

It was seven o'clock when Alfie's Grandma got up and started to move around downstairs, starting the breakfast. Alfie had already been awake for two hours, which was very unlike him. He had woken at five and was simply not able to return back to sleep. He cursed, for he was tired and propped up his pillows before siting up.

Alfie wasn't sure if he preferred to be asleep or awake. His dreams had been plagued by horrible nightmares and three times in the night he woke in a cold sweat. He could still remember most of his dream, though he tried his best to forget—it involved hundreds of wailing, dismembered bodies crawling across a huge barren black desert, through a big hole in a tree walked the man in red who took down his hood and the gang members face greeted him, smiling devilishly with razor sharp pointy teeth and purple eyes. Then he turned into the shadow and they chased him across the desert into his school. Alfie saw Tommy waiting at reception for him with Nigel. Tommy put a cowboy hat on and in an instant his hands turned into tentacles, which rose into the air and grabbed Alfie, sucking the life out of him. Nigel stood and watched playing with a green electrical current in his hands—which sparked and flew at Alfie's face.

That's when he woke and decided it best to stay awake. Gradually light began to seep underneath his curtains and the chickens in Nigel's garden began to cluck and coo. The milk man came and went, a paper boy on a bike rode past and one man in a suit left his house early.

Alfie looked around his now tidy room—his Grandparents had watched him pick up every last thing and return it to its usual place (if there was such a thing). Alfie's ears were still ringing from the telling off his Grandma had given him.

He looked at the spot where the horrible tentacled thing that caused the devastation had been. There was no evidence that it had been there at all. No slimy sludge patches or greeny-brown goo, no leftover tentacles—only a smart dent in the wall where Alfie hit his head. He had been an inch away from turning round and telling his Grandparents exactly what had happened, but he knew too well that his Grandma would just shout at him and say *"Don't make up foolish lies to try getting out of tidying up!"*

Alfie got up, washed, dressed and had breakfast. He left five minutes earlier than normal to knock for Nigel, thinking rather hopefully, that if he spoke to Nigel about what happened last night, then he wouldn't go telling the whole school and town that *"Alfie had superpowers."*

However, when Alfie did knock and ask a sleepy, messy-haired Nigel about the previous day's events, he had absolutely no idea what Alfie was talking about. Alfie went back indoors feeling rather confused and tried to convince his Grandma that he was too ill for school today. But then she felt his head (Alfie winced) and told him that he was fine, Alfie sighed.

Alfie's thoughts at school were plagued by the horrible tentacled monster that stole his shadow. It caused Alfie to be something of a shadow himself in school. He jumped in Art when someone had made a model using an old hoover tube painted green—he was trying to think about the previous day, yet none of it made sense. He had never heard of anything like a huge tentacled monster coming to steal your shadow before, not in fact or fiction. He choose to keep quiet about the tentacled monster for fear of being called a nutter, or a freak, and to be honest with himself Alfie was struggling to comprehend how anything like that could be real. It was just a dream, he repeated over and over in his head, or some sort of hallucination. How could it be anything other? It was ludicrous, unreal and downright crazy to think that something like *that* could exist.

His Grandparents were already worried about him after thinking he smashed his room up for no reason. The first thing Tommy said when he saw him before school was: "What's that massive lump on your head?"

Alfie said that he had… walked into the kitchen door.

Tommy smarted. "But you don't have a kitchen door." Alfie ignored him. Tommy knew something was up, he always knew when Alfie was hiding something from him. Alfie knew he had to spill the beans at some point—Tommy however, was going on and on about the *"ghost corridor"* as he called it, and would have told the whole world if he could, Alfie had to kick him several times as people walked past.

"The *ghost* corridor—*Ow!* What?" he said, hoping on one leg.

"Be quiet! People will think we're crazy or something." Alfie said in an undertone, but Tommy just shrugged. "Everyone already thinks we're crazy." This was true.

The initial shock of the event passed as quickly as the next few school days. The daze that had clouded Alfie's thoughts subsided. But it wasn't long before something else strange and mysterious would happen to Alfie...

Alfie was sitting in the living room thinking. His Grandma had laid his homework across the coffee table and begged him to do it. Alfie promised that he would *try,* and he had, but ten minutes was enough, so he packed it all away and sat back. It was the weekend after all. His Grandparents were out for the day so Alfie sat in the comfy chair, picked up the remote control for the TV and was about to switch it on, when... the mirror above the fireplace glazed over—just enough to catch Alfie's attention.

Alfie frowned, he was sure something just moved *inside* the mirror. Putting the remote control down, he slipped off the chair. The surface seemed to be rippling slightly, as if it were water. He saw his own reflection, messy haired and confused—suddenly fade away. The mirror now resembled a window. Shapes, fuzzy at first, began to form. Until, Alfie was looking into someones kitchen... and there was someone in it. Sitting at a round wooden table, wearing an apron and drinking from a mug was a small and very old woman. She obviously hadn't noticed anything because she was staring into space, in a world of her own. Alfie could hear the tick-tock of a loud wall clock and the tap dripped rhythmically. All of a sudden, the old woman sat up straight and looked around the room. Then, out of nowhere a cat jumped in front of the mirror. Alfie fell backwards into the coffee table with the shock.

"*Ahh!*"

The cat poked it's head through the mirror as the view of the kitchen faded, a pale mist clouding the surface. The tabby cat gave Alfie a long look, turned back into the fog and disappeared from sight. The fog swirled then settled before a short popping sound echoed around the living room. The mirror returned to normal. Alfie, who was sprawled across the coffee table didn't move. His eyes fixed to the mirror. Did that just happen?

The doorbell rang shrilly causing him to jump. Alfie shook himself out of the daze and went to answer it. Tommy stood grinning on his doorstep, next to his, looking down at his shoes was Sparky.

"It's ok if Sparky comes in isn't it Alfie?" said Tommy walking in before Alfie could answer.

"See," said Tommy to Sparky, who was still on the doorstep. "It's fine."

Sparky looked up and smiled at Alfie before flicking his eyes away. He looked a lot more comfortable in the clothes he now wore— a very large, baggy black t-shirt, jeans and trainers. Both sat down on the sofa, as Alfie passed he glanced up the mirror.

"This was on your doorstep," said Sparky handing him a small piece of folded paper. Alfie took it and sat down in the armchair—probably a note for his grandma. Alfie usually got notes and people popping round to relay a message for his Grandma about the upcoming coffee morning or so. But this note seemed different. It was a small, folded piece of thick, cream paper. Turning it over he saw his name written in scrawly writing. Curious, Alfie opened it. It was probably from his neighbour, or the milkman or something... but there was no message. In fact, it looked like it had been ripped out of a book, for there was a paragraph of writing above, of which only half the words were visible. Underneath that were six bullet pointed words, the look of which Alfie had never seen before—they looked like utter gobbledegook, or foreign words. Alfie rubbed his head and sighed putting the note in his pocket. Perhaps it was Nigel sending him a special code?

"Nice house," said Sparky.

"Thanks," said Alfie not listening. "Did you see who left this note?" Tommy and Sparky shook their heads. Alfie frowned, peeved more than anything else that he had another weird thing to *think* about, as he was sure this had something to do with all the other strange nonsense that had been happening.

"What is it?" said Tommy.

"I have no idea, you tell me." Alfie handed it to him. Tommy looked at it, Sparky glancing across his shoulder, but they too were at a loss. Tommy glanced at Sparky who was looking at the words intently and then up at Alfie who had stood up and began pacing.

"This all just gets weirder and weirder doesn't it," said Tommy shaking his head.

"What does?" said Sparky.

Tommy looked at Alfie, he wanted to tell Sparky about the ghost corridor, in fact he looked positively excited that he could let someone else in on it, Alfie nodded at him in agreement, it was only fair he supposed.

"Is anyone in?" said Tommy. Alfie shook his head. "Good. Right, sit down Sparky…"

"I am sitting down," he mumbled, looking a little worried by Tommy's sudden burst of life.

And then they told him—Alfie starting to explain the story—not well enough by Tommy's standards as he pulled Alfie back on every little detail (what shade the stone work was, how many buttons the man in red had on his jacket and even the correct shade of green of the lightning).

"And we didn't know who either of the men were or what happened to them," he said for the seventh time. "And that green lightning bolt!" said Tommy with an awe struck tone. "It was so loud and hard that it blew us out the corridor!"

"Calm down," said Alfie growing weary of circling the story over and over.

Sparky sat where he was with a large frown on his face obviously wondering what he had let himself in for by befriending these two.

"I've got something else to say," Alfie sat down in the arm chair. For a moment he stared at the ceiling trying to think where to begin. "When I came home that night after the ghost corridor, I saw Nigel outside being chased by the gang. I stepped in to help him and we got cornered by them. But when one of them went to hit me, he sort of… *couldn't.* I had my hands outstretched like this and he just slid back across the ground away from me. And then there was this green electrical spark from the lamppost which started shooting out at them. It saved me, because they ran away." Alfie trailed off from the suspitious frown he received from Tommy. "Honestly, I'm not *lying*!"

Neither Tommy or Sparky said anything for a while, Tommy chewed his mouth—he thought Alfie had gone nuts and Sparky was inspecting the thread of the sofa—he thought they were both nuts.

"So," said Tommy and Alfie could spot the scepticism. "You think you *moved* this person?"

Alfie muttered back that he thought so, yes.

"Impossible," Sparky mumbled, still looking at the thread.

"I am just telling you what happened. You think I'd make something like this up? To what, impress *you*?"

43

"No," said Sparky sounding scorned.

"Show us then," said Tommy.

"But I don't know how it happened. Nigel was there, but he seems to have *forgotten*..." Alfie trailed off knowing how ridiculous it all sounded.

"Look mate, you need to get a grip. This last week you've been like a ghost. I think that corridors done something to you."

Too right, thought Alfie.

Then he braced himself for a tirade of scepticism. "Do you want to know how I got the bump on my head, and why I've been a ghost at school?" Tommy glanced at the bump on Alfie's head and shrugged. "Now, I might have been dreaming... but that same night, straight after the incident with the gang, *that you don't believe me about,*" Alfie mumbled. "I came upstairs and there was this like, *hurricane* in my room and well... a massive creature appeared—" Alfie told them in detail all about the tentacled thing and how it took his shadow. "The tentacle wrapped right around my shadows waist—" Sparky's eyes had drifted to a place just behind Alfie, his eyes searching for something, then he suddenly clapped a hand to his mouth. Alfie stopped talking.

"What?" said Tommy looking back and forth.

"Y-y-*your* shadow..." said Sparky pointing at him. "You-you haven't got one!"

"Exactly!" said Alfie. "That's what I've been trying to tell you!"

"Oh *yeah*," said Tommy his expression far away as he searched for Alfie's shadow on the wall. "That is *weird*. So that monster thing must have stole your shadow!"

Sparky sighed. "But, but a shadow isn't independent! It's the thing that a physical mass casts, it's not something that can be stolen!"

"Thank you Einstein, we know how shadows work. What we're trying to work out is how and why Alfie hasn't got one."

Alfie picked up the lamp on the side table, clicked it on and waved it around himself, but there was not a single flash of shadow upon the wall—the only shadows were the ones rebounding off the furniture. It was as if he didn't even exist.

Tommy shifted in his chair. "Do you think that this might all be down to you know… *magic*?"

Alfie and Sparky spluttered.

"What!" Alfie laughed. "Out of all the things I thought you were going to say, I was not expecting that!" said Alfie through Sparky's tumultuous snorts—Tommy sat in silence, offended.

"Yeah but," he offered leaning forward. "We can't explain that ghost corridor can we? And you can't explain why you *apparently* moved a person." Alfie didn't bother correcting him. "Or that giant octopus you told us about, unless it was a dream?"

"It most certainly was not a dream!" said Alfie, pointing to his head. "I've got the bruise to prove it."

"And no shadow…" said Sparky, who wasn't laughing anymore.

Tommy asked for the scrap of paper and looked at it closely—it was thick weighty paper of good quality and the writing was scrawly and untidy. "What do you think?" said Tommy passing it back to Alfie and standing over his shoulder as if they were a couple of scholars.

"It's a bit curious," said Alfie. "That this piece of paper with my name on lands on my doorstep the day after everything that happened yesterday."

"It could be that person who tried to kill you in the corridor?" said Sparky wide eyed.

"If he did know where I live then I'm sure he would just come in and kill me rather than leaving me a little note of obscure words?" said Alfie.

It could have been the man in the cowboy hat though, he had been right outside last night.

"Read the words out loud... if it's magic then it might do something," said Tommy gleefully.

Sparky mumbled that Tommy was talking nonsense and of course it wouldn't work, they were just funny words and could, if anything, be a riddle. Alfie had to agree with him.

Tommy glanced at Sparky and winced, obviously wishing he had not invited him round.

"*Magic* is something in fairytales and stories, not real life." Alfie chuckled as Sparky nodded sagely.

Tommy huffed loudly and started counting on his fingers. "Ghost corridor. Giant octopus. No shadow. Weird words. Men in red bloody—"

"Alright! We get it," said Alfie, he wanted to add weird *window mirrors* to the end of the list but thought better of it. "I just don't think it's magic, there has to be another explanation. Anyway, a minute ago you didn't believe me when I said I moved someone without touching them, now you believe in *magic*!?"

"Just say a word, let me see the *proof*, if nothing happens I'll never mention it again," said Tommy.

Fine, thought Alfie, anything to shut him up. Alfie looked down at the words on the note. The first was *Dulcis,* a funny shiver ran down his spine as looked at them and he felt strangely reluctant to say them. "Dulcis."

He was unsure if he had even said the word correctly. Tommy looked around the room frantically, but of course, nothing happened. Tommy pursed his lips then when no fireworks exploded he sat back deflated.

"Told you," said Sparky in a soft voice, as if he was consoling Tommy over a recent loss. "Magic doesn't exist, its just, you know, fairytale stuff."

Tommy shook his head then sat forwards again. "I think you should have said it as if the *C* is an *S*, like Dul-*Sis*."

Alfie was about to tell him to drop it, that it was not magic! Until—they all heard it together.

"*Meow...*"

They all stood up very slowly for there was a lot of commotion outside.

"What's happening out there?" whispered Tommy looking at the living room windows. Alfie pulled the curtains wide then staggered backwards into Tommy.

"Ahh!" said Tommy pointing frantically at the window, where around a hundred cats had collected in Alfie's small front garden. There were more cats out there than they had ever seen in their whole lives. Black cats, white cats, ginger cats, tabby cats, cats with too much fur and one cat with no fur at all.

"CATS!" screamed Tommy jumping on Alfie's sofa. "Loads of them!" Tommy started to laugh. Sparky stood by the window quite stunned as they pawed at it to be let in. Alfie didn't think he had enough milk to feed all this lot. And what on earth would the neighbours think seeing all this?

"Alfie! That word," Tommy shouted jumping up and down. "That word is *magic*, it is! It is!" He climbed off the sofa pointing frantically at the slip of paper in his hands. "It makes cats come to you!"

They all started to laugh, half in shock, half in wonder.

"*Meow... Meow!*"

Sparky jumped as one of the cats head butted the glass. "There getting vicious!" cried Sparky standing back from the window looking terrified. Alfie shouted at the cats through the window to stop head butting the glass, but for some reason they ignored him.

"My Grandma hates cats!" he cried. "If she comes home now she's gonna freak out!"

"Say the word again," said Sparky manically waving his arms around. Alfie told him that he didn't want any more! Tommy was standing in the corner giggling to himself, he found this hilarious.

"In most *magic*," said Sparky using his hands as inverted commas. "The same word said again has the opposite effect, like a sort of counter-spell."

Alfie and Tommy glanced at each other as the meowing became louder and louder. "How do *you* know things like that?" said Tommy.

"Dulcis," said Alfie. The effect was instant, the cats shook themselves, almost realising where they were as if they had been sleepwalking and one by one started trotting off. Some of them started fighting.

Watching them all leave, they then turned and looked at each other with wonder in their eyes.

"You were right Tommy…" said Alfie. "This is *magic*!"

5

The Disapearing Clothes

Alfie was lying in bed. He had tried for sleep but to no avail. He'd watched his clock turn twelve, then one, then two, then three. But sleep never graced him. His head was swimming with thoughts, ideas and... *magic*. At school Alfie had felt nervous and on edge, the lack of shadow was gaining him some unwanted, curious glances. He would be walking down the corridor and feel one or two pairs of eyes double take at the space around him—where they thought, a shadow should have been. They could tell something was not quite right, but couldn't quite put their finger on it. But, what would they do to him when they realised he didn't have a shadow? Send him away for scientific tests probably. Alfie shivered. Some of the neighbours had started talking too. The old couple next door who never went out, were sure as anything that they had seen hundreds of cats jumping through their garden. His Granddad had laughed about it after they told him and suggested (in private) that they probably needed to get out a bit more and were: "Bloody seeing things again!"

Alfie sat up, taking the little scrap of paper out he looked down at the list (for what had to be the thousandth time that day) and looked at the little scribbled words:

Dulcis

Laravatus

Vanearo

Consisto

Petivo

Alfie daren't read any more out (much to the annoyance of Tommy who wanted him to say them all), he was in all truths a little apprehensions about what they would do. He also didn't want to get too carried away with Tommy's idea that it was—*magic.* His brain kept telling him how ridiculous he was to think such ludicrous things. *"Coincidence!"* his mind would shout, or *"You were imagining things."*

But here he was with a tiny scrap of paper that had six funny words scribbled all over it, the like of which when read aloud would make a hundred cats come to his front door. Alfie wondered how peculiar it was that only cats should come to him, why not dogs, or elephants? Perhaps that's what the other words did? Alfie shivered again.

He slept most of Sunday, getting up around lunch time. His Grandma was buttering some toast in the kitchen for him when he eventually made it down.

"I wonder why you aren't sleeping?" she said coming over to feel his forehead. "Might be the stress of the last school year," she said. Alfie wished that was true. "I forgot to say, Thomas and Daniel called round early this morning," she passed him the toast. "Seemed quite concerned for some reason when I told them you were still in bed, don't know why. Do you want a cup of tea?" She smiled.

After finishing his toast, Alfie said he supposed he'd better go and knock for Tommy. "Well put your winter coat on," said his Grandma. "There's a chill in the air."

Alfie trudged along the cold roads towards Tommy's and wrapped the knocker. Almost instantly, the door flung wide open. "We thought magic had killed you!" Tommy cried the instant he saw him. "We were debating whether you had been trampled by a thousand cats or something!"

Alfie sniggered. "I just overslept."

"So…" Tommy said letting Alfie inside and pushing him upstairs where Sparky lurked on the landing. "Anything else *happened?*"

Alfie assured them both that if anything did happen they would be the first to know.

The first lesson on Monday morning was English.

"Ok class," said Mr Woodbridge who was tall and gangly, which led to some rather amusing nicknames which cannot be repeated. "Today we're going to be carrying on with our exploration of…" *Bla bla bla*, thought Alfie and his train of thought wandered immediately.

He looked out the window. Suddenly someone zoomed past the window with a big stick, causing Alfie to lurch backwards with fright.

"You ok Alfie?" said Mr Woodbridge.

It was the new girl Gracie—hockey stick in hand as she raced with the rest of her class up to the top field. "Yes Sir," Alfie smiled, he was so jumpy at the moment.

Tommy poked him in the ribs gently before whispering —"Stop looking at the *girls* playing hockey."

"I'm not!" Alfie hissed, looking away from the window.

Half way through the lesson Alfie was bored stiff and the little scrap of paper in his pocket kept playing on his mind.

"Now, I want you to all…" said Mr Woodbridge pointing down at the board. "Copy these sentences from the board and underline the *adverbs*," he said sitting down (knees rising above his desk).

The class began chatting away discussing what an adverb was. Tommy turned to speak to Sparky who was sitting behind them on his own. And this was his chance—he knew what word was next on the list, he'd read them all so many times he knew them off by heart. Alfie had been waiting all day for the perfect opportunity to read aloud one more of the words. He knew it was reckless to do such a thing. He knew it was foolhardy, that people could get injured—but if anything bad happened he could just repeat the word again and all would return to normal. Hopefully. The thing was, in his pocket were words that made things happen. And he really wanted to know what they did.

He sat forward, palms sweating as he braced himself for a hundred dogs to come falling through the roof, a herd of elephants to storm out the stationary cupboard or an invasion of furry guinea pigs.

"*Laravatus*," Alfie said as quietly as he could. Alfie felt a small rush of adrenaline.

Tommy turned back round and looked at him. "Did you say something?"

"No…" he smirked, one eye on the board. Alfie had seen what had happened almost instantly, the words on the board had started to twitch and wriggle of their own accord—then all at once they began floating around the whiteboard like jellyfish, some of the letters (L, Y, X and Q) had left the board completely and had started climbing the walls like mountaineers—Y and X

52

pulled a few of the I's and an S towards them before using them as a rope and hook to latch onto the stationary cupboard door.

It took only a few seconds before everyone in the class looked up and saw what was happening, some of them became unable to speak—a J had landed on Mr Woodbridge's head and he went bright red when he saw everyone staring at him open mouthed—Tommy was the last person to see it.

When he saw what was happening he did a double take. Ever so slowly he turned his head to Alfie very slowly. Sparky grimaced, he was still annoyed that he wasn't right about magic as the class started to yell and woop.

— "How is it doing that?!"

— "What is happening?"

— "That W just fell off! Look!"

Poor Mr Woodbridge tried calming them down. "Now, *now!*" he said, but after five fruitless minutes trying he gave up and pulled a small manual from his drawer, called: *'Your Interactive Whiteboard and You.'*

In Maths, Alfie, Tommy and Sparky were struggling with algebra, not helped by the fact that the classroom was always hot and stuffy. It was an old room with cream walls and plastic orange seats and wobbly tables about a hundred years old. Alfie hated Maths and hated the teacher Mr Taylor-Clarke even more. He was an inwardly evil middle aged man who frowned at noise that the class was making and barked at laughter. After twenty minutes, Alfie was staring into space. From the window he could see Mr Woodbridge, the Headmaster and a few caretakers roping off the English classroom. The chatter and excitement about the letters that had *"taken on alife of their own"* had been quelled immediately by Mr Taylor-Clarke who hated excitement and barked at them to stop making such an awful noise—he was in one of his moods.

Sparky leaned across to Tommy.

"I can't do these..." he said as silently as he could. Mr Taylor-Clarke and his ginger moustache suddenly prickled like an antenna, then turned to stare at them with cold accusing eyes, he didn't like people, or children and he especially didn't like know-it-all teenagers—if he could have his way he'd have the cane back in schools, it never did *him* any harm.

"One of these is wrong," moaned Sparky under his breath, not spotting the stare.

"YOU!" cried Mr Taylor-Clarke at the top of his voice, causing Henry Goofham to fall off his seat in shock. "Did you speak?"

Sparky's lip quivered and he mumbled that he had.

"Detention!" said Mr Taylor-Clarke—his favourite catch-phrase. "*All* next week." Sparky's jaw dropped. Joel cackled silently with Christian.

"That's not fair!" Alfie cried.

"I decide what's *fair* in here Brown!" Alfie felt the blood boil in his veins.

"Sparky—er, I mean, Daniel was only saying how hard these are," said Alfie. Sparky sunk a little in his seat.

"Hard? I used to do these in my sleep!" he spat, ginger moustache quaking.

"God help your wife then," Alfie said without thinking. This caused the class to erupted into hysterics.

"FUNNY! You think this is funny do you? You ignorant child!" Spit flew across the room and children shielded themselves as best they could with workbooks from Mr Taylor-Clarke's wayward spittle. "Stand UP!"

"Noop," said Alfie simply as some of the class began muttering excitedly—typical Alfie getting into trouble again.

"NOW!" bellowed Mr Taylor-Clarke going purple and Sparky jumped so hard, his pencil flew into the air and hit Joel in the head.

"Say… *please*," said Alfie leaning back on his chair and smiling up at Mr Taylor-Clarke's cantankerous, enraged face. The class went silent, but loving every second, unable to believe Alfie's bare faced bravery (except Joel who wished that Alfie got expelled for this). Sparky slid down so far in his seat he was practically under the table.

Mr Taylor-Clarke seemed to compose himself, and walked towards Alfie ever so slowly. "You will stand up, you will be escorted to the Headmasters office and you will do a *months* after school detentions—now STAND!"

"Firstly," said Alfie who was surprised about the casual tone of his voice. "Take the detentions away from Sparky and me, then apologise. If you want me to do something, then address me like a person… I would say please but I fear *you* are not a person, but a monstrous creature of some sort that doesn't deserve to be addressed as such."

Everyone in the class, even Tommy was staring open mouthed between Alfie (whom they didn't know possessed such a way with words) and Mr Taylor-Clarke who looked set to spontaneously combust.

He suddenly roared, unable to speak any longer and charged at Alfie like a Rhino, his left eye twitching murderously.

Alfie knew what he was going to do but didn't have long to think about it.

"*Vanearo*," he muttered. Then pandemonium… the class erupted into utter disbelieving shrieks—as a stark naked Mr Taylor-Clarke stood before them. He stopped charging mid flight towards them, realising he had no clothes on. All rage vanished, but the red face remained. He took one long confused look at Alfie and ran out of the classroom screaming. It took a few seconds of silence for everyone to actually compute what just happened—then they exploded.

"Did you… did you see that!?" said Daryl Mears through tears of laughter.

"You couldn't help not to! *Ahaha!*" Ursula said over the wails and cries.

"Well I thought it was disgusting…" said Jessica Curdle.

Even Henry Goofham was rolling round on the floor in fits of hysterics and Alfie couldn't help but smile from ear to ear when Tommy and Sparky turned to face him after several claps on the back for his barefaced argument with "rage-monster-Clarke."

Alfie, Tommy and Sparky were seated at a clunky wooden table, staring at the periodic table. Tommy had been watching Alfie like a hawk all break time, thinking he was going to do another bit of *magic* without telling him. Alfie sat quite still, a thin smile on his face. He couldn't believe what was happening—the words on that little scrap of paper, left on his doorstep did magic. They made impossible things happen, like make words jump off whiteboards and a teachers clothes to spontaneously disappear into thin air! Alfie had to keep reminding himself that this was not a dream, this was real, and it was by far and away the coolest, most brilliant thing he had ever done.

Tommy casually leaned across and whispered in his ear: "Tell me when you do another. I want to see it all."

"I'm not sure this is a good idea," said Sparky whose worry lines had grown exponentially. "You've already done enough."

It was true, people were talking. In fact, Alfie had listened to several amusing accounts of what had happened in class—the story about what happened getting twisted until it resembled something out of a fairytale with potential UFO involvement and secret technology finding it's way into their English department, to potential nervous breakdowns of teachers that like to strip all their clothes off. Alfie smiled to himself, no one knew it was him causing all the mayhem.

The next word on the list was *Consisto.* Alfie wondered what it would do—he didn't wish for their science teacher Miss Davenport's clothes to disappear, apart from being a ghastly thought he also felt a bit sorry for her. With the anticipation rising, Alfie braced himself, he had to wait for the perfect opportunity. Tommy started banging his head on the table in apparent frustration at the periodic table causing the class to laugh, Alfie used the distraction.

He looked up at the blackboard and Miss Davenport next to it. "*Consisto.*"

Nothing changed—perhaps this one was a duff word, or perhaps he'd said it wrong? Sparky had noticed something and nudged Alfie in the side pointing to Miss Davenport who had stopped speaking and had seemingly frozen to the spot, her actions fixed in one motion—pointing up at a chemical. No one in the room noticed.

"You told me you'd tell me!" whispered Tommy with quiet rage.

Alfie shushed him and said the word again as quietly as he could. Miss Davenport instantly carried on speaking, but she stopped and looked back at the class, almost realising that something had just happened, but she just shrugged and carried on nevertheless.

So, *Consisto* made things freeze! Tommy leaned across and wrote in Alfie's book: *'it makes things stop!!!!'*

Sparky looked the other way, rubbing his head as Miss Davenport asked the class if they would work in pairs and test each other on the periodic table. Muttering broke out as they all paired off and began the exercise, except no one was talking about chemicals, metals or gases.

"Sparky's a fat git," whispered a low deep voice behind them. "Oi, Sparky fat boy, look at me."

"Sod off Curtis," said Tommy turning round to look at the large, dopy looking boy.

"What about... no," said Curtis dimly, he was a weird boy, as tall as he was wide with a lumpy head and one squinty eye—a rugby injury. Alfie saw why the four large bullies had decided to pick on Sparky—Joel, Alfie's enemy sat grinning to himself some way off. He had put them up to this, Alfie just knew it.

"Just ignore him Daniel," said Jessica shooting a nasty glance at Curtis.

Curtis and the bullies cackled before imitating Jessica. "Yeah *Sparkly* just ignore us. We're gonna *get you* new boy."

"Oi!" said Alfie. "Why don't you cork it Curtis, you dumpy git!"

Curtis and Frank stood up, their chairs scraping backwards against the floor. "Now, now boys," said Miss Davenport in a small ineffective voice. All of a sudden Curtis leapt over the table in one lunge as everyone gasped. The floor shook as he landed. He stood over Alfie, who didn't move from his seat. He rather thought Curtis's breath smelt very strongly of beef crisps.

"What are *you* going to do potato head?" said Alfie, fists clenched as Curtis's eyes bulged. Then he went bright red.

Miraculously, with his head low, Curtis loped away back to his seat. Alfie couldn't believe it and nor could Joel who looked positively outraged, he would've paid good money to see Alfie get punched in the face.

Miss Davenport looked relieved. "Right now that's settled, I am sure we would…"

Alfie still had his eye on Curtis. And he was right to. When Curtis reached his seat at the back of the room, he turned away and clutched something, he spun round quicker than Alfie, or anyone else expected. A small bottle of acid clutched between his hands.

"N-*No!*" cried Miss Davenport. But Curtis threw it. It flew across the room. Straight towards Alfie's head. The class screamed. But the bottle stopped, frozen in mid air, an inch from Alfie's nose. He clutched it quickly. There was a long pause, in which the class gaped open mouthed.

"Nice catch Alfie!" said Tommy looking round at the class, then turning to wink at him. The class awoke and then applauded, nodding their heads.

"He caught it?" some of them choruses, confused.

"Reflexes of a *cat*!" cried Tommy as Sparky climbed out from under the table.

"*You*," said Miss Davenport. "May just be the luckiest boy I know."

It's not luck, thought Alfie, he had said *Consisto* just in time. Then Miss Davenports gaze came to rest on Curtis. "Whereas you are about to be the *unluckiest*, follow me." She sounded stern and Curtis didn't argue, his gaze fixed at the floor. "Class dismissed."

Everyone cheered, picked up their bags and left. Joel looked utterly bewildered.

"That. Was. Brilliant!" said Tommy hugging Alfie, then regretted it, so patted him awkwardly on the shoulder instead as Sparky followed them shaking his head.

Drama was one of Alfie and Tommy's favourite lessons, mainly because they could prat around doing silly voices and get told well done. However they both had a sneaky feeling that it wouldn't be Sparky's favourite lesson, he wasn't one for being in the spotlight.

"Hi Daniel," said a sweet voice as they entered—it was the new girl Gracie. Sparky smiled awkwardly and nodded in her general direction.

"Oh don't talk to them losers," mouthed Ashley Di Marco, the snob.

Alfie still felt a little shaken by what happened in the last lesson. Even when he was asked by Mr Drake to do a double act with Tommy, Alfie fell silent and couldn't think of anything to say. Which was very unlike him.

At the end of the lesson Mr. Drake handed round a form that needed to be signed by their parents. It was for a combined Drama and Art trip to London in around a months time. Ashley positively squealed with excitement while Sparky shrank in his seat, muttering that he didn't like London. Alfie and Tommy were surprised they had been handed a sheet, so were the rest of the class. They assumed that they were still banned from school trips—especially school trips to London. Last time they went, a few years ago, they had been banned from three large department stores in a row and the teachers decided that they would not take them anymore.

Mr Drake gave them both a long look. "I am trusting you both." They looked at each other and smiled.

"Thanks Sir."

It had started to get dark as they walked home through the park. The leaves crunched beneath their feet. They stopped at a newsagents on the way home to get sweets. Alfie was helping himself to Tommy's because Sparky didn't agree with sharing. As they walked, Alfie could hear the birds tweeting and was sure we could smell someone's dinner in a nearby house—spaghetti bolognese. He was starving.

"Give us another sweet old chap," said Alfie.

"Here you are," Tommy said, passing him the bag.

"What a day!" said Tommy. "I can't believe all that stuff you did!" Tommy could barely contain himself. "I mean its actual *magic* isn't it!"

"Tommy shhh!" said Sparky chewing on the end of strawberry lace. "What if people hear? I think Alfie has attracted enough attention today already."

Alfie agreed that it was probably better to talk about it later when people wouldn't be able to hear them. Alfie was thinking specifically of Joel and Christian who were walking over the railway bridge a hundred yards ahead.

"But," said Alfie whispering. "I figured something out. The words must work with *thought*." Tommy was concentrating so hard on Alfie and what he was saying that he nearly walked headfirst into a lamppost. "Because I was looking at Miss Davidson when I said *Consisto* and she froze—I was looking at the board when I said *Laravatus* and at Mr Taylor-Clarke when his clothes vanished."

"That was the best one!" said Tommy laughing. "Magic-ing his clothes away like that!"

"I don't think he liked me mentioning his wife," said Alfie

replaying the scene again to tumultuous roars from Tommy. Even Sparky giggled.

Joel turned around to see what all the noise was about, he and Christian were having their own hushed conversation. Just then two girls brushed past Alfie. He suddenly smelt the sweet smelling aroma of Sarah Ashdown. As she passed she turned her head looking straight at Alfie and smiled. Pink lipstick glittered in the fading light, blonde hair shimmered like a golden waterfall. Alfie's attention was captured, his stomach fluttering faster than a cage full of butterflies.

She looked away then caught her friend up, glancing once more over her shoulder at him. Alfie struggled to breath for a few seconds, his heart feeling like it had fluttered away.

"Woah," said Tommy who had also seen it and started to inspect Alfie. "I can't believe that. Do you reckon magic has made you better looking?" Sparky snorted. "Honestly though, the way she looked at you. I think she fancies you, as much as it pains me to say that."

Alfie laughed. "Girls like her, do not like boys like me." He said, even though he'd love to think otherwise.

"Must be magic," said Tommy frowning to himself.

"Keep your voice down about the *you-know-what*!" said Sparky.

"Oh shut up! Listen, I think this is brilliant Alfie, all this stuff. But *erm…well…*" Tommy bit his lip and squirmed.

Alfie rolled his eyes. "What? Spit it out!"

"Well do you reckon the magic words would work for me?" Alfie shrugged, he'd never thought about it, but for some reason he felt quite possessive over them.

"Another sweet?" Tommy offered.

6

Raining Top Hats

The canteen was far too small. But it beat soggy homemade sandwiches. At the end of the canteen was the school stage, used for assembly's and school plays. Tall windows lined the hall showing a misty, cloudy day outside. The tree's were sparse and the ground laden with orange and brown. Autumn had well and truly bedded in.

Alfie, Tommy and Sparky had been waiting in the queue for ten minutes and Sparky was beginning to get restless. "I mean are we ever going to get served?" he kept muttering, throwing nervous glances at the dinner ladies.

"Hey Alfie, why don't you magic us to the front of the queue?" said Tommy, causing Sparky to look even more frantic.

"We are NOT, I repeat NOT supposed to be talking about… the *M word*."

"He's right," said Alfie. "People are talking."

"But…" appealed Tommy, but Sparky and Alfie both shook their heads. Eventually having got their food, all three having gone for the days special—fish fingers, chips and beans—they went to find a table. Joel looked up and glared at him—he had found out that it was Alfie and Tommy who stuffed his locker full of paper. Joel gladly called to Alfie that he'd be reporting him to the Headmaster. Alfie wished Joel the best of luck, and he would have a hard time convincing the Headmaster it was him, without any evidence. Joel scowled back.

Sparky found three seats in a flash—and shoved a whole fish finger in his mouth. There was a high pitched giggle behind them. Alfie glanced over, Sarah Ashdown and the pretty gaggle of girls were hunched together whispering.

Alfie sat down, tucking into his chips, trying to pretend as if he hadn't seen anything, his heart beating a little faster than usual.

"Well, it's quite nice all this time off isn't it?" said Tommy who was referring to the fact that they had only had one lesson that morning. Science had been cancelled while they were clearing the rooms of all acids and dangerous chemicals. English, because they were installing a new whiteboard and Maths because Mr Taylor-Clarke was off ill. But everyone thought it was because he had a mental breakdown and ran through the school naked.

Henry Goofham had been walking round with a new found freedom the past few days as well. Curtis had been suspended, for how long Alfie didn't know, but he heard someone say it was a couple of months. Not everyone was happy about the suspension. The rugby coach Mr Cairns was giving Alfie the evil stare from the teacher's table—Curtis was his best player and they had a very important match coming up.

What with all the events of the day before when Alfie had said aloud the strange words, people had started talking. I mean, it's not very often that whiteboards start acting of their own accord, a boy nearly gets his face burnt off and a teachers clothes completely disappear. Alfie, and his class were the ones under the microscope, it was all their lessons that had all the *'weird stuff'* going on. And now, prefects had been ordered to patrol the school and report back anything that might be deemed remotely suspicious. Alfie saw Nigel sitting at the teachers table in the corner discussing something important with the English teacher. Poor Nigel, who was writing the school newspaper looked frantic and had been inundated since the strange activities in school. He had to rope in extra helpers to stay behind most lunch times, and after school, interviewing ten people at a time—all had different stories. The final edition of the Westbury School Newsletter ended up being more like a weekend broadsheet newspaper.

"Alfie has to be careful Tommy—" Sparky stopped as a patrolling prefect walked past their table. "Look what's happening, posters and patrols all because of…"

"So?" said Tommy. "Don't tell me you're scared of a few *prefects*? Some of them are in the year below anyway. I'm not scared of them and neither should Alfie be—no one knows it was him… and even if they did he could just use it again to… I dunno—seal their mouth shut or something."

"Hmm," sighed Alfie suddenly glad it wasn't Tommy who had the magic words. Mind you sealing someone's mouth up would be good (especially on Tommy) and he wondered if any of the remaining words would do that.

After the recent heightened security, he didn't feel wholly comfortable reading aloud more words in the vicinity of lots of people.

Sparky told them that he was going to tell them all about his dream he had last night, more for changing the subject than anything else. Alfie and Tommy looked at each other as he recounted standing on top of a large building as he saw a flying dragon, "except it was sort of like a person with a face and body."

"Really?" said Tommy feigning interest and then realising something.

"Yeah, but it was like a person, the dragon I mean..."

"Very interesting—Alfie look..." said Tommy pointing at Ashley and Gracie who were carrying trays of food. Gracie stopped and stared at Alfie as if he was a rare artefact, he looked away quickly. Ashley guided her over to a table where her friends Edward and Lucy were sat. Why had Gracie looked at him like that?

"I reckon she fancies you too!" said Tommy reluctantly as another prefect walked slowly past their table. Alfie and Sparky rolled their eyes, Tommy was off again. "I'm just saying, that look she just gave you, looked like she fancies you." Tommy said worldly as Sparky chuckled.

"Not every time a girl looks at you means they fancy you!"

Alfie was about to laugh when he saw a flash to his left. Across the hall's stage, someone dressed all in black skirted across it and behind the long dark curtains. That was strange. No one was allowed on the stage at lunch. Alfie looked at Tommy who was chewing a chip, and Sparky who was still recounting his mysterious dream through a mouthful of beans. No one else had seen it. Alfie looked back, in the darkness of the wings of the stage, he saw two gleaming purple eyes. *His* purple eyes, and they were looking straight at him. Ever so slightly it moved forwards, into a shallow pool of light. Alfie swallowed hard. His shadow was wearing a tall black top hat with a long, black undertakers coat. It's face was as pale as moonlight and transparent, with crusty red smatterings about its mouth. Then in a flash of coat tails, it was gone. Alfie stared after it. Was he dreaming? Or hallucinating? Or could it be that... his shadow had come after him?

Alfie turned back, rubbed his head and made a snap decision.

"Come on," he said standing, abandoning the rest of his lunch, he was going to follow his shadow. Tommy took one look at Alfie's pale face and stood, Sparky however didn't look as pleased to be leaving his lunch.

Alfie marched from the canteen and began to walk up towards the playground.

"What is it Alfie?" said Tommy as they hurried to keep up with him.

"I've got asthma," panted Sparky behind them.

Alfie glanced behind him, but kept his pace. "I saw it."

"Saw what?" said Tommy jogging up the stairs.

"My shadow," Alfie saw a dark flash at the bottom of the corridor through a sea of people. "There!" he pointed sprinting up the long corridor, bumping past several groups of people. Sparky shouted for them to wait but Alfie didn't slow, he skidded round the corner and sprinted down the adjoining corridor with Tommy just behind him looking charged—but then Alfie slowed—they were in the oldest corridor of the school. And it was completely empty and quiet.

"Hey," said Tommy. "This was where the ghost corridor was."

"Shush!" said Alfie quickly freezing still as he saw something move across the wall. They both saw it. Standing at the very end of the corridor, facing the wall... was the shadow. It was feeling around the wall for something. A purple door faded into the wall with a small pop! It pulled the silver knocker quickly

67

and went inside.

Alfie felt rooted to the spot, it hadn't seen them follow it and now it had gone into the ghost corridor. The one they had both found. But, the shadow didn't exist until hours after they left the ghost corridor, so how on earth did it know of it's existence? More importantly, what was it doing in school?

Sparky stumbled up behind them. "Oh—my—god!" he panted.

Tommy didn't look away from it. "It went into the ghost corridor." Alfie started to walk towards it, he had to find out where it went.

"Where are you going?" said Sparky.

But Alfie carried on walking. Tommy caught up with him. "Do you really think we should go in there after what happened last time?"

"Oh no…" said Sparky, seeing the purple door. "That's—that's never been there!"

Tommy grimaced. "That shadow did look a bit… *scary.*"

"Are you coming or what?" said Alfie turning to them both.

"I'm not going in there," Sparky pointed. "If Tommy said it looked scary, then I'm going nowhere near it!"

"I'm not scared!" said Tommy joining Alfie's side. Sparky whimpered.

Alfie slowly approached the tall purple door. He took the silver knocker and pushed. His heart beating a million miles an hour, Alfie felt the chill run down his back again as he crossed the threshold. The stone was damp and slippery with moss and puddles of water glittering in the flickering blue light. The door clicked shut behind them, Sparky whimpered as it faded away to stone. Shiny fire brackets sparkled with blue light showing ten purple doors with silver knockers standing each side. There was a dripping noise, and small scuttling sounds.

"It's the ghost corridor," said Tommy. "But sort of *different*."

Alfie agreed, there was definitely something different about it. Perhaps the blast of green light had damaged it somehow.

"This is weird," said Sparky in a small voice. "I don't like it, lets go back! *Pleeeeease*!".

"I want to find out where the shadow went," said Alfie looking to see if any doors had been left ajar.

"Are you sure that's a good idea?" Tommy said anxiously.

"What's behind the doors?" said Alfie reaching for a handle.

"Wait!" cried Sparky. "We can't just rush into this."

"It's just a ruddy door Sparky, stop being so paranoid, if we get into trouble Alfie will use his magic words." Tommy looked at Alfie expectantly, waiting for him to agree, Alfie nodded.

"Fine!" said Sparky standing out the way.

Tommy took the handle and with a daring expression on his face turned the handle. A torrent of sunlight flooded into the corridor, causing them to dive backwards.

"What the ruddy hec!" said Tommy stunned, Sparky leaned forward quickly and closed the door. He was breathing hard and looked on the verge of madness with his hair up all over the place.

"I must admit, I thought you two were mad when you started going on about all this... but I believe you now... but please, I think we've seen enough."

Alfie and Tommy hadn't seen enough, they were curious, their interest had been caught, the smell from the place behind the door was of coconut, sand and sea.

"Lets go in," said Alfie.

"No!" said Sparky blocking their way.

"Why not?" said Tommy.

"Because," started Sparky with a deep breath. "We are in

school, its Autumn outside, fog, mist, maybe some rain... and we are underground. So how is there a door leading outside!?" He gesticulated wildly, then took out his asthma pump and took three large breaths.

Alfie pushed Sparky aside and opened it. Once their eyes adjusted they could see bright blue sea, a golden beach and palm tree's. A sweet breeze blew in through the door as they listened to the rhythmic sound of the soft patter of waves. Alfie felt himself drift through the door. The sun was hot and the sand softer than silk. When all three made it through, they looked back and saw the open door like a patch of material that had just been cut out of the world.

"The physics are all wrong..." muttered Sparky feebly. "It is lovely though."

"It's not lovely, it's magic!" said Alfie.

"Yeah!" said Tommy his eyes ablaze with wonder. "It's a tropical beach and we're at school! Hey..." he said. "This is better than that school trip to Scarborough." They laughed.

They were standing on a large tropical island, with a shallow blue sea stretching lazily across a golden sandy beach. Alfie picked up a coconut at his feet and wondered if he could open it with magic, although he didn't really like coconut. Tommy walked to the shore and, taking his shoes and socks off, started paddling in the water.

"This doesn't feel right," said Sparky. "I'm not talking about the physics, I mean the feeling..."

Alfie nodded again and looked around. There was no one else here and the only sound came from the small waves.

They joined Tommy paddling but Sparky refused to take off his shoes.

"Ah!" cried Tommy pointing. "Look a little crab!"

They all laughed as a bright red crab scuttled out from the sea and made its way up the bank. There was something in one of it's claws. Alfie noticed it and peered closer. It was what looked like a tiny, black top hat. Black clouds suddenly appeared in an instant across the sky and began to pour with rain.

"Ahh!" Tommy cried, trying to shelter himself from it. But then, they realised... it wasnt rain that was landing on their heads. When Alfie caught some of it in his hands, he realised it was raining tiny, black top hats. Sparky made a funny noise.

A grating, gravelly voice boomed out across the island "BE CAREFUL WHAT YOU BELIEVE TO BE REAL!"

"*Ahhh!*" They all screamed and Tommy fell over in the blackening sea.

"Come on! Let's get out of here!" Alfie cried and they began to scramble back up the sand bank to the door. The whooshing sound echoed again, and when he glanced around to see what it was, he almost toppled over in fright. A humungous tsunami, a hundred double-decker buses high was shooting through the now black sea towards them.

"Quick!" he cried charging up the sand.

Tommy had seen the wave too. "Ah! WAVE! A BLOODY MASSIVE WAVE!"

Sparky was almost crying as he ran as fast as his legs would carry him across the rising tide of tiny top hats. Alfie began to panic, they weren't going to make it! He saw a dark flash past the door and a long dark hand reached round, feeling for the handle.

"No!" cried Alfie. "It tricked us! It's gonna close the door!" Alfie pelted towards it faster than he had ever run before, as a dark hand closed around the handle.

"CONSISTO!" cried Alfie.

The door juddered and froze. The long, dark arm yanked and yanked. There was a flash of red light and the door moved again. Alfie lunged himself through the air, ready to get anything between him and the gap. The door swung as Alfie flew through the air. His foot just about poked through the gap as...

CRACK!

"ARRGH!" he screamed as pain shot up his leg.

"Quick!" Cried Tommy as he and Sparky ran over wrenched the door open. The dark hand disappeared suddenly and they fell to the floor gasping for air.

"Ah, my foot!" Alfie cried.

"QUICK!" cried Sparky diving into the corridor as the whooshing wave loomed overhead. Tommy sprung to his feet and dragged Alfie by the arm through the door. Sparky slammed the door shut. As soon as he did there was a humungous THUD. The door bulged and bent, then returned to normal.

Alfie clambered up as quickly as possible. A door at the end of the corridor slammed. The shadow had gone.

"That was close!" said Alfie, his foot throbbing. He glanced around the dark corridor. "Just watch out for shadows, you know like moving ones. That thing might be around here somewhere."

And it could do magic, thought Alfie as he limped along the wet floor. It had made the effect of his *Consisto* disappear with a red flash. If the shadow had been a little quicker Alfie, Tommy and Sparky would be long gone, in a sea of tiny black hats. And they knew it as they began to walk quietly away back up to school.

"I don't think we should come down here again," said Tommy who was soaking and had left his shoes behind on the beach.

"Every time we come here we nearly flippin' die!"

Sparky turned to them both. "I told you," he said in a small voice, looking traumatised.

7

The White Rabbits Lift

The weekend couldn't arrive fast enough for Alfie who had done barely any homework for the last month. However he knew a walk around town with Tommy and Sparky would be a lot more fun than staying in all weekend looking at boring text books.

He was also a little cautious about opening another textbook anyway. When he had got home on Friday evening and raced upstairs dumping all his books on the floor and getting the list of magic words and putting them safe in his bedside draw—he noticed one of his books wiggling a little. His English work book was moving ever so slightly. Upon opening the book and flicking through the pages he almost had the shock of his life. A large letter "J" sprung off from beneath the pages and started bouncing round his room. Alfie couldn't believe it. It was one of the letters from the English lesson in which he used one of the magic words. It must have found a way into his book and been there ever since! Alfie managed to catch it and put it in an old shoe box, which he tucked safely at the back of his wardrobe. Alfie wondered how many other strange things he would encounter that were the result of this mysterious power.

Alfie, Tommy and Sparky had barely discussed what had happened in the ghost corridor. Every time Alfie or Tommy mentioned it Sparky went pale and started to shush them, trying to forget that anything even happened.

In Alfie's rare quiet moments alone, two parts of his brain were telling him two very different things. One said that there is no way that all this could all be real, who's ever heard of a shadow parting and walking around independently by itself? Or corridors that only appear to you? But the other side said that if it was all in his head then how had Tommy and Sparky seen it too?

Saturday morning and the air was crisp. Golden brown leaves detached themselves and fell to the road—the tree wasn't wrapping up warm in time for Winter but Alfie's Grandma insisted he wore his old puffy jacket with the toggle buttons. Alfie hated it. It was so thick that it was a struggle to move his arms in it. But his Grandma insisted that if he was going to town, then he would wrap up warm. She also tried to wrap his Granddad's scarf around him but he told her that it wasn't *that* cold.

On the way to the bus stop, Sparky walked in-between them both. At the newsagents, Tommy assured Sparky that they'd wait outside. Sparky frowned and went in to get sweets.

Tommy turned to Alfie and looked like he was going to explode. "I tried not to tell him about going into town, so that you and me could talk about what happened. Beacuse he wont let us talk about it! But, he managed to find out somehow."

"You wenr't going to invite him?" said Alfie frowning.

"What? We need to talk without him stopping us. I was even

75

going to try and leave early, before he came. But he was at my house this morning at seven—seven o'clock in the bloody morning Alfie! We're never going to get to talk about this stuff if he keeps…"

Sparky poked his head outside and looked at them suspiciously. "I forgot to ask if you want anything?" Alfie and Tommy shook their heads.

They made their way to town by bus—It was comparatively empty for a Saturday and they sat on the top deck.

"Just think," said Tommy getting comfortable. "We're pretty lucky we are going to town today, we could still be in that…"

"Shh!" said Sparky leaning across. Tommy sighed, it was getting on his nerves now.

"But yeah," said Alfie. "We are lucky."

The bus stopped and looking out of the window in a mood, Tommy noticed something and pointed, Alfie leaned over and looked out, but he couldn't see what Tommy was pointing at.

"The car," said Tommy. "It's Gracie's isn't it? Well not Gracie's but her parents car, she must be going to town today too."

Alfie shrugged. "So? I don't care," he lied.

Tommy and Alfie groaned suddenly as Joel and Christian walked up the bus stairs. Joel saw them and looked like he wanted to go back downstairs, but instead, he pretended as if they weren't there and took a seat near the front.

As they made their way off the bus Tommy shook the drivers hand and thanked him—the bus driver looked quite perturbed but shook it anyway. Joel walked just ahead of them off the bus and announced. "Well I am surprised he could afford the bus fare!"

Westbury was a large market town and every Saturday there was a hustling, bustling market that sold everything from pegs to hog roasts, from hats to books, to electrical goods—whatever you wanted, there would be a market stall for it.

They rounded the corner into the High Street which was bustling with people, Alfie hated crowds and it was particularly noisy.

"Oh get out of the way!" Alfie stopped exactly what he was saying and stepped back in shock as he looked at Gracie's rather shocked face. "Oh hi…" he said.

"Hello," she said, looking as taken aback as he was.

Ashley Di Marco was in a world of her own. "I think we should go to Porshley's next—*ohh*," she said, noticing him and wincing. "What are you doing here?"

"Didn't think we'd see you lot!" said Tommy bounding forwards and shaking all the hands of Gracie, Edward, Lucy and a reluctant Ashley. "What you doing here?"

"Shopping, of course!" said Ashley.

Gracie looked up at Alfie and muttered so no one else heard. "Why are you limping?" she looked curious.

"Oh," said Alfie. "I just… sort of tripped, playing football the other day." Alfie couldn't even bring himself to look at her, the butterflies in his stomach were fluttering wildly and his mouth felt dry. She was beautiful, with dark wavy hair that fell over her shoulders and dark brown eyes. Alfie wished he could spend the rest of the day with her, but he was too nervous to ask. Gracie's dark eyes narrowed a jot, and she was about to say something, before Ashley butted between them.

"Bye then," said Ashley pulling Gracie by the arm and turning away.

"Never mind," said Tommy watching them leave.

Sparky tutted at the two boys as they watched the girls leave. "Where can we go for lunch then?" he said smacking his lips.

Tommy peeled his gaze away. "I swear the only thing you think about is your stomach!"

Alfie continued to watch Gracie and Ashley saunter away with a funny feeling in his stomach. That is until, he saw someone watching him. An almost familiar man was leaning against a wall in the shadow, staring straight at him, from beneath a cowboy hat. The man wore a long black undertakers coat with dark shoulder length hair that spilled out underneath his hat. Alfie swallowed, unable to take his gaze away. It was the man who saved him and Tommy in the ghost corridor.

Perhaps, thought Alfie as he stood struck-dum in the middle of the street, this man was an undercover police officer, sent to find people who could do magic. The theory was soon dashed. Flashing blue lights appeared from the corner of the street as five police cars came storming down the road. Everyone in the surrounding streets turned to look.

Tommy saw him now too. "It's the man from the—" but his words were drowned out by the sirens. The man darted away as police began to jump from cars towards him.

"FREEZE!" one of the Policemen cried, but the man didn't freeze. He darted down the alleyway and stopped before an unassuming grey door. The police raised their tasers and batons surrounding him. "LOWER YOUR HANDS!"

The man slowly raised his hands into air. One of the police cars suddenly roared to life behind them, of it's own accord, for there was no driver. Then, without any warning began to speed towards the police. It sped towards them like a bullet. There was nothing else they could do except jump out of the way.

With a swish of his long coat, the man opened the grey door and slipped inside. Shutting it before any of the police had even got up.

The driverless police car screeched to a halt. The police were up on their feet instantly and charged towards the door.

No one in Westbury high street had ever seen anything so peculiar. Neither they nor the police has ever seen anything like this before, as from the van they fetched a long steel pole and tried to smash the door down. But to no avail.

One of the policemen shrugged. "He's gone." Two of the officers ran over to the car but left scratching their heads when they couldn't find any sign of a driver.

Alfie was crunching through the leaves on his own as the sun was beginning to set. Sparky had made them all go home because they had homework that was due in, apparently. Alfie thought it was because he didn't want to talk about what they had seen—he was scared.

As he wandered home alone, Alfie couldn't help but wonder about that man. Who was he? And why did he keep following him? Alfie had now seen him in the ghost corridor, outside his house and in town. Turning into Mulberry Drive, he heard something rustle in the bushes. Alfie carried on walking, his peripheral vision picking up something moving through Mrs Henderson's garden to his right.

Something was moving through the shadows. A shiver running down his spine. Alfie preyed it was a cat, or a dog, or anything other than what he knew it was. His heart began to race, breath caught somewhere in his throat. An shadowy outline of himself wearing a dark blood splattered coat, a tall top hat and glistening purple eyes climbed out of the bushes.

Alfie stood stock still where he was, gripped by fear. He was alone. The shadows white transparent face glittered, a line of blood trickled from the side of its mouth. It was more solid and less transparent than the last time he had seen it.

"What do you want from me?" said Alfie, his voice quivering uncontrolably.

The shadow smiled its dirty brown pointed teeth. In a flash of black, it was next to him. Cold clawed hands gripped his shoulders so tight Alfie suddenly realised he couldn't move. It's breath was putrid and hot. "What do you want?" said Alfie straining, watching the gnashing of its sharp, dirty teeth.

It's face contorted with effort as it spoke. "I am growing… stronger and… stronger. At some time I will… take *your body*!" Spit flew from its mouth burning Alfie's face. He couldn't break free of the grip but he knew this was the time he had to act!

"Vanearo!" Alfie said (hoping this would make the shadow vanish) there was a ripple in the air between them. A pulse of energy drove a wedge between them with a loud SNAP!

Alfie felt the grip release and found himself flying backwards. Toppling backwards, off balance, he hit the side of the pavement. Alfie didn't stop to think, he turned and ran as fast as he could. The shock of the shadows surprise visit had made Alfie's legs turn to jelly. His sore foot, the bruise from the last time he'd met the shadow stung as he ran. He risked a fleeting glance over his shoulder, the shadow was dancing along the walls towards him. Alfie ran back in the direction he had come. But he didn't know where to go—would the shadow catch him eventually? Alfie was already tired and felt a stitch start to blaze in his side.

Just when all hope seemed lost. When Alfie's stitch threatened to topple him. Just when the shadow was gaining, he saw something up ahead. A small, white rabbit. Standing up against a lamppost next to the newsagents. Then, it darted away. With the last remaining ounze of energy, Alfie gritted his teeth and ran after it. Alfie followed it up the long road as some passer-by's turned to watch. The shadow was still in the corner of his eye and the stitch in his side burned terribly, but he had to keep running up the hill!

The rabbit darted into an alleyway to the right. Alfie spun on the spot, sprinting after it. Then his heart jumped into his throat. A high stone wall at the end of the alleyway blocked any way out—he was trapped.

The shadow stopped at the entrance to the alleyway, silhouetted by the orange lamp light behind it. Alfie realised with a sinking feeling that he must have been tricked.

But through the darkness, Alfie could see the white rabbit trying to signal something to him. It began jumping up and down, as it had done before. It jumped onto a bin and head butted the wall. Alfie got the hint straight away. He knew what to do this time. The wall looked like any other—just like the one in his school. But he knew better than to assume thats all it was by now. Alfie glanced up at the shadow. It was smiling gleefully, before... it charged. Alfie lunged at the wall, putting his palms to the stone.

The shadow zoomed through the darkness in a cloud of black smoke. Alfie's hands were not touching stone anymore. They were touching cold, silver metal. Two silver doors had materialised in front of him. The shadow realised what was happening and roared. The doors slid open. Alfie diving in after the rabbit. The doors snapped shut as the shadow charged into the door.

BANG BANG BANG!

Three huge dents carved deep into the metallic doors.

Ding! Went the lift as it juddered into movement. Alfie breathed hard clutching his side, before, all at once, the lift dropped. Alfie thought he might lose his stomach. He hit the roof and held on for dear life as the lift exploded like a bomb. This was no ordinary lift! Alfie thought he might pass out, the stitch was burning his side, his chest rattling, his sore foot pounding and he was hurtling towards the centre of the earth with no idea where was he going.

8

Nikolas Wiseman

Alfie rubbed his face. He'd just face planted the floor because the lift had very suddenly and without warning—stopped. Now, Alfie had an imprint of the corrugated metal floor on his face. The white rabbit scrambled to its feet as the lift came to a juddering halt.

The lift slowed to a crawl. Alfie's stomach gave a little jitter, he had absolutely no idea where this lift was heading. The florescent lights above their heads flickered. Light between the doors of the lift came in long intermittent green strobes. The lift stopped and as a bell tinged, doors parted slowly. Alfie kept to the sides, not knowing what could be awaiting him. The white rabbit burst from the lift, jumped through the doors and scampered away. As Alfie didn't move, undecided about the strange place he was now in, the floor of the lift made the decision for him. It rose up and flipped him out. Alfie tumbled forwards, as the lift bell tinged, shut its doors and disappeared.

Alfie sat dazed for a short moment, head spinning. He was sitting on lush, red carpet with gold trim. The walls were white stone and were very tall and wide. Long corridors sat to either side of him. The closer he looked the further the corridors seemed to go, reminding Alfie of an everlasting mirror. The ceiling was high and sparkled with candlelight, hot wax dripped from overweight waxy chandeliers, but vanished before it hit the floor.

Something small and peculiar darted across his vision. Alfie had the shock of his life. Something was flittering in mid air, just in front of his face. Alfie wondered if it was the hit on his head that had made him start imagining things. A tiny human-like head peeped out from behind long thin arms. Two stumpy legs hung useless, while its four tiny translucent wings beat furiously to keep it up. This resulted in a noise that sounded like a wasp trapped in a jar. It's little face gorped at Alfie as if he was the odd one in this scenario. The tiny creature started to giggle in a high pitched tone before pulling on Alfie's nose. It darted back in shock when Alfie yelled, batting it away and rubbing his sore nose. The tiny creature looked terrified and whizzed off screeching.

Alfie sat stunned, his heart still beating hard, where on earth was he? He had never seen anything like that. He blinked and thought maybe, just maybe it was just his imagination—probably the bump to the head he took in the lift.

He felt uncertain on his feet after the chase with the shadow. Slowly he started to walk down the long corridor to his left. The candle light in the chandeliers above flickered casting odd shadows on the walls, which made him nervous.

What was he doing here? It didn't look like anywhere he'd ever been, or seen before. And where had the white rabbit gone?

After a few minutes walking Alfie realised that every corridor he turned into was exactly the same as the last, no matter if he went left or right. The same red carpet with gold trim, the same brown doors and gold handles, the same candles burning in the same chandeliers. And what was behind these doors? Perhaps someone who could help—tell him where he is and help him find a way out of here. Alfie wished Tommy was here, just so he wasn't on his own. He felt oddly uncertain without his best friend next to him.

Alfie hesitated before a door in the middle of the corridor. He just needed to ask the person who answered where he was, explain that he's lost and got here via a lift and hopefully they should be able to send him in the direction of his home.

Knock, knock. Alfie waited, then listened for movement, but there was no sound. He knocked again... nothing. Alfie pushed the door very slightly, it clicked and slowly began to open inwards.

"Hello?" Alfie said softly. But there was no one inside. It was a dusty room and looked to have been vacant for quite a while. It was large and empty, with greying walls and dust ridden carpet that rose as he walked across it and got stuck in his throat. There was a large white stone fireplace, a tall mullioned window with long heavy hanging beige curtains.

So, he couldn't be *underground* like he first thought? For there was a dull light shining through the misty window.

The door behind him creaked. He looked up with a sudden, horrible, ominous feeling in his stomach. A pair of hands grabbed his shoulders.

"Aow!" Alfie cried as his hands were wrenched behind his back. "What are you doing!"

Alfie spun round. A young man was standing some way from

ALFIE BROWN: THE BOY WITH PURPLE EYES

him by the door with a cold expression. He didn't move, or say anything. His eyes were dark and heavy and he wore a smart waistcoated suit with golden buttons.

Alfie couldn't move his hands, they had been tied and bound behind his back by a thin glowing blue string. Every time Alfie struggled against the impossible stuff, it tightened.

Ten more tiny, flittering creatures zoomed into the room, squawking and squeaking, chasing after each other and tumbling through the air. Alfie reminded himself that he wasn't dreaming, these tiny things were actually real. The man clicked his fingers and they froze in mid air and drifted into line, standing to attention.

"We have a visitor," said the young man. The tiny things burst into rapturous applause. "It is *NOT* a good thing!" he barked and they fell silent. "Who are you?"

He was cut short as one of the things farted. This caused them to erupt into high pitched hysterics. The man clicked his fingers again and they froze solid.

The young man took a step closer. "Who are you?"

"I'm Alfie *B-B*-Brown…" Alfie stuttered, wishing his heart would stop beating so hard. "I came here by that lift in the wall." Alfie pointed towards the corridor. "I was being chased," said Alfie hopefully.

The man didn't look convinced, he turned to the little things. "Can you go and fetch the *Dedicere*," he said calmly.

Alfie didn't know what that was, but didn't like the sound of it. "Wait! What is that? It wasn't my fault I came down here, I just followed it. I just followed the white rabbit!" Alfie cried, feeling on the verge of tears.

The young man clicked his fingers again. "Cancel the Dedicere," he said and the little things flew back into the room looking disappointed. "Why didn't you mention white rabbit before? Then we wouldn't have had to go through all that nonsense. Follow me," he said, suddenly warm and friendly.

As Alfie stumbled after him, the glowing blue string fell away and dissipated like steam.

"I am Theodore. I am the servant here at Whiteholl Estate."

Alfie swallowed, immense relief flooding through him to not be bound and interrogated any longer. One of the little things glared at Alfie as it zoomed over his head. "What are those things?" he said.

If Theadore was frosty a moment ago, he had completely thawed out now because he was positively bubbling with warmth. "Those *pain-in-the-behinds* are Imps. Creature's from the Faerie world. Devilish little buggers. Have to show them whose boss you see otherwise they'll walk all over you."

Alfie followed Theadore down five flights of stairs. The stairs led to a plain stone floored room, lit only by one solitary candle light with four doors on each side of the room. Theadore looked at the doors for a second, then seeming to make his choice walked over to the furthest on the right and touched the handle. He looked back at Alfie and smiled. "Good luck," he said. "You'll need it."

Alfie grimaced and walked into the dark room. Theadore shut it behind him with a loud click. The room was quiet and dark, the curtains were sealed shut, but he could make out by the low orange embers of the fire that it was very large room.

Sitting in an large, high backed armchair reading was the man in the cowboy hat. The man who had saved Alfie and Tommy in the ghost corridor. Then outside his house after the incident with the gang. Then in town earlier today.

Without looking up from his book, he held out a hand signalling Alfie to sit in the chair opposite. The man didn't close his book, but laid it neatly on his lap.

"I did wonder when I might be seeing you," he said grey eyes piercing the darkness.

Alfie smiled awkwardly and sat down. The two chairs were the only pieces of furniture in the room. Other than that, it was crammed with hundreds and hundreds of old books that were stacked in tall, tottering piles.

"My name is Nikolas Wiseman." His eyes were dazzling, bright and fierce like a wolves. In the firelight Nikolas's face looked deep and old, yet Alfie would have said he was perhaps mid-thirties, at most. There was something else, maybe the way he held himself which made Alfie feel that Nikolas, was a lot older. His coat and cowboy hat sat beside him, next to a pile of books he was using as a drink stand. He too, like Theadore was dressed in a smart waistcoat, trousers and shirt, and wouldn't have looked out of place in victorian London (bar the hat). "But please, call me Wiseman. Everyone else does."

Wiseman put the book down on the floor, the spine read, in gold writing—*Hidden Places and Where to Find Them.*

"You've been following me," said Alfie uncertainly. "You know what's happening to me don't you?" Alfie was reminded of the first time he had seen Wiseman, in the ghost corridor—that was the first, of many weird things to come. "It's just, I've seen you everywhere—when you ran away from the police, you were in the ghost corridor..."

Wiseman burst into laughter when Alfie said *ghost corridor.* It looked like the first laugh he had in a long time.

"Oh that has cheered me up!" he said before chuckling again.

"That *ghost corridor* as you called it—"

"Well *I* didn't call it that," said Alfie hurriedly. "My friend Tommy did."

"Your friend saw it too?" Wiseman nodded quickly to himself and carried on. "That corridor, is actually called a *LeyDoor*. It's an ancient piece of Magic that allows passage between the walls of the world."

Alfie looked at him for a long moment. "Did you say… *Magic?*"

Wiseman leaned forward. "I certainly did say Magic." He reached across and took a book off one of the tottering piles. "All these books in here are about Magic." He passed it to Alfie. It was heavy and had a green leather bound cover. In scrawly gold writing it read: '*Magick: The Art of Charming Inanimate Objects.*'

"Oh," said Alfie. "You spell Magic with a K at the end?"

Wiseman took the book back and muttered that it was the *real* spelling. Alfie chuckled to himself.

"What's so funny?" said Wiseman raising a tall eyebrow.

"It's just… my friend Tommy, he said right at the start that all this was magic. And we told him he was a nutcase, but it really is isn't it?" Wiseman nodded sagely, before jumping up and announcing he needed a drink and bounded from the room like an exuberant toddler.

As he sat Alfie had the strange sense of feeling outside time. This feeling proved stronger by the fact that the three clocks in the room had all stopped, purposely or not, on eleven minutes past eleven. He knew it would be dark at home by now, but the window in this room had light creeping in from behind the curtains. Alfie wished the fire was a little hotter, he kept shivering with cold, even the duffle coat he was wearing wasn't warming him up.

Wiseman didn't seem too bothered by it though. He returned, sweeping into the room with two Imps behind him carrying a tall glass filled with thick red juice with a small paper umbrella and straw in the top. He sat down and sucked happily.

"You, my boy are not just a normal human being. But I am sure you already guessed that didn't you? I, too am not a normal human being." Wiseman sat back and grinned. "I belong to the Mage. We're a race of Wizarding folk separate from…" Wiseman looked up searching for the right words. "Normal human beings. You know the *sleeping ones*—we like to call them *dormies*—unofficially of course.

"Dormies?"

"We're not supposed to call them that, but it just means sleepy ones. Ones that haven't awoken yet. One's that are dormant in the area of magick."

"So you mean everyone had the potential to do magick?"

"Exactly. It's innate and born into all humans."

"Ok," said Alfie slowly. "So how do I know that your not just some nutter?"

Wiseman stared at him and Alfie realised maybe that was the wrong thing to say. Wiseman began undoing his tie a little, then his first couple of shirt buttons. He pulled out a pendant on a long chain.

"This," he held it up. "Is a *skry*." It looked like a clear, shiny black stone. "It's a magickal material that holds all a wizards personal information, proving the wearers magickal identity."

Slowly, glowing orange words faded onto the surface of the skry: '*Nikolas Wiseman — Wizard — Level 33.*'

"Wow," said Alfie wishing he had one. "You're an actual *Wizard* then?"

"Of course!" said Wiseman taking another slurp of the red

drink. "Don't worry I'm not crazy and I haven't made a mistake by inviting you here. I know what you are. I've been watching you."

"It was you who put that note of magic words on my doorstep wasn't it?"

"Note?" said Wiseman confused.

Alfie swallowed and changed the subject. "You said I am not a dormie human. So... what am I exactly?"

Wiseman took a long slurp and put the drink down on the tottering pile of books at his side. "You're like me. You can do magick. You've woken to you innate magickal abilities. You are a wizard." Wiseman grinned at him across the firelight.

Alfie swallowed. "I am a... a wizard?" he shook his head and chuckled. "But, I can't be. I mean, I am just... normal."

"Don't worry, your mind takes time to adjust. It's a big change. Your ego won't like the change, it will put up a fight," said Wiseman matter of factly as if he said these things everyday. "It's lucky that we managed to get to you in time, many people who wake up and find their magickal power go off the grid. It can send them crazy. Others are locked up because they turn to crime and others manage to blow themselves up because they don't know how to channel their new found powers correctly. Either that or they're taken," said Wiseman trailing off.

"Taken? By who?"

Wiseman took a long moment to answer. "You remember in the..." he smirked. "Ghost corridor? The man dressed all in red?" Alfie nodded. "His kind—collect wizards. Not unless we can help it though."

"Where did the LeyDoor come from? And how did that man in red know I would be there?"

"I made the LeyDoor. I wanted to have the chat with you that

91

we are having now… perhaps it was too soon, in hindsight," Wiseman looked into the blazing fire and brushed his hair back. "The man in red, there's lots of him. They can read the future and like I said, they collect wizards. They can't operate in places without Magick, for the only thing keeping them alive is their Magick. Therefore they probably saw the LeyCorridor as the perfect place to intercept us," Wiseman winked. "Didn't succeed though did he?"

"The main aim for you, Alfie Brown is to get you inaugurated into a mage as quickly as possible. You cannot, *officially*, do any Magick until you have been properly inaugurated into a Mage by the Magicity Council—when you receive one of these," said Wiseman flashing his skry pendant. "But…" he said walking around his chair and prodding the fire with a long poker. "There is no WAY that you will be inaugurated until you are rid of that demon."

"So you know about—"

"Know about it? Of course I know about it! It's been following you everywhere. Goodness knows what damage it's caused!"

Perhaps Wiseman like Alfie was thinking about the red blood spatters around the shadows mouth. Alfie forward in the chair, a hundred questions in his mind about all that had gone on. Wiseman seemed to know the answers. "What's the Magicity Council?" said Alfie, but Wiseman ignored him.

"I must also say Alfie," Wiseman grabbed a log and chucked it on the fire. "It is not common to have a shadow demon after you on day one." The fire caught the log and the room lit up. Wiseman's face looked more lined in the dancing firelight as he sat down. "It's not my job to worry you Alfie," he said softly. "But I feel it's my duty to alert you. It's not common, even in the magickal world to have a demon like that after you. While researching you, I only came across a couple of examples. All were highly trained Sorcerers, two died, one survived."

Alfie must have looked puzzled because Wiseman back-tracked. "A sorcerer is a rank above my own, a wizard, and I class myself as extremely proficient in Magick. Your priority, if you want to remain alive is to avoid the shadow at all costs. I will research as well as I can for you," Wiseman glanced the room looking for something. "I have found a collection of spells and charms that will hold the creature at bay, but for how long is hard to say."

"But *why* is there a shadow after me?"

"Hard to say, I've not had much dealing with them. Ah…" said Wiseman looking around at his books. "Now where was it?" He held out a long arm and a book zapped into his outstretched hand.

The side of the book read: *'Magick: Beasts, Creatures and Harm-Dooers from Down Below.'* Wiseman flicked through the pages.

"Aha! Here it is, listen up…" said Wiseman who began to read. "*Er-hum*… a *lynch demon* can only be raised to take the form of something the victim finds revolting. Usually sent to a victim to kill or possess. The lynch demon can only be raised by the highly trained. If the victim miraculously expels the demon from their body, then it will take the nearest thing—usually, the shadow of the victim—leading some to call it the shadow demon. The shadow demon takes a form similar to the victims. It's form grows with the ingestion of blood, which the aggressor will usually provide, however the shadow is adept in finding its own. The shadow demon will do as the aggressor instructs, usually to kill, spy, haunt or reattempt possession. The shadow demon hunts it's victim by tracing the victims used magick.

Only the victim can retain possession of their shadow, to say, only the victim can kill or banish the demon. They cannot hire someone to do it for them. It is not known how to kill the demon. However some claim there is a sword, name not know, that has power over all demonic life—" Wiseman looked up. "And that is the end. That's all I've found."

He took another swig of the red drink and they sat in silence for a minute. Alfie sighed as Wiseman slurped again.

"What is that?" said Alfie. "That drink I mean." It looked a lot like blood to Alfie and he wondered vaguely if Wiseman was some sort of blood drinking creature—it would certainly explain the darkened rooms.

Wiseman smacked his lips together. "Strawberry and blood-orange Daiquiri," he smiled happily. "My new favourite."

Wiseman could obviously tell what Alfie was thinking, for he gave him a wide smile, bearing his teeth, slurped again, then laughed.

Alfie sunk a little lower in his chair. The demon had been set on him by someone, but who? Alfie was just about to ask when Wiseman clicked his fingers and an Imp appeared in mid air in front of him. "Fetch me another," he said, handing it the glass.

"What's a Dedi-cere?" said Alfie, he wasn't sure if he said it correctly. "It's just Theadore said he was going to fetch the Dedi-cere?"

"A *Dedicere*," said Wiseman correcting Alfie. "Is a magickal memory specialist, they can hide people's memories. Comes especially in handy when you think you have a brilliant new wizard and it turns out they haven't a single magickal bone in their body," Wiseman tutted. "I don't know why Theadore would have sent for one, I am quite a good Dedicere myself."

"So it was you," said Alfie pointing at him. "You wiped Nigel's memories!" Alfie stood up out of his chair, more out of triumph for working something out. "The morning I knocked for him... he couldn't remember a single thing about what happened the night before with the gang!"

Wiseman didn't say anything, but smiled contentedly. "We don't *wipe* memories, we hide them. You're not allowed to wipe peoples memories."

Alfie agreed, but pieces of puzzle were slowly sliding into place about the past six weeks. "Which means..." said Alfie recalling the night in question. "You were the one who made that green electricity shoot out of the lamppost at the gang!"

Wiseman chuckled. "You should be a detective."

"You-*hoo*..." came a rather croaky noise. The door opened and a middle aged woman dressed in a pinafore with greying hair tied in a tight bun on the top of her head, came into the room backwards. She had a feather duster in her hand and was frantically pawing at the mass of cobwebs round the door. "Oh look at it in here!" she said in a gravelly voice. "It's absolutely filthy! But he won't let me clean it will he? Oh no."

"Good afternoon Mrs Foot," Wiseman called.

"OH!" cried Mrs Foot, dropping her duster. "I didn't see you—I was just dusting Sir. You know you really ought to try and keep this place looking tidier. If you'll just let me sort these books into nice, neat piles..."

Wiseman waved a hand at her. "It's fine."

Mrs Foot's eyes lingered on the books around the room for a second, and it obviously pained her to leave them in such an unorganised mess. She was frumpy and common looking and in Alfie's head he struggled to imagine her doing magick, or even belonging to a magickal world at all.

"Well I'll be off then," she said. "The dining room needs a good scrub." With that she was off.

Wiseman chuckled to himself. "That's my resident cleaner."

"Can't you just use magick to clean?" said Alfie, saying what to him, seemed obvious.

"I could, but I like Mrs Foot," said Wiseman. "She's a Dormie. Her poor mind is so closed off to Magick, she could see a twelve foot table hoping round in front of her and still think it had been caused by a nasty breeze that had blown in from somewhere."

Alfie frowned. "What, even though she could see it happening in front of her?"

"Absolutely," Wiseman pointed fervently. "Some people in this world can only accept their own reality. If something happens to counter that reality, their mind will fill in the blanks. Anyway, I like having her around."

Suddenly a loud crash echoed around the room. Alfie jumped half a foot in his chair with fright. It sounded like an elephant had been let loose, the chandelier shook above them.

"What was that?"

"Don't worry, it's probably just Gareth," said Wiseman matter of factly, as if Alfie knew exactly who *Gareth* was. "He's being a bit of a pain recently." Alfie could hear running footsteps and more crashes, but Wiseman carried on talking nonetheless. "I would like to know one thing before I am called away. It intrigues me. The magick that you performed in your school... originally I thought it was just your power naturally occurring. But you found some spells didn't you?" Wiseman's voice had gone cold.

Alfie all but froze in his chair. He had already established that Wiseman hadn't given him the note but that only led to the question—who did? The long pause gave him away.

"The note on your doorstep?" he said. "Do you have it on you?"

Alfie got in out of his pocket and passed it across. Wiseman took it and held it before his face, inspecting it thoroughly, turning it over in his hands. "Strange, strange..." he kept mumbling.

"What is?"

Wiseman looked at it a while longer, then passed it back, a deep frown forming on his face. "There's no magickal trace on it. Usually a Mage will leave a trace on it, bit like a finger-print. But whoever gave you that didn't want anyone to know."

BANG! CRASH! came another huge explosion of noise above them. Wiseman ignored it, but Alfie was worried about what on earth this Gareth was doing. The next moment, the door opened.

"Wiseman," called Theadore in a resigned voice. "It's Gareth again."

Wiseman rolled his eyes, looking peeved. "It's this Knark I've been unable to get rid of—causing me all sorts of problems."

"Wiseman!" called Theadore as another *CRASH!* vibrated the walls.

"What's a Knark?" said Alfie above the noise.

"An old demon. Don't worry he's harmless. Just gets a little... upset sometimes," said Wiseman and Alfie made a note to never bump into a Knark.

"Theadore could you escort Alfie home," said Wiseman as Theadore bowed looking relived.

"But..." Alfie had so many questions! He didn't want the meeting to end! Where had the white rabbit gone? And was it magickal in some way? When would they meet again? What did he do if he came face to face with the shadow again? "What happens now? I mean with the shadow and everything?"

"Do not worry about the shadow for now, I have it at bay, but Alfie…" Wiseman took Alfie by the shoulders so that Alfie was forced to look into his powerful stare. "Promise me that you won't use your magick, or those spells. No if's or buts…" All Alfie could do was nod into the piercing grey eyes. "Promise me also that if you see the shadow, you run. I will be in contact with you in the near future. Now go, I am a busy Wiseman."

Theadore appeared by Alfie's side as Wiseman marched from the room and disappeared out of sight. Alfie followed Theadore out of the room and back the way they had come. Long, loud crashes reverberated the stairways as far off shouts of complicated sounding magick seemed to quell the demon.

Theadore led the way silently along a long old corridor which was lined with many photographs in frames. There were hundreds, mostly black and white, that stretched up as high as the ceiling on both walls. They all, in some way or another, had Wiseman in them. One of the pictures suddenly caught Alfie's attention, causing him to double-take. Then stop abruptly. As a trickle of uncertainty and confusion seemed to flood his brain. He had to look closer to see it wasn't just a trick of the light. In a small black and white photograph, in a small silver frame, a little charred round the edges was someone he recognised. Alfie's heart skipped a beat. Nikolas Wiseman was standing with an arm around Alfie's French teacher… Mr Sapiens.

Alfie blinked rapidly, trying to see if it really was him and not just someone who looked like him. But the more he looked the more he was certain, the dark olive skin and stubble, smart dress and confident smile of a younger looking Mr Sapiens.

Theadore noticed his pause. "You coming or not?"

Alfie apologised and followed, with a feeling that he was falling down a very long and dark rabbit hole.

9

The Disapearing Teacher

Sunday morning was a gloriously sunny. The radio was on downstairs and Alfie could hear his grandparents laughing at whatever was on. His Grandma had woken him ten minutes ago by pulling his curtains wide—she always did this and it really annoyed him. She told him to get up and start revising. To spur him on, with what she thought was an incentive, was a plate of buttered toast (cold now) and a cup of tea (cold now).

As she left these on his table she mentioned that Tommy had rang the house that morning. But she told Tommy that Alfie had to stay in and revise.

Alfie didn't mind this too much, he didn't think he could face another barrage of questions from Tommy, especially about every thing he had been told by Wiseman. He could barely compute it all himself. He just wanted to be on his own for the day, with his own thoughts, in peace. The doorbell rang, and Alfie suddenly remembered, his Grandma was hosting a coffee morning at their house today. Oh no, around twenty people would be pilling in soon. He would have no peace. Alfie sighed.

After getting dressed and bypassing the cold tea and toast,

Alfie took himself off to the park. His Grandma stopped him in the hallway before he managed to get out the front door, as she went to fetch more biscuits. "Where are you going?" she said sternly.

"*Erm…* left some of my revising books at Sparky's," Alfie said quickly.

"Well be quick," she said before frowning. "Whose *Sparky?*"

"Friend at school."

"Why does he have *your* books?" but before she could finish his Granddad called from the kitchen.

"Beryl! Another coffee for Margaret." His Grandma sighed.

Alfie took his chance. "Bye! Be back soon," he nipped out the door before she could stop him.

"Don't be long!" she called, through the open letter box. "Mr and Mrs Henderson want to say hello to you!"

It was such a warm sunny day for December that Alfie decided he didn't need his puffy duffle coat. Walking along Mulberry Drive he wondered what Nikolas Wiseman had meant about keeping the shadow at bay. Every shadow he now saw, cast long in the midday sun, made him jumpy.

As he walked alongside the park—he noticed the tall iron railings being re-painted by the park keeper, an old man who always wore a funny blue bobble hat. Alfie's heart jumped for joy, the park was empty! Time to think properly at last.

It was a large park, with an adventure play area at one end, a small forest of trees at another and a large green expanse that, come summer would be teeming with people. Alfie sat down under a large oak tree with a big hole in its root, the warm glow from the sun felt like a cosy blanket and Alfie felt fully relaxed. Alfie reasoned that he should be digesting everything Wiseman had told him yesterday, but his mind brought up the last thing he had seen before he left his house—the photo of Wiseman and Mr Sapiens. He knew what Sparky would say if he told him—coincidence!

If he could just speak to Mr Sapiens and find out how he knew Nikolas Wiseman that might give him some answers? On the other hand, he could just ask Wiseman the next time he saw him... but, when on earth would that be? There was a sudden gaggle of noise from a few people that had just entered the play area. Oh great, thought Alfie, he couldn't get peace to think anywhere.

He turned over on the grass and looked over. He knew those people. Alfie's stomach did a little flip—it was Ashley and Gracie. There was triumphant sound as a boy swung from the swings and soared through the air and landing perfectly.

It was Christian—then Alfie's stomach lurched as Joel came waltzing in from behind the slide. What were they all doing in the park together? Alfie watched transfixed, unable to move in case they saw him.

Half an hour later, they decided to leave—Christian called something to Joel and they began to walk off. Joel looked quite pleased, he and Ashley had sat in silence at opposite ends of the climbing frame while Gracie and Christian were on the swings together.

Alfie ducked down as close to the ground as he could get as they all walked away from the play area. Christian took Gracie's hand in his as they disappeared together over the bridge. Alfie rolled onto his back, suddenly a horrible pain spasmed in his stomach. He felt sick. Alfie realised with a dawning realisation that he was jealous, of Christian, who was walking away hand in hand with Gracie. The lovely, beautiful Gracie.

When he got home, Alfie ran straight upstairs and jumped on his bed, burying his head in the pillow—the image of Christian and Gracie holding hands burned into his mind, impossible to shake off. His stomach twisted as he tried to let go of the image of their interlocking hands. Alfie sat up and swallowed, he told himself not to be so stupid and that he didn't stand a chance with her anyway, so its best he just forgot about her. He didn't even understand why he felt like this, it was totally irrational. He had never felt like this about anybody—it was horrible.

Alfie sat back on his chair shaking his head of the image and trying to think of more important matters. Alfie wished he had recorded everything Wiseman said. It spun through his mind in one complicated mass of confusing information.

But Mr Sapiens his French teacher was in a photograph at Wiseman's house. Wiseman was a wizard, so what does that make Mr Sapiens? Surely not just a French teacher?

Wiseman's words echoes around his skull—*"The main aim for you, Alfie Brown is to get you inaugurated into a mage as quickly as possible. You cannot, officially, do any magick until you have been properly inaugurated into a mage by the Magicity Council..."*

So, if Alfie managed to defeat the shadow, he would become like Wiseman, a wizard and a mage. At the moment he wasn't allowed to do any magick at all. But how on earth Wiseman expected him to figure out how to defeat the shadow? He had all but said it was next to impossible.

Alfie shook his head and rubbed his eyes. He felt dizzy trying to think about it, what with everything else—Gracie, and studying and now the mystery of Mr Sapiens.

Perhaps he knew what was happening to him?

The long and short of it was Mr Sapiens was connected to

magick and Alfie needed to speak to him about his connection to Nikolas Wiseman.

By Monday morning Tommy was giving Alfie the cold shoulder. When asked why he wasn't around, Alfie lied and said he had been feeling 'a bit ill all weekend'.

Alfie debated in his head about telling them what had happened, but somehow it felt easier keeping it to himself.

Sitting on the benches in the playground Alfie felt detached—there were conversations happening that he was observing but not taking in. Wiseman's words were echoing round his head. The photo of Mr Sapiens next to Wiseman plastered across his vision. Followed by Christian and Gracie's hands and rather sick, jealous feeling. Alfie felt like time had bypassed him completely when the bell rang for the end of the day.

"What's been up with you today?" said Tommy, as they were walking up the main corridor to leave for home. "You've been spaced out."

"Yeah you feeling ok?" said Sparky in a concerned voice.

"Will you two stop asking if I'm ok. I'm quite able to manage myself," Alfie snapped. "Anyway, I'll er… speak to you both later."

"Why?" said Tommy looking haughty. "Where are you going?"

"I've got… extra French lessons," said Alfie turning away, hoping they wouldn't spot his lie.

"You never told us?" said Tommy slowly.

"I forgot," Alfie smiled but it was probably more of a grimace.

Alfie felt them watching him as he walked in the direction of the languages department. Tommy knew something was up—but Alfie just couldn't find the necessary action to either

104

tell them what was going on, or at least pretend like everything was normal. Instead, he had invoked Tommy's suspicion, and that was never a good thing.

Why should he tell them anything anyway? He didn't have to, Alfie thought as he made his way back along the sparse corridors, glad he was on his own at last.

Alfie opened the door to the French block. A small alcove cast suspicious shadows on the walls that unnerved him—shadows seems to attract his attention a lot more these days. He walked over to the French room and looked in through the small door window. Darkness.

Where could Mr Sapiens be? Teachers normally stayed later than the pupils to do *stuff*. Alfie went along and peered inside all the other windows, but all were empty.

"And what are you doing, skulking around?" A sulky voice rang around the walls. Alfie nearly jumped out of his skin with fright and turned to see Joel, standing in the doorway of the French block—standing a bit taller than usual and puffing his chest out. Obviously aware that it was just him and Alfie.

"I could ask you the same thing," said Alfie regaining his composure.

The image of Gracie and Christian in the park flashed across his mind and he felt the burning jealousy in his stomach reignite.

"I am a prefect of course. On duty, making sure there is no one… up to no good," said Joel tapping the little gold badge on his chest and daring a few steps forwards. "I am sure the Headmaster will be interested to hear that you've been creeping around the French block."

"You tell him, you tell exactly what you saw… me walking around looking for Mr Sapiens to have a look over my home-work. You tell him that, I'm pretty sure you'll get a medal for your daring vigilante work."

Joel rolled his eyes. "I've been entrusted with the other prefects to find out who and what is going on with all the... weird stuff," said Joel stepping forwards.

"I couldn't care less."

"And my prediction..." said Joel ignoring Alfie. "Is that its all down to *you*. The weird stuff happening was in every class you were in. And there isn't anyone else in this school with disgusting PURPLE EYES! I mean, it's not *natural* is it?"

"Sounds like jealousy to me. Just because I am different." Alfie had enough, he pushed past Joel and went to leave the French block.

Joel suddenly smirked. "On the subject of jealousy. How is Gracie?"

Alfie stopped—how did he know? Joel must have seen him at the park. Now he was smirking from ear to ear. Alfie regretted promising Wiseman that he wouldn't do any magick, because he sincerity wanted to use some now. It took all of his inner strength to bite his tongue and walk off, ignoring Joel's loud laughter and stomped all the way to the main building.

Some teachers were milling around at the top of the stairs where the staff room was—Alfie, feeling apprehensive poked his head round the door. Three teachers sat, two he didn't recognise and Mr Taylor-Clarke who took one look at Alfie before disappearing behind a large shaking newspaper. Mr Sapiens wasn't in here either.

Alfie stomped around the school for the next twenty minutes, silently cussing Joel under his breath, and searching, but Mr Sapiens was no where to be found. He would have to wait until tomorrow, when he had French.

Alfie had a plan in his head to wait behind after class and talk to Mr Sapiens when every one had gone, which was a good plan—or so he thought.

He sat down in the French class before anyone else, watching Tommy walk in with Sparky looking puzzled.

"You really do want to do well in French don't you!?" Tommy joked, slightly unnerved.

Alfie grimaced, he felt apprehensive and as the rest of the class entered felt a rising tension. He scanned Mr Sapiens desk, there was nothing on it that suggested he was out of the ordinary—let alone a Wizard! Perhaps he wasn't, perhaps he was just someone Wiseman thought was a wizard, but turned out wasn't so hid all his memories? For why would a Wizard teach French in an small English town?

Mr Sapiens opened the door and walked in. Causally propping his satchel against his desk and facing them all. Alfie stared. Here he was. The rugged good looks, olive skin and intelligent eyes of Mr Sapiens whom he never even gave a second thought to at the start of the year—but now Alfie felt paralysed.

Alfie waited patiently the whole lesson, doing his work in a dream. Thinking the whole while what he could say to Mr Sapiens when the rest of the class had gone.

As soon as the bell went Alfie's heart leapt, at last! He sat patiently folding his bits and placing them into his bag as slowly as he could. Everyone else was rushing and already out the door.

"You coming or what?" said Tommy peering at him from the doorway. "It's break time!"

Alfie stood slowly picking up his bag. "You go ahead, I just need to speak to Mr Sap—" but when Alfie looked up, Mr Sapiens was not in the room. Alfie spun round, the room was empty. He didn't even see him leave. Where on earth did he go?

On Wednesday, Alfie left English early saying he needed to go the toilet. Once free Alfie went to the French block and waited outside Mr Sapiens classroom. He could see him inside. He could hear him inside. Alfie swallowed, he would definitely catch him this time.

But, as soon as the bell rang, Mr Sapiens did not come out when the class exited. Alfie looked in the room and saw it completely empty—the funny thing was, unless he left via a window there was no other exit.

On Thursday, Alfie waited on a bench next to the language block and Alfie had a good view of him through the window and of the hallway—Alfie would be able to see exactly where he went. Or so he thought… the class piles out and Alfie craned his neck for the sight of Mr Sapiens in the classroom or hallway. But he was gone. It was as if he had vanished into thin air. One second he was there teaching his class, the second, the was gone. Alfie moved inside, this was ridiculous. He wasn't in his classroom and Alfie hadn't seen him leave. Alfie started to think that maybe, just maybe, Mr Sapiens didn't want to be found!

On the last day of the week Alfie was at his wits end. He hated feeling powerless—he just could not work out how Mr Sapiens was so hard to find. Alfie had hardly spoken to Tommy or Sparky all week, in fact he had hardly spoken to anyone all week. He did get the occasional smirk from Joel but that was to be expected. At the end of the day Alfie waited for everyone to leave, by sitting on a bench at the back of school—he wasn't even sure why he was still trying—in lessons Mr Sapiens was there but as soon as Alfie tried to be alone with him, he vanished.

Alfie made his way to the French block one last time, he had to find out how Mr Sapiens was vanishing like this. He peered in through the window, but again—empty. Alfie heard footsteps approaching the language block and glancing to the left he saw it was Mr Sapiens. At last!

Alfie tiptoed up to the coat racks and hid behind some left behind coats, holding his breath. Pushing a dank green jumper to the side, he watched as Mr Sapiens unlocked his French door, went in, and returned carrying a small satchel.

Then the amazing happened, just what Alfie was hoping for—Mr Sapiens locked his French door and instead of walking back out the block, he took two steps to his right and facing the blank wall put his hand to it. Closing his eyes as he did so, until, a door faded into the wall with a small pop. He walked straight through it, before the door disappeared with another small pop.

Alfie moved from out of the coats slowly and walked to the wall, where there was no door anymore. Mr Sapiens *was* different. He was a wizard. He had walked through a LeyDoor in the wall. Now all Alfie had to do was go through the door and speak to him…

Alfie put his hand to the wall, in exactly the same place Mr Sapiens had done. But nothing happened. He waited, and waited, he took his hand away and tried the other hand. When that failed he tried different parts of the wall. Perhaps you had to speak French to it, thought Alfie, but he was rubbish at French so that wouldn't work.

"Oh COME ON! OPEN!" he cried, frustration boiling over, kicking the wall and stubbing his toe. Alfie ran at it and shoulder barged it. "AHHOOW!" He cried and fell to the floor, furious with it.

"'ave you quite finished?" said a deep gravelly voice. Mr Sapiens stood in the doorway of the LeyDoor looking down at him. Alfie got up quickly and Mr Sapiens looked stony. "Can I 'elp you?" he said.

"Mr Sapiens…" said Alfie standing up and brushing himself down. "I've been trying to talk to you for ages!"

"Why?" he said sternly. "What were you doing out 'ere making all 'dis noise?"

Alfie felt relif at finally finding Mr Sapiens flood through him. "Trying to get into that LeyDoor Sir."

Mr Sapiens looked so shocked, he stumbled back into the wall. "You-*you* mean you can see it?" he said looking behind at it.

"Er *yeah*?" said Alfie. "It's red, with a gold handle. I've only ever been through purple LeyDoors."

Mr Sapiens didn't say anything for a long moment—seemingly shocked into silence, his mouth slightly open, eyes blinking unbelievingly as if he had just awoke in some fanciful dream.

"Follow me…" he said turning and going through the Ley-Door.

Alfie grabbed his bag and followed Mr Sapiens down a small flight of carpeted stairs, which led into a long gothic stone corridor. They walked in stunned silence to the only door that had a sign on it that read: '*Silviu Sapiens.*'

The room was large with a high jutting ceiling made of hundreds of wood beams and three stone arcs. The walls were made of large warm coloured stone, reflecting the candlelight, which—like in Nikolas Wiseman's house—came from a tall and immense chandelier with hundreds of dripping wax candles.

It was like stepping into an ancient magical castle. Mr Sapiens could challenge Wiseman for the amount of books he had, but his were organised and sat in neat rows across tall bookcases. One comfy leather armchair sat in one corner next to a large ornamental window. A fire at the other end of the room was blazed, with a tidy desk in front of it.

"Take a seat," said Mr Sapiens sitting down gingerly, a puzzled frown etched onto his face. "How do come to know of LeyDoors?"

"Nikolas Wiseman told me—" said Alfie, sinking into a seat before the desk.

Mr Sapiens blinked rapidly and looked away as if he hadn't heard him right. "Wiseman? But—you couldn't—" he stammered.

"That's where I saw the photo of you and Wiseman, at Whitehollˍ…" said Alfie.

Mr Sapiens leaned back on his chair and brushed his hair back. "C'est impossible," he said to himself muttering what Alfie presumed was French under his breath, before regaining his posture and sitting forward. "What do you know about the Wiseman and how did you come to find yourself in Whitehollˍ?"

"It all started when I followed a white rabbit. I was being chased by my shadow and I took a lift-type-thing, like a LeyDoor, in the wall in an alleyway and then I was in this dusty old manor house with Imps and a Knark and a servant called Theadore." Mr Sapiens chewed his pen and watched Alfie intently. "He told me about magick, and wizards and stuff."

"You mean to tell me, you actually spoke to him?" Mr Sapiens said as if this was impossible.

"Yeah I did Sir."

Mr Sapiens got up from his chair and walked around the same

spot for a minute. Alfie carried on. "Me and Wiseman talked for a bit, then as we left I saw a picture of you and Wiseman together and I didn't think it was real. My French teacher, next to the man that just told me magick exists and that I was a wizard… I had to find you to ask what you knew, if this was all real, or all some big practical joke?"

Mr Sapiens took a deep breath and leaned back on his chair. "What did he say about magickal training?" he said, looking up at the ceiling.

"I can't do anything until I get rid of my Shadow…"

"Shadow? You don't mean… a Lynch Shadow?" said Mr Sapiens incredulously. Alfie nodded.

"But *how*?"

"Well it was sent by someone—"

"No, no I don't how did it get to you," said Mr Sapiens, waving his hands. "I thought it was only… but you are only a boy…" Mr Sapiens struggled, before frowning. "How did all this start? Tell me *everything*."

Alfie sat back, took a deep breath and began to tell Mr Sapiens everything that had happened since the start of the year, it took a while but Mr Sapiens sat listening intently.

"… And Wiseman said that I am not to do any more Magick…" said Alfie with a grimace.

"That's probably for the 'ze best, you don't want you blowing up the whole school." Mr Sapiens took a deep breath and fiddled with some pens on his desk—obviously thinking hard about what he was to say next. He looked out of the darkening window. "I knew Wiseman a long time ago. When I was a teenager, growing up in a small town in France. I knew I was different. I had a power. It got me into all sorts of trouble at first and the thing is, I couldn't use it willingly. It would just 'appen. At first being different did nothing good for me, I had no friends and my parents pretended I wasn't theirs. I know can you believe that? I moved away to the city and 'ad a hard time working as a chef. My abilities, as Magick often does, leaks into things you do, when you don't know how to channel it. The food I created was brilliant but all the while I kept seeing this man follow me—a good year it took him to finally pin me down. He was a young man called Nikolas and he told me I was a wizard and could do magic. He took me all over the place to strange places and showed me amazing things and introduced me to people that could do Magick the same as me. A year laster I was inaugurated into a Mage and finally I felt like I fitted in. I had some wonderful years working at the White Council. But then strange things began to 'appen… prophecies and…" he stopped and rubbed his chin. "We were warned to give up the work we were doing. They kept to their word and our secret centre was infiltrated and burnt to the ground. Along with many Mage. Others were scared off. Included me…"

"So who infiltrated the White Council?"

"I don't know," said Mr Sapiens darkly, fiddling with a pen on his desk before standing and stretching. "So that was my story. Now onto yours. I have only known two people that had a Shadow after them and neither of them are alive to tell the tale."

"Wiseman said he'd keep it at bay for now. But I am going to have to find a way to defeat it."

Mr Sapiens raised his eyebrows. "I think Nikolas Wiseman has high expectations of you…" the fire crackled. "He always talked about someone who—"

"Who what?" said Alfie, but Mr Sapiens looked away.

"I…" he stuttered, before changing the subject. "I noticed that strange things have happened around the school the past few months. I am just guessing that some of it is down to you?"

"All of it I think…" Alfie said smirking—he couldn't help it.

"Where did you get the spells from? What book?"

"Are they *spells*?" said Alfie. "I got them from a note left on my doorstep."

Mr Sapiens eyes narrowed and he looked to the ceiling. "Wiseman is right to ask you not to use Magick, until you understand it. Magick has rules… use too much you'll go bad and blow your spark. Use the wrong Magick and it can take over you. It can become addictive and will soon become hard to differentiate between the wizard and the magick. You might witness it one day, someone who blew their Spark—we call them *Scabs*," said Mr Sapiens in a disgusted voice. "I would be wary of using Spells that you found on your doorstep, sounds particularly strange."

"Wiseman said he couldn't trace who put them there."

"Did he?" Mr Sapiens looked very worried for a second. "Then I would trust his judgement," Mr Sapiens pointed. "It's also important too that you stay off the radar. Magick can be traced straight to you, there are some people who would see you as an ideal target. A young wizard, unprotected by Mage law, is a sitting duck." Mr Sapiens finished, sat back and saw the darkness outside the window and decided it was time they adjourned. There were still so many questions Alfie wanted answering but bit his lip, there would be more opportunities.

They walked back out of the LeyDoor and into the French block, Mr Sapiens walked Alfie to the school gates. "I must stress," he said, turning to Alfie. "That you cannot talk about this to *anyone*."

114

10

The Old Library's Secret

Alfie had the whole weekend to think about what Mr Sapiens said. Tommy had called, but his Grandma said Alfie was not to be disturbed as he was revising. He wasn't, he was just pretending. Having laid all his school books out over his desk, before laying down on his bed. When his Grandma came in to check on him he would jump over to his desk and pretend to be deep in concentration. When she left, he would go back and lie down again. On the third visit, his Grandma caught him lying down.

"I'm allowed a rest aren't I?" said Alfie.

His Grandma gave him a long, cold look. "You've only been revising for an hour!"

After that it was fine, because his Grandparents went out, so Alfie could think in peace. He thought about the conversation he had with Mr Sapiens last night. At first Mr Sapiens seemed surprised that Alfie had spoken to Wiseman, as if that was somehow an impossibility. Then he too suggested avoiding the magic spells that were left on his doorstep.

It was strange, now Alfie came to think of it—he would have

put money on it being Wiseman who put the spells there. He was the one who followed Alfie and knew where he lived. But quite obviously it was someone else. Alfie didn't know anyone else, apart from Mr Sapiens, who was connected to magick. Mind you, he'd already found out his french teacher was a wizard, so who else could be?

Alfie, Tommy and Sparky were walking to school, Tommy was crunching through the leaves with gusto. Alfie still hadn't told them about Mr Sapiens or Nikolas Wiseman and the burden of it was wearing him thin. He had however, confided in them what he saw in the park the week before.

"I can't believe Gracie and that bloody creep Christian. He's so posh and ergh..." said Tommy. "Did you know he can speak four languages!" he said as if this just proved beyond any doubt that Christian was a complete creep.

"I know," said Alfie and they talked about Christian's silly posh accent and his horribly pristine hair—this made Alfie feel a lot better.

"When did you see them at the park?" said Sparky.

"Oh—" Alfie suddenly remembered that was the day he'd pretended to be ill so he didn't have to see Tommy and Sparky. "Christian's an idiot isn't he!" Alfie said, choosing to ignore Sparky.

But Sparky had opted for a suspicious tone. "And how was extra French classes Friday night?"

"Fine, just fine..." said Alfie glancing down at his feet.

"Learn any new words?" said Tommy, oblivious to the lie, as he crunched through more leaves.

"Not really," said Alfie wishing they'd talk about something else.

Sparky snorted. "You mean you didn't learn—"

"Shut up Sparky!" said Alfie, before laughing. "I mean, who wants to talk about work and school and stuff anyway?"

"Yeah," said Tommy. "You're such a nerd sometimes Sparky."

Tommy carried on nattering away to Alfie about anything and everything. Alfie could tell however that he wanted to ask *something*.

"So," said Tommy. "Do you reckon you're going do any more... you know *magic*?" he whispered.

Alfie knew it, Tommy was dying for Alfie to do some more and had dropped so many hints recently. But Alfie couldn't say: '*No, I can't do any more magick because Nikolas Wiseman told me not to*'—for that would mean he would have to explain who Nikolas Wiseman was. And then they would find out that he hadn't been entirely truthful with them.

"Guess what," said Tommy. "It's the school trip tomorrow!" He cried jumping into a large pile of leaves.

Alfie told his Granddad about the trip the night before and he made Alfie a special packed lunch. It included big crusty bread cheese sandwiches, crisps, an apple and some money for a chocolate bar and drink. Alfie smiled as his Granddad packed it all into a large tupperware box. Alfie suddenly had a flush of emotion. He wanted to tell his Granddad everything. Everything that had happened to him the last few months to do with magic... But then, the phone rang. And Alfie knew that he couldn't tell him. He couldn't tell anyone.

It was the day of the school trip to London. Mr Drake and Miss Cairney stood by the coach, clipboard in hand marking off the names of everyone who boarded the coach. Alfie, Tommy and Sparky got on, marching to the back of the coach and were told rudely by Frank and Bruce that they should push off if they knew what was good for them. So they took some seats in the middle. Then slowly, the rest of the class made their way on. Jessica Curdle and Sarah Ashdown took a seat together in the middle, Sarah looking decidedly bored already as she looked longing out the window for her real friends who were stood in a huddle outside in the playground giggling. Then Gracie, followed by Christian sat down in their seats together. Alfie glared, along with Tommy.

The coach drive felt long, Miss Cairney tried to alleviate some of the boredom by reading out the *itinerary of the day*. Alfie kept glancing across at Gracie and Christian. He couldn't help it. He had a good view of them from here and they didn't seem to be talking. After two long hours, they had made it, the coach driver dropped them off and Mr Drake led the way to the art gallery.

The art gallery was big, and did indeed have lots of art in it. They were to wander around on their own and meet up in a few hours. Alfie struggled to comprehend how he could spend a *few hours* in here. They had to leave Sparky behind, out of frustration, he was moving from picture to picture, staring at them and making crooning noises.

After an hour Alfie had been round three times and seen everything. "I'm going outside, you coming?" he said to Tommy who was staring into the distance.

"I'll follow you out in a minute."

"Ok," said Alfie, who followed Tommy's gaze to Ashley DiMarco, who was walking around with Joel.

It was hot and sunny and the midday sun beat down across the crowds on London's streets. It felt better to get some fresh air, and get out of the boring art gallery. Tommy would be along soon and Alfie was sure they could find something better to do around here. There was street of small shops to the right, away from the crowds, that would do. Alfie didn't like crowds.

Then Alfie froze. Was that? No, it couldn't be. In amongst the crowds of people, he was sure that he had just seen... his Dad? He had not seen his Dad in ages, his last birthday if he remembered correctly. And even then he didn't stay long. But there he was, Alfie was sure of it, in the quiet street walking along hunch shouldered. Alfie stared. His Dad went straight into a small bookshop about thirty paces away. Without thinking Alfie tripped blindly towards him. It was small and had a bright blue sign. He didn't know why he was nervous, but opened the door and went inside. A small bell above the door tinkled. There were two men in the shop, one was a lazy looking man sat behind the counter, the other a tall man with his back to Alfie. Where had his Dad gone?

"Excuse me," said Alfie approaching the small counter. "Did you seen a man walk in just now, small, hunched, brown beige jacket?" said Alfie glancing round to see if he was hiding behind any corners.

The lazy looking man, glanced up from his book. "I aint seen no one who fits that description pal." He returned to his book.

Alfie was sure he saw his Dad walk in here. Perhaps he really had imagined it—but it seemed so real. He moved round the shop once more, just in case. Alfie looked down disappointed, he would give anything to see his Dad right now. He wanted to tell him everything that had happened. He might understand, have some advice, that's what Dad's did wasn't it?

He was being stupid, if his Dad wanted to speak to Alfie, he would have come and seen him. With that, Alfie sighed and turned towards the door.

"Aoh!" cried a voice. Alfie had accidentally bumped straight into the tall man, knocking all the books out of his arms.

"Oh, I'm so sorry!" said Alfie, bending down to pick some of them up. The large man bent down too.

"Don't worry, I'll get them."

As Alfie was about to say he insisted, he happened to glance up and at the man's face, and gasped. Alfie had never seen anyone else with them. He stepped back in shock. He couldn't believe it. The tall man…had bright purple eyes!

"Y-y-you…" said Alfie pointing into his face. The man was staring back at him too, with the same expression.

"Well I never," he said.

"But, *but*… I didn't think anyone else—"

"—Nor did I," said the tall man with purple eyes before looked around briskly. "Wait here, let me just get these."

He quickly took his books to the desk and got them wrapped and paid for. Then carrying them by the top of a string knot, marched from the shop. "Come," he said looking at Alfie. "Follow me."

Alfie followed the tall man to a small café across the street. The plastic tables were greasy, and the chairs were fastened to the table but Alfie didn't care, he just wanted to know who this man was whom shared his rare eyes.

They sat at a table in a dark corner and ordered two teas. Alfie sat staring into perfect identical purple eyes. Now Alfie knew why people found them so strange, it did look peculiar. The tall man was well kept, but not particularly good looking. His cheekbones were too high, his face pinched and nose was too long. His neck was too thin and black hair too short—the

120

overall impression was of an underfed meerkat. He dressed impeccably and wore a long black wool coat, underneath a grey shirt, grey tie and black waistcoat. The only colour this man possessed were his eyes, which sparkled like a perfect starry night sky.

"I thought I saw my Dad go into the shop," said Alfie.

"You did?" said the man. His voice smart and clipped. "And, he wasn't?"

"No, he wasn't. I could have sworn I saw him go in."

"Does your Dad have…" the man leaned in closer and whispered. "Purple eyes?"

Alfie chuckled. "No." His Dad had brown eyes.

"I *see*. I am Found, by the way," said the man, reaching out a hand. "Richard Found."

"I'm Alfie Brown." He said sipping his tea. "I've never seen anyone who has the same eyes as me."

Richard nodded. "It's most peculiar," he said. "I have read many books about it. But never actually *seen* anyone else with them."

"Really? There are books about it?" said Alfie who had never thought of the possibility. "What do the books say?"

"Well, I have my own theory. But generally, I think they have something to do with…" Richard leaned in closer again. "*Weird* things."

Alfie stared at Richard. "Weird things? Like what?"

Richard leaned back in his seat and smiled. Then he picked up his tea cup and dropped it on the floor. It smashed, sending hot tea and shards of china all over the floor. "Why on earth did you do that?" said Alfie, feeling for a moment that in was in the company of a nutter.

But Richard just smiled, bent down and picked up a small

shard of the broken tea cup. He put it down on the table and lay his hand over it, muttering lazily. *"Hexplicoo."*

The shard of cup immediately grew, morphing into its original cup shape. It bulged for a few seconds, before tea began to refill itself in the cup.

"Magic," said Richard.

Alfie gorped. The waitress came over with a damp cloth in her hand and began to wipe the mess up. Then she stopped noticing he still had another cup. "I ordered another one, a few moments ago." Richard smiled at her. She nodded politely and carried the broken shards away.

"She noticed," Alfie whispered.

Richard waved a hand dismissively. "They don't notice anything."

"So, are you a wizard?" said Alfie excitedly.

Richard half-nodded. *"Hmm* sort of. Do you have a shadow demon after you as well?"

Alfie nearly exploded. "Yes! I am trying to find a way to get rid of it. Do you mean to say that you got rid of yours?"

Richard grinned wide and sat back looking content. "Why yes I did, as a matter of fact."

Alfie's brain was working overtime, what had Wiseman said? He had known only three sorcerers with a shadow after them, two had died and one survived. Richard Found must have been the one who survived! Or was he just jumping to conclusions?

"Are you a sorcerer?" said Alfie quietly.

Richard frowned. "What makes you say that?"

"You said you weren't a wizard, but you can do magic. And Nikolas Wiseman, this man I know, he said he only knew one person who survived from a shadow demon attack—"

"—I would stay away from that man if you know what's good

for you," said Richard curtly. "He's nothing but trouble."

"What you know Nikolas Wiseman?" Richard nodded and looked serious. "*But...* he seemed really nice to me. He told me—"

"Well, my dear boy, he would because he…" Richard was now face to face with Alfie over the table, and looked fiery. "He is not what you think he is. It's very well known that this image of him being the amazing one who introduces you to a world of magick, as I guess he has already done, is just a smokescreen. Beware, you will only end up doing his bidding. The only reason he has an interest in you, is because you have something he wants—and with those eyes I wouldn't doubt that possibility for a second."

Alfie sat back and swallowed some more tea. "How did you get rid of your shadow?"

Richard calmed. "Well, I was hoping you'd ask me that." He took a swig of tea and was about to speak as two faces swam into Alfie's vision. Tommy and Sparky were looking through the glass, then spotted him.

"Alfie," said Richard quickly. "You must never, under any circumstance mention me, or this meeting do you understand?"

Tommy came wandering in slowly looking confused. "Alfie everyone's looking for you, you just disappeared. Who were you talking to?"

"This is…" Alfie stopped. Richard Found had vanished from his seat. Alfie hadn't even seen him go. His tea was still sitting there steaming. "Oh," said Alfie remembering what Richard said. "No one, just some bloke who… bought me a tea." He couldn't think of anything else.

"Why did you come in here?" said Sparky.

"I was waiting for both of you and I got bored ok!"

"Well, whatever, come on, let's go before they start panicking!"

said Tommy walking out the café.

Alfie kept glancing back over his shoulder to see if Richard was still in the café. He was gone. Alfie cursed Tommy and Sparky as they walked back to the gallery, if only they waited five more minutes! Alfie was about to find out how Richard Found had defeated his Shadow! Alfie silently seethed and barely spoke all the way home.

All night Alfie tossed and turned, dreams sliding into his mind and dissolving away again—the face of his Dad walking up to him, about to speak, before vanishing. Then Alfie was staring at a large crowd of people all pointing and laughing at him maliciously. There was Wiseman and Mr Sapiens and just behind them with his finger to his lip was Richard Found. Then looking closer at the crowd, Alfie saw the old doddery couple next door, then Nigel and his parents, then all his teachers from school, then Jessica Curdle, Sarah Ashdown, Joel, Christian and Henry Goofham all laughing because they were all wizards and he wasn't.

"Ha-ha!" Joel laughed. "And he didn't even know!" They roared with laughter as Alfie felt his blood boil and raised his hands to spell him, but Joel reacted and sent Alfie flying backwards into the mud.

Alfie turned and ran away, just up ahead was a hill. Over the top waiting for him was Tommy and Sparky, who looked sad and bedraggled.

"We didn't think you were coming back..." said Sparky in a sad voice which echoed around Alfie's head.

Tommy was tapping his watch. "It's bloody broken!" he said as a loud ticking noise echoed across the plains. *Tick-tock-tick-tock.*

The crowd of people from below the hill were now standing abreast of it, all looking down at him, Tommy and Sparky. A giant pendulum hanging in the air behind them—*tick-tock-tick-tock*—as they began to laugh loudly. Black bags under their eyes as thunder struck the ground before Alfie's feet.

Alfie woke with a start. Sweat was pouring from his brow. He was lying the wrong way round in his bed and the covers were on the floor. He sat up and scrambled for the glass of water, he was desperately thirsty. Once he had finished, he put it on the side table and noticed something odd. The time read: *11:11*. But it couldn't be 11:11, it was almost morning. Alfie picked up the clock, it was still ticking loudly—perhaps it had got jammed?

Alfie wiped his brow and stood up, how odd after what he had just been dreaming. Putting his dressing gown on and plodding downstairs—to get another glass of water and find out the real time—Alfie discovered his Grandma at work in the kitchen. He stood quietly in the doorway watching her mix some ingredients in a cake bowl.

"Aooh!" she cried as she turned, spotting Alfie and nearly dropping the mixing bowl. "Goodness gracious me, you gave me the shock of my life! Don't creep!" She looked slightly manic and had her dressing gown on too. "What are you doing up at this time? It's half-past-five!" she said.

"I could ask you the same thing," said Alfie nodding at all the ingredients on the table.

Alfie sat down and had a cup of tea with his Grandma, he didn't see any reason to go back to bed. Was it him or did the clock in the kitchen seem exorbitantly loud this morning? Perhaps that was just because it was so quiet. Far away he could hear his Granddad slowly snoring.

Alfie took a sip of tea. "So are you going to tell me why you're making a cake at five in the morning?"

His Grandma blinked rapidly for few moments then sighed. "You know what day it is today?" she said. "November 11th… your mothers Birthday." Alfie's stomach twisted. He had totally forgotten, of course it was! Alfie didn't know what to say, he opened his mouth but nothing came out. "I was making a lemon drizzle cake… it was her favourite."

"I know," said Alfie smiling. Everything he knew about his Mum came from the stories his Grandma would tell him when she was in a melancholy mood.

"And look, I made this little bee out of roll on icing to go on top," she said, showing him an intricate carving in icing of a bumble bee. "They were her favourite, Bee's—for some reason—that's why we always called her Bee."

"I know…" said Alfie again in a small voice.

For the rest of that morning, the walk to school, and the first two lessons Alfie could hear the same malicious ticking noise from his dream. It wasn't loud, but annoyingly persistent. The strangest thing was, no one else could hear it. Alfie wondered if he was getting some form of tinnitus, and wondered about going to the school nurse. At break time Alfie had to go the toilets, he was having trouble hearing people speak for the *tick-tocking* noise was growing louder and louder.

"Are you sure you haven't anything lodged in your ear?" said Tommy as they walked to Drama. "I knew a guy once who was deaf for about a year, until the doctor had a poke around and found a crayon lodged inside his—"

Alfie and Sparky returned perplexed looks. "No, Tommy I don't think Alfie accidentally turned over in the night and got an alarm clock stuck in his ear!"

Tommy straightened up. "Well, it wouldn't fit…" he said quite seriously.

Alfie slapped himself on the side of the head. It was becoming unbearable. *Tick-tock-tick-tock*. He didn't understand why no one else could hear it—it must have had something to do with the dream last night, but what? Alfie closed his eyes. He couldn't even think straight above all the noise.

It was at the end of lunch when Alfie finally cracked. The bell suddenly went and Alfie clamped both hands to his head at the horrible cacophony of noise!

"Shut up! Please just SHUT UP!" he cried. The lunch hall went quiet, and stared at him slightly open mouthed. "Not you!" he called, making a quick exit. On the way to science class Alfie kept shaking his head in an attempt to dislodge the noise. As they approached reception, the ticking noise in Alfie's head became louder and louder with every step. He winced. The old deserted corridor stood dark and opposing. This was the loudest the ticking had been all day! Did it have something to do with the old corridor in front of him?

Alfie had a sudden, burdening thought—the ticking was not going to stop until he went back into the corridor where the magick LeyDoor had been.

"What are you doing standing here?" Sparky shouted in his ear. Alfie pointed down the corridor and Sparky shook his head. "I thought we agreed?"

Tommy looked concerned for Alfie's wincing face, against the now cacophonous parade-like ticking noises, as if a thousand clocks were inside his head. With each step down the corridor it became louder and louder. There was no light down here, only what was left over from reception. They marched down the corridor, with Alfie clutching his head for fear it would explode. Tommy and Sparky cautiously following, unsure if their best friend was losing the plot. But then, as Alfie got half-way down the corridor, the noise, all at once, abruptly and miraculously, stopped. Alfie blinked and rubbed his streaming eyes.

"Oh my god… it's stopped!" Alfie glanced around as normality resumed—he was standing directly outside the door to the old library. It was locked and it was dark inside, a banner stretched across warning people away.

"It's stopped?" said Tommy. "Just like that? I reckon you must have accidentally said a magic work and made that sound in your ears."

"It's not that," Alfie muttered.

Tommy tapped his chin. "Well maybe it has something to do with this corridor. It might be something to do with the ghost corridor?" Alfie winced at this last statement—it just reminded him of Wiseman laughing at his use of—this reminded Alfie that he had not told his best friends anything about it.

"I think it must have been a sound that wanted you to come down here…" said Sparky. "As much as I wish it wasn't."

Alfie grinned. "I think you're right." The door to the Old Library was ajar. Alfie put one finger to the door and pushed slowly, the door swung open silently. As much as he didn't want to go inside, he didn't want the horrible noise in his head to return even more. As he stepped cautiously over the threshold a plume of dust greeted him. Alfie held his nose and took a few steps inside. His head was still ringing from the horrible ticking. He heard Tommy's quick breath behind him and small grunt at the dim, grey room, then Sparky's almost inaudible whimper as the door clinked shut behind them.

THE OLD LIBRARY'S SECRET

The old library was very big. The bookshelves were tall, strong looking and made of dark oak and lined the tall library in neat, efficient rows. A spindly old ladder sat before the nearest shelf, and something about this dusty old room filled with books reminded Alfie of Wiseman and his room. The carpet was so dusty and covered in residue that it was hard to make out the pattern or indeed colour underneath. The air was damp, and a small far off scuttling noise made his skin crawl. It was very dim, the windows had been boarded up, but some of the panelling had fallen away causing odd stretches of light to carry through.

BONG! BONG! They all jumped as a loud grandfather clock rang out. It sounded loud enough to carry throughout the whole school. *BONG! BONG!* But Alfie had never heard it before? *BONG! BONG!* It echoed in long clanging notes. *BONG! BONG! BONG! BONG! BONG!*

"Ok, ok!" cried Tommy. "Be quiet already!"

It stood against the wall behind a small alcove in amongst a set of cushy looking chairs. It was very large and ornate looking with a grey face and a long pendulum—*just like in his dream...*

"*Pffft,*" Tommy tutted. "It's got the time wrong! It's nearer to half-one, not eleven."

Alfie stopped and looked closer. Tommy was right, it was the wrong time. The grandfather clock had stopped, just like his own clock this morning, incredibly on: *11:11.*

What were the chances of that? Alfie felt like his head was about to explode. Just then, Sparky stopped stock still, he had heard something. "*Shhh!*" he mouthed, tapping them. "Someone else is in here."

He was right. They heard footsteps, from behind some of the bookshelves a long way off and then a voice.

"It's stopped!" called a strange voice. "That bloody awful, scrounging ticking noise has stopped!" The voice was odd, it was a man's voice but constricted, shrill and mad sounding.

"Yes! Yes! Yes! At last, at lasty, lasty, last! This calls for a celebration!" Called another with a similar shrill, childish sounding tone.

Alfie, Tommy and Sparky didn't move from the alcove. They certainly didn't sound like teachers, or anyone at this school that they knew of. The footsteps grew louder. Alfie raised his hands. Two men turned the corner and stopped, spotting them immediately. Alfie swallowed, both men were wearing long billowing rags and even in the dim light, Alfie did not like the look of these men one bit. No one moved.

"W-what are you doing here?" said Alfie, his voice flailing.

"Others?" said one of the men to his compatriot. "Others, in *our* place." It didn't speak the words, more spat them. Tommy and Sparky backed away into the bookcase.

"We," said the other man importantly. "Are here because of the…" he convulsed. *"Ticking!"*

The other man, stepped forwards and sung. *"For where we smell a trail of Magick, Magick will ultimately be…"*

"We have faced the most incredible woe, outcast from our places!" It cried dramatically, long rags flying around. *"We've been treated like vermin."*

"But through it all, we always knew, that we would find our treasure and reignite our spark again!" It walked into a stretch of light and it's face suddenly illuminated. Alfie, Tommy and Sparky gasped. It was the most repulsive thing they had ever seen. It quickly darted out of the light again, embarrassed. It's voice now higher, ringing out. "We have faced this kind of ridicule and persecution always!"

Alfie wasn't surprised. It's face looked like a melting wax

work, one eye clinging to the less saggier part of its face. Huge green blobs all over and no teeth.

Alfie put his hand to his mouth for he knew what they were. "You're *Scabs*?"

"*Wahhhhh!*" They screeched. "How dare you call us that!"

"Nice one mate. Now you've annoyed them even more," said Tommy glancing around for the exit.

Alfie swallowed. "What are you doing in our school?"

The shorter one out of the two stopped wailing. "A school? This is a *school*?"

"Yes, our school, what are you doing in it?"

"We're in a school Dee! A school, a school, a school!" It jumped around with joy and linked with his partner, doing a merry dance. "We're here because we heard the *tick-tock tick-tock...* for where mysterious things occur, magick is often behind it. And we so desire our powers back!"

"Alfie," Tommy whispered. "Use your magick to get us out of this." Very suddenly the Scabs stopped dead still.

"You," said one of them. "Can do magick?"

"Yes I can..." he said, hoping this would make cautious around him, for he would Spell them if not. Instead they began singing and dancing even louder.

"*We must, we must, we must... this is our treasure, treasure, treasure!*" they sung. Then they slowed and began walking towards Alfie.

"Stay back, what are you doing?" said Alfie raising his hands, but they ignored him.

"Alfie..." said Tommy in a small voice. "Do *something*."

The Scabs tip toed towards him, arms reaching out slowly. Alfie backed up against the grandfather clock.

"We simply must have you. Then we will be magick again."

They spat, slime spilling from its mouth.

Alfie didn't have many choices left. The promise to Wiseman not to do magick was about to get broken. A long scabby hand reached out from beneath battered old rags for Alfie's throat.

Alfie had an overwhelming feeling engulf him to use the last spell on the list. The one he had not used yet. He recalled the spell in his mind and cried. *"Petivo!"*

An almighty rush of air surrounded him. His arms came together in front of him. In one moment the air froze and time stood still. A ball of shimmering, dancing, purple light fizzed between his hands. The ends of his fingers crackled, hundreds of purple electric sparks crackled on the surface of his skin.

He looked up slowly, everything had frozen: the repulsive face of the scab contorting slowly into a terrified fury. Alfie glanced to the right at Tommy and Sparky's wide, terrified eyes.

The spinning purple ball of light between Alfie's hands grew in a split second. Before a sudden rush of air and sound as time resumed. The ball shot from his between his hands like a whip. Smashing the Scabs full in the chest with a shower of purple sparks. The Scabs were launched off their feet and flew across the library, screaming at the top of their lungs before hitting the far bookshelf with a sickening *crunch!* The bookshelf began to topple forwards, away from the wall and fell with a *crash!* on top of them.

The Scabs lay unmoving, twitching as purple jolts of energy jumped from the end of their rags.

Tommy and Sparky turned to Alfie, who was breathing very hard. He felt as if a huge amount of his energy had been snatched away. But, he was enormously glad he used the last spell on the list—something inside him, a feeling, told him to use it.

"Woah..." said Tommy and Sparky in unison.

"That was amazing!" said Tommy mouth agape.

Alfie nodded, looking down at his hands. "That was the last spell word."

"That was the *best* spell word."

"I shouldn't have done it though," said Alfie remembering what Wiseman told him.

"Why not?" said Tommy frowning. "There aren't any prefects in here! And need I remind you, if you hadn't have done that spell, we would be dead!"

Sparky took out his asthma pump and took a deep breath on it. "That spell was exactly the same colour as your eyes."

"Those things are absolutely disgusting. I'd rather take Joel out for a romantic, candle lit dinner than have another conversation with one of those." Tommy prodded one of the Scabs with his foot.

"Do you think it is dead?" said Sparky.

"*Naa*," said Alfie hopefully.

"I think its just knocked out a bit... what's that?" said Tommy, pointing at the wall, where a light was coming in from the a crack in the wall behind where the bookshelf had fallen. The crack was only very small, but the light must have been bright because it pierced it like a laser. Alfie stood on top of the bookshelf and had a closer look, softly rubbing the wall as grey stone fell away, it was so old and crumbly he barely need touch it. More light spilled from the crack. He looked at Tommy and Sparky, who both looked puzzled.

"Get this stone off!" said Alfie as all three started to tear away bigger and bigger clumps of crumbling stone as dust showered them. The strange light shone into the room. It was a dazzling, beautiful, radiant light that made Alfie feel warm and cosy.

Continuing to rub away stone, it wasn't long until they felt something different. Underneath was a smooth, clear stone like worn glass. "What is it?" said Tommy, as if he were leading an excavation.

"No idea, looks like glass," said Alfie inspecting the smooth glassy stone.

Dust and brick continued to fall quickly until finally they stood before a huge glassy stone wall. Stepping back together, they blinked at the light pouring out, which was a dazzling pearlescent white. Yet now, the glass-stone was the same shade of purple… as Alfie's eyes.

After ten minutes of staring at it and not knowing what to say, the three boys looked at one another. "This just get's weirder and weirder…" said Tommy, who was so covered in dust he looked like statue. Alfie had to agree, they were standing before a huge wall of purple glass and he had no idea why. In fact, it hurt his brain to think about it.

"What do we do about them?" said Sparky pointing at the Scabs.

Tommy shrugged. "Just leave them. Not our problem. Unless you want to take one home with you?"

Sparky grimaced. "Yeah but, what about the mess in here? They're going to know it was us that did this!"

"We'll go to the bathrooms straight away and get cleaned up!" said Tommy with a look at Alfie who nodded back in agreement.

That night Alfie was exhausted, once he made it home, it took all his strength not to fall straight to sleep. A large slice of lemon drizzle cake was waiting for him on the kitchen table. It had atop it, a large bee made out of icing.

Alfie swallowed hard. The house was empty and cold. Taking a small bite of the cake, he looked out the window into the sky.

"Happy Birthday Mum, wherever you are."

11

Sampson's Void

First lesson back the next day was Art. Alfie, Tommy and Sparky were sat around an easel, pencils in hand but with no intention of using them. Alfie was staring out of the window as the teacher, Miss Cairney began asking the class about what they saw in the London art gallery, before droning on about various paintings in complete amazement.

Alfie was thinking whether or not he should tell Mr Sapiens about the drumming and what happened in the old library, he might know what it was? Perhaps it was an initiation ceremony that all wizards had to go through? But why was a *purple wall*, of all things, in the old library? Mr Sapiens would surely want to know about it, especially if there was something magickal happening in the school. Would he be annoyed if Alfie told him he used magick again? But, like Tommy said, if he hadn't they would be dead—killed by those disgusting *Scabs*.

Alfie's mind wavered to the last spell—*Petivo*. What a glorious feeling that was, Alfie recalled the end of his fingers fizzing, and time slowing right down for just a few seconds, before an almightily rush of air, blasting the Scabs away. Alfie would be lying to himself if he said he didn't find it exciting, cool even. He imagined Christian and Joel being blasted across the school playground, then Gracie running to his arms saying how interesting and wonderful Alfie was.

He had spent half the night running through what happened in the old library, trying to get it all into perspective, but it stubbornly resisted to make any sense. It was all linked together somehow—the purple doors, the purple wall, his purple eyes. On top of all that, his Grandma had gone on full nag-duty. She was worried that Alfie didn't care about his end of year exams. And she was right, Alfie didn't care one jot. If only she knew what he was up against—exams really were the least of his priorities.

"What I always thought was strange," Tommy whispered as Mrs Cairney asked them all to start drawing. "Is that the school closed the old library about four years ago, when we first got to the school. But it's bigger than the new one we have now, strange huh?"

Sparky cleared his throat. "Not that strange," he said. "The old library has got lots of damp, and is really far from the centre of the school. I suppose they opened the new one to be easier to get to, and less damp."

"What I want to know is," said Tommy ignoring him and lowering his voice as Miss Cairney passed. "Is that drumming in your head led you to the old library right? So someone wanted you there for a reason: to be killed by those *things*, or to find the purple wall…"

"Right?" said Alfie wondering where Tommy was going.

"So… who wants you to get killed? Or who wants you to find a magic purple wall?"

"Well, it would help if we knew what the purple wall was,"

said Sparky. "It might just be a purple wall, nothing more."

"What? Exactly the same shade as his eyes?" said Tommy pointing.

Alfie nodded, he had been asking himself the same questions. Was it Wiseman? Was he trying to get into contact? In Wiseman's house, his clock was stuck on 11:11—just like the clock in the old library.

But what about the Scabs? Why were they there? Perhaps Wiseman had sent them to kill him? Richard Found, the man with purple eyes he'd met in London, had told Alfie to *beware of Wiseman*. Those words echoed around his head now. Alfie couldn't voice these theories however, because he still hadn't told Tommy and Sparky about Wiseman, Mr Sapiens or Richard Found.

"What about that scabby thing," said Tommy shaking Alfie from his slumber, as Sparky convulsed.

"I'd to know how they got into school! And what they are!" said Tommy frowning.

"Like they said, they followed a magick trail," said Alfie. "Which I assume was the purple wall, but I don't know."

Sparky looked up with an even bigger frown. "In the old library, you told us that those *things* couldn't do magick?" said Sparky accusingly. "How did you know that?"

"*Erm...* I don't know," said Alfie floundering. "Anyway you'd both be dead if I hadn't have saved you!"

When they finished Art they agreed to go and check on the old library. They decided that if anyone went in there and saw loads of dust and rubble, they would make the connection to them immediately. Alfie had the idea to use *Consisto* on the door to make it freeze shut, so no one would go in there—he would be using a little bit of magick again, but he was sure Wiseman wouldn't mind, just this once, if it meant not getting caught.

But when they got to the entrance of the corridor, next to reception, and making sure no was watching slipped into the darkened corridor and made for the old library. When they got there, the door was tight shut. Alfie made to open it, but it was locked and wouldn't budge. He turned to Tommy and Sparky who looked bemused. None of them knew how to feel about this. Had someone been in, saw the damage and then locked it up? There was no sign of the white or purple light creeping under the door frame. Neither was there any dust. Tommy got on his hands and knees and tried to peer under the door. "It looks normal…" said Tommy.

Alfie got down too, he could just make out a very dim purple glow from the wall at the very back. But there was no dust, or rubble, or Scabs.

The next three weeks were strange, the weather got colder and colder. Alfie now lived in his old puffy jacket. Tommy had tried to keep the conversation between the three of them about the old library up—but gave up when he realised Alfie wasn't interested. Alfie had had enough of pointless speculation, he wanted *more*, he needed actual answers. And yet, Mr Sapiens was not around.

Every day for the next week Alfie was on the look out, but there was no sign of him at all. Alfie was getting increasingly worried—was he avoiding him again? No. Their French lessons were replaced by a different teacher called Miss Jolly. A great sinking feeling arose inside him every time Miss Jolly entered the classroom and not Mr Sapiens. Where on earth was he?

"Why do you want to know where he is so much?" said Sparky

139

suspiciously, after Alfie asked Miss Jolly (for the tenth time that week) where Mr Sapiens was before she repeated the same answer.

Alfie was worried. Worried that his french teacher and one visible link to the magick world had gone.

At the end of the day as they began to pile out of school, Tommy turned to them. "Oh my god! I forgot to tell you guys!"

"What?" said Alfie and Sparky together, alarmed at Tommy's tone.

"It was in school yesterday when I discovered it, you need to see this!"

Tommy ran towards the front of school and into reception where a few people were milling around putting decorations on the tree.

"What? What is it!" said Alfie, he wasn't sure he could cope with another LeyDoor or mystery purple wall to contend with. Tommy leaned in close to Alfie.

"I've got a power, like you!" Tommy whispered.

Sparky exchanged a worried look with Alfie who's stomach churned.

"Watch…" said Tommy. He walked up to the school entrance, waved his hands in a wild extravagant fashion. The doors opened, sliding apart.

"You see?" said Tommy.

"Tommy," said Alfie thankfully. "You do know there automatic doors?"

Tommy spluttered with laughter. "I got you both, your faces!" he proceeded to laugh hysterically and roll around on the floor. The receptionist had to ask him to be quiet because she was on the phone.

"I've gotta go, I'll speak to you guys later." said Alfie, hoping they wouldn't kick up a fuss, he was trying to find a way of going to find Mr Sapiens without them following or getting suspicious. He reasoned that if he could get into Mr Sapiens LeyDoor in the French room, he might be in there or there might be a clue where to find him.

"Where you going?" said Tommy getting up.

"Extra french lessons." Alfie said without stopping.

"But Alfie," said Tommy who was standing with his hands on his hips. "You know Mr Sapiens is away?"

"I know," said Alfie thinking fast. "I've got… Miss Jolly instead."

Tommy shrugged and walked off waving his arms at the automatic door, but Sparky stood watching him, a curious look on his face. He definitely knew something was up.

When Alfie got to the languages block he scanned the area to make sure there was no one nearby and pressed his hand to the wall. If Mr Sapiens was not in school, that wasn't to say he wasn't *in* the school somewhere. Alfie wondered why Mr Sapiens had been away? Was it to do with him? Perhaps he was scared about the consequences of being too close to a wizard with a Shadow after him?

Alfie stood with his hand to the wall for five minutes, until he realised that the door was not going to appear. What on earth was going on? Alfie knocked upon the wall.

"Mr Sapiens!" he called. "Mr Sapiens, it's Alfie Brown. Can you let me in?"

But Mr Sapiens did not open the door in the wall. Alfie left the languages block feeling despondent and walked home alone in the dark and cold.

A week later and Alfie had all but given up on Mr Sapiens, he'd been away for over three weeks and Alfie didn't think he would ever return. He had already started plotting an idea to use the Christmas holidays to go and hunt down Richard Found. He would return to the bookshop, see if he could get Richard's address, or wait for him—it was a long shot, but Alfie knew Richard had the most important information he needed, he knew how to get rid of a Shadow.

Alfie was sitting on a bench blowing into his hands to warm them up, waiting for Tommy and Sparky to return from the canteen. They turned the corner, arms full of small bags containing cakes and pastries which they proceeded to lay out on the table.

"Here you are, your doughnut," said Tommy, passing him a sticky bag.

"We saw Mr Sapiens," said Sparky biting into a large cinnamon roll.

"What?" Alfie said, looking up at him sharply and spitting out the bit of doughnut he'd just bitten into.

"He was walking back to the languages block, he had a cut across his face," said Sparky drawing a line with his finger.

"Looked nasty," added Tommy.

Alfie got up and abandoning his doughnut and friends, running towards the languages block.

"Where are you going!" cried Tommy, but Alfie didn't care, he needed to see Mr Sapiens.

Alfie saw him through the window of his French room. He didn't knock, instead he burst inside making Mr Sapiens jump.

"There you are!" said Alfie breathless.

"AH!" he cried. "Please knock next time," he said, picking up the books he'd just dropped. "How can I help you Alfie?" said Mr

Sapiens as if he was expecting an enquiry about a particularly tricky bit of French.

Alfie saw the gash across his face, it was almost healed now but stretched halfway between his nose and ear.

"How did you get that? I mean, where have you been?" said Alfie speaking too fast, unable to help it.

Mr Sapiens got up and grabbed Alfie's shoulder. "We cannot talk 'ere," he said in a hushed voice. "Come back tonight after your last lesson and I will tell you." Mr Sapiens ushered him away and out the door.

Alfie breathed a huge sign of relief, Mr Sapiens was back at last. Now, all he had to do was answer to a scowling, confused Tommy and Sparky.

When the bell struck for last lesson Alfie snuck off through the crowd without saying goodbye to Tommy and Sparky, it was easier than pretending he had extra French lessons again—Sparky had asked the head of French and languages if he too could have extra French lessons and was told they wouldn't be doing those for another few months. When Sparky queried Alfie about this, he made up another lie and said his Grandparents were thinking about getting him a private tutor for a couple of subjects, nothing to do with school. Sparky was very sceptical.

Making sure no one was around was tricky, so Alfie hid in the toilets for ten minutes. He did this for two reasons, first to hide from Tommy and Sparky and second to make sure the crowd of people leaving would not all spot him hanging around, acting suspiciously then going through a door in the wall that isn't normally there. There was only one problem with hiding in the toilet cubicle, there was only one and the lock was dodgy.

Alfie sat with the toilet seat down for a few minutes, holding his breath. He tried hard to blot Tommy and Sparky's face from his mind, he was going to have to come up with a pretty good excuse this time—something that he wasn't used to doing with Tommy. They usually told each other everything.

Alfie listened for a few more minutes as the noise of the crowds in the hall swelled and then died away. Just as he was about to unlock the toilet door, he heard footsteps, then voices.

"And you can see it's literally tearing him up inside. He's not the same person." Alfie knew that voice, it was Joel. "He's never going to get over this."

"Yeah," said Christian.

"I told you didn't I? I said, if you get with Gracie, Alfie Brown will be so distraught!" Alfie put a hand to his mouth, a sudden writhing bubble of anger in his stomach. Joel was talking about *him*!

"I told you it was a good plan, well I've got him back, good and proper for all those times he wronged me," said Joel and Alfie could imagine his weasely face, smiling smugly. So, they planned to meet Gracie on purpose, just to make Alfie jealous?

"But well, thing is…" said Christian. "I think I really like her."

Alfie was about to explode. He could almost feel the tingling sensation on the end of his fingers as he Petivo'd both of them into the bathroom wall. He took a deep breath.

"Just her face, and her eyes and her hair and she's so sweet and clever and kind…"

"Alright Casanova," said Joel. "As long as you don't mess it up. That would make Alfie happy, if you split up," said Joel to himself.

They left. *The conniving son of a…* Alfie swore loudly. Joel planned it? Going out with Gracie just to annoy him? Well Joel really had it coming to him now, Alfie was going to prepare something extra special for him after this was all over—Alfie couldn't wait.

Alfie pressed his hand to the wall, this time the door faded up straight away. Checking back one last time Alfie pushed the door open and went in. The corridor echoed as the door clinked shut, the fire burned a little brighter in their brackets, noticing Alfie's presence and illuminating the stone pathway to Mr Sapiens office. His footsteps echoed all the way along the corridor, fire brackets causing dancing shadows all along the wall. Alfie couldn't stop thinking about what Joel had just said—what Spell could he use on him? *No, no*, now was not the time for revenge.

Alfie approached the doorway to Mr Sapiens special office. He was stood by his desk looking out of a grubby window. The room was a little messier than last time, a few books were out of place, and his desk didn't seem as tidy and ordered. There was no fire blazing away, and Alfie was sure the room temperature was a couple of degrees lower than it was in the school—he was glad he had his coat on.

Mr Sapiens turned slowly and smiled. "Come, take a seat." He offered and Alfie took the chair facing the desk. Mr Sapiens looked tired, with deep black bags under his eyes.

"I suppose you want to know where I 'ave 'bin?" He said, looking back out the window. Alfie wondered what was out there. Mr Sapiens rubbed the scar on his cheek. "I went in search of Nikolas Wiseman."

"You searched for him?"

"Yes, before I saw you 'ere in my office those weeks ago I believed Nikolas Wiseman to be dead."

"Dead?" said Alfie in a small voice.

"For fifteen years," Mr Sapiens got up and paced around his chair. "Fifteen years! I thought my old teacher was dead."

"He was your teacher?" said Alfie, wondering how—Nikolas Wiseman didn't look more than forty years old.

"Yes, 'e was Chief of the White Council... the one who found me and told me what I was, the one who taught me everything I know..." he sprayed his arms wide. "When 'ze building was blown to shreds, I was in his office with 'im, sitting opposite as we are now. We went off to 'elp and well, that was the last time I saw 'im." Mr Sapiens looked away. "It came as a great shock to me to 'ear you say you 'ad seen 'im. If only they knew 'e was still alive," he said to himself. "Anyway, we spoke again. And of you, and it was decided 'dat I... teach you a few things."

"Teach me?" said Alfie confused. "Teach me what?"

"Magick of course," Mr Sapiens smiled. "Wiseman agreed with me that you cannot learn too much, only being a wizard and unqualified Magi, but a little bit cannot 'urt..."

Alfie smiled—he was going to learn Magick? He was not expecting Mr Sapiens to tell him this.

"But Mr Sapiens, I mean, how did you get that scratch?" said Alfie as Mr Sapiens squirmed.

"Wiseman proved partially... tricky to find," he said looking out the window and smiling. "He is very good at 'iding..."

"Hiding?" said Alfie, trying to clarify.

"Yes, 'iding, 'iding..." Mr Sapiens flashed his hands impatiently. "Long ago, when I knew 'im, he could do such great Magick. He made 'is own h'ouse completely disappear. A passer by would walk past where his house used to be, and not see or notice a thing. Not even a the highest level wizard would realise. If you took a map the place where 'is h'ouse used to be would shrivel up and disappear... rendering 'imself virtually invisible... 'e has many enemies. Anyway..." said Mr Sapiens jumping to life. "Enough about Wiseman. All you need to know is, 'e 'as agreed to let you do some Magick. So without further ado: *lesson one*, Magick."

A blackboard popped into the air behind Mr Sapiens head, a piece of chalk flew up and scribbled all by itself: *Lesson One, Magick.*

Mr Sapiens took a seat behind his desk and pressed his hands together. "Human's are born with an innate talent—through their will, to control the elements and the physical world around us. Most people on this planet will die having never explored them. It is a power that doesn't discriminate or belong to one person more than another, it is true in everyone and exists in abundance. The ancients knew about these powers actively encouraging it for the better of all existence. Today, normal people are discouraged from thinking anything of the sort, if you do your nutty or a crazy person. They 'ave crafted a nice system in our societies for automatically disregarding magickal phenomena, the people's brains and minds are not focused to see, not allowed, too concerned instead with the accepted intellectual dummies to suck upon instead: technology. The un-woken mind will turn away from magick, not see it, make an excuse or say it never 'appened."

"That's why I've had to be careful," said Alfie. "People get scared by this stuff."

"Yes," said Mr Sapiens. "The mind is like an open flower field full of white light—the light is magick. People erect walls around the field, creating borders and compartments, blocking out all the light because? Everyone else is. It's what they've always done. Apparently it is the status quo to live in darkness. If you can smash these down then you can do anything."

Mr Sapiens lifted his hand into the air. The pen directly beneath it rose slowly into the air and into his outstretched hand.

"You can do this," said Mr Sapiens pointing at him with the pen. "Normally when someone starts realising 'dat they are a wizard, they get freaked out or scared and erect more walls because this world that you are waking-up in is not set up for us, there is no support system, not anymore anyway. But I digress... *spells*." The blackboard began writing. Mr Sapiens strode into the middle of the room and asked Alfie to stand so he was facing him. "Spells," he said looking in his element. "Are words that can change the physical world around us. A spell is also known as a *Word of Power* or *Power Word*. And it works like this: a word is simply a vibration made by our throat. This physical world is made up entirely of vibrations. Everything is a vibration. Thus a spell can change a physical object by combining the two vibrations into one, or changing a particular part of the vibration in conjunction with the wizard's will, thus causing an effect—in the way that we see and interact with it."

Mr Sapiens asked Alfie if it made sense or not. Alfie agreed that it did, even though his brain felt hot.

"I want you to say... Promoveobarduss." Mr Sapiens then said it slowly pronouncing each syllable. "Pro-move-eo-bar-du-ss."

"Prom-oveo-barduss," Alfie said feeling a little stupid as Mr Sapiens winced.

"No, no, no... think about what you are saying. Do you not want to know what the spell does?"

"You asked me to say it."

"Then ask," said Mr Sapiens stamping his foot like a spoilt

child. "You need to know what a spell does before just saying the word! This spell is something to attract an object towards you. For example, if it's a pen in front of you, it will jump into your hand. But there is a snag…" he said looking around with a little smirk. "To really do this spell, you have to mean it—you have to really want what you ask for… as you can tell it is 'ard to build up that sort of desire for something simple, like a pen. So it takes practice to find and replicate this desire…"

For the next twenty minutes Mr Sapiens taught Alfie how to say the spell word: *Promoveobarduss* properly, by making the word big in his mouth and by speaking with a deep voice. Mr Sapiens told Alfie to visualise the object he wanted to come to him in his mind. Alfie closed his eyes and saw the object floating around inside his head—(he imagined his school bag that sat just across the room).

"Just feel the word… just feel it. Sometimes it's good to use the passion of wanting something else, something that you really want and use that desire to make the object come to you…"

Alfie thought about all the things that he wanted; money, a big house and… *Gracie*. As hard as he tried to get her out of his head, she would pop up again—her golden skin and light brown eyes floating across his vision.

"Ready Alfie?" said Mr Sapiens.

Alfie, with his eyes closed tried with all his might to imagine his school bag—and slowly Gracie's face faded away.

"I'm ready," he said.

"Now, say the word and your bag should fly towards you."

Alfie braced himself, opened his eyes and cried "Promoveeobarduss!" His bag stayed where it was. "Promoveeobarduss," he said again, staring intently at the bag. Mr Sapiens chewed his lip.

"Come on," said Alfie. "What did I do wrong?" he said looking at Mr Sapiens.

"Ah well," said Mr Sapiens picking his school bag up. "It is moving… a little." It was true, the bag was twitching, but only ever so slightly—Mr Sapiens said that maybe they will try something else.

"Does that usually work?" said Alfie.

"Well, I suppose it is quite tricky, even if it is a *level one spell*," Mr Sapiens said in a small voice.

They came to sit back at Mr Sapiens's desk. "I don't know why it didn't work," said Alfie. "I mean, I've done others and they worked."

"Yes I know, it was quite foolish of you to do so. I mean you didn't even know 'who they are from!" said Mr Sapiens and Alfie didn't mention the fact that he still didn't know.

"So… how many Spells are there?" said Alfie hoping this was a legitimate question.

"Oh thousands, but Alfie I must stress Wiseman still doesn't want you practicing magick on your own—it's dangerous."

Alfie shifted in his seat, feeling uncomfortable, he hoped Mr Sapiens wouldn't shout at him for what he was about to disclose, what he had had waited three weeks to tell him. "Those spells that were on my doorstep… well I found out what the last one does a few weeks ago…" Mr Sapiens looked at him with a little frown and Alfie carried on hurriedly. "For the whole day I could hear this ticking, thought I was going mad… and I sort of followed the noise—it was coming from the old library. When we got in their—"

"We?" said Mr Sapiens.

"Me, Tommy and Daniel Sparker…" Mr Sapiens sighed and looked up at the ceiling. "We went in and there were two Scabs, waiting. They could hear the ticking too. Well, they tried to attack me and we got scared so I used the last spell on them. They flew and hit the wall and the bookcase fell away and behind the wall was this purple transparent sort of stone or glass. Like a large shining purple sort of… stone thing."

Mr Sapiens was staring at Alfie's eyes and looked horror stricken for a second, then he regained his composure and asked in a non caring sort of way—"What 'appened when you said the last word? Can you tell me what word it was?"

Alfie told Mr Sapiens that it was called Petivo and described the effects, a purple ball, the slowing of time, the blast of energy. Mr Sapiens nodded as if he understood exactly what it was and he smiled.

"Very impressive. That's a wizard spell."

"Is it?" said Alfie. "What do you mean a wizards spell?" Alfie imagined that he had perhaps stolen the word from a wizard.

"It means…" said Mr Sapiens. "That you did a wizards spell. To do a wizards spell you have a be a wizard," said Mr Sapiens talking to Alfie as if he was a toddler. "When you are inaugurated as a Mage you start on level one and learn your way through The Levels. When you get to level thirty-three—you become a high wizard and there are thirty-four levels of that until you become a Sorcerer."

"I see, so how come I can do a wizards spell then?"

"Isn't it obvious?" said Mr Sapiens. "You're a wizard—one who has awoken to their innate powers. Because you have not been discovered yet, you are slightly in danger. Good job you met myself and Wiseman. But, as you are not inaugurated by the magick council you are off the radar, you're undiscoverable—the magick that restricts wizards from performing spells above their level are not applicable to you… yet."

"Oh," said Alfie suddenly understanding. "So when, if, I become a Mage, you're saying I wont be able to do them anymore?"

"Yes." He said simply. "Going back to what I said earlier about magick being dangerous. I meant it. It can really damage some people psychologically. Mr Taylor-Clarke for example hasn't fully recovered yet after you used that *Vaneoro* spell on him." Alfie sank a little in his seat and grimaced. "The mind is a fragile thing."

"Well, how do I put it right?" said Alfie. "I mean, I can't get his clothes back or anything like that can I?"

Mr Sapiens smiled even wider. "As a matter of fact, you can…"

"What?" said Alfie confused. "How?"

"There is a place where all the things that are vanished magically go." Mr Sapiens walked towards him and held his hand out. "Take my hand and I will show you…"

Alfie took Mr Sapiens cold hand and felt slightly apprehensive. "Not a lot of people know about this place. Wiseman told me about it years ago. *Ipsum-Vaneoruss.*" Mr Sapiens said it so quickly Alfie barely had time to register the room disappearing before his eyes. He felt himself falling, like he did in his dreams—stomach first, then the rest of him. Then another sensation of landing somewhere safe, but Alfie couldn't see anything, as hard as his eyes searched, the sooner he realised that wherever they were, the darkness was impossibly impenetrable. But then, tiny sparking shoots of red light started to appear. Stretching out before them was a fizzing, popping red tunnel of light. Inside the tunnel was black, outside was millions of snapping, popping red lights knitting together like pulsing fabric. Mr Sapiens held Alfie's hand tighter as very suddenly they began to shoot forwards at breakneck speed. Whizzing, popping noises became more frequent the faster they went, the red light began to blur… Alfie felt strange… then feint… he shut his eyes, unable to cope with the terrible speed… reminding him of some horrible roller-coaster… then solid ground met his feet. Alfie slowly opened his eyes, feeling dazed and confused.

The best way to describe the room they were standing in was… blank. The walls were so smooth grey they looked like nothing in particular. The only stand out feature was a lone, wooden oak door standing tall ahead of them. Mr Sapiens was already to it and walking through. Alfie glanced quickly around and followed him—inside was a small light and airy foyer, with a wooden desk counter. Behind the counter was another large door exactly like the one they had just come through. The whole foyer was small and with plain white walls with nothing on them whatsoever. Up above them the ceiling darted upwards where a large skylight was letting in a beautiful sunny blue sky. Alfie blinked at it, for he knew from his partial experience that time was always different in these places.

Behind the counter now appeared a jolly man with a huge grin which beamed at them. "Silviu Sapiens!" he cried giggling. "How lovely to see you again!" he reached across and shook Mr Sapiens hand merrily. "And nice to meet you too young man!" who lent forwards and took Alfie's hand and shook, introducing himself as: "Parsons… just call me Parsons."

Parsons was short with a huge grin, messy beard and blue overalls, a small bald patch on the top of his head shined in the sunlight from above.

"Hello," said Alfie relinquishing the tight grip.

"And to what do I owe the pleasure?" said Parsons beaming at them both—and looking as if he had not seen a soul in a long time, for he gazed at them madly.

"Well," said Mr Sapiens conspiratorially. "This young man here did not know about *The Place Where Vanished Things Go*, and we've come to retrieve some items that he vanished here."

"Aha!" cried Parsons. "By mistake was it?" Mr Sapiens gave Alfie a funny look before nodding. "Well, you've come to the right place! By the way, we don't call it *The Place Where Vanished Things Go* anymore. It's Sampson's Void now," he giggled pulling out the largest bunch of keys Alfie had ever seen from the back of his overalls and flicked through them. Then inserting a long one into the door behind him. The door made a loud clunking noise and squealed as Parsons pushed the doors wide open. Inside was a huge warehouse, or what looked like a warehouse. Mr Sapiens guided Alfie round the counter, following Parsons into the humungous place. It was quite dark—candle brackets fixed to each corner of shelf supplied some light, but it wasn't enough. But there were what looked like, hundreds of bright flashes going off all over the place—not unlike a camera flash, and then sudden noises of thuds and clatters. The warehouse was lined with hundreds upon hundreds of solid oak shelves. Alfie could see them stretching upwards forever, into the ceiling—if there was a ceiling for it was taller than a hundred cathedrals and seemed to stretch on forever. Ahead of them, the warehouse, if you could call it that, stretched so far in front of them that it bent over the horizon.

"Whenever someone vanishes something magically, whether they meant to or not, it comes here…" said Parsons. "Those flashes are things coming and going."

Alfie saw something flash on a shelf quite near to them that looked like bowl of fruit, a second later it flashed again and disappeared. "It's quite interesting," said Parsons. "If you wanna hear it?" Alfie nodded. "This is the seventh version of this type of Void. Way before, it was just chaos! Things would get damaged and the Mage would complain and not wann'ing ta' vanish their stuff. So we had to iron out the creases. There was a time…" said Parsons, laughing into his hand. "An elephant appeared, with a little hat on its head. It crushed a ton of inventory! Turned out it was from a circus, some kid wizard who didn't know his own powers demonstrating to the Dormies a *'magic-trick'*, and he only went and vanished the bloody thing! magically!" Parsons roared with laughter, then stopped. "Of course, the elephant wasn't happy at all, damaged a lot of our stuff that day… took weeks to clear it all out…" he said quite seriously. "But anyway, everything now is instantly categorised, numbered, and comes and goes without a problem."

"Well Alfie, would you like to ask for Mr Taylor-Clarke's clothes back?"

"Sure," said Alfie wondering how on earth Parsons would be able to locate Mr Taylor-Clarke's missing old clothes. "Do you know where I could find them?"

Parsons put a pair of spectacles on and pulled out a small notebook. "Rough date you vanished them?" he said peering over his glasses.

"*Err*…" said Alfie thinking. "About the end of September?"

Parsons scanned the notebook faster than light, then with an "Aha!" put three fingers to the entry in the book and flicked them upwards into the air—a small swelling of air rushed about their feet. Before a loud screeching sound began to echo. A drawer from a filing cabinet a hundred feet long stretched out in front of them, bending round the corner to meet Parsons who pawed through the brown papers inside. Then after a few seconds, pulled one out. Going back to the counter in the white room, he clicked his fingers and the filing cabinet drawers zapped around the corner, disappearing. Alfie and Mr Sapiens followed the man back into the little white room.

"September... *September*... Aha! You vanished... a pair of brown trousers, a belt, an orange-y shirt and brown tank top with matching tie, vanished from Room. 53b, Math Department, Westbury High School, Westbury?"

"That's the one!" said Alfie open mouthed.

"Ok!" said Parsons excitedly. "Number *one-one-five-three-four-nine-five*." Parsons clicked his fingers. There was a sudden whoosh as five items of clothes came zooming through the door. Alfie and Mr Sapiens had to duck to avoid a low flying belt. Parson grabbed them. "Here we are, signed off and ready to be handed back. Ok?"

"Thanks!" said Alfie, taking them and passing them to Mr Sapiens who held them rather distastefully. After giving their thanks to the overactive, giggly middle-aged man called Parsons, they left. Alfie feeling rather nervous about travelling back though the red tunnel thing again.

"What is the red tunnel thing Mr Sapiens?" said Alfie as they closed the large double doors and stood back in the blank grey room.

"A wrinkle-road we call it. There is no other way to get to a Void," he said, noticing Alfie anxiousness for travelling back.

And in fact there was no reason to worry, the way back was far easier than Alfie anticipated—he felt the same falling sensation, then flying through the red tunnel of light, then landing softly on Mr Sapiens stone floor barely twenty seconds later. Mr Sapiens put the clothes down on a chair straight away.

"I'll make sure 'e gets them, probably not a good idea for you to hand them over," he said smirking.

Walking home Alfie felt optimistic. Not even the biting cold could dampen his spirits. He had travelled to a Void with his French teacher—a magical Void to a place where all the things that are vanished by magick appear and disappear. It was unbelievable—Alfie giggled to himself, he couldn't believe this was happening to him.

As Alfie walked over the railway bridge and through the park he could saw two people through the darkness he thought he recognised—Tommy and Sparky were on the swings sitting quietly. Alfie, on a high, finally felt ready to tell them everything.

"Hi guys, what you doing here?" he said opening the playground gate. "You're not going to believe what's happened!"

"Oh so your speaking to us now then?" Tommy snapped not looking at him.

"I'm a wizard and I am going to be taught real magick!" said Alfie breathless. "Except I am not supposed to say anything, I don't suppose."

"So what!" shouted Tommy. "Isn't that great for you!" Tommy didn't look pleased for him at all, in fact he looked mightily sore.

"Tommy please!" cried Sparky looking anxious, his face pleading. Alfie could sense Tommy on the offensive, his face maddened.

"Well come on!" he shouted back. "He tells us nothing for weeks, then now decides to swan over and tell us everything that's actually happened. Well thanks mate, you're such a pal!" he spat jumping off the swing.

Alfie was taken aback by Tommy ferociousness. "Tommy, I didn't have to tell you. I was asked not to tell *anyone*."

"Well then maybe you SHOULDN'T HAVE TOLD US ANY-THING THEN!" cried Tommy.

"Look, I'm sorry okay? I was just… confused and—" Alfie stammered.

"*Ahhww*… BOO-HOO!" Tommy yelled. "We are your friends, I am, and always have been your BEST friend, but you have been LYING TO US! And FRIENDS DO NOT LIE TO EACH OTHER!"

"I was going to tell you, tell you both—" said Alfie pleading, he needed to make them understand. Sparky was sitting with his head in his hands. "I just didn't know when to, because… I didn't understand it and…I needed to know more, and the time was never right to—"

"NOT GOOD ENOUGH!" Tommy cried as Sparky whimpered again.

Tommy turned and marched away. "Come on Sparky!" he yelled. Sparky looked at Alfie quickly, then at the ground before waddling after Tommy.

Then he stopped and turned. "You should have told us the truth." He said quickly, looking at the ground. "We could have helped, we are you friends. You didn't need to lie to us…" Sparky quickly trotted after Tommy who was marching off across the green.

Alfie stood motionless, breathing hard against the dark, cold night, watching his friends leave, unable to believe what just happened.

Over the next few weeks Alfie lost what optimism he had. Tommy and Sparky were still not speaking to him and Alfie had to sit next to smelly Chris in lessons, facing the occasional glare from Tommy. Break time's Alfie sat on a bench the other side of school and made sure Joel didn't see him—he would love to see Alfie on his own with no friends. This was the first time he had a real argument with Tommy and didn't really know what to do.

The morning after the argument in the playground Alfie had knocked for Tommy as usual, hoping all had been forgotten—but his Mum answered and told Alfie that Tommy had already left. At school that morning Alfie found Tommy and Sparky sitting on a bench, but when he got closer, they saw him and walked away without a word.

Alfie felt very alone, not even a spell could save him now. A small part of Alfie felt angry that they would leave him, now of all times—just when he was about to confide everything to them—but another part of Alfie knew this was his fault, he should have told them sooner, a lot sooner.

Alfie was in his room, a few days before they broke up for the Christmas break. Things were pilling up in his mind. He had homework that should've been done, but lay in a pile on his desk—he didn't care, but his Grandma was nagging him furiously and had been through all his books and written him a homework schedule. Alfie was getting increasingly worried by the revision and kept wondering if their was a spell that he could use to make him remember everything he read. On top of that, his Granddad was nagging him about what he wanted to do once he left school, Alfie didn't know, he was more concerned with staying alive. And he had no one to talk to. Nikolas Wiseman hadn't contacted him and whenever Alfie asked Mr Sapiens, he changed the subject. Tommy and Sparky were avoiding him at all costs. Gracie and Christian were all wrapped up in each other and even Joel seemed extra happy these days, continually sniggering when Alfie walked past muttering. *"Billy no mates…"* under his breath. Just to compound Alfie's misery, Curtis had returned to school—just to put the cherry on top of Alfie's worst ever week at school. Curtis had been removed from all Science lessons which was good, but had cornered Alfie at break time the second day he got back, flanked by Bruce, Frank and Titan, swearing vengeance upon Alfie (even though it took him a couple of attempts to say the word). Yet Curtis seemed wary of Alfie, seeming to sense from his previous encounter that not all was what it seemed with this short, skinny messy haired individual who was half his size. After Curtis and the gang walked away, Alfie spotted Joel cackling to himself with Christian.

Alfie was extremely glad to be breaking up for Christmas.

No one seemed to care or even remember his problem, his major problem. Alfie wondered if everyone had been memory wiped. His problem was not just an adolescent teenage problem like everyone else's, no, a massive, terrifying magickal demon was dead set on killing him—sort of problem. Alfie's only saving grace in that department was the fact that since meeting Wiseman at his house, Alfie hadn't seen the Shadow once. Or at least, he didn't think he had. There were occasions when he was walking home when he thought he saw someone watching him from behind a nearby tree, but when he got closer there was no one there. On one particularly cold night as Alfie walked back through the dark park stomping across the soggy park he saw the gang that had tried to hurt him and Nigel at the start of the year. They were sitting around the swings and glared at Alfie as he passed. He tried not to think about the amount of enemies he had built up this year. A few moments later, he heard them scream and run from the park. When he turned he didn't see anything, but swore he saw a black shape dart behind the slide.

On the last day of term before Christmas the teachers played games in the lessons, which was fun, for everyone else. Alfie didn't join in. He knew if he said anything he'd get glared at by Tommy, or Joel. But, was it his imagination? Did he just catch Gracie staring at him? He must have been mistaken.

Alfie sat alone at lunch—the hall was completely full for everyone was tucking into a special Christmas lunch. He even pulled the cracker with himself putting the hat on his head and sighing.

That night was the school's Christmas party. The school hall had been decked out with decorations, balloons, party food, fizzy drinks and was blaring out Christmas music. Alfie stood in the foyer feeling miserable as he watched everyone excitedly piling in. Tommy and Sparky who made straight for the food, Joel and Ashley who were singing together, Christian who tugged Gracie in, Henry Goofham followed by Nigel with his pen and paper in hand, Sarah Ashdown and her giggly friends were followed by all the teachers, who were wearing paper hats. Alfie sighed, he would just spoil it by being there, so turned on the spot and walked out of school.

Alfie lay on his bed. He felt sad that he didn't go to the Christmas party. What would be the point in going? He'd just sit there by himself, get glared at by Tommy, endure being called *billy no mates* by Joel and have to watch Christian and Gracie snuggling up to each other for the dance. No thank you, Alfie much preferred his freezing cold room contemplating whether to get the train to London to search for Richard Found. But what would he tell his Grandparents? Mind you, he didn't have any money for the train fare, let alone a hotel! And even if he got there, how would he know where to look? Richard Found could be anywhere.

And it was his birthday tomorrow.

12

The Magickal City of Magicity

It was the early morning of Saturday December 21st and Alfie woke early, blinking at the bright sunlight streaming in through his room. Alfie smiled, he was sixteen! Jumping out of bed like an excited puppy, and regretting it instantly, for he suddenly registered how cold it was.

"Ah, ah…" he cried, hopping around on the bitterly cold floor. He managed to pull a sweater, jeans and some thick woolly socks on, before running downstairs three at a time and found his Grandparents sitting waiting for him at the kitchen table, with a small bundle of presents. His Granddad was wearing his battered old gardening clothes, with the newspaper open before him. His Grandma was wearing her flowery apron and a big warm smile, her hair all frizzy—a sign that she had been rushing around to get things sorted.

"Happy Birthday Alfie!" they chorused as he sat down at the table, beaming.

"Right," said his Grandma. "We have bacon, sausages, beans, hash browns and fried bread for breakfast…" she smiled. "But I think we should open these presents first?"

"I think that's a brilliant idea," said his Granddad. "Here," he slid them towards him.

"Ah presents!" said Alfie pretending to have just seen them. "Thanks Granddad, thanks Grandma."

"Well come on and open them," Grandma said, sitting down.

Alfie took the first present, which felt a lot like a book, the wrapping paper was brown and tied up with string. Alfie unwrapped it carefully, he was right, it was a book.

"Do you like it?" said his Grandma looking anxious.

"Of course I do, thanks, this is really... useful," said Alfie, smiling inwardly, he should have known—the book was called 'Your Exam Passing Schedule'.

His Granddad passed him a large bundle which looked suspiciously like clothes— which wasn't like his Granddad and if he had to guess Alfie would say it was a big woolly jumper, seeing as he always went on about clothes being better than heating. Alfie would have probably swapped a woolly jumper just to have the heating on for one day, he was sick of seeing his breath in front of him. When Alfie did open it, he was shocked. It wasn't a woolly jumper at all. It was a black leather jacket, exactly the one he had dreamed of for ages—in fact he had dreamed of one like this for ever and had been on his last five Birthday and Christmas wish lists.

Alfie held it up, it wasn't new but it looked fantastic—it was like an American baseball jacket, something straight out the 1950's and it smelt brilliant.

"But how?" asked Alfie.

"It doesn't matter how sunshine," he smiled. "Go on try it on."

Alfie put it on, it was the best feeling in the world and fitted perfectly, it was as if it was made just for him, tight round his waist and long enough on the arms. Alfie felt a massive surge

164

of power wearing the jacket.

"Oh Alfie it's brilliant…" said Grandma, putting her hands to her mouth, looking like she was about to cry.

"This is the best present ever!" Alfie said.

His Granddad looked immensely happy with his decision and sat for the rest of the morning, reading his paper and smiling. Alfie felt so happy, he didn't ever want to take it off—it was the first proper fashionable piece of clothing he had ever owned. His Grandma usually got his clothes from the charity shop, so invariably the shirts were either too big, too small or just disgusting. Alfie now decided that he would care a lot more about what he looked like—if was ever going to attract girls like Gracie, he thought, then he'd have to make a bit more effort. Just after breakfast Alfie went upstairs to get changed. He pulled out all his clothes and tried them all on to see which ones went best with his new leather jacket. Eventually he decided that his best jeans, old black boots and plain white t-shirt went together brilliantly and Alfie was impressed with how cool he now looked, what a transformation! He wished he could do something about his hair, which fell in twisted strands across his gaunt face.

Just as he was finishing admiring himself, Alfie thought he heard something. It sounded like a shuffling and creaking. He looked round his room, but nothing was out of place—must be the mice underneath the floorboards again.

Gggggggggwwwwwwwwrrrrrrrrrrrrrrrrrrrrrr!

Went the noise and Alfie stopped stock still.

"Hello?" He moved slowly to the window and looked out. The street was bare, spare a few seagulls.

"I'm not outside am I?" said deep, sarcastic voice.

Alfie darted round, but there was no one in his room. Could it be... the Shadow? Had it broken down Wiseman's defences?

"Who's there?" said Alfie backing against the wall.

"Oh come on..." The voice was very deep, grumpy and sounded like creaking wood. Alfie tip toed across to his bedroom door and opened it, there was no one on the landing—he half thought that maybe his Granddad was playing a trick on him.

"Getting warmer," said the voice again. "Oh, I'm *here* you thicky!"

Alfie's wardrobe doors burst open, drawers moving like a mouth and the wood bending into the shape of a face. "How long does it take?" said the wardrobe. "Seriously... wandering about the room like a little scared mouse."

Alfie's wardrobe was talking!—The doors and drawers resembling a large grumpy face. Alfie backed against the wall again, this was surreal.

"But you're... you're my wardrobe!" said Alfie incredulous.

"Well if you don't want to hear my message," it said. "Then I'll just be off."

"No it's ok!" Alfie said quickly, at the same time wondering how his wardrobe could just *be off*. "Do you have a name?"

"Of course not! I am a wardrobe for god sake! Dear oh dear, the children of today. Oh, and can you put that flipping enchanted letter in the shoe box somewhere else before I completely flip out! It's driving me bonkers!"

"I'm sorry..." said Alfie. "I will... sure... but erm... how can you talk? I mean, can you see? Are you *always* alive?"

"So many questions and he said you were one to watch. *Talk, see... alive?* None of this matters. I have a *message* for you, then I will resume to being your wardrobe, got it?"

166

Alfie said that he definitely got it, and sat on his bed taking in the surreal scenario as best he could.

"Now listen carefully because I'm afraid I will only say this once, got that once… not twice, or thrice… just once."

"The message?" said Alfie eagerly.

The wardrobe frowned, two knots of wood bent and creaked, then it sighed and said in a monotone voice—"Wiseman says he will meet you at Westbury Churchyard in ten minutes… good luck!" it mumbled, then suddenly it lost all face and returned to normal. Alfie stared. Had that actually happened? His Wardrobe, had just come alive and relayed him a message?

Nickolas Wiseman wants to see me? Smiled Alfie—this must have been what he meant when he said he would contact me, Alfie thought—mind you, ten minutes? He would have to run, the Churchyard was a good twenty minutes walk from here. Before sprinting downstairs, Alfie tentatively approached the wardrobe and reached for the shoes box on the top shelf. Inside he could feel the letter *J* jumping around. He put it under his bed and backed out of the room, watching the wardrobe.

"Grandma, Granddad I'm just off out, I'll see you later!" said Alfie, bounding down the stairs.

"Where are you going?" said Alfie's Grandma coming from the kitchen.

Alfie thought quickly. "*Err…* meeting a friend," he said, trying not to lie.

"What friend? You didn't tell us sweetheart."

"I know, I only just remembered, I've got to run because I'm going be late!" said Alfie reaching for the door handle.

"Who's going?" she said looking down her nose at him, she was suspicious.

"Er, Tommy and Sparky... might be," said Alfie, wishing they were.

"Ok," she sighed. "It would have nice to see you on your Birthday, but never mind—just be careful."

She kissed him on the cheek and Alfie felt bad, but he knew he couldn't tell her the truth, for one she wouldn't believe him. He opened the door and ran.

The air was crisp and chilly. Alfie pelted up the road and towards the churchyard. Puffed out and breathing hard, the Church loomed up into the sky before him. At last, he was at the entrance to the gates but there was no sign of anyone there. The small gravel car park was empty, only a few crows occupying the surround, sat atop gravestones. Alfie walked through the stone archway and into the gravel courtyard. As soon as he did, a car appeared to his left. It wasn't there before he'd walked under the stone archway. It was a very nice car, sleek and old looking with shiny silver-blue paintwork like moonlight and a black soft top. A tall man got out the passengers side—cowboy hat first, Nikolas Wiseman.

"Do you like her?" he called to Alfie. "She's a *Morgan...*" he said looking smitten. "Beautiful isn't she?"

"Yes," said Alfie noticing the registration plate which read—W1sem8n.

"Magically engineered of course, I always find cars these days have very little leg room... Perhaps people are shorter nowadays." Wiseman puffed his chest out. "She's got all my own little inventions and tweaks."

The driver window slowly wound down and Theadore smiled warmly at Alfie, then addressed Wiseman.

"Should I take her home?" he said.

"Yes, but wait for my call. We might need you later," said Wiseman and Theadore did a little nod. Alfie watched the car reverse and drive off, as it crossed the stone threshold to the churchyard it flashed once, a bright moonlight flash before vanishing completely.

"I have something here which should tell us," said Wiseman walking into the graveyard and fishing for something in the deep confines of an inner pocket. "Where the pesky LeyLine is."

"LeyLine?" Alfie queried, thinking maybe he'd heard Wiseman wrong.

"Aha! This map," said Wiseman triumphantly wrestling it from his pocket. "Has gone all faint! Must be old I expect, here look at this…"

Wiseman turned a grubby pile of paper towards him. "This is a LeyLine map. A terribly exciting way to travel magically."

Looking at the map Alfie realised, incredibly that it looked a lot like the London Underground map. Lots of different coloured lines all connecting to each other. There were tiny names next to dots all along the lines and read things like: *Whitegate* and *Happy Gnome.*

Alfie wondered what they meant, he had been into London quite a lot with his Grandparent's, they always went by train because his Granddad hated driving around London. Alfie remembered when he was little watching the underground map all the way, counting down the stations until it was their stop.

"There is a means of travel across the whole world that isn't hindered by the slow progress of technology," said Wiseman. "These invisible lines pave almost the entire world. The ancient world used to map these lines by building monuments on top of them. Just like this rather extravagant church," said Wiseman looking up at it. "Magick runs thick through LeyLines, like water through rivers." said Wiseman, mysteriously. "Odd things are always reported to occur around LeyLines that cross."

"Like what?"

"Well you know, ghost sightings, time slips, weird noises, smells… you know, all the weird stuff people like to read about in magazines," he said waving his hands. "Now, these coloured lines on here are the LeyLines," he pointed at the map. "All we have to do now is find the blasted thing."

"Find what?" said Alfie confused.

"The LeyLine of course!" Wiseman began looking around the churchyard.

"So you can see them?" said Alfie, looking around for a coloured line.

"No, they are invisible!" Wiseman rolled his eyes. "But there is always something that sticks out, maybe a tree that mysteriously cannot be cut down, a gargoyle's face that changes, or a mysterious gnome that moves by itself when no one is looking. Aha!" cried Wiseman, who became tangled with a bush. "In this case a gravestone!" he called triumphantly and waving for Alfie to join, who did so anxiously. Wiseman had stopped before the oldest, grubbiest looking gravestone in the yard. It was surrounded by a dead prickly bush, under a dead looking tree.

"Just look at that gravestone. What is there about it that looks different?"

"It looks old?" offered Alfie, who certainly didn't think it looked magickal in any way.

"No!" barked Wiseman. "Read the inscription."

Alfie tried to read the words, but they were very faded. "Er, it says… Leonard E. Yelling with a message beneath… *I travel… beyond?"*

Wiseman looked at him expectantly, but Alfie just shrugged, he had no idea.

"Look," Wiseman began to walk around it. "It is the only gravestone around this area, it is under a tree that I presume cannot be cut down and the inscription… *Leonard E. Yelling…* is a part-anagram of LeyLine. Then the quote: *I travel beyond* which could be a metaphor for death, but it could mean to travel— magically," Wiseman said with his arms wide, as if it was obvious.

"And no date of death," said Alfie nodding.

"Well spotted, this is not a gravestone, tis' a LeyLine key!" Alfie smiled, it did make sense he supposed. "Now, I want you to look at the map," said Wiseman who shoved the grubby paper under Alfie's nose. "Can you see where we are?" It smelt like tobacco and whisky.

"No," said Alfie, all he could see was blurry coloured lines.

"Look!" Wiseman pointed to a spot near the left edge of the paper where a large red arrow stood reading: *'YOU ARE HERE.'* A tiny picture of the church lay next to it. "And we want to go here."

Alfie followed his finger all the way up a smooth red line to the centre of the map to a perfect round purple circle, with what looked like a white blurry line surrounding it. Inside the purple circle read *'MAGICITY'* in big, bold letters.

"Magicity?" asked Alfie, he'd never heard of it.

"That's where we are going," said Wiseman looking excited. "To travel by LeyLine is pretty simple," Wiseman fixed Alfie with a hard stare. "You need to jump up and down on the grave shouting *I'm a little fairy short and stout…"*

"What?" said Alfie, that sounded a little childish and he scanned the graveyard to make sure no would see him.

"Go on," said Wiseman hurrying him forwards. "That way if we're spotted in the graveyard they just think we're crazy…"

"Then what happens when I do that?" said Alfie.

"The giant fairy turns up and whisks you away to Magicity in a giant pumpkin pulled by magick horses of course!"

There was a pause, Alfie gazed at him for a second trying to work out if Wiseman was being serious or not. Then he cracked up, spluttering into laughter at Alfie's perplexed expression.

"I'm sorry, I'm sorry," he said. "I couldn't resist!" he laughed again, clutching at his sides bent over double while Alfie stood wondering what on earth he was getting into.

After Wiseman had calmed himself down, he explained that Alfie should repeat Magicity three times in his head. "Then just put your hand upon the gravestone and poof!"

"Poof?" said Alfie. "What's poof?"

"Well," said Wiseman. "It means you *go*… you fly."

"Fly?" thought Alfie. "What in?"

"Oh for goodness sake come on!" said Wiseman checking his watch.

Wiseman watched as Alfie cautiously reached out for the old stone, *Magicity, Magicity, Magicity* he repeated. He waited, hand touching the cold stone. But nothing happened. "Was that a joke as well?" he said frowning up at Wiseman, who didn't say anything—he just grinned. The next second Alfie knew why. All at once, with the strength of a tornado, he was wrenched up into the air feet first, faster than lightning.

"AHHH!" Alfie left his stomach behind as he was turned upright, soaring upwards into the sky and swearing loudly.

The force shot him forwards at electrifying speed through the air. The graveyard and land beneath him a blur. As he self-righted falling stomach first which was cushioned by an invisible cushion of air, he saw a pulsing red line like the one on the map. It looked like a shining red river. The wind was strong and noisy, if Wiseman was shouting orders at him, Alfie couldn't hear him! Did he not know Alfie hated heights! All of a sudden he stopped going upwards. The invisible thing that had taken charge of him pointed him forwards and for a split second he hung in mid air. He had never been this high! It was incredible and terrifying. Now, all at once, he burst forwards. The wind battered his face as he soared high above the houses and town below. He could see tiny windows with Christmas trees, tinsel and decorations. Alfie stopped himself from crying out, he was terrified of heights and now he was in the hands of some invisible force, a current blowing him along—and it was uncomfortable. One minute he was on his stomach, the next he was upside down and he couldn't seem to keep straight. Alfie wondered if anyone could see him! He soared through the sky at a dizzying pace, sinking lower now, over cars and houses, his school, past churches and fields, woods and rivers following the translucent red line.

Wiseman suddenly soared past him, swirling in the air, his long coat billowing in the wind. He was laughing a deep bellowing laugh, clearly enjoying himself—turning on his back and putting his hands behind his head.

Alfie felt exhilarated and alive as he soared up higher into the wet clouds, watching the towns and cities below him, which didn't look entirely real from up here.

"We're nearly there now Alfie!" bellowed Wiseman. "I said... WE'RE NEARLY THERE! Watch the descent it can be quite...

BUMPY!"

Wiseman zoomed forwards and out of sight. Up ahead he could see what looked like, a huge circle of mist, which glittered like a cloud made of silver glitter. It was unlike anything he had ever seen. It seemed to encircle a town below and not an ordinary town. This must be what the white outline next to the purple circle had been on the map. All at once Alfie's heart leapt into his throat.

"AARRGHH!" he screamed. The invisible force that had been carrying him had now—let go! Alfie began to plummet towards the earth at break neck speed—the ground crashing towards him faster and faster—the wind blasting his ears as he turned summersaults in the air. Alfie cursed everything about this mode of transport. But then as quick as a flash the invisible force caught him and cushioned his crash landing—just as he was about to smack straight into the grass hillside. He hit the floor running and stopped before Wiseman's feet, who was smoking a pipe and looking amused.

Alfie felt totally disorientated, his legs felt like a wobbly jelly. He collapsed into the road and face planted the floor, staying there for a good minute.

"You get used to it," said Wiseman at his side, picking him up.

"Hmm," was all he could manage.

They were standing on a tall grassy hill with a small belt of trees on the left. All around were towns, far below and all around the bottom of the hill. Alfie looked back, the hill down was quite steep. Along it stretched a stony path leading all the way up through bushes, rocks and a small forest. Wiseman tapped Alfie and pointed ahead. At the top of the hill was a thin swirling, silvery mist.

They walked up the stony path towards the wall of mist. Every step closer they took, the mist seemed to thicken and bulk, sensing their presence. Objects and shapes appeared thought the mist, twined with odd noises like far off battles, cries and shouts. Alfie looked up at Wiseman who did seem deterred. The hill levelled, the mist just fifty feet ahead. A small white hut stood just before the mist like a small ticket theatre ticket stall. Just in front of it was a large ornate gate with swirling mist encircling the bars. Inside was a friendly looking man with small round spectacles, he wore a bright red jacket with silver buttons with a black flat hat strapped under his chin. Glancing over his book at them, he smiled and put it down.

"Tickets and tag's please," he said in a showman's voice.

Wiseman began rummaging around in his pockets. Alfie felt his heart race, as he was sure he just saw two red eyes staring at him from inside the mist. "Here we are," said Wiseman handing a small grubby bit of paper to the man in the booth.

Alfie watched the cold red eyes inside the mist. It was a knight statue, he thought, wearing huge amounts of metal armour and proudly sporting the Saint George cross, sitting aboard a humungous grey horse. The red eyes peeped out from underneath slits in the headgear.

"And here is mine," said Wiseman, getting the Skry pendant out, yanking it off his neck and passing it to the man in the booth. The man inspected both casually and waved them on ahead, passing the Skry back to Wiseman. The gate made of mist silently swung open and as they walked forward the sound of a thousand charging horses suddenly erupted into the air. Alfie jumped and subconsciously grabbed the back of Wiseman's coat. Through the mist a shape appeared. It wasn't a statue, it was moving! The knight aboard the horse stopped before them.

It looked monstrous as it trotted up to them. As Alfie looked closer, he saw that it wasn't made of stone at all—it was made of the silvery mist. Alfie stood as still as he could next to Wiseman, heart beating ferociously.

"Pendragon…" called Wiseman in his deepest voice.

The Pendragon tilted its large head judging Wiseman and stared at them both for a long time, it's large hand stroking a sword hilt. Then ever so slowly it bowed softly to the Wiseman, who did the same. Then it turned and blew, a small tunnel appeared ahead of them through the wall of mist.

"Walk," whispered the Wiseman to Alfie, pulling him by the arm through the tunnel of mist. Alfie looked back and saw the Pendragon's glaring red eyes watching him all the way, the mist swirling round his head until it disappeared.

"What was that?" said Alfie unable to hide the fright in his voice.

"The Pendragon, Protector of Magicity… he decides who comes in and out."

They walked further through the thick mist which smelt funny, like a flowery pungent incense. Eventually it became thinner. Sounds echoed toward them as they got closer to the end. Then, the mist fell away abruptly and Alfie's eyes suddenly adjusted to bright sunshine. They stood atop the lip of a cliff, beneath a small stone ruin, below them—beneath the cliff, into the valley—was the most spectacular sight Alfie had ever seen. He gasped as sun glinted across a wide horizon, sparkling off the top of buildings in a small, sprawling city below.

"This is no ordinary place—this," said Wiseman proudly walking forwards, throwing his arms out. "Is *Magicity!*"

Alfie stumbled forward to get a better look joining Wiseman

at the edge gazing across the wondrous expanse below.

Magicity was held inside a valley. The layer of silvery mist could be seen shining and sparkling in the sunlight on top of the hills that surrounded it.

Perched high on the rocks to the east was a monumentally large and extravagant castle. It had been carved into the mountain side and looked out across Magicity. It had a long piece of rock that protruded outwards from the mouth of the castle like a tongue. Water poured from the hole, cascading down in a giant waterfall with a small rainbow cast above. The river below stretched and winded through the city glinting white from the sun.

In the north of Magicity Alfie could make out a large stadium, with wooden rafters and white glass body in the shape of a egg. Inside was a grass pitch and white lines—Alfie wondered, peculiarly, if they played football here?

Directly below them and nearest the cliff edge, was a very large open square that was full to the brim with people. There was a market, with hundreds of stalls and wooden wagons with shouts and cries echoing off the vast stone buildings encasing the square. Directly in the middle of the square was a tall grey rock that stretched high above the surrounding buildings. There were steps going up the rock and a tiny protruding thing in the top that Alfie couldn't make out. In amongst the market stalls were what Alfie assumed were—street performers. Fire erupted from the mouth of one man, whose ball of fire turned into an orange elephant which grew and grew, then went charging off down an alleyway. The noise that echoed from the square was ridiculous, there were all manner of bells, whistles, flutes, drums, and sounds that Alfie had never even heard before.

The cobbled stone streets looked uneven and were full of shops, with enclosed bridges stretching out of the roofs to other shops. Nothing was symmetrical or even, or the same. Just off the square were lots of terraced houses lining the streets with pretty iron gates and mullioned windows. Tall, wide front doors of all colours had moving steps up to them. Chimney pots with smoke billowed into the sky, past a park with a flying adventure play area with slides that ran for miles, swings that swung themselves and tree houses the size of mansions!

A train line ran around the city. But the tracks were not ordinary, they sailed up into the air and over the city into many spirals before shooting down and vanishing into a dark hole beneath. It reminded Alfie of some sort of monstrous roller coaster and was sure that wizards only travelled in ways that made you feel sick.

Then, one of these *trains*—if it was called that—darted out from a nearby station. But, it was as far away from a *train* as you could get. It appeared to be flying, but was actually clinging on the invisible rails, green sparks shooting from beneath it, more resembling a giant, gothic, black snake—with hundreds of different sized cogs spinning round powering it. Alfie could just make out tiny people, sitting inside pod-like carriages and didn't seem bothered that it was lurching round in the air and turning summersaults.

Alfie reluctantly tore himself away from the view as Wiseman pulled him onto a wide stone elevator which cut through the side of the cliff top and seemed to take them straight down to the cobbled street below, leading, just ahead, to the busy square far below. Alfie stepped on cautiously and with a grinding noise it started moving, he gripped the stone rail and swallowed—it was a long way down—he held onto Wiseman's coat. The drop was quite frightening, so to the cliff edge, which to Alfie did not look secure.

Wiseman chuckled."Don't like heights eh?" he murmured above the noise of the grinding elevator. "Well, we'll soon have to change that."

Alfie tried to ignore the comment, especially if it meant going on the *snake-train*.

The cobbled street was light and open with small, dark shops either side of them. A wooden archway stretched across the street just before the entrance to the square. Alfie suddenly felt nervous, were they all wizards? Was he allowed here? Was he dressed correctly? He partially hid behind Wiseman as they entered through the crowd into the square. Thankfully who he presumed were wizards, were dressed quite normally. Almost all the men wore tight tailcoats, top hats and were very smart, while women wore petticoats.

But everyone seemed to have added in some colour, or something wacky to their outfit which added to the carnival atmosphere—some were dressed outrageously with papier-mâché heads, at least, Alfie hoped that it *was* papier-mâché fancy dress.

Small cramped shops all the way around the edge of the square were filled with fascinating things and begged a closer look. Street performers filled every nook and cranny that wasn't filled with a market stall and reminded Alfie of the performers he often saw in London, yet none of the London performers could do *these* tricks.

One man in a battered blue bowler hat, waved his hands. A small cloud formed in mid air, he waved it over to a small girl in front of him and the cloud began to snow. The girl laughed and jumped around gleefully, trying to catch the snowflakes in her mouth—a sign next to the man said: *Sweet Snow*.

A clown wearing a huge pair of dungarees, with a white face and green nose blew up a balloon in one breath and without touching it, made the balloon twist until it resembled a green puppy. He pulled a handful of sparkly yellow powder from his pocket and blew it over the balloon. With a small crackle and explosion of silvery vapour a green puppy began to yap and lick the nearest persons face.

There were endless stalls selling hundreds upon hundreds of different nik-naks. Things were whizzing overhead, there were loud explosions, clouds of silvery smoke and shouts from stall owners—Alfie didn't know what to look at first and he didn't dare blink in case he may miss something. Wiseman noticed Alfie's delirium.

"So," said Wiseman stopping. Alfie was still walking and he had to put a hand on Alfie's shoulder to stop him. "This occasion is only here once a year..." said Wiseman, walking out to a small clearing at the end of the market stalls. "See here at these shops around the square... you have Thyme the magical herb store..." Wiseman pointed to a shop on the right, with grubby windows but a huge selection of pots and jars filled with (mostly green) herbs. "Ah, now see over there..." Wiseman pointed straight ahead to a shop with lots of shrivelled up things dangling in the window. "That sells Talismans."

Alfie didn't have a clue a Talismans was.

"Over there is Bernie's Beasties, they sell animals—alive ones mostly, but I wouldn't recommend going in there unless you know precisely what you want, some of the animals can get a bit... *excited.*" Wiseman rubbed his hand where a small scar lay across his knuckle. "Just here," he pointed to, what had to be the prettiest most attractive shop around. "Is *Mellini's* sweet shop." Wiseman smacked his lips together, looking hungry and Alfie made a note to go in there as soon as he could.

"*Delicias* the Charms place, over there, but if you are wise I'd suggest going to *The Bellús* which is just off Merlin Street. It's much better and I know the owner,"

"What's a charm?" said Alfie eyes still darting.

"A Charm is an Enchantment. An example would be… your wardrobe," Wiseman smiled then led him around the square.

"I *seee*," said Alfie, remembering his grumpy wooden friend.

Wiseman guided him around the stalls, darting in and out of the people. Alfie recognised most of the things on the stalls—jewellery, food, pots and pans, even furniture—but more often than not there was something magickal about it. Alfie overheard a man on a cheese stall asking the owner if the 'Jumbly Wumbly Cheese,' made with the milk of a Tunderwacker (what that was Alfie didn't know), would make him go bright green for a week. The owner laughed hysterically and said "No, that's the *Girdle Scream Cheese.*"

As they walked through the hundreds of stalls Alfie noticed that Wiseman was getting quite a lot of attention. While one owner of a stall called out to him and shook his hand, another refused to serve him. Some of the people looking around, smiled from ear to ear as if Wiseman was a celebrity and asked him to do strange things like: 'touch my talisman'—Alfie assumed that it was a bit like signing an autograph in his world.

One family with a small child passed by Wiseman as he was looking at an old copper kettle, the small child pointed up and said: "Nikolas! Nikolas!" Wiseman looked around at the child as the parents looked embarrassed.

"Oh," said the young woman. "It is you. Well, it's an *honour*—he knows who you are, he has a poster of you in his room…" She giggled nervously. The father looked too petrified to speak. But Wiseman, using all his wealth of charm had a short conversation with them. Alfie stood around awkwardly as Wiseman began to pick the small child up.

"And you young man are going to be a fine athlete. *Ahh* yes, I can see it now, star of the Magicity Games it's… *Toby Herbert!*" cried Wiseman and the small boy laughed and giggled at his hero.

Several minutes later when the young family scuttled away, Wiseman picked up a large leather bound book and told Alfie that it was a: *'spellbound book'* which meant that the secrets inside usually black magick could only be opened by a powerful wizard. "And I like a challenge!" he said. But as he went to buy it, the man on the stall took one look at Wiseman, snatched the book off him and said: "I don't want you, or your business! Be off before I call a Guard and tell him your trying to Spell me into knocking the price down to zero!" spat the immensely angry man.

Wiseman left quickly, looking put out, but it didn't stop him calling the man a: "Barnacle-nosed-old-bigot!"

Wiseman, in rather a hurry, marched off down an alleyway away from the stalls and out of the main square until they reached a tall white building. A huge sign read *'The Cupio Cantara Café.'* The writing vanished suddenly, before—as if being written by an invisible hand—appearing again.

People were sat round the outside on tables, drinking from tall glass tankards. A small bridge led across a stream, or mote that surrounded the cafe. Going inside, Alfie saw that it was huge. It was light and airy, with sun streaming in through the windows high above them. Ivy vines stretched around the windows lazily, occasionally they would stretch a little further. Waiters and waitresses were gliding between tables picking up trays without touching them—Alfie could hear the running water now, which only got louder as he followed Wiseman through the café and up some stairs to the top of the building. Stretching down one corner of the café, was a waterfall. It wasn't big, but through the glass ceiling above Alfie could see the rest of it. The small waterfall inside was merely floating into the café through a funnel, where it filtered through long stone pools which encircled the café. At first Alfie would have assumed this a bit of a waste of space, but when they sat down he soon realised what it was for. Wiseman and he took a seat on a nearby white table that seemed to be growing out of the floor, so too did the chairs which Alfie sat down on rather tentatively. Wiseman clicked his fingers and two tankards appeared on the table instantly.

"I wanted to take you here for a couple of reasons…" said Wiseman taking his tankard. "Firstly, because its one of my favourite café's. And secondly because, I don't know what you drink in your world, but I imagine our tastes are pretty dissimilar." Alfie nodded glancing around at all the wizards and feeling mightily out of place. "So, I think this is the perfect place. You take your tankard and put it in the water…" Wiseman dipped his tankard in the stream that passed next to their table—when he pulled it out, the clear water began to change colour. Wiseman watched licking his lips, until it resembled a dark orange colour.

"Aha!" he called triumphantly. "Strawberry, passionfruit and mango daiquiri!"

Alfie blinked, pointing at it. "But…" he said.

"It's a magick waterfall, it gives you the drink you most desire at the time of filling it up."

Alfie chuckled, before grabbing the tankard and dipping it under the cool waters surface. Small bubbles started to pop just under the surface of the water, but the colour didn't change. A few slices of lemon, some ice and a straw suddenly popped into his drink. When he took a cautious sip he realised it was lemonade!

"Haha!" Alfie cried, pointing at it and looking at Wiseman who smiled. "It's lemonade!"

Wiseman nodded. A couple of people around them gave Alfie a snooty look.

Alfie and Wiseman chinked their glasses together. "Cheers!" they chorused and took a sip. Alfie suddenly felt his throat constrict and he started to choke—but then Wiseman did the same.

"Er-*huh*!" he coughed. "Bummer! I forgot," he said, wiping his mouth and handing Alfie a tissue—his eyes were streaming, the bubbles had gone right up his nose.

"Ergh, what happened then?" Alfie said, inspecting the drinks.

"I forgot to… put a Bit in the water didn't I. Silly me. My fault. Here," Wiseman handed him a small golden coin.

"What's a Bit?" said Alfie.

"Just chuck it in and I'll tell you. Don't wanna choke again do you?" Alfie certainly didn't, so chucked the little golden coin into the water, the current dragged it along and out of sight. Wiseman did the same. "If you don't pay as soon as you fill up, it either chokes you, or empties the glass all over you." Alfie was rather glad it hadn't emptied all over him and his nice new leather jacket. "It's important that I tell you about the difference in some of the rules in this place and yours," began Wiseman. "As we have just gathered from that…" he said pointing at the water. "The money is different from your… *pounds?* As you've just seen."

Alfie had twenty pounds in his pocket that he'd got in a card that morning from his Uncle. "So, it's a different currency?" said Alfie with a sinking feeling, perhaps they wouldn't accept his money here.

"Yes and no. The currency in Magicity is called the Bit. This is OneBit—the smallest amount we have in coin." Wiseman got one from his pocket and passed it over. It was about the size of a penny, but a little thicker with five tiny circular groves all around the outside. On the first side it read *1Bit*, round the outside tiny words read: *'spend wise, receive wise'*. The other side had a cats face, the eyes of which stared hypnotically back into Alfie's own eyes.

"Why is it a cat?—"

"And then after that is…" said Wiseman ignoring him. "A CamBit, a GamBit, a OctaBit, a PentaBit. But you can use your pounds in these shops too." Alfie breathed a sigh of relief. "It's not so strict and you can haggle with anyone. People won't be offended like they seem to be in your *supermarkets*." Alfie giggled at the thought of Wiseman haggling with someone in a supermarket. "It wasn't funny. It was embarrassing, why call it a market if you can't haggle? But," he said, returning to the point. "There's also—*Cambering* as the locals call it, which basically means to barter. You can offer your professional experience, if you have any, instead of money or even offer a swap."

"That's brilliant," said Alfie, who knew the embarrassing effects of never having any money.

One of the street performers walking past on the street outside suddenly made a massive jet of water shoot out of his mouth into the air. It exploded like fireworks and turned into hundreds of different coloured balloons. They floated down and some children nearby laughed and jumped for them.

Magicity felt a million miles from home. It was the most amazing place Alfie had ever been to. Alfie wondered what the time was, somehow time in Magicity felt different—as it seemed to in all these magical places.

"What's the time?" said Alfie curiously. Wiseman looked around and pointed out towards a shop facing the square with lots of mirrors in the display. On the side wall of the shops facing the square was a large painting of a white rabbit with a clock in the middle of its stomach. It was almost Midday.

"White rabbit," said Alfie jogging his memory. "Whatever happened to that white rabbit at your house?—" Alfie said turning back round, but Wiseman was already standing and moving for the café exit. "Could've told me we were leaving," said Alfie.

"Sorry, didn't realise the time!" he called. "Hurry."

Alfie was blown away by how beautiful Magicity was—the large turreting buildings seemed to move and sway, the stonework seeming to shift imperceptibly. Gargoyles on the side of buildings greeted you *good-day*, in a croaky, hoarse tone. Flags reined down from every shop round the square emblazoned with flashing images of the shop's logo. There were some buildings around the square that seemed to be competing to see who could climb the tallest, for they all wobbled and teetered ominously as their spindly tower stretched skywards.

Alfie found the shops all so perfect, there was nothing

arbitrary about the products they were selling, all the things had a use for something. Like the duvet that floated into the air when it was time to get up. Or an enchanted alarm clock that jumped away from you when you tried to switch it off. Toilet seats that lift themselves up and down. Talking TV's that called for you when your favourite programme was about to start. Enchanted furniture like the sofa that turned into a bed if you fell asleep on it. The kettle that boiled itself and made you a cup of tea when you asked it to. The salt and pepper set with long legs that walked around your kitchen table seasoning your food. The self sorting cutlery drawer. The bookshelf that organised books in any order you liked. The sock drawer that sorted all your odd socks and paired them. The nervous cooker that called you when something was burning, and immediately turned its own heat down. The phone that told you who was calling and hung up if you didn't like them. The notebook that scribbled down the thoughts that you knew you would forget.

Alfie was simply bowled over by the ingeniousness of it all. Magick was brilliant.

There were books too, loads and loads and loads of books, with all sorts of interesting names. And all about Magick. Alfie had never had much interest in books, but now found that he longed for nothing more than a seat by the fireside and a hundred or so of these books to read through. The spine's read things like:—*"Ambleside's Home Spell Compilation: All You Need For Your Home."*

"Magick: A Secret Study of Spells You Shouldn't Know..."
"Magick Hero's Guide to: How to Charm Your Enemy."
"Merlin's Secret Spells for Securing a Starry Night."
Alfie's eyes strained as he tried to read the spiralling gold letters on the spines as he was being hurried away by Wiseman,

who was paying for his large pile of books and having them wrapped and sent to his home. On and on the titles went, each one sounding better than the last and now he understood completely why Wiseman had so many books.

Wiseman and Alfie went back out to the market stalls in the square. "Hopefully that imbecile has gone now," said Wiseman gruffly.

Alfie was just about to go looking for something that he could give to Tommy and Sparky as a Christmas present, until he remembered that they weren't speaking to him. A stone dropped in his stomach, he'd forgotten about that. But, what if he got them a present? Surely they would forgive him?

Alfie was pleased with what he found.

"*Gnarlus Paper…*" The dirty, unwashed man on the stall called it. "All you gatta' do is write ya' question on it and it'll givya an answer, quite *rare* that is." The dirty man hitched up his trousers and grinned.

"How much?" said Alfie.

"Well this is a very rare art'e'fact i' this ya see, there aint none overz like this anywhere, in the 'werld. So we'll say a *WamBit*."

Alfie stood looking blank, wondering what on earth a WamBit was? Wiseman was speaking to someone a way off so he couldn't ask him. The man noticed Alfie's pause and his sellers instinct kicked in. "How much ya got?" he said—Alfie pulled out the £20 note, some paper clips and an old stick of chewing gum that had been in his jeans pocket for ages.

"Whatsat'?" said the man pointing at Alfie's hand.

"This?" asked Alfie holding up the £20 note.

"No, no!" said the man inspecting Alfie's hand. "*This…*" he picked up the chewing gum sounding amazed.

"Oh, that's just some chewing gum."

"*Chewing-gum*," said the man as if he had never heard of such a thing. "From the Outside?" the man pointed towards the mist.

"Yeah…" said Alfie. "From the outside."

The man seemed to think about it for a minute, turning the chewing gum over in his fingers. "Swap ya' the Gnarlus Paper for the *chewing-gum?*"

Alfie duly agreed and the man shuffled off to wrap the paper up in some more paper and string.

Just before Alfie left, the man asked him. "What does' I do wiv' it?"

"You put it in your mouth and chew," said Alfie, thanking the man and leaving quickly. Alfie tucked the Gnarlus Paper into his back pocket and caught up with Wiseman who was inspecting some talking pens at another stall and asking him how much a WamBit was worth.

"Oh you wouldn't be able to afford a WamBit, it's nine-hundred and ninety-nine Bits. And, in your money… *hmm,* let me think… quite a lot, why?"

"No reason," said Alfie, tucking the Gnarlus Paper inside his jackets inside pocket for safer keeping. That was Tommy's present sorted, now just to get something for Sparky—there was a lot of market stalls selling food, thought Alfie, where was that place that sold cheese?

"Just one more place to go for me," said Wiseman.

"Where's that?" said Alfie.

"The old carpet shop off Twist Street."

13

The Sword in Magicity's Stone

Alfie waited outside The Olde Carpet Shoppe on Wiseman's orders. It was a good few streets away from the square but the noise and commotion still reached him from here. The shop itself looked small and dark, and was part of a long street of thin, three storey terrace shops, that shrouded the small, uneven cobbled street in darkness.

After a short while Wiseman emerged with the cheerful looking shop keeper. "And as I say," said the man, leaning in the doorway. "If you need it in an hurry, then ya' know what a'do," he winked.

"Thanks David. We'll pick it up on the way back." Wiseman waved goodbye and they left.

"Did you buy something then?" said Alfie, wondering why Wiseman was buying new carpets.

"Certainly did. Happy Birthday," said Wiseman matter of factly.

"It's for me?"

Wiseman nodded smiling. "It is, but it's too heavy and lumbersome to carry, so we'll pick it up later."

"What is it?"

"A carpet. I thought that would be obvious."

"A carpet?" Alfie asked, what on earth did he want with a carpet?

Wiseman rolled his eyes. "Not just any old carpet, a very old and tatty, second hand carpet!" he called triumphantly.

"Thanks…" Alfie said, putting on his most sincere voice. Wiseman chuckled as they found themselves in the main square again. There were now even more people around and Alfie could hardly move through the excited, buzzing crowd.

"What's happening?" he asked looking up at Wiseman, who pulled his cowboy hat a little lower over his face.

"It's festival day!"

"Festival day?" said Alfie, trying to squeeze through the crowds behind Wiseman who stopped near the front where the crowd seemed to have gathered around the large rock centrepiece in the middle of the square. It was a huge mound of grey rock, taller than anything else, even the tottering buildings, with steps carved intricately all the way up to the top where something was sticking out. The whole statue seemed to glow, pulsing with energy. Alfie had a strange feeling of deja-vu, he was sure he had seen this rock before. All the people in the square were now gathered around and sounded extremely excited.

A squawky voiced man behind him said: "Do you think this will be the year?"

Another voice said. "I dreamt this moment the other day and *I* pulled it out! Do you really think it could be me?"

Chat and conversations carried on this strange vein for the next five minutes and left Alfie utterly bemused—he had no idea what was going on and Wiseman was standing silent, eyes closed in the shade of his hat.

Suddenly lots of men dressed in shiny red suits marched into the square out of nowhere with blaring trumpets. The people hushed as the performance began. Street performers stopped what they were doing and the people in the shops came out and joined the crowd. Some started to point upwards at a spec in the sky. As it got closer Alfie realised that it was a man, dressed in a red suit like the trumpeters. He was flying towards them, holding his hat above his head like a parachute. As the man landed perfectly in the middle of the square, the trumpeters blew deafening loud and fireworks crashed into the air all around them. The crowd roared as the man withdrew a stick and shouted:

"ROLL UP! Roll up! One and all, I am the bestest ringleader of them all!" The man was huge and his voice carried. He had a massive moustache and a big fat head. "Who will be the bravest? The strongest? The fearsome-est of them all? Who will go first? Will it be you!?" he pointed with his stick at a young girl at the front who nearly feinted.

Alfie could hear some sour voices in the crowd muttering quietly behind him: "I don't know why they still bother, I mean its not like someone's going to pull that thing out is it?"

"I know. No ones removed it in like five-hundred years? Or a thousand? What makes them think someone will do it now?"

But then the Ringleader roared again. "Our FIRST person to come up please. Let me release the DECIDER!" The crowd screamed.

As the trumpets blared again, the people screamed. The ringleader walked to the edge of the rock and tapped it with his stick. A ball of bright white light collected at the top of the stick. The ringleader flashed his stick into the air, releasing the ball

THE SWORD IN MAGICITY'S STONE

of light which zoomed over everyone's heads zigzagging and darting all over the place, zapping to and fro—for what reason Alfie had no idea. Then it stopped above someone's head. Alfie joined everyone else who was craning their heads to get a better look—he wished he was taller. Everyone moved away from the person, creating a passage for them to the front, staring silently at this chosen one.

"We have our first challenger!" cried the ringleader meeting the small man at the front who looked very nervous. The whole crowd watched silently, holding their breath.

"What is your name?" bellowed the ringleader.

"…C-Colin," stammered the small man. "Colin Headspell."

"Ahh," said the ringleader knowingly. "Another Headspell… well Colin Headspell, good LUCK!" The Ringleader slapped him on the back and stepped to the side to let him pass. Colin walked slowly towards the rock in silence.

At the top Colin waved as he stopped before… a stone sword? Alfie was sure that he could make out a thin stone sword—Colin put his hands around the hilt of it as the crowd tensed. Colin yanked. Then yanked again and pulled and tugged, but nothing happened. Alfie could see him trying desperately to pull it out, but it still looked like stone—Alfie suddenly realised that this was a competition to pull the sword out of the stone, like the old story with Merlin and Arthur. Alfie looked up at Wiseman and wondered what was really going on.

"*Ahh* Colin…" roared the ringleader. "Never mind!" Colin trudged back down the stairs as people began to get excited that it might be them again.

Alfie watched on for a good hour as several more people attempted to pull the stone sword from the stone, it was all very exciting stuff but Alfie could feel he was getting cramp in his legs standing still for so long. He could also sense Wiseman getting quite agitated. The food he had bought for Sparky was zipped up in his pocket—Alfie hoped it would keep—he wondered how magick cheese was different.

"Now, we have only time for two more volunteers to come and have a go to pull the sword from the stone, if neither of the next two can pull it out, then we wait for *another year*."

The crowd groaned.

"So, will the next person pull it out? And who will it be? Let the Decider, DECIDE!" The ball of light immediately flew back into the crowd. Alfie didn't bother watching it, he could sense where it was for the crowd were *ooing* and *arw-ing*.

The Decider seemed to be taking a long time.

Alfie looked up and had the shock of his life. As he turned, a thousand faces were staring at him. Eyes from every conceivable place were staring… straight… at… him!

Looking up slowly, he realised with absolute dread that the light has stopped above his head. The pulsing ball of light bobbed silently above him. Alfie looked at Wiseman pleadingly, he didn't want to go up there, in front of all these people—he didn't even belong here!

Wiseman placed a sturdy hand on his shoulder without looking at him and guided him forwards. Very slowly the crowd began to move apart to let Alfie through. His legs felt like jelly. This was a mistake. He could feel the crowd looking at him with a mixture of apprehension and jealousy—Alfie would gladly swap.

Tentatively he walked. His heart beating faster than a frantic drum. His breath caught in his throat. Sweat beads forming at his temples. The ringleader greeted him with a huge stage smile. Alfie looked up at him, his moustache didn't look real up close.

"And what is your name then boy?" boomed the ringleader, his voice carrying loud across the square. It was surreal, every single face was looking at him—thousands and thousands of eyes all looking up at *him*.

"A-A-Alfie B-Brown," he said, voice quivering.

"ALFIE BROWN!" roared the Ringleader and the crowd roared back. Then he whispered "It's not a name I've heard before, where are you from?" Alfie didn't know what to say, he just pointed towards Wiseman. "Ah, I *see*..." the ringleader looked towards the crowd and Alfie saw his look of suspicion. "Well go on then," he said, before booming. "GOOD LUCK ALFIE BROWN!" The crowd roared again and then silenced.

Alfie walked slowly toward the stairs in the glowing rock face. The large grey, glistening rock loomed down over him. Alfie begged his legs not to fail him with thousands of eyes burning into his back. As he put a foot onto the step, a sudden warming sensation crept over him. The glowing light of the rock felt welcoming—the only way he could describe it was—the feeling of being home. Halfway up the stairs all he could see were all the people down below staring up at him, waiting, watching.

Then he was facing it. A long, heavy looking sword, stuck into the stone, facing toward him. The sword, although stone, seemed to glow with an imperceivable elegance. There were no sides to the rock up here, and Alfie didn't like heights. The stairs finished, and there was a three pace walk to the sword. The crowd held their breath as Alfie stepped off the last step. His palms went sweaty and stomach flipped as he saw the drop.

As he took the first step forward, heart beating fast against his chest, he glanced down and saw Wiseman looking up from under his hat, eyes sharp.

Alfie reached out slowly and touched the hilt. He saw and felt the sword change at his touch. The rough grey of the stone faded away, like it was being washed off—revealing underneath a beautiful purple hilt and silver blade.

Ever so gently, he pulled. It slid easily from the stone, so deft and purposeful. Alfie was clutching the hilt. It felt as if the sword was willing him to pull it. With one strong, elegant swish the sword fully withdrew. The crowd gasped. Some screamed, but most looked struck dumb. There were a few thuds as people feinted.

A tingling sensation rose up Alfie's arm and into his head as the sword thrust itself into the air. Alfie stood atop the rock, wavering as the sword held itself high above his head.

But the crowd did not cheer. They stared at the boy who pulled their sword from their stone.

Alfie stood, struck dumb atop the rock—he saw Wiseman, who subtly waved at him to come down. Alfie turned, and came over quite dizzy. He carefully began to walk down the stairs. Sword clutched by his side. It wasn't heavy, which was strange, but felt perfectly weighted in his hand. Was this supposed to happen? Alfie guessed by the looks he was receiving, that it was not. As he got to the bottom step the ringleader said nothing—he too was struck dumb. Alfie couldn't tell if it was curiosity or disgust on his face. A crumbling sound made everyone jump.

The whole rock suddenly shuddered. Then, it started to melt before their eyes. Melting away like it was just a sandcastle being washed away by the tide—until all that remained was a small, round water fountain, glittering in the sunlight. A stone hand emerged from the middle of the water. It's fingers rolling and curling, pointing and turning rigid. Alfie followed the finger with everyone else. From what he could make out it was pointing towards the white rabbit with the clock in its stomach.

Alfie turned around and faced the crowd whose sullen faces slowly turned from the fountain to him. Should he give the sword back? He didn't want it, he didn't even know what it really was—it obviously meant a lot to them.

Wiseman put a hand on his shoulder and walked him towards the crowd, who parted silently. Looks of disgust, outrage and confusion on their faces. Alfie tried not to look at them. It was deadly quiet, the only sound was his and Wiseman's muffled footsteps on the cobbled floor. When they got to the edge of the crowd Alfie felt the Wiseman release his grip and whisper hurriedly: "Just keep walking Alfie, just keep walking."

Alfie did, he daren't look back. Alfie and Wiseman emerged from the crowd into a long wide dusty street that lay out ahead of them. It felt weird to have every eye watching him, in a place he had never been, by thousands of people he didn't know. People were hanging out of windows watching them walk casually away.

And then, his worst fear materialised—just ten steps past the crowds edge.

"*THIEF!*"

Then—pandemonium.

The crowd, as if waking from a slumber began to scream and shriek and charge towards them. The street performers, the shop owners, smartly dressed men and women suddenly became demonic.

"RUN!" cried Wiseman dragging Alfie away by the collar and sprinting. "This way!" he cried turning right at high speed into a long, dark deserted street. Alfie sprinted after Wiseman, the sword was clumsy and kept banging against his hip. The screams behind them grew agonising as parts of the crowd drew in on them—they didn't look so nice now. Wiseman's coat was flapping behind him wildly flicking up dust. Alfie wasn't sure if he could outrun these people whilst clutching the sword. All of a sudden, Wiseman pushed Alfie into an alley.

"There!" shouted Wiseman pointing ahead, and bursting down another small and very dark alley behind the shops. "Here it is!" he said charging through a muddy puddle, straight towards a gleaming green door with a golden knocker, which was at odds with the dark alley. Wiseman wrenched the handle and yanked the door open. But then let out an anguished cry. All that stood behind it, was—another green door. He opened that only to find another green door.

"NO! It's a bloody Prism!" he screamed.

Alfie could feel the crowd pounding down the alley towards them. The walls shook. Wiseman sprang off again, Alfie could sense Wiseman's rising panic. They emerged from the alley into a long cobbled street, people stood to the right and left of them. Everyone stopped. Alfie glanced behind at the crowd now closing in. "Oh bugger…" said Wiseman, taking a deep breath before shouting. "Straight ahead!" Alfie accelerated as fast as he possibly could. The crowd from either side charged. Wiseman jumped the cobbled road, pulling Alfie by his coat over an angry dog and into another alley. Wiseman skirted the wall and jumped clean over a pile of old cauldron's. Alfie jumped stairs three at a time and landed hard into a large puddle of muddy water. A fizzing crack and burst of blue sparks above his head illuminated the alley. Wiseman, instead of turning left into another alley, burst straight through a grey door. Alfie charged in just behind him, straight into someone's dining room. Wiseman fell into a long decorative table and it crashed to the floor, candles and plates smashing around them. Wiseman pulled Alfie away, turned quick and cried something at the door behind them where hundreds of people were charging for them. The door swung shut with a snap and hardened.

By the time Alfie turned, breathing hard and trying to catch his breath, he saw Wiseman already up the up the staircase. Alfie charged after him and into a small candle lit bedroom. Wiseman stood on the small bed and yanked the window open. Outside was another dark street, but quiet.

"We need to get onto the roof," he said before leaning out, and clumsily climbing onto the window ledge.

"No way," said Alfie suddenly hearing the door downstairs crash. The crowd were inside. Wiseman poked his head back in.

"Alfie, come here!" he said menacingly—it was not an invitation. Alfie jumped to the window as he heard the people crashing up the stairs. Wiseman whispered something and the door instantly turned into bricks. Wiseman pulled Alfie out through the window—Alfie struggled, his heart in his mouth as he looked down.

"Ah! *No!*" he cried, trying to pull himself back into the room. The sword sweaty in his grip.

"It's ok," said Wiseman. "Look!"

Slabs of wood started to appear, leading up into a spiral staircase. "Walk!" Wiseman cried, as they both heard the crowd of people trying to blast their way into the room. Alfie thought his heart might pop out of his chest. Swallowing hard, he stepped onto the first step. Wiseman stepped behind him and encouragingly pushed him up the spiralling wooden stairs that lay themselves where he stood, all the way to the top of the building. Alfie scrambled onto the angled roof, and clutched at thick black tiles, the sword dangling under his arm. There was a blast and the roof shook.

"Quick!" said Wiseman dragging him up and across the roof. Magicity certainly looked different up here. Alfie could see, quite unwillingly, across the tops of all the houses and chimneys, and black tiled roofs. Wiseman began to run along them, his coat flapping and eyes darting around for an idea. Alfie scampered after him, some of the tiles slipping from beneath his feet. There was a cry behind them. Wiseman turned as Alfie just caught him up. Alfie took a quick shelter behind the nearest chimney. Three identical men in masks had jumped up onto the roof. Then, they began to run at Alfie and Wiseman, who both let out a little cry and burst ahead. Suddenly Alfie saw Wiseman slip on a roof tile before sliding away out of view. A blast of red light seemed to propell Wiseman back up onto his feet. But more trouble lay ahead. Alfie saw the roof end, a wide street cutting off their escape plan. It was a very large gap and he swore Wiseman hadn't see it.

"Wiseman!" said Alfie pointing at the end of the roof. But Wiseman shook his head, and raised his left arm. Silver wood and rope shot from his hand as if made of water, forming solid in mid air—into a bridge across the roof gap. Wiseman charged across it. Alfie following as best he could, getting thrown around by the motion. Screams suddenly echoed from below. They were running across the rooftops of the square's shops below. People were pointing up and watching on transfixed. As soon as Alfie and Wiseman touched the adjoining roof, which was a lot steeper, Wiseman flashed his arms and the silver wooden bridge collapsed in mid air. The three masked men skidded to a halt. Wiseman clambered across the roof, to the other side, facing away from the square.

"Alfie, come here…" said Wiseman, Alfie clambered across too and joined him, perched out of sight behind a chimney. "They have blocked off all the routes… close your eyes." Alfie did, then felt a cold shiver run down from his head to his spine.

"What was that?" he said.

"Just something to try and make us a little harder to spot." He said, doing the same to himself—a blue haze now surrounding him. "I have a small plan." Wiseman looked at the sword, held his hand to his face, covering his mouth and muttered something. The sword in Alfie's hands jolted.

"What are you doing?" said Alfie.

"I was going to duplicate it, but it won't seem to let me. There's no way we can…" Wiseman held his head, lines appearing across his face. Wiseman stood and looked around, then popped his head over the roof, scanning the square below. "Right, it's time for plan B," he said. He held out his right hand high in the air, closed his eyes and began muttering hard under his breath.

"Stand!" called a voice. "Both of you." The voice was deep and commanding. A masked man was standing on the opposite roof, facing them. Wiseman tensed. The masked man began to raise his arms.

"Alfie," Wiseman whispered. "When I say go, jump over this roof and into the square…" Alfie swallowed—this was madness.

"I asked you both to stand." Alfie and Wiseman slowly stood. "Now raise your arms." Alfie began to raise his arms slowly. He really didn't want to jump over this roof, but readied himself. Terrified, Alfie stood waiting. The sword still clutched between his balmy grip. There was a rumbling, scraping sound below them. Alfie looked up and saw the snake-like train coming by, very near them. Alfie saw Wiseman's hands tense.

"Go!" Wiseman cried, jumping over the edge. The masked man roared as Alfie catapulted over the roof top after Wiseman—the wind soared in his ears as his stomach turned flips. This was madness—as he sailed, plummeting down, before... now Alfie saw why Wiseman said jump. They were about to land on the snake-train. Suddenly a flash of red burst across Alfie's vision—he felt like he'd been punched in the face. He sailed away from the snake-train and hit the ground. There was a thud as Wiseman landed next to him coughing hard. Shouts and screams suddenly filled the air as the crowd closed in on them. For a second Alfie just lay where he was, holding tight to the sword—trying to catch his breath. He saw the masked man who spelled him, looking down from the roof above.

"Seize them!"

"Grab them!"

"Stop them from getting away again!" cried the voices in the crowd. Rough hands pulled Alfie and Wiseman up. Alfie clutched the sword to his chest.

"STOP!" cried a loud authoritative voice. People began to move out the way "Guards!" they began muttering. "It's the Guards..." the crowd began to move out of the way quickly and kept their heads down, daren't to look up.

"Everyone move back!" cried another who was pushing the crowd back. All ten of them were immaculately dressed in dark blue trench coats that fell to their ankles. Silver buttons stretched from the neck to the midriff. They wore heavy black

THE SWORD IN MAGICITY'S STONE

boots and looked immaculately tidy. All wore blank white masks and stood in a circle around Wiseman and Alfie. Alfie's head was pounding from where he had hit the floor. One Guard approached them both slowly.

"Wiseman, didn't think we'd be seeing you so soon," some of the Guards sniggered.

Alfie noticed the man had a nasty tone to his voice. "Trying to steal Magicity Sword are you? Well I think perhaps you should just give it back to me, right *now*, it is Magicity property, not yours!" spat the senior Guard with disgust.

"No it isn't mine," said Wiseman with resonance. "It's Alfie Brown's. *The boy who pulled the sword from the stone...*" He announced, causing some of the crowd started to murmur.

"WHO!" bellowed the Guard. "Ruined a priceless relic of Magicity and who is attempting to STEAL the sword, we cannot have that. Pope is on his way."

"Pope," muttered the crowd. "Pope?" they murmured over and over.

Alfie suddenly became afraid. Who was he?

"Oh god," whispered Wiseman. "I hate Pope." Then he announced again: "The legend of the sword in the stone says that the one who pulls the sword from the stone, is the real owner. What is the point in holding a festival every year if you are expecting no one to take it?"

"The sword is property of the Council of Magicity," stated the senior Guard.

"I think I can deal with this," said a tall man suddenly appearing out of thin air. The murmuring of *"Pope"* grew louder as it spread through the crowd.

"Pope," said Wiseman with as much forced pleasure as he could. Alfie could see the man clearly now. He was tall with a pale face and smart greying black hair, he was a hard looking man with a full length black coat buttoned up to his chin with a silver badge on his left breast. He too looked immaculate.

Pope walked forwards slowly, gloved hands behind his back, people backed off a little more. Alfie could sense the cold malevolent air coming off him in waves.

"I would like to ask what you think you are doing?" His voice was measured but sharp. "You are no longer welcome here old man, and nor are your students. Do I make myself… clear? I will ask you for the sword once. If you do not give it to me. I will make sure you never leave. Is that clear?"

Alfie's heart was beating so fast, he thought his chest might explode.

Wiseman grimaced. "Oh Pope, you know the rules. I know you have everyone in Magicity bowing at your feet…" Wiseman stood and leaned a closer to Pope. "But things are changing… the sword belongs to Alfie. He pulled it out."

"You used Dark Magick to steal that sword," said Pope loudly so that the crowd began muttering. "All we want is to give it back *to the people*," he said looking round at all them. They murmured in agreement. Pope looked at Alfie, his cold eyes staring straight through him. Alfie's arm twitched and began to raise—what was happening? Alfie couldn't move his arm! Pope reached out a waiting hand for the sword. Alfie tried to pull his arm back, but it kept moving, against his will!

"NO!" cried Wiseman. There was a tiny red flash and Alfie's arm fell back down. "How dare you!" said Wiseman furious.

"We will get it either way…" said Pope chuckling.

Wiseman suddenly noticed something and smiled—Alfie heard it too, a whooshing sound. "Oh…" said Wiseman, confidently. "You really think so?" A dark shape in the air shot towards them.

It was a big carpet! Guards began firing Spells at it, but the carpets lapels battered them away like flies. It whooshed towards them, Pope ducking as Wiseman grabbed Alfie's collar and hoisted him up into the air, landing on the carpet and scrambling for something to clutch as wind blew hard. The next second Wiseman soared high into the air and landed on the carpet before it curled up and burst into the sky with horrifying speed. Alfie clung on for dear life as the carpet went higher and higher. There was a huge roar of disapproval from the crowds below. As the carpet levelled out Alfie regained a more comfortable position, even though he tried not to open his eyes or look down. Alfie clutched the sword as well as he could, between grabbing edges of the carpet.

"I knew we would need a plan B," Wiseman cried above the noise of the wind.

"This is a flying carpet?!" Alfie roared. "This was my birthday present?" he said and Wiseman grinned.

Down below he could see the town square and all the people watching them fly off. He could see Pope, a tiny figure, now marching off, followed by the strange masked Guards. Magicity looked very strange from above. It started to look hazy, like a mirage and Alfie suddenly had a thought.

"What about the mist?" he shouted in the Wiseman's ear.

"It's ok… we're going over it."

"Over it? But I thought you said nothing could get past it?"

"Ah, well we shall see… *Ahhh!*"

A cloud blew into Wiseman's face and he choked. "I'll explain some other time." Alfie felt his stomach turn but then elation filled him as they soared upwards through the clouds, he couldn't even see Magicity anymore. "This is it," cried Wiseman. "Brace yourself."

Alfie clutched the tassels harder with his cold numb hands as the carpet suddenly shot upwards and tore through the clouds. Alfie felt the instant penetrating cold, thick wet cloud soak straight through him. It was unbearably cold. With the wind in his ears, his numb hands and cold soaking wet clothes Alfie wondered if this was the best idea. But then, they were greeted with a beautiful golden sunlight. They had broken through the clouds and mist. The carpet slowed to a crawl as clouds below them looked like a huge brilliant white duvet. The sun cast an orange blanket across them and the mist below glittered.

"Beautiful isn't it?" said Wiseman releasing his grip on the carpet and sitting cross legged. Alfie took a moment before answering.

"It's... mad," was all he could think of. "I am flying on a carpet that you bought from a shop, and we just escaped from a town, place, that I never even knew existed. I pulled a sword from a rock. Could this day get any weirder? I am in a dream aren't I?"

"Happily... or however you may see it, no, you are not in a dream and I have to admit this has been a rather eventful day for me too." Said Wiseman brushing mud from his trousers and watching the muddy flakes fall gracefully down to the clouds below. "I think it might be time to go home."

Alfie agreed. He was exhausted, but so heartily pleased that they had escaped. "Won't they come looking for me?" he said. "You know, now I have their sword?"

Wiseman sighed heavily. "Yes, probably."

They landed back in Westbury graveyard, the carpet landing softly and sliding them off onto the gravel. The carpet stood and

206

shook the dew from its fabric like a dog. Alfie stood and rubbed his eyes. It was completely dark now, the journey had been long and he had nearly fallen asleep. Alfie knew his Grandparents would be worried sick.

"So what does this mean?" said Alfie, holding the sword up for examination in the moonlight.

Wiseman stood and stretched his back. "That sword has not been lifted, they think, in over a thousand years. Legend has it that, well, perhaps we'll save that one for another time." Wiseman stared at Alfie for a long moment. "If you wouldn't mind Alfie, would I be able to take the sword? I would say its imperative I look it over."

Alfie handed it to him without question, today had been too weird and long to start questioning now.

"Meanwhile Alfie, take care of yourself."

"And you, but when will I see you… I mean, will we meet again?"

Wiseman smiled. "I will be in contact."

Alfie nodded, turned and started to walk home, but then remembered—the carpet, it was his now wasn't it? "The carpet…" But when Alfie turned, there was no one there. Wiseman had gone, carpet, sword and all.

14

The Shadows of Christmas Past

Alfie woke with a start. He had slept like a log, but his ears still rang with the telling off he received from his Grandma when he returned home late last night. She told him very loudly (and very probably waking all the neighbours) about what time he should return home in future, especially in the winter when he could catch cold.

His Granddad had left early to tend to his allotment and his Grandma must have been out because Alfie couldn't hear her downstairs. He felt guilty that his Grandparents waited in all day on his Birthday to do something nice with him, but he ended up running off — albeit for a wacky, crazy adventure to a magical city. Alfie got up and changed as quickly as he could, finding the biggest, thickest jumper in the bottom of a pile of clothes on the floor and slipping it on. He sat on the end of his bed for a while, gathering his thoughts. He felt as if he had awoken from the most monumental long and crazy dream. When he stood, he felt strangely uneven on his legs, as if they hadn't been used in a year. He hobbled over to the window and looked out across the suburban street.

How could everything look the same, yet so different? The world was not as grey and boring and ordinary and rubbish as he had always thought. Because magic was real, and he could do it. But now he had annoyed the residents of a magical city, stealing their prized possession—he didn't know that did he? Was that what Richard Found was warning him against? Wiseman must have known what he was doing, why else would he take Alfie to Magicity on that specific day? But Alfie wanted rid of the shadow, and to do that he needed the sword.

Looking back up the street Alfie saw two people turning into his front garden.

Ding-Dong.

Alfie crept downstairs feeling nervous and paused before opening the door. Tommy and Sparky stood a little hunched against the cold in jumpers and scarves, smiling awkwardly.

"Oh… *hi*…" said Alfie shocked. Neither Tommy nor Sparky said anything. "Do you… want to come in?" said Alfie.

Tommy and Sparky sat on the sofa and Alfie perched on the end of his Granddad's chair. Nobody said anything for a long moment, the clock on the mantelpiece ticking loudly. Eventually Sparky looked up.

"So… Happy Birthday!" he said a little too enthusiastically. "For… *err* yesterday."

Alfie smiled. "Cheers!"

Tommy sighed. "I'm really… *sorry* about stuff," he mumbled fiddling with his shoes laces.

"It's fine," Alfie mumbled back. "I'm sorry too. I should have told you guys."

"Yeah you should have," Tommy said and Sparky shot him a sharp glance. "Where were you yesterday?" Tommy raised his eyebrows suspitiosly. "We did knock, but your Grandma said she thought you were out with *us*."

209

"I…" Alfie took a breath and smiled—it was time to tell the truth. "I went to a magickal city called Magicity with a wizard called Nikolas Wiseman."

Tommy and Sparky didn't say anything for a long moment while they tried to work out if Alfie was joking or not.

Tommy frowned hard. "What… *really?*"

Alfie nodded. "You want the truth, I'm telling you it. I didn't tell you before because I didn't understand anything that what happening. I know it would have helped to tell you guys, but I can't change the past—I don't think. I'm sorry."

Tommy stared at him for a moment, chewing on his words. After a long moment he nodded and smiled. "Yeah I'm sorry too, for… overreacting."

"I'm…" said Sparky in a small voice. "I'm not apologising because I haven't done anything wrong."

Alfie and Tommy jumped up together, laughing at Sparky's cheek, even though he looked quite serious. They picked up a cushion each and started whacking him.

"Oi! Gerrof! Stop it! Alright… I'm sorry too!"

"That's better!" said Tommy. "You were involved."

They all laughed heartily.

"So," said Tommy sitting down. "You've said you'll tell us the truth? I want to know everything that's been happening the past few weeks. Start with this magic city."

Alfie got comfortable in his chair. "Right well, where to start?" He started talking about the day before—his Birthday—receiving the leather jacket from his Granddad, going to meet Wiseman in the graveyard, finding the LeyLine and going through the mist, past the Pendragon into Magicity. Tommy and Sparky listened with open mouths as Alfie described each thing in explicit detail: the café with the waterfall, the money—Bits, the sword in the stone festival which he won! Apparently the first person in a thousand years. Then the escape using the magic flying carpet. Even as Alfie said it all, he couldn't believe it all actually happened. It sounded like a terrific story (of a madman), but not *real*.

Tommy and Sparky listened to the whole story, mouths agape for an hour—for it took a long time to tell.

"Oh yeah! And my wardrobe was enchanted! It spoke to me!" Every time Alfie remembered a new facet of information, Tommy and Sparky's face would turn a different expression of surprise and wonder. Alfie felt so glad to be able to talk to his best friends again.

"So," said Sparky taking a deep breath. "There is a magic city which we, normal people aren't allowed to go to?"

"Yeah," said Alfie. "It's surrounded by this magic mist and this creepy ghostly guard called the Pendragon."

"I bet it's like those corridors that we've been down, the whole city just defies physics," said Sparky.

Alfie was pleased that Sparky was understanding and not *freaked out* or sceptical in some way. He and Tommy must have rubbed off on him more than he thought.

"But," started Tommy. "You said you pulled some sword from a rock? Where is the sword now? Can we see it?" said Tommy glancing round the room.

"Wiseman took it," said Alfie.

"Why?" said Tommy indignantly. "And who is this Wiseman? When did you meet him?" He sounded suspicious, like a parent warning his child away from dodgy strangers.

Alfie sighed. "Well, again, this is a long one…" Alfie recalled the events of walking home from town, the Shadow cornering him and chasing him, of following the white rabbit into an alley, then into a lift that stopped the Shadow from getting him. The lift taking him to a manor house underground. He remembered the Imps, Theadore, and then Nikolas Wiseman. "You'd both recognise him. He's the man from the ghost corridor with the cowboy hat Tommy? And Sparky, he's the man we saw in town that day, again, in the cowboy hat, who disappeared through that door."

"And he's a wizard?" said Tommy. "That's so cool."

Alfie resumed, telling them about everything Wiseman said. How he had blocked the Shadow for now, but Alfie must find a way of killing it.

"How does he expect you to do that?" said Sparky. "You have no experience."

"I know," said Alfie. "I think that's why he took me to Magicity, to get the sword. That's the only thing that will kill it."

Sparky shifted in his seat. "But Alfie, what if this Nikolas Wiseman just used you to get the sword for himself?"

Alfie shook his head violently, he wouldn't have done that, somehow Alfie just knew Nikolas Wiseman was on his side.

"What was it like?" said Tommy greedily. Alfie could only describe it as… *shiny purple.*

Sparky rubbed his face as if he couldn't believe it. "Shiny purple? The sword is *purple?*" Sparky looked at Tommy who nodded, understanding the connection. "This purple is a recurring theme isn't it?"

"And you got chased by the whole bloody town?" said Tommy breaking the silence. "Then flew home on a magic carpet?"

Alfie just nodded and laughed, he just wished he had some proof, perhaps they were pretending to believe him just to be nice.

"Wow man, bloody wow!" laughed Tommy as Sparky winced

at his language.

"And," said Alfie, recalling the rest of the story. "When I left Whiteholl—that's what Wiseman's house is called—I saw a picture of him and Mr Sapiens on the wall."

They both looked, mouths agape. "We knew there was something to do with you and Mr Sapiens! But we couldn't for the life of us work out what or why!" Sparky said very fast. "When we asked about having extra French lessons and Miss Evans told us that they wouldn't be doing them for a couple of months, we twigged properly that you were sneaking off somewhere alone."

"So we followed you," said Tommy. "When you said you were going to do extra French lessons again, we followed you, into the languages block, but well, you just disappeared! We couldn't find you anywhere inside."

"What did Mr Sapiens have to do with it all?" said Sparky.

"He's a wizard too," said Alfie.

Tommy laughed. "That's mental! A wizard teaching French!"

"He told me about spells and stuff and he showed me this place…" Alfie told them about Mr Sapiens taking him to Sampson's Void.

"Oh wow, imagine the things you could find in there!" said Tommy with a greedy expression.

"So," said Alfie out of curiosity. "Why did you decide to come round today?"

"Well," started Sparky as Tommy stared down at his shoes. "It was Tommy really, we were in the school disco and a song came on… I think it was Queen—Friends are Friends."

"Friends Will Be Friends," Tommy corrected.

"Yeah that one, and Tommy went all quiet and went looking for you."

"Alright, alright!" Tommy flapped. "Anyway, it's over now... isn't it?"

Deciding it was lunch time, Alfie attempted to make some sandwiches for them, not very well, so Sparky took over. Sitting in the living room again—belly's full and feeling content with a roaring fire, they continued to talk over and over about Magicity, Mr Sapiens and Wiseman. Alfie chose carefully to omit Richard Found from his new truthful pact with Tommy and Sparky. Found was the only one who actively told Alfie not to tell *anyone*.

Alfie stoked the fire with the long poker, recounting the size and scariness of the Pendragon, making Sparky recede into the sofa, before suddenly remembered something—he did have some proof that he went to Magicity!

"Ahhh!" he cried causing them both to jump, he didn't mean to make that noise. "Sorry," he said jumping up out of his seat and going into the hallway where his coat was hanging on the banister and pulling out the two different shaped brown packages tied up with string. How could he have forgotten? Walking back into the living room he handed the two parcels to Tommy and Sparky.

"Now remember," said Alfie conspiratorially, sitting back down and feeling very excited. "I got these from a *magic shop.*"

Tommy and Sparky looked at each other, eyes lighting up. Sparky went first, he peeled the strings off and pulled the brown paper away carefully, to reveal a small round, smelly green cheese. Sparky took one sniff and quickly rolled it back up in the paper. "Thank you," he said in a small voice. Alfie nodded smiling smugly, if only he knew what it did.

Tommy unwrapped his carefully, until it revealed the sheet of brown Gnarlus paper. He looked perplexed at the dirty brown parchment between his hands for a moment then turned it over to see if there was anything on the other side. Tommy frowned and held it at hands length as if it were a joke present and were about to squirt water in his face.

"It's a piece of paper?" said Tommy perplexed.

"I got it from a real magic shop, he told me that it's called *Gnarlus Paper*." Tommy nodded still confused. "You can write any question on it, and it will give you an answer."

Ever so slowly Tommy's eyes started to swim with untold possibilities and he looked back and forth from the paper to Alfie.

"What," he started, a big grin expanding across his face. "You mean this bit of paper knows everything?"

"Apparently."

"Woah. Think what I could do with this!" cried Tommy punching the air and jumping round the room.

"Just think how handy it will be in the run up to your exams!" said Sparky.

"I'm not using it for exams! Actually I might," said Tommy. "Alfie, pass me a pen." Alfie chucked a biro at him. "Right, so I just write any question? Okay, so…"

Alfie and Sparky went and sat closer to Tommy as he wrote—*'what is my name?'* Tommy wrote very carefully and small, in one corner. Nothing happened for a long moment. But then, the ink at the top of the page swirled round, swimming towards the middle of the page where it formed slowly into new letters: *Thomas Edward Eagles.*

All three gorped at the dirty piece of paper. *"Woah…"* said Tommy. He looked the gobsmacked. Alfie wished he had kept this for himself, how useful it would have been!

"This will be really useful for you, if you need to know anything I can just ask it, you know for magic," Tommy grinned.

"Do another question," said Sparky who still looked slightly sceptical, as if it was a trick. But Tommy put the pen aside and carefully folded his paper back up.

"I think that's enough for now," he said propping the paper carefully next to him.

Sparky picked up his school bag and pulled out two presents. "Seeing as we are exchanging presents."

Tommy grinned and chucked Alfie a large round thing. "We need to start playing again," he said as Alfie unwrapped a football.

Sparky handed a curiously shaped present to him and grinned. It was a thin parcel shaped like a large egg. Alfie unwrapped the polka dot paper and looked in wonder at what came out. It was a beautifully detailed mask in the shape of a lions face. It was made with a thick hard wood with intricate carvings and a fluffy lions mane that went all the way around the outside.

"Sparky thank you so much. I mean, where did you get this?" Alfie looked up at Sparky who looked slightly awkward.

"I made it," he said in a small voice. Alfie and Tommy looked at him their mouths a little ajar.

"You made *this*?" said Alfie holding it up to inspect better the faultless carpentry.

"Yeah, I like to do art and make stuff in my shed. I couldn't think of anything to buy you, so I thought I'd make something. What with everything that's happening, I thought it could come in handy. Use it to hide your face and stuff, that's why I added the strap at the back."

"Sparky, you should be an artist or something because this is amazing!"

Tommy agreed. Sparky shrugged it off, his red face smiling. Alfie felt a warm glow return to him. He had his friends back, this was the best Birthday present of all.

The day before Christmas Eve and Alfie's Granddad was getting increasingly excited. He marched home with a large Christmas tree over his shoulder and proceeded to drag it through the front hallway, causing his Grandma to yell—she promptly got the hoover out to get rid of the hundreds of needles that littered the floor as Granddad potted the tree in the corner of the living room.

"Got it from Jim..." he said proudly, breathing hard. "Right, now where are those decorations?"

For the rest of the afternoon they put the decorations on the tree, saving the porcelain fairy until last.

"And there's Gary on top to cap it all off..." said Granddad standing back to admire the tree as Alfie laughed.

"We do we call the fairy Gary?"

"Because," said Grandma folding the decorations box up away. "When we got it, we asked you what we should call it and you said Gary. You were only three..." she conceded. "I think it was the only name you knew."

"Only name I knew? Who was this Gary then?" said Alfie curiously.

Grandma sighed softly. "He used to come round when you little, he was a friend of your Dad's."

Alfie did faintly remember a jolly man with a beard, but it was a hazy memory.

"Where is Dad?" said Alfie, more to himself. He had wondered earlier that day why his Dad hadn't been round—he usually made a quick appearance on his Birthday—but not this year.

Perhaps something had happened to him? What annoyed Alfie the most was he didn't have any way of contacting his Dad, he didn't have a phone number, he didn't know where he lived or even what he did. He was like a ghost-dad that only half existed.

His Granddad gave a short cough, the excitement from putting up the tree fading. "I'm sure he'll turn up some time…" he gruffed, glancing at Grandma who looked pale. She didn't like Alfie's Dad.

"Right," said Granddad trying to inject some excitement back into the room. "I've got some chestnuts in my bag, who fancies roasting them?"

The night before Christmas Alfie was sat up in bed. He couldn't sleep. His Grandparents were downstairs watching the TV with a glass of sherry each (no doubt).

Alfie kept getting this feeling that he'd forgotten to do something. And now, sitting in bed he remembered what it was—he had forgotten to wrap his Grandparents presents! In all the confusion of the last few weeks he hadn't had time to get any wrapping paper either! Pulling the sheets back, Alfie crept out of bed and winced, the floor boards were freezing! He pulled open his wardrobe doors, which he did carefully these days, in case it might shout at him. He reached into the topmost compartment and pulled down the two rectangular boxes of the *'Finest Chocolate Brazil Nuts'*. They were his Grandparents favourite and he knew there was some wrapping paper somewhere in his room from last year.

After he'd finished wrapping, he crept downstairs. His Grandparents were half-asleep watching carols on the TV. Alfie slipped into the room, holding the boxes behind his back. His Grandma was half-singing along and didn't spot Alfie slide the boxes under the Christmas tree. Alfie saw that a few more presents had materialised since he had gone to bed. He smiled, excited to wake up in the morning.

"What are you doing up, out of bed?" said his Grandma, spotting him.

His Granddad stirred. "What? I'm not…" he said waking with a start.

"Not you," said Grandma pitifully. "Alfie."

"Sorry," said Alfie laughing and going back up stairs. "Night everyone, Merry Christmas for soon!"

"Yeap," called his Granddad. "Merry Christmas for in forty-nine minutes…"

Alfie laughed and made his way back upstairs. As he crossed the threshold into his room, he suddenly felt an awfully strange feeling come over him. That strange feeling of being outside time. Shrugging it off, Alfie got back into bed. As he flicked the covers back, something landed with a small thud on the floor. He leaned out of bed and looked around. Lying a few feet away, was a small brown package tied up with string. Alfie frowned, that wasn't there when he was up here a minute ago… he lent over and grabbed it. It was small, but weighty. It couldn't have been his Grandparents giving him an early present, because he would have noticed them come upstairs.

Laying back in bed, Alfie carefully pulled off the string and unwrapped the delicate parcel. Inside was a small, round, battered leather box. Very slowly Alfie opened it. A small shimmering shard of purple stone, splashed purple light across the room. It was like nothing he had ever seen before. The purple stone shone with radiance, but more than that, there was light coming from inside it. But it wasn't a blinding light, Alfie could look into it still and watch the shimmering, sparkling, dancing light beneath the surface of the strange stone. The stone was a rough pendant shape on a sleek silver string. When Alfie touched the string it felt cold like metal but soft like silk. He picked it up and held it high in front of him wondering what it was. Alfie thought, without a doubt, that there had to be something magical about it. As he gazed into the stone wondering who could have gifted him such a thing, he noticed words starting to appear inside the stone.

'I Am The Desire Stone', swam the words. Alfie nearly dropped it with shock. The words changed again like ink through water: 'Wear Me'.

Alfie did as it said, taking the two ends of loose metallic string and putting it round his neck. There was an instant sealing sound as the two ends connected and sealed. He let it drop to his chest. As it touched his skin, it emitted a bright flash which lit the room, shimmering purple rays bouncing off the walls.

Alfie swallowed hard, who on earth was it from? And what was a Desire Stone? It reminded Alfie of the stone wall in the old library. Why was everything the exact same colour as his eyes? Alfie took the grubby bit of paper and string, he thought he could see something else inside. He rolled it out flat. There was small, scrawly, writing in one corner.

Alfie,

Enclosed is the Desire Stone,

P.S. Don't trust HIM.

Alfie tucked the note away in his side draw, his mind whirring.

Just before he went to sleep he tried to take the Desire Stone off, but couldn't. The silky string wouldn't come apart. So Alfie lay in bed watching the dim, deep swimming purple. He fell asleep thinking, not about how excited he was for the Christmas Day, but who on earth the person could have been to give him this magical Desire Stone.

Alfie woke with excitement rippling through him. It was Christmas Day. Sitting up, the Desire Stone bobbing on his chest, he glanced out the window, the morning was still night and the dark sky was covered in a thick layer of grey cloud and Alfie imagined all the people waking up around the country. All the children waking with joy and fits of excitement. The smell of the Christmas tree, the glow from the lights, the crackle of a fire, the roasting of dinner. Alfie grabbed his alarm clock from the side table—6.47am—a perfectly reasonable time to get up.

On Christmas day his Granddad was usually the first up. He would get the turkey ready, make a fire in the living room and lay out the stockings at the end of everyone's beds. Granddad was like a child when it came to Christmas.

After a minute of hunting Alfie found it hanging on the door of his wardrobe. Alfie swallowed and took it off carefully. It was a long red wool sock, that felt weighty with hidden wrapped goodies. He jumped into his big woolly sweater and crept across the hallway, into his Grandparents bedroom.

"Merry CHRISMAAAAAAS!" Alfie cried.

"OHH!" his Grandma shot up and nearly fell out of bed. "Oh Alfie, I wish you wouldn't shout, you'll wake the neighbours!" she hissed.

His Granddad was already sitting up in bed with a cup of tea, grinning broadly. Alfie sat on the end of the bed and they all opened their stocking presents. His Grandma sat up looking shaken and grimaced at the time on the alarm clock.

"Are you wearing a necklace?" she said suspiciously.

Alfie went red. "Oh," he said, looking down—the silver string was visible. "Yeah… it was a present from a mate at school, anyway…" he said quickly to change the subject. "What's that?" he pointed to an odd shaped present his Grandma had just pulled out of her snowman stocking.

All in dressing gowns, they traipsed downstairs, sat down and had a lovely breakfast around the kitchen table, with the radio blaring out Christmas carols. They ate croissants and butter, toast and marmalade, cereals and all with a big pot of steaming hot tea. His Granddad was in top form, insisting that they pull a Christmas cracker so they could see who wore their paper hat for the longest. Grandma took hers off straight away for it was "too itchy!" After breakfast Alfie opened the living room door, inside looked magical—the tree and lights and the presents sparkling underneath, reflecting the flickering light of the fire. With the fire burning they sat together around the tree and began to open their presents. Carols in the background and much joking and laughter. His Granddad making fun of a present his Grandma had received from her sister—a miniature cactus.

"What on earth?" said Granddad as Alfie laughed. "Was there a point to sending that, or was it just left over from a tombola?" he chuckled.

"Yes," said Grandma. "It is a bit strange," she said turning the cactus round in her hands.

Alfie received a brand new, knitted navy jumper from his Grandma who smiled warmly, Alfie put it on to please her. It had a small reindeer on it with snowflakes.

"Keep the cold out better than any heating that," said Grand-dad and Alfie told him to say that when he wasn't sat next to a roaring fire.

"Good point," Granddad conceded.

Alfie also opened a couple of nice shirts, more chocolate, and a leather polishing kit. His Grandparents looked extremely grateful for their chocolate brazil nuts and ate three each straight away.

After they had finished opening presents they went and got washed and dressed. Alfie wondered what Tommy would be getting, or if he had just been playing with the Gnarlus paper, Alfie wished he'd kept it for himself and got Tommy something else. It would've been extremely useful. He already had a very long mental note of all the questions he wanted to ask it.

Alfie was sat in the armchair by the fire having a well earned rest. His Grandparents were washing up in the kitchen and he could hear them both chatting away. It was dark outside now and orange street lamps began popping on, except the one opposite them which still hadn't been fixed. Alfie's thoughts drifted to the stone around his neck, and the note:

'*Don't Trust Him.*'

Don't trust who? Alfie pulled out the stone from under his shirt and gazed into it, the firelight flickering across the glassy purple surface. As Alfie stared a black inky substance began floating around inside, joining together.

'*I Am The Desire Stone... I Can See Into Your Heart... I Can See Your Desires.*'

Alfie frowned at it, what was this thing? He contemplated it being some kind of joke toy from Tommy—he loved pranks.

But that theory completely dissipated as the next word faded up:

'*Gracie.*'

Alfie's heart gave a shudder. How on earth could it know that? Underneath, more words appeared.

'*Send Her Your Christmas Greetings*'

Alfie rubbed his eyes, his heart beating six to the dozen, an equal measure of confusion and embarrassment. This was a magic stone that told ones *desires*. Why had someone given him this? And who? More importantly *why*?

Alfie was embarrassed that it knew he liked Gracie. Her face had been a contender for a lot of Alfie's thoughts over the last few weeks, even with everything else that had been going on and it pained him to keep thinking of her and Christian, but at the same time he knew that there were more important matters—staying alive for one! Alfie kept telling himself that she was out of his league—she was beautiful, with her golden skin and dark eyes and long dark wavy hair, while Alfie was short, scrawny and odd looking. And now this stone wanted Alfie to send her his *Christmas greetings*?

Alfie sat in the chair reasoning why he should? If this was a magic stone then perhaps it knew something he didn't. But at the same time, why should he trust this stone left by someone he didn't know?

He sighed, it couldn't hurt could it? No one would think anything over, say, a Christmas card would they?

Only one problem, Alfie didn't know where Gracie lived.

Alfie didn't know why he followed the Desire Stone's advice. He decided he would have to hand deliver it, presuming she lived close. If only he had the flying carpet, he could be there and back and no one would even notice.

But Alfie did know how to find Gracie's address… the Gnarlus paper. Without waiting Alfie went to the hall and picked up the phone, glancing over his shoulder he made sure his Grandparents were busy. Alfie was nearly deafened by Tommy shouting "MERRY CHRISTMASS!" so loud down the phone that Alfie had to hold it at arms length.

Alfie gave Tommy a few choice words and proceeded to explain why he needed Gracie's address, and told Tommy in hushed tones about the Desire Stone. Tommy immediately sounded serious and went to fetch it.

"This magic paper is awesome!" said Tommy returning.

"Good. The address Tommy?"

"Right, right… Thirteen Ashcombe Road. Oh…" said Tommy, his voice sounding grave. "That's the *haunted house* isn't it?"

It was true, Thirteen Ashcombe Road was the old haunted house at the top of the hill, surrounded by iron gates and high brick walls. Alfie thought it was derelict, for as long as he could remember that spooky house had not been lived in. Gracie couldn't live there surely?

Alfie went to the kitchen where, under the sink was a box of Christmas cards with snow scenes on. He wrote *To Gracie, Merry Christmas!* Then couldn't decide whether to put his name or not, finally he signed it *from Alfie*.

Putting on his navy Christmas jumper, leather jacket and scarf, he headed outside. He closing the door as quietly as he could. He pulled the Desire Stone out again:

'*Gracie.*'

'*Send Her Your Christmas Greetings*'

It still read.

Alfie marched off up to the top of the hill. It was dark and frosty now and the walk was bitterly cold. The walk wasn't long, past the graveyard and through the park, then at the bottom of the park across a deserted, quiet road stood the large and opposing building, framed against the night by a low moon. It had high iron bar gates with spiked railings. Their were some lights on inside and as he approached the gate he couldn't help feel as though he was intruding on such a private day. Alfie paused before the gate. This felt like madness, he felt incredibly nervous, his heart hammering hard in his chest. The gate was slightly ajar and squealed as it opened. He crunched across the gravel, past a large black car with black windows, to a big front door. It had two supporting stone pillars either side and a large chain that Alfie assumed was a doorbell. Cautiously he reached out, yet it suddenly dawned on him what awful madness this was—why was he giving Gracie a Christmas card? He had hardly even spoken to her, what if she told everyone? He'd get teased about it constantly, especially if Joel found out!

Yank. He pulled the chain and a heavy bell bonged ominously. After a long agonising few seconds, a tall man with a kind face opened the door. The man looked at Alfie, he had a paper hat on and a woolly jumper that would have put his Granddad's to shame.

"Can I help?" he said, before staring open mouthed as he saw Alfie's purple eyes—it was a common reaction.

"Hi, erm, I was here for Gracie, is she in?" Alfie stammered. The man shook himself before smiling awkwardly.

"I'll… just go and get her." He smiled and went to turn away. "*Oh*, what's your name?"

"Alfie Brown."

The man paused again before regaining his composure. "Right yes… yes of course… Ah Alfie, Merry Christmas, I am Gracie's

226

Dad Jonathan." He lent outside and shook Alfie's hand.

"Nice to meet you," Alfie smiled as warmly as he could in the cold.

Jonathan turned and went off back inside. The inside of the house looked amazing. Through the crack in the door he could see a white stone floor hall with a large grand staircase with red carpet and gold trimming. A few moments later with Alfie's heart picking up at a rate of knots, Gracie came slouching to the door looking confused, she too had a paper hat on her head.

"Alfie?" she sneered and he suddenly felt very awkward.

"Hi Gracie," he said fast. "Erm, I just wanted to give you this. It's nothing really. Just a card."

He handed her the card. "Merry Christmas," he said fast, turning to leave. He could feel his cheeks growing hot.

"Oh," she said softly. "Alfie wait."

Alfie spun on the gravel. Gracie's expression softened and if he was not mistaken, she looked pleased. "Merry Christmas," she smiled back.

The butterflies in Alfie's stomach suddenly took flight. He smiled, turned again and crunched away.

There was a short pause before he heard the door shut and Alfie walked back out the iron gates, he felt weird, she smiled at him in a nice way. He looked up the street and saw someone else walking towards him. He kept his head down, not really wanting to be bothered, he hoped it wasn't Christian. He looked up again and… was he imagining things? The person in the road ahead had vanished.

"Alfie!" screamed Gracie who suddenly came sprinting up to the iron gates. "Alfie, I just… I just saw *something…*" she said leaning against the gates and pointing up the street.

"What was it?" he said scouring the darkness ahead, trying to see past the lines of cars and front garden walls.

"There!" screamed Gracie pointing again. Alfie whirled round—it was the Shadow. It was standing in the middle of the road, fifty yards away. It walked towards him, head bowed beneath its top hat, eyes glowing deepest purple.

Alfie felt terror grip his insides like a vice. Wiseman's spells must have broken! Or the Shadow had found a way around them!

"Alfie RUN!" screamed Gracie, but somehow he couldn't, his legs felt fixed to the spot. The message from his brain to his legs had got stuck, they would not move.

"Go back inside," Alfie called as calmly as he could. Gracie looked terrified and backed off as a beam of orange lamp light crossed the Shadows face. Alfie knew he couldn't outrun it again. Alfie's mind whirred. The Desire Stone had told him to come here… perhaps Wiseman gave him the Desire Stone to lure him here because he wants the sword all to himself!

The Shadow stopped in the road ahead of Alfie and looked up from under its hat. It had dried blood all around it's disgusting gaping mouth. Alfie felt a cold wind flash up his spine as the Shadow smiled. He felt it's cold presence, he could sense the hate and murderous intent pouring off the Shadow.

Then, in one heart stopping moment, it was sprinting. In a flash it was there, right in front of him. It was all he could see. Its hot breath on his face, the putrid smell almost chocking Alfie to death. Before Alfie could even register what to do, the Shadow swiped the air. Alfie buckled as pain shot through his stomach.

"AHOOW!"

He fell to the floor, sick rising in his throat. He heard Gracie

228

scream before looking up and seeing a dark fist aiming for his face. He scrambled backwards as the fist missed. The Shadow laughed and flew at him again. Alfie swerved out of the way hearing a fizzing sound as it passed his ear. Alfie scuttled backwards as quickly as he could and raised his hands at the oncoming Shadow.

"*Petivo!*"

Alfie felt the rush of wind build up around him, the high pitched whistle and the contraction of air. The Shadows attention was caught. Purple light erupted, the air splitting with a huge CRACK! The ball of purple light flew from between Alfie's hands, smacking the Shadow square in the chest. It toppled and fell, skidding across the tarmac. Alfie's heart jumped with joy, but felt an instant draining of energy. The Shadow rose immediately and barred its dirty brown teeth. A hole in its chest sealed over as it marched towards him fast again.

Alfie didn't know what else to do, he hadn't learnt how to fight shadows!

"*Consisto!*" Alfie shouted but the Shadow didn't stop.

"Laravatus!" the Shadows hat turned into a black rabbit and bounced away. Alfie grew pained. Nothing was working!

"Vanearo!" he cried, the Shadows jacket vanished but it carried on marching fast towards him. It grabbed Alfie's hair and pushed him to the ground.

Alfie felt his head smash into the road, then a sharp elbow in his side. He yelped with pain and struggled against the impossibly strong hold. Gracie was yelling for Alfie to run, but he couldn't! Alfie felt the Shadows rage, as it punched him swiftly in the gut again causing him to lay helpless on the road, gasping for air as the Shadow stood over him chuckling softly.

There was a sudden, huge flash of green light that lit up the entire road. The Shadow looked up dropping it's grip on Alfie. Then looked back at him pulling Alfie close to his face. "I will… get you." Slime fell out it's mouth as it struggled to speak. Then it relinquished its hold and vanished in a whistling, whirling, black column of smoke. Alfie felt hot air rush past him, as he fell back to the ground. Gracie opened the iron gates and ran towards him.

"Are you ok?" she cried desperately. "What the hec was that thing?!"

"I'm ok," said Alfie trying to catch his breath again, his stomach and head feeling sore and the salty taste of blood in his mouth.

"Whatever you just did Alfie, it was pretty incredible!" she said sounding impressed. "That was some nice Spell work you did there."

"Thanks… I mean, what?" said Alfie rubbing his head, thinking he'd heard her wrong.

Gracie helped him up to his feet. "That's a nasty graze you have on your head," she said ignoring Alfie's incredulity, as her Dad came runnig out of the house.

"What's going on, we heard shouting?" he bellowed looking accusingly at Alfie.

"Here I am!" called another voice from behind them all. Nikolas Wiseman was strolling up the street, with his black coat, cowboy hat and cane. "Alfie's with me, nice to see you again Jonathan."

"Wiseman?" said Jonathan who looked taken aback.

Alfie looked from Wiseman to Jonathan to Gracie. Alfie swallowed. "You know the Wiseman too?"

"Oh well yes of course!" said Gracie smiling.

"Is someone going to tell me what just happened?" said

230

Jonathan.

Grace sighed. "Alfie just got attacked."

"By who?" said Jonathan, looking up and down the street looking outraged.

"His Shadow," said Wiseman looking at Jonathan with a knowing look.

Jonathan looked horrified. "A shadow? And your still... *alive?*" he said seeming to grapple with facts he'd never assumed possible.

"Thanks to me," said Wiseman. "I expelled it, for now."

"Well of course," said Jonathan looking stricken. "Only the one who's Shadow it is can kil—"

Gracie stamped her foot. "—Kill it, yes we know Dad, but I am sure Alfie doesn't want to be reminded of this now."

"Quite," said Wiseman.

"Is someone going to tell me what's going on?" Alfie stammered, not knowing what to say first. "How do you all know each other? And how did the Shadow find me? I thought you had made it go away?"

"Shall we go inside?" said Wiseman turning and walking through the iron gates without an invite. Alfie, Gracie and Jonathan followed.

Gracie's house was magnificent, inside they were greeted with a large, wide staircase with red carpet with gold trim, with pictures in frames lining the walls. The floor was white stone with several rugs and carpets scattered around—Alfie wondered if any of them were flying ones. The house was nothing like the derelict, broken down old haunted house he remembered it as. They went immediately into the room on the left. It was a large drawing room, with a huge open hearth fire and a large framed mirror resting above the fireplace. Four red leather chairs sat by the fire looking warm and inviting, and there was some noise coming from the kitchen down at the end of the hallway.

Gracie sat down and poked the fire. "That's just mother and my silly younger brother, he's helping wash up, for once."

Wiseman undid his black coat and threw it. A hat stand popped out from the bottom of the coat and landed in the corner. Jonathan closed all the doors.

"That was quite a close call there," said Wiseman sitting down, eyes resting upon Alfie. "If it hadn't have been for me being in the right place as usual I'm pretty sure you'd be dead."

"Well, thanks again," said Alfie rubbing the bump on his head, which twinged.

They were all looking at him. Alfie wished they would all stop looking at him. "But I thought you said you'd stopped it, from coming near me?"

"I did, but…" Wiseman mumbled. "It must have broken through, stronger than I thought. Anyway, you'll be glad to know that I've finished my inspected the Sword."

"The *sword*?' said Jonathan. "*Ahh*. So it was you who took it? I heard rumours but I wasn't sure. You know what this means?"

"It wasn't me who too it," said Wiseman cutting in. "It was Alfie."

They all turned to look at him again. Gracie and her Dad looked alike, their jaws dropped at the same time.

"But you do know what this means?" he said quietly. Wiseman looked cautious and mumbled that he had *no time for tales*. Alfie suspected that he didn't want to talk about it in front of Alfie, as if he was some sort of bomb that might explode if he heard the wrong things.

"But that means," started Gracie. "That Alfie is—"

"Yes, yes!" cried Wiseman shushing Gracie before she said anything more.

"What does it mean?" said Alfie wishing they would just tell him what was going on. "And how does Gracie know about all this?" he said looking at Wiseman.

Gracie looked pityingly towards Alfie for a moment before saying: "Because we are wizards too…"

Alfie felt the breath being taken away from him for the second time that day. "I return to my original point," said Wiseman sternly. "I have examined the said sword thoroughly and… there's something wrong with it."

"What do you mean?" all three chorused.

Wiseman shifted uncomfortably. "It's not real. It's a fake."

Alfie didn't say anything—a stone dropped in his stomach. The sword was what would save him. It would kill the shadow and end all this. "However," Wiseman continued. "It might be a clue."

"A clue? We went to Magicity and pulled that out and all the trouble afterwards just for a bloody clue?" said Alfie feeling sick to his stomach.

"It would make sense," said Jonathan biting his lips. "It's too dangerous to put the real one there, but that just raises the question… who took the real one out?"

Wiseman was gazing off out of the far window.

"But it felt right in my hand," said Alfie. "It felt good."

"Just an illusion, I had the same feeling when you passed it to me," said Wiseman. "But, I do think that whoever took the real one left a clue to finding it. But now it just begs the question—where is the real one?"

"I think I'm confused," said Alfie slumping back in the chair, it

233

was getting late and Alfie had been way longer than he planned, his Grandparents would be worrying where he was.

"Yes I think we all are," said Jonathan, his Christmas hat sliding over his face.

Wiseman stood sharply. "These questions matter not right now," he carried on before Alfie was about to interject. "What matters is finding the real sword. If you want to eliminate the Shadow, then the real sword is the key."

"Is the sword the only thing that can kill it?" said Gracie. Wiseman swiped at his long nose and wrinkled his face up, as if he thought that the answer was in the back of his head somewhere. In the same surreal moment, Alfie sat back in the chair and realised how strange this situation was. He was sat in the house of a girl he fancied, whose family were also wizards, and knew the famous wizard who was helping him. It made his mind hurt.

"So where could the real Sword be?" said Gracie.

Wiseman shrugged. "We certainly can't continue our search in Magicity unless we go in disguised."

"You still wouldn't be able to," said Jonathan. "Security has been tightened tenfold since the incident."

Wiseman chewed his lip. "I toyed with the idea of giving the fake sword back and patching up, in some way, the relationship with the City."

"Yes, it may go some way." said Jonathan. "But they'll never forgive you."

"I don't want their forgiveness, I am doing this for more than their affection, or personal gain," said Wiseman loudly. "There is rather more urgent reason we need to find that Sword." Wiseman tapped at the mirror above the fireplace. "I taped this earlier."

The mirror crackled and a spinning logo flashed up onto the mirror that read *WizTV*. An odd looking presenter with a tall triangular hat greeted them and there was a picture of Alfie on screen next to a sign that read: *FUGITIVE*.

"What is this?" said Alfie unable to hide the incredulity in his voice.

The screen flashed up several images of Alfie, the day he and Wiseman were in Magicity. The news reporter began: *"The theft of the Sword of Magicity is still being tracked by City officials. Guards have said that the two suspects, one being wizard Wiseman, the famous eccentric level thirty-three wizard who is in hiding with an accomplice, a boy unknown to the authorities, but believed to be from the Outside. There are hundreds of witness to the event itself, one, a Terrance McDummit, said that he even had an argument with Wizard Wiseman earlier that day after he tried to steal something from his stall. The theft of the Magicity Sword is top priority for Magicity Guards who are working furiously to seek and return Magicity's most prized possession. This and more from our leading story to come later on..."*

The footage zipped forwards. *"In other news, there have been increased reports of attacks on thirteen innocents by vicious cloaked entities, believed by some to be Lynch Shadows, although Guards have reiterated that this is an unlikely scenario..."*

The Wiseman waved a hand and it disappeared. There was a short silence and Jonathan looked uncomfortable.

"My Shadow has been attacking people in Magicity?" said Alfie feeling sick.

"Yes, that's what makes this all the more *urgent*," said Wiseman. "Officials are brushing off any reports that it could be a Lynch Shadow. But it's only a matter of time before they blame the attacks on you." Wiseman clutched the fireplace and rubbed his

235

chin in thought.

"For starters, it looks like you. Secondly, you stole the Magicity Sword so if they can lock you up for anything then they will."

Alfie recalled the Shadows blood smattered face and shuddered.

"Anything we can do to help Wiseman?" said Jonathan softly and slowly all their eyes turned towards Alfie who swallowed. They were looking at him as if he was already dead. Alfie couldn't disagree with them—it wasn't looking very good. They sat in silence for ages just listening to the clattering of Gracie's brother doing the washing up. Alfie didn't dare mention the Desire Stone—for in case they decided to have a look and see the word Gracie floating in it.

What then did Richard Found mean by it? And the note that came with the Desire Stone? thought Alfie, glancing at Wiseman who was tapping the edge of his chair.

So, apparently the fake sword was a clue, like that hand that pointed at the white rabbit on the side of that shop, Alfie was sure that they were signs left by whoever took the Sword last. Alfie was also sure that the real Sword would be in Magicity, since whoever removed the Sword had to be a Mage. But the question was:

The sword was a fake—but Wiseman thought it was a clue. A clue to what though? The person that took the real sword could have been anyone in the last thousand years. Alfie recalled the hand coming out of the fountain and pointing. But where did it point to? The person who last took it, must have been a wizard because you must know exceptional magic to be able to steal Magicity's most prized possession and replacing it with a fake

236

without ever being caught. Something inside Alfie clicked like a clock—the sword, or the clue to the real sword was in the centre of Magicity. He didn't know how he knew that or why, he could just *feel* it.

"How do I get back into Magicity?" said Alfie, causing Jonathan and Gracie to splutter out laughing.

"Did you not pay any attention to the newscast? They will lock you up forever!"

"Yeah Alfie, my Dad's right — if you go back there it's suicide."

Wiseman was not laughing, he stood contentedly quietly smiling to himself.

Alfie swallowed and looked at Wiseman. "I just know that the sword is still in the centre of Magicity. I have to go back."

Alfie didn't know, he didn't know anything. But something inside him felt compelled to return. Jonathan looked at the Wiseman with an exasperated expression, but Wiseman just smiled.

"The signs will appear to guide you along the path you choose."

15

The Dice Duchess

The Shadow had broken Wiseman's defences and attacked Alfie and no one seemed to know what to do about it. Alfie lay in bed, dull purple light flickering from under his sheets from the Desire Stone. He thought, how cruel this all was, how confusing, how downright terrifying. In some tiny fraction of his mind he still held onto the belief that he was in some wild, sporadic dream and that very soon, he would wake up and everything would be nice and normal again.

Alfie turned over in bed. He was wondering about Richard Found—he couldn't help but think that he was the key to unlocking the mystery behind killing his shadow. They had met by chance and Found had said that he had defeated his own shadow—that meant, he knew how to kill one. The problem was, Alfie had absolutely no idea where he lived, or how to find him. Should he confide in the others about what Found had told him? But then they would be annoyed that he hadn't told them sooner. And Found would not be happy, he had specifically asked him not to tell anyone of their meeting.

Alfie and Sparky went round Tommy's house on Boxing day.

After a big lunch they retreated upstairs where Tommy showed them all his presents, of which he wasn't too bothered. He had, as Alfie guessed, being playing with the Gnarlus Paper.

Alfie sat down on Tommy's sofa at the end of his bed and told them about what happened the day before—getting attacked by his Shadow, the Desire Stone, the fake Sword and Gracie.

"That's mental!" said Tommy pacing round his room unable to convey the right words to explain what he felt. "I can't believe I missed it! I mean, I should have been there!" Tommy looked immensely pained, as if he'd slept right through Christmas day.

"So…" said Sparky trying to make sense of everything Alfie told them. "Your Shadow found you and attacked you, after this Desire Stone thing told you to go an post a card to Gracie?"

"That's pretty much it yeah," said Alfie, and Sparky puffed his cheeks out. Obviously struggling to take on so many new developments.

"There seems to be something new happen every day!" said Tommy wildly.

Sparky sat back dumfounded. "And Gracie Hitchin is a—a wizard?"

"*And* they all know Nikolas Wiseman," said Alfie. They all stood and shook their heads for a minute.

"Anyway, I've been searching the Gnarlus paper…" said Tommy changing tact and pointing to it, where it sat proudly in the middle of his desk. "But honestly, whenever I ask about magic its so cagey!"

Tommy repeated that he had asked it in several different ways how to make a LeyDoor appear in a wall, but the answers he received were: '*You can't*'—'*I am not telling you,*' and '*This question again?*'

Alfie chuckled. "Sounds like it has a wicked sense of humour."

Tommy rolled his eyes and ran his fingers across the bed post and said chargedly. "What are we going to do about the sword then? Where could it be? Where should we start searching?"

The first Monday of January and they were back at school. Alfie had mixed feelings about returning. On the one hand he was glad to be in a different environment with his friends, but on the other hand his end of year exams were coming up alarmingly fast and with everything that was going on—he didn't have the time or heart to care much about them.

On the first day back, they were out of luck—it was freezing! For some reason the heating was faulty in school so they had to wear their coats during lessons. This made simple things like writing awkward and combative, even talking was tough, being done through a mouth that kept chattering with cold. However this did little to dismay a very buoyant Alfie who walked around school with his two friends again. He knew he didn't need to, but made them both swear on their lives that not under any circumstances would they reveal *ANY* of what he had told them, Tommy and Sparky had put their hands to their heart and said that they wouldn't.

"I still can't believe it!" said Tommy incredulously as they walked the corridors. "I mean she's an actual—"

"*SHHH!*" said Alfie jumping and clamping his mouth shut. "You swore!" he said, pointing.

"I know, *jeez*, I wasn't gonna say was I?" Tommy said in a hushed voice. "It's just well, I was thinking last night how just this gets weirder and weirder doesn't it?"

It bolstered Alfie's mood further now that Gracie would regularly come over and speak to him. On Thursday Alfie bumped into Gracie in the new library. Alfie had been sent out of a lesson for not copying anything off the board, so wandered about the school, which was good thinking time. He liked the library, it was quiet and smelt dusty like his house. He was absent-mindedly glancing at some books, when he turned and came nose to nose with Gracie.

"*Ahh!*" he said shocked by her sudden appearance, a torrent of butterflies whizzing through his stomach.

"What are you doing Alfie?" she said suspitiously, her dark eyes narrowing. "Shouldn't you be in lessons?"

"I was just… got sent out… just thinking," he stuttered.

"You shouldn't wonder *alone,*" she said in a hushed voice, then sighed and looked around the library. "Come sit down, over here…" she pointed to a table in the corner out of the way.

When Alfie sat down at the table, he expected Gracie to sit opposite him, but she sat directly next to him. It was almost *too* close. Her gaze drifting up to the graze on his forehead. "That's cleared up nicely hasn't it?"

"It was quite a Christmas day we had wasn't it?" said Alfie.

"Certainly was," she smirked, glancing away and watching the three remaining people in the library leave, until it was just them. "I still can't believe what happened and that you are a…" she said flustered. "It's just… I mean, please tell me about, you know, *everything*. From the start."

As he did, Gracie sat and listened intently, nodding her head. It felt magical, staring into her dark eyes and letting her in on his darkest secrets and every detail of his recent plight,(omitting only one or two bits to save embarrassment).

Once he had finished Gracie just gazed at him, then a worried expression crossed her face. "And the note said *don't trust him?*"

Alfie nodded. "I thought it meant Wiseman at first."

"No, Wiseman's fine, it couldn't mean him," she stopped and

chewed her lip. "Unless… he thinks you could be…" she sighed and hummed to herself.

"What? Go on…" said Alfie.

"Well," she sighed. "It's common knowledge that Wiseman and Venusias—quite a famous wizard—were due to be married. Everyone loved her, honestly she was stunning—she had the greenest eyes I've ever seen! One day, she just vanished. And has never been seen again. You can imagine what happened, the Mage were divided between support and condemnation of Wiseman, some believed he was to blame—either that he killed her had something to do with her disappearance—but others believe that it was just a plot by Magicity Council to bring Wiseman down. They had been looking for reasons to for ages. He went into hiding, hid his house from the maps and everything…"

Alfie smiled, that's what Mr Sapiens had said too.

"But, well the theory is that Venusias—and Wiseman will tell you the same if you have the guts to ask him—was taken by the Faeries."

Alfie laughed, thinking she was joking. "You serious? *Faeries?*"

Gracie frowned. "You think Faeries are those little things with wings don't you? Well they're not. Faeries are a tricky, devilish humanoid people. They look just like us. But they are poles apart in personality. They are harsh, cunning, and nasty, they thrive on the pain of others—mostly wizards and humans. The Faeries have waged war against wizards since, *forever.*"

"Where do they live then?" said Alfie.

"They're not allowed in either of our worlds, they have their own, hidden somewhere." Gracie waved. "But I don't care and don't want to know," she shuddered.

"Why did they take Venusias?"

Gracie's golden face carved into a deep frown. "They like… collecting pretty women. And because they knew that Wiseman was a threat to them, taking Venusias is their way of saying *back off*, I suppose."

"So," said Alfie. "What does Wiseman think *I* might be?"

Gracie stared for a long moment and Alfie could sense she was struggling internally with what to say. "It's prophesied that the person who pulls—I shouldn't be telling you this…" she sighed and leaned in closer. "The person who pulls the sword out of the stone has been called many things like The Talent, the Infinite One and The *Wizardues*, a prophesied wizard who comes with great natural power, and defeats the Faeries. If the Faeries were defeated then he would get all those girls back and stop the oppression they have over our worlds. And it would help people like Wiseman whose obsessed with finding the Faerie worlds." Gracie stopped speaking and pulled her scarf round her neck a little tighter against the cold. "You do know that if you don't find this Sword, it's the end of you. I don't know of anyone in living magical history who has ever survived a Shadow."

Alfie sighed. "I just wish I had some concrete clue."

"I know. I've read into it and so has Dad, but we can't find *anything*. All we could find was stories of wizards who put powerful dark woven spells of concealment over themselves, to become pretty much invisible to their Shadow. But, invariably the Shadow is never far away, always searching—their whole lives. And if the wizard gets ill or sloppy and their powers wane, that's them done for," she leaned back on her chair. "If you want to live Alfie, you're going to have to do what no wizard or sorcerer has managed to do in living magical history. Find the Akashic Sword."

"The Akashic Sword?" Alfie said, the word vibrating around his head—it sounded like a memory, he knew it from somewhere. "Is that what it's called?"

"Oh, it's called many things hasn't Wiseman told you?" she said incredulous. "People call it the Sword of Excalibur, Magicity Sword, The Arthurian Sword—loads. But its all just different names for the same thing."

The bell rang ear split-tingly loud, shattering any chance of more questions. Gracie stood quickly. "I've got History. I'll see you later," she said softly and touching his arm ever so gently before walking out of the library and down the corridor, her long wavy hair bouncing behind her. The butterflies in Alfie's stomach quadrupling.

A week later Alfie found out Gracie was *officially* 'going out' with Christian. Alfie couldn't help but feel a large sinking feeling, quite similar to being punched in the stomach by the Shadow. Somehow after the chat they had all Alfie could think about was her. It was the Desire Stone that made it happen, it told him to go and see her, and now they were on speaking terms. Alfie had other things to worry about, at least that's what he told himself. Since Christmas Day he was forever checking over his shoulder—the Shadow could be anywhere, it could be following him to school, it could be hiding in the toilets or waiting in his bedroom when he got home. He could not relax. Alfie replayed the conversation with Gracie over and over in his head at night. She had told him so many things he had never known before—but now, when he saw her in the corridor, she was with Christian with Joel usually just behind them looking smug. Christian was somehow, always nearby.

If Alfie was honest with himself he hadn't thought much about the Sword. It was like looking into a deep, pitch black well searching for a penny. He was attempting to do something no wizard had ever done. The ominous feeling of something bad approaching was getting stronger and stronger. He ran it through his head often, the fake sword, the rock turning into a fountain with a hand, coming out and pointing at the white rabbit with a clock in its stomach... but nothing solidified, they just swirled round in his head like a puddle of nonsense.

Alfie, Tommy and Sparky discussed his situation but nothing ever came of it. Even Mr Sapiens had proven unhelpful, muttering something about the Sword being *a myth* and that he should be looking at *alternative avenues*, however Mr Sapiens proved even more unhelpful when Alfie asked him "What avenues?"—Mr Sapiens merely shrugged and picked a nearby book up to read.

Alfie also asked after Wiseman, to see if he could get some answers out of him, but again he was disappointed—Wiseman being *away*, or *not available*. The Shadow was bound to turn up soon and Alfie would not be able to do anything about it. The only people who seemed bothered by Alfie's impending situation were his friends. Alfie already kept seeing dark flashes when he walked home—from behind tree's and down dark alley's, when he would turn round corners, there would be a flash of a tail of shadow—as if someone heard him coming and ran away. But he didn't know if this was the Shadow, someone or *something* else. Tommy would encouragingly guide Alfie away and try and make a joke, while Sparky trotted along mostly always terrified. Unless Alfie found a way of getting into Magicity undercover and started looking, he would, very soon, be in deep trouble. But, said a small voice in Alfie's head, even the people that live there haven't found this Sword, so what chance did he have?

Some things had changed though, Tommy was getting curiously good marks in all of his subjects of late. The teachers were becoming increasingly confused and surprised with him getting hundred percent marks in maths, science and history tests. Alfie didn't need to ask why. Tommy had kept his grubby piece of parchment carefully wrapped in a linen cloth, in a special pocket inside his bag. Alfie saw him casually taking it out half way through a lesson, keeping it resting on his knee under the table and out of sight.

But it was on the way out of the lunch hall after a particularly grubby meal of soggy pie and lumpy mash that a sudden desperate thought exploded into Alfie's head—the Gnarlus paper!

"Tommy," said Alfie fast. "Have you got the Gnarlus Paper?"

"Yeah why?" said Tommy suspiciously, he was very guarded about his magic paper.

"Right, let's find an empty room!"

They walked the corridors hurriedly searching for an empty room, which was tricky because it was raining very hard outside, causing almost everyone to be indoors, playing chess or doing work, or eating lunch. "Oh fine…" said Alfie who marched into the nearest toilets. As soon as he did, Bruce and Frank, who tried to hide something behind their back, glared at them, a small tail of smoke rising behind their backs.

"What?" said Frank is a dozy voice.

"Get out…" said Alfie quickly.

"Why?" said Frank squaring up.

"Because there's a GAS leak in here!" Alfie cried.

"Ahh!" they both screamed running out of the toilet faster

than Alfie had ever seen them move before. He raised his hands at the door and said: "Consisto." It sealed shut. "Get the Gnarlus Paper out."

"Okay, but why?"

"Why? Why didn't I think of it before! I've been so stupid… all we do, is ask the Gnarlus Paper where the Sword is!"

"Okay. But I told you," said Tommy unwrapping the paper like it was a new born kitten. "It gets cagey about answering *magical questions*."

"What have you asked it exactly?" said Sparky.

"Well," said Tommy counting on his fingers. "I asked it about LeyDoors, all I got from that was they are *a magical time transportation system*."

Alfie deflated. "Can we at least try?"

Propped up against the sink, with the sound of the rain battering the windows outside, Tommy pulled open the dirty smudged parchment flaps.

"Okay," said Alfie, getting his pen out and moving towards it.

"Woah…" said Tommy moving it out of his reach. "*I* write."

Sparky shuffled on the spot checking his watch. "We need to hurry, we only have eight minutes before the bell rings for the end of lunch time."

Alfie told Tommy to ask it where the sword was. Tommy wrote slowly and made the letters clear "because otherwise it doesn't understand," he said.

The question—'*Where is the Sword?*'

Returned the answer—'*Swords can be found in various places all over the world…*'

"I think it's confused," said Tommy. "You need to be more specific."

So they asked it—'*Where is the sword in the stone?*'

The answer faded up—*'In the stone.'*

"No, this isn't right," said Alfie, then slapped himself on the head—what had Gracie called it? "Try… where is the *Akashic Sword?*"

Sparky looked at his watch. "We have two minutes until bell."

"Okay!" said Alfie as Tommy wrote the letters carefully. When he finished, the sentence took a little while until it faded away, sinking as if being pulled through a plug hole. Alfie, Tommy and Sparky leaned over awaiting the answer that could save his life.

The answer they got back was—*'Hidden.'*

Alfie blinked, unable to believe it. Then the word vanished. He looked at the paper with disgust, he had really thought that could be the answer to his prayers.

The bell rang.

Tommy muttered that his magic paper was fickle. Alfie felt like punching it.

Two week later and Alfie felt more frustrated than ever. It was a week full of the same questions going round and round his head. He was sick and tired of waiting around trying to figure out how to save himself from the Shadow. He felt like he had waited very patiently for the signs that Wiseman had promised, but they still hadn't materialised. Yet, just when Alfie was at the end of his tether the aforementioned *signs* made an appearance…

The strange day started with Alfie waking with a jolt. The Desire Stone lay beside him on the pillow, in front of his eyes and as he woke, a tiny picture inside the stone ebbed and flowed under the surface and as his eyes slowly adjusted he saw a tiny picture of a white rabbit, holding a ticking clock. The picture faded and Alfie sat up, shaking it, trying to make it come back. Then a new word swam in deepest black ink: *'Magicity.'*

When Alfie went downstairs for breakfast he realised he was the only one in. He flicked the radio on for company, there was a crackle, before it tuned into a song…

'The answers in the looking glass…'

It stopped abruptly and returned to the normal station, with some people talking about the news. Alfie looked up at it frowning before putting some toast under the grill.

On the way to school Alfie walked slowly up the three streets to Tommy's house. When he looked up into the sky, he saw one cloud, in the shape of a hand. The hand moved slowly, the fingers rolling and pointing—just like the hand in the fountain in Magicity.

Alfie, Tommy and Sparky were sat in a boring history lesson. Alfie was thinking about the strange things he had seen that morning. As he fiddled with the Desire Stone under his shirt, he sat back and pulled it out just a little. *'Magicity,'* it read. Perhaps he could show Gracie the Desire Stone, now that it didn't have her name floating in it? He looked across the room at her. She was concentrating hard, hand scribbling away at the questions Alfie had given up on a long time ago. Joel looked round and saw Alfie's gaze, sniggered and nudged Christian in the ribs, whispering something in his ear—Alfie didn't know what, but he sure wanted to know, it made his blood boil that Gracie would go out with a slime ball like Christian.

That morning had been strange, but now Alfie was sure something was trying to send him a message. The rock that he pulled the Sword out of turned into a fountain, and a hand pointed at a picture of a rabbit with a clock in it's stomach. The picture in the Desire Stone this morning was the same. Then the cloud with the pointing hand in it.

Alfie rubbed his forehead, the graze didn't hurt anymore but his mind did. Tommy had finished his phrases, the Gnarlus paper laying on his lap under the table. Alfie tapped him and borrowed it hurriedly, ignoring his muffled yelps as Alfie began scribbling all over it. Alfie wrote as quickly as he could.

'What is the white rabbit, in connection with magic?'

The black ink slowly coiled away and formed into an answer: *'The white rabbit symbol is synonymous with the magical world and wizards in particular, often appearing to them as a vision or guide.'*

Alfie knew the white rabbit was a sign that he had to follow. Something was burning inside him white hot—he thought he knew where the Sword could be. He needed to follow the white rabbit which was painted on that wall with a clock in it's stomach. A white rabbit that had probably been painted there a long time ago—that was now, crumbling off—painted long enough ago for the Sword to have been taken and hidden somewhere—like inside the walls where the painting of the white rabbit was? Alfie swallowed excitedly, his mind was racing ahead way too fast, but he didn't care. The Desire Stone went cold in his hand, looking down, new words had faded up:

'Now you know what to do...'

Just below the words, a small purple hourglass appeared. It turned. Purple sand starting to fall.

Alfie started breathing heavily, it was time to act. He leaned into Tommy.

"Tommy, Sparky we have to go now. If you want to come?" Alfie hissed at them, half standing.

"What?" they both said turning at once and looking alarmed. A few people round the classroom looked over absentmindedly at him, then back to their work.

"I think I know where it is…" Alfie hissed standing up. "*Erm, excuse me Mr Ward, would you mind if me, Tommy and Sparky leave*—we have to go and…" Alfie tried to think of a good lie as a few of the class looked up from their work and frowned—*Alfie Brown was trying to sneak his way out of class again.* "A meeting, with…"

"Who with?" said Mr Ward suspitious.

"He's right sir," said Gracie standing. "I do too, I nearly forgot. Thank you for reminding me Alfie!" she said confidently. "We four have a meeting with the student advisor team with the headmaster in five minutes."

Mr Ward buckled and looked at Gracie and nodded. "Fine, off you go," he smiled.

"And me sir," said Christian who stood too, looking perplexedly toward Gracie.

Gracie snarled at him. "Sit down Christian."

"Sir that's not fair! How come they get to leave early?" said Joel in a smarmy voice, glaring at Alfie as he began stuffing books in his bag. Then muttering broke out in the class about how unfair this was, that some people should be allowed to go early and not others.

"The headmaster wants to see them!" called Mr. Ward. "And very soon I dare say, you'll have yours."

All four walked from the classroom hurriedly, Alfie walking briskly ahead out of the block and into the playground. The fresh air felt good, the thoughts solidifying in his brain. Tommy guffawed at Mr Wards stupidity at letting them out early but then caught sight of Alfie's determined expression.

Gracie caught Alfie's arm and pulled him back. "Well?"

she said, stopping him just before they reached the deserted playground, she looked expectant. "Are you going to tell us what's going on?"

"It's up to you if you want to join me or not," said Alfie. "But this is what you wanted, to be told and involved in *everything*."

Tommy walked up and stood next to him. "Whatever it is, I'm in..." Sparky was more hesitant but eventually nodded.

Alfie glanced at the Desire Stone, the hour glass was just visible, the sand disappearing quickly—he knew whatever they did had to be done fast. Alfie didn't want to know what would happen once the sand ran out. "When I was in Magicity, there was this side of a shop that had a giant painting of a white rabbit on it, with a clock in the middle of it's stomach. Later on, when I pulled that fake sword out of the rock, the stone melted down and turned into a fountain. A hand appeared and pointed towards the white rabbit... the painting is on the side of a shop."

"The magic mirror shop?" said Gracie, her eyes glazing over—realisation dawning.

Alfie knew it all made sense, he was sure the sword would be inside the white rabbit, which was—inside the side of the shop it was painted on—which, happened to be a magic mirror shop. Alfie remembered seeing it, pointed out by Wiseman. That's what jogged the memory of the mirror in his living room at the start of the year and the line from the song this morning: '*The answers in the looking glass.*'

Alfie feeling the adrenaline pump through him as the weight of the decision he was about to make nestled on his shoulders. "Are we ready?"

"Woah!" said Gracie. "We can't just go charging in there. And *you* certainly can't. You're a fugitive, and these two are Outsiders, I am the only one who will be welcome there."

252

"Ok," said Alfie looking away from her mesmerising stare and trying to think straight. "I'll go alone," he said, before they drowned him out.

"We're coming!"

Sparky whimpered. "What about Mr Sapiens? I think you should tell him, he might be able to help?"

Alfie shook his head. Mr Sapiens would only stop them from going. "No," he said glancing at the diminishing sand in the hour glass. "We go now."

They were standing in tiny a dark room all looking at Alfie. "Why are standing in the broom cupboard?" said Sparky shielding his nose from the smell. "I thought you said we were in a rush?"

"We need to make a pit-stop, if we have any chance of getting into Magicity." Alfie looked towards Gracie in the dim light. "Have you ever been to Sampson's Void?"

Gracie looked curious, or as curious as you can in near pitch black. "No."

"Take my hands," Alfie said again. "We're going to need some tickets and some sort of disguises."

Slowly they took his hands and stood in a circle. "Where are we going?" said Sparky whimpering.

Alfie swallowed. "Sampson's Void."

Alfie had never gone there by himself and was taking a huge risk. He concentrated and held Tommy and Gracie's hands tightly, bracing himself.

"It doesn't hurt does it?" said Tommy looking concerned.

Quick as a flash Alfie said the magic words: *"Ipsum-Vanearo!"*

The broom cupboard fell away like a mirage, now they started to fall, as if the floor had given way. He retained as tight a grip as he could with Tommy and Gracie's hands as red lights popped and fizzed around them, knitting into place to form a tunnel ahead of them. All at once they picked up speed and began to zoom along the fizzing red tunnel. It was a little bumpier than Alfie remembered. All sound had disappeared but he could see Tommy's mouth open screaming. Sparky's too. Gracie had her eyes closed as her hair whipped back. Alfie closed his eyes as a wave of nausea blasted through him. The next second, he felt air and sound return, in a flash of blue light they landed. Tommy wobbled, and Sparky bent over breathing hard. Alfie relinquished his hold and they all stood a little shaken. Alfie felt the relief pour through him. It had worked! He was so unsure it would—using the vanishing spell to vanish themselves into Sampson's Void was either madness or genius. But now, they were standing in the warehouse as tiny tags began writing themselves and attempting to attach to them—like all the other vanished items.

The small door which creaked open straight ahead of them at the end of the warehouse creaked open. "Ha-ha! I said you'd be back!" cried Parsons, marching towards them.

"Hello Parsons," said Alfie quickly. "Do you think—"

Parsons held up a finger. "Its nice to meet you all. My name is Parsons. Welcome to Sampson's Void." He shook their hands formally. "This is where all the things that are vanished magically come."

"Wow," said Tommy gazing up the shelves upon shelves of stuff, stretching far into the ceilings which seemed to go on forever. Alfie was about to speak again, before Parson's beat him to it. "You need help, that's why you're here. What do you need?"

* * *

"Are we sure we've got everything we'll need?" said Gracie looking at the small pile of stuff. "Four tickets to get into Magicity. Four black coats and…" she giggled as Alfie looked at a smelly plastic halloween mask, they had found in the confines of the warehouse. Parsons looked at the pile.

"Are you sure you've got everything you'll need?"

Alfie said that he thought so, as they put their coats on. "Wait!" said Parsons. "And this…" he grabbed a nearby bowler hat and added it to Alfie's head.

"There's so much stuff in there!" said Tommy looking at Parsons who grinned.

"Just make sure you vanish all this stuff back again, when you've finished what ever your doing."

Alfie grimaced. "We are—"

Parsons held up a hand. "I dun' wanna know…"

Alfie smiled, and slipped the mask over his face. It smelt horrid. The face itself had boils and spots all over it and an anguished face with slanting mouth and eyes. Alfie was dubious that this would work at all, but couldn't think of an alternative. They knew his face in Magicity, it was all over the news.

"Hmm," said Gracie as Sparky recoiled away from him. "It just looks like a mask."

"We haven't got time for this!" said Alfie.

"Just wait." Gracie screwed her face and began reciting something under her breath, as she did the plastic of the mask began moulding to Alfie's skin, it was a strange feeling.

"Much better!" they chorused.

Gracie looked pleased with herself. Alfie put the black hat on and pulled it as far over his face as it would come. The mask was very itchy. "Are we ready to go?" he said glancing back down at the Desire Stone, the sand in the hour glass running thin.

Gracie held the tickets which were small and square on yellowing paper, with moving ornate scrawly writing. Tommy put on a black hooded robe and Gracie a black wool jacket with the collar up. They looked a bunch of complete miss fits.

"Thanks Parsons," said Alfie. "Can you vanish us back?"

Clattering back into the broom cupboard, Alfie grabbed them and began to run. Down the corridors, straight out through reception, much to the receptionists dismay and through the town. The others followed right behind him as he charged on through the town towards the churchyard. His side burned, and the air felt hot in his lungs, but he kept pace. Arriving at the churchyard, puffed out and holding each other they stopped to look at Alfie.

"Was that necessary?" said Sparky, taking several puffs from his inhaler.

Alfie walked over to the old gravestone under the tree and turned. "We're going to Magicity. There might be more running involved." Alfie gave Sparky a sharp look. "And there might be danger, just remember what we're looking for and stick by me and Gracie." He took a deep breath. "Tommy you go with me, and Gracie you take Sparky."

"Sure," said Gracie. "Hold my hand Sparky."

"What?" said Sparky alarmed.

"Oh for god sake, just hold my hand!" Gracie grabbed it, closed her eyes and touched the gravestone. With a wild gust of wind and an extremely loud whooshing sound, they both shot into the sky faster than a gunshot.

Alfie took Tommy's hand, closed his eyes and touched the

repeated in his head: *'Magicity, Magicity, Magicity'*, then he touched the cold stone and... *Whoosh!* They were pinged hard into the air. Alfie heard Tommy swear loudly as they exploded into the sky faster than lightning. Alfie could see Gracie and Sparky just ahead, their hair flailing wildly in the wind. Alfie felt his stomach churn as the wind slashed his ears. The cold frost whipping and biting their skin. Then, all of a sudden, the warm invisible force enclosed around them, soft and comforting as they began hurtling along at breakneck speed across the country.

"Woah!" screamed Tommy. "This is MENTAL!"

"Brace yourself Tommy, it's a steep drop." Alfie called still holding as tight as he could to Tommy's arm.

"Sure!" Tommy shouted back. They saw Gracie and Sparky just ahead fall at an amazing speed towards the ground. Alfie and Tommy felt a momentary pause before they felt the invisible force leave them. All at once and they began to plummet through soggy clouds towards the ground which yawned beneath them.

"*Ahhh!*" They both screamed through the wind, stomachs turning flips. He closed his eyes and shielded his face. At the last second the warm cushion caught them swiftly and tilted them upright until their feet met the ground with a hard thud.

Tommy wobbled then fell over. "My insides hurt."

Alfie turned to see Gracie helping Sparky up, who looked disturbed, his hair all over the place.

"You alright Sparky?" asked Alfie with a little grin. Sparky quivered, and went a pasty green colour.

"Never, ever, ever, ever, ever make me do that again!" he said hiccupping.

"Seconded!" said Tommy with his face still in the side of the hill.

"What next?" said Gracie looking anxious and Alfie looked up at the wall of swirling mist. Just before it the small booth, and past that a tall iron gate and a pair of red eyes.

Alfie glanced at the Desire Stone again, the sand was now nearly half gone, Alfie shuddered. He didn't know what would happen when the sand ran out, he just knew he needed to keep going. "Come on, we haven't got long."

With his hat pulled low over his face, Alfie marched fast towards the booth. His heart was beating fast. What would happen if they got caught? Gracie walked just ahead, tickets in hand. A man in a red uniform, black hat and grumpy face peered down at them.

"*Yeees?*" he said slowly. "Tickets or Skry stones please."

Gracie pulled out the three ticket and passed it up onto the counter. Alfie kept his head bowed under the hat. Tommy and Sparky stood just ahead of him as planned, trying to look as normal as possible—but Alfie could see, by their eyes how terrified they looked. The man looked at the tickets, then his gaze drifted over his glasses to Gracie, then to Tommy and Sparky. Then to Alfie.

"Excuse me sonny, can you take your hat off," he said.

Alfie glanced at Gracie who mouthed for him to do so. Ever so slowly Alfie began to take the hat off. The man in the booth recoiled. "Woah! I mean… sorry, it's just… leave the hat on sonny…" he laughed nervously. "And er… on you all go now."

Alfie couldn't believe it, the mask worked! He pulled the hat back on quickly and stumbled along after Gracie.

The wide iron gates slowly opened outwards and the white mist swirled upwards. Red eyes glared across at them.

"Pendragon," Alfie whispered and led them up the short hill through the gates towards it. When they reached the edge of the mist Alfie felt his heart beat in his chest, probably loud enough for them all to hear.

"This is it," Alfie said turning to them with Sparky cowering behind Gracie and Tommy. "If he starts to attack just run for it."

"We won't have time to run!" Gracie hissed.

A huge grey horse trotted forward agonisingly slowly out of the mist towards them. A pair of red eyes materialised slowly and came resting upon them.

It's voice suddenly boomed across the hillside. "ALFIE BROWN," it boomed. "YOU RETURN."

Alfie swallowed and took a step back, it knew it was him, even through the pathetic mask. "YOUR DARK ACCOMPLICE INJURED MY PEOPLE. YOU STOLE FROM MY PEOPLE, AND ESCAPED PERSECUTION. AND NOW YOU INSULT US BY RETURNING IN DISGUISE TO PLUNDER MORE MAGICAL ASSETS."

"No—it's not like that..." Alfie stammered.

"NO?" The horse stamped its front legs hard into the ground, making them all jump. "YOU ARE A FELON!" Spat Pendragon his face glowing white hot. It withdrew it's sword quickly and held it aloft. "YOU THINK YOU CAN PASS ME AGAIN!"

Alfie felt a sudden burning in his chest. Purple light erupted from the Desire Stone. Alfie shielded his eyes, the Pendragon framed monstrously as it wielded the sword.

Gracie screamed. "Alfie! Do something!"

"WHAT IS THIS?" said the Pendragon suddenly, the sword still above its head. "This light?"

Alfie pulled out the Desire Stone which was glowing hot,

light pouring out illuminating the whole hillside purple. Breath heavy in his throat he said. "It's my stone—" Alfie stopped for the Pendragon's face dropped, red eyes widening. It dropped the sword to the ground as the horse whinnied. "YOU POSSES THE AKASHIC STONE? WHERE DID YOU GET IT?"

"I was gifted it this Christmas. I don't know who from."

The Pendragon looked deep into Alfie's eyes. "YOU DO NOT LIE." It said to itself, frowning.

After a long pause, the Pendragon's eyes flickered from Alfie to the stone. Then, it turned and blew a hole through the mist. The Pendragon sheathed its sword, eyes not leaving Alfie's. Heart hammering in his chest Alfie moved forward. The Pendragon didn't say another word, but watched them walk through the mist in silence. Gracie put a hand to Alfie's back as they walked. Sparky was whimpering beside them and looking back at the red eyes which followed them all the way. Tommy was looking from Alfie to the stone and back, his mouth agape.

They walked on through the mist. As it faded, they saw the large stone pillars which topped the entrance, atop the hill with Magicity stretched out beneath them. The sun just beginning to set behind a mountain. Dark clouds hovering overhead as a spittle of rain began to fall. Down below there were no people like there were before. In fact, the town looked desolate.

They took the stone escalator down to the old cobbled street. Tommy gaped around at this new world, eyes ablaze with wonder, while Sparky just clung to the railings whimpering softly. When they reached the bottom Gracie guided them towards the main square. Which was virtually empty bar a few people walking hurriedly past with hoods up.

The square was bleak, there were no stalls or street performers. Just the large opposing grey rock standing tall in the middle of the square. Stumbling closer over the cobbles Alfie saw a sword proudly poking out of the top.

"Wiseman must have returned it," Gracie hissed.

Alfie looked up at the rock, it didn't look that magical anymore, no more than any other lump of old stone. Up ahead, past the rock facing the square was the large faded painting of a white rabbit with a clock in the middle of its stomach.

"This way," said Alfie leading the way towards it.

"And you are sure the hand pointed to *that*?" said Gracie. Alfie whispered back that he was certain, just as a woman with a large nose eyed them suspiciously from the window of a magical herb shop. Alfie fixed on the crusty painting of the white rabbit. They were the only ones in the square now. Alfie walked past the spot where he and Wiseman were trapped by Pope and the guards before flying away on the carpet. Alfie felt an anxious weight pull on his chest. They stood before the shop that had the white rabbit on the side of it. 'Merve's Magical Mirrors' read the large sign, only half the letters flashing neon gold. They peered through the window at a huge selection of mirrors. Mirrors hung on the walls, mirrors on the ceiling and mirrors lined up on cases. Even the assistants desk had mirrors all over it. Alfie, feeling his heart beat furiously in his chest, turned to see Gracie nod at him—even though he felt uncomfortable—they had come all this way, and all he had was a hunch.

Alfie opened the door and went in, a small bell ringing through the silence. The others trotted in after him. A short, fat woman poked her head above the desk and suddenly screeched. "Can I *heeeelp*?" This nearly caused them all to collide with a collection of mirrors behind them. The woman stepped forwards around the desk to get a better look at them. She was very odd looking as she peered down at them through huge jugular glasses that looked like that were made for thick round windows, not for seeing better. She was also small and round, like a dumpling.

"Erm," Alfie stammered. "We're just *looking*." He kept his head low under the hat.

"*Fine!*" she screeched. "Look away me dears."

Alfie scurried off out of her way. The shop really was crammed to the brim. There were tall mirrors, circle mirrors, triangles mirrors, mirrors of no shape, mirrors with gold frames, silver frames and even fire encased mirrors. There were mirrors which made you look beautiful and ones that made you look ugly (which did nothing to Alfie's mask), there was every kind of mirror you could ever imagine.

But there must be one that must be different—one that showed a picture instead of a reflection. That's what was in Alfie's mind anyhow, all the clues had led him to this mirror shop. And why? The only connection he could make was what happened near the start of the year—when he saw someone in his mirror at home. An old lady sitting at her dining table. He already knew that magical mirrors did all sorts of strange and wonderful things. Wiseman had made the TV work on one. But, now he had a countdown on the Desire Stone to try and find what the clues were leading to. He just needed to find what it wanted him to find.

As he searched around, he grew frustrated. None of these mirrors showed any sort of picture, just his own rather disgusting shadowy face in a number of amusing shapes. After a while of fruitless searching Gracie tapped him on the shoulder.

"What is it?" said Alfie a little too loudly, hopeful she had found something.

Sparky and Tommy stood awkwardly together, with one eye on Alfie and another on the woman, who was still ducked under her desk. Gracie pulled him slowly towards the woman's desk. "Ask her what you're looking for."

Alfie glanced at the Desire Stone, it had barely a quarter left. Keeping his head low Alfie said: "I wonder if you can help? We are looking for a mirror…"

The woman did not look up from under the desk. "Well that's a given!" the woman cackled.

"Well, a different sort of mirror…"

The woman stood slowly, looking curiously at him. "Go on… you have my interest."

"What we are looking for…" said Alfie keeping the hat over his face. "Is a mirror that instead of reflecting, shows a picture."

The woman's huge eyes narrowed. "You mean a looking glass?"

"Yes we do!" said Gracie before Alfie could answer.

"Because I have some more mirrors and things like that downstairs," said the woman pointing down at the floorboards. Gracie asked politely if they could be taken to them. "Of course!" she smiled. "No one ever goes down there, they are all the rubbish—broken half of 'em, the others are defective or like you say, barely reflect. People don't want looking glasses na' more."

As she hobbled to the back of the shop, Alfie risked a glance at Gracie who gave him an excited, meaningful look—whereas Alfie couldn't help frown, he didn't want a looking glass. He wanted a mirror with a picture in it! They went down a rickety pair of stairs to a dingy, dark basement. The only light came from a small dirty window all covered over in dust, but it cast a modicum of grey light across the cluttered roomful of mirrors. Or what they presumed to be mirrors, for they were all covered in greying sheets—it could have been anything under there.

"*So…*" the women screeched again. "That your after a looking glass?" Alfie nodded, not exactly sure if that was what he was after, but Gracie seemed pretty sure.

The woman stroked her chin. "I trust you do not have much knowledge of mirrors?" They all shook their heads. "Mirror magic is a much maligned and misunderstood thing. Did you know that there is means, some say, to travel in between every mirror in the world? Or that you can talk to loved ones who've passed over? Or see the future reflected and the past shadowed?" Her saucer shaped eyes floated off for a moment, before returning sharply. "Any mirror in the world can turn into a looking glass if *it chooses.* But there are not many mirrors that are *exclusively* looking glasses."

"So, do you have one?" said Gracie.

"Hmm," she said spinning around and peering under sheets. "I know of only *one* in here. Not sure where it is." She waved a dumpy fist and the sheets nearby flew into the air and fell to the floor in a cloud of dust causing Sparky to cough loudly.

"Alfie look…" said Tommy quietly, so the woman didn't hear. And he pointed to a mirror just behind the woman. It was twice her height and had a large ornamental dark oak frame. The greying sheet partially covered it, but a small glimmer of light was coming from the mirror face.

"I think we've found it," said Alfie aloud.

"What?" screeched the woman who followed their gaze. "*Hmm.* So that's where it was." She hauled the sheet off with a flick of her hand, underneath the mirror face was dusty and grubby. Alfie moved towards it wiping some of the dust and muck away with his sleeve. As he did so, more light shined out from underneath. Through the patches of dust and dirt, he could see green rolling hills and a small cottage with pretty flowers round the sides. In a tree beside the cottage was a snoozing cat laying on a thick branch. The front door of the cottage opened and a very small and elderly lady began to walk towards them. As she got to the tree she gazed directly at Alfie and waved. She could see them. Alfie felt Gracie, Tommy and Sparky move in closer.

"Greetings to you all," said the old lady smiling as she came closer. "I trust you are not disappointed that I cannot give you direct access to that which you *desire*." Her eyes flicked to Alfie's and he guessed with a huge plummeting feeling that she meant *the sword*.

"Who are you?" said Alfie. She wore a pastel pink cardigan and stood rather hunched over a stick used for support. The old lady's eyes flickered to the shop owner behind them and she looked concerned for a second. "I am the Dice Duchess." She said in a croaky voice. "And I wonder if we cannot have a chat, alone."

Alfie turned to the shop owner. "Would you mind?" he said in his politest tone.

The shop owner frowned and looked like she might shout at them all. "I... well..." she went to make a point about this being her mirror after all and anything it did say she should hear it, but then glancing round at their faces she deflated and smiled bleakly. "I'll go and see if there's any more customers upstairs..." and off she went, clapping up the wooden stairs and closing the door behind her.

"Alfie Brown," said the Dice Duchess peering through the glass at him. "We meet again. We did meet very briefly in September if you recall?"

Alfie suddenly gasped. "It was you in my mirror at home!?"

The Dice Duchess nodded and leaned on her stick. "Mirror magic is a fickle thing, often works when you least want it to." The cat in the branches got up and stretched. Gracie gave Alfie a short look, they needed to hurry.

"So…" said Alfie. "Do you have the sword?"

The Dice Duchess stared for a long moment. Alfie's heart beating hard, he really hoped she did, or could at least direct them to it.

"I never had it. It belonged to the looking glass we're speaking through now but—"

"What do you mean *belonged*?" said Gracie. "You mean it was in this mirror?"

"And now it's not." The Dice Duchess looked down, her face wrinkling—it was hard to tell if she was happy or sad. "It was taken. It is lost."

Alfie swallowed hard. "But who took it?"

The Dice Duchess looked stricken. "I cannot say," she whispered softly as the wind rustled the tree branched. "*He did…*" she shook her head softly. "Fifteen years ago it was taken. But you, you are the one who should be taking it." she said anguished, on the border of tears. Alfie rubbed his head hard.

"Why are you here to tell us? Did you have it, or look after it or something?"

"No, no!" she shook her head violently. "It belonged to the looking glass, as do I. But *found* a way he did… such dark eyes." She shook again and pulled a hanky from he sleeve drying her eyes.

Gracie huffed. "So you won't tell us who took it?"

The Dice Duchess suddenly looked fierce. "I don't tell, I advise. I am a seer, I see things. I saw the man who took it, but it will do

266

you no good knowing who it is, believe me, I see." She sniffed again as the cat came to her heels. "I'd advise you not to go after him. He's evil. Different. Not to be trusted. He tricked me." She swallowed. "Your problem has few solutions. I can see the paths people take. I can see what's ahead of them—life is like a dark and unlit lane, you cannot see more than three feet ahead of you in any direction. But I can see your path as if lit by a blanket of moonlight. I advise those I must and I only deal in appointments."

Tommy sighed—even though he was staring into a magic mirror, he still thought seers, psychic and mediums were a load of codswallop. "But we need to find the sword. Can you help us with that?"

"You have been walking along a narrow path that will soon turn into a fork. You can go left or right. One carries on, the other is a dead end." She spoke gravely as the wind rustled the branches of the tree again. "I can see destruction and chaos that you bring to this world if you find the Akashic Sword. You will reign fire and fury over two lands—you are the spark that ignites a great fire between two warring races." She cut off, as the cat brushed against her leg. "I have waited many years to read aloud this prophesy, but I cannot read it all. For it would lead you to the wrong path if I did. That is all I can tell you for now."

"What do you mean?" said Alfie, who just wanted answers, not riddles.

"I can tell you no more," she waved her hands enough.

Gracie cleared her throat. "Why should we believe you?" she said tartly.

"Oh Gracie Jane. Why should you exactly? I am just a batty old woman in a mirror."

The cat stretched again, then climbed down and strolled towards them. The Desire Stone vibrated slightly and burned against his chest. Alfie quickly glanced down at it—the sand in the hour glass had gone.

"Ah," Alfie blinked at it. "I just don't know what I am supposed to do next," he said pleadingly.

"Forget about the sword for it only leads to a deal with the devil. And the devil comes in many disguises…" the mirrors image started fading slowly. "There is always another solution."

"No wait!" Alfie cried as the mirror face went completely blank. Alfie stared in disbelief. "Come back!" he said pleading.

"I know who you are," said a sharp voice behind them. Alfie turned, at the foot of the stairs stood the shop owner looking gleeful. "I listened to your conversation. You are Alfie Brown." She smiled excitedly. "Guards are on the way, so no funny business!"

"You alerted Guards?!" Alfie cried absolute panic rising in his chest.

"Well of course I did!" she said coming down the stairs slowly. "There is a price upon your head. I'll get a lot of Bits for this, and I'll be famous. The woman who caught the sword thief," she cackled.

Meow.

Looking down they all saw the cat from the mirror sitting quite calmly in the middle of the floor watching them.

"How did that get in here?" she screeched. The cat began to lick its paw—it must have come through the mirror.

Gracie moved as quick as a flash, she drew her arms out wide and a ball of blue flames lit the room, blasting towards the shop owner. She nimbly flicked her hands and deflected it. The blue fire hit the wooden stairs and burst into flames.

"Whoops," said Gracie, as the shop owner danced out of the way of the flames which spread quickly up the stairs chasing her. She reacted by jumping over the hole in the stairs and shouting at the top of her voice, swinging her arms around her head. A violent force blew all four of them into the surrounding mirrors. Alfie felt himself lifted bodily from his feet and clattering into the mirrors behind him, sending shards of sharp glass cascading around them. Gracie was standing up before she hit the ground, a furious look in her eyes. The fire was spreading, sending acrid smoke into the room. Tommy yanked Sparky up, who was laying in the remains from the looking glass. The shop owner had just realised that her baggy green trousers had caught fire and she whimpered trying to stamp it out. There was a crack and sparkle of fireworks as two large nearby mirrors sprang into the air from either side of the shop owner and sandwiched her with a *crunch*! She crumpled to the floor with a groan.

"Nice one!" Alfie called as Gracie peered through the smoke at him and coughed.

"Come on!" she called. "Let's get out of here!"

Tommy and Sparky lumbered towards him through the smoke.

"Watch the glass!" cried Sparky. "Watch the glass, it's really sharp!" Sparky was clutching his hand which was streaming with blood.

"He's cut!" cried Tommy.

"STOP!" cried a large booming voice. A Guard stood at the top of the stairs. Gracie raised an arm but the Guard just laughed, the fire on the stairs diminished and disappeared as he passed. His long dark coat and white mask covering his face and body, he looked at each of them in turn as they coughed against the smoke. "Got you at last," he said, eyes in the mask resting on Alfie. The fire had stopped and smoke began to clear, but it did nothing to stop the panic that coursed through Alfie. He had to get them out of here, somehow. The cat that had come through the mirror now trotted forward and stood in front of Gracie.

"I don't think you have actually," said Gracie looking down at the cat—which suddenly did something amazing. It peered up at the Guard, then poised ready to pounce. They watched in slow motion—mid flight, the cat changed. It's features grew three times it's original size, it's head growing a long dark main of hair, from it's jaw protruded large bottle sized fangs. It's tabby coloured fur became golden and it's front paws into the size of dinner plates which landed squarely on the Guards chest, flattening him to the ground.

The lion roared, almost deafening Alfie who found himself running straight up the stairs without invitation. Gracie, Tommy and Sparky following closely. There was a loud blast and the shop shook as mirrors fell off the walls. The lion roared again as the light of a hundred flashes and bangs cascaded up the stairs. Glancing back, Alfie saw the shadow of the lion and the Guard cast long on the wall.

"What do we do now?" said Tommy whose face was caked in soot.

"We get out of here, as soon as possible!" Alfie cried moving for the door and walking out into the sweet fresh air of the desolate town square, it was empty and quiet. Bu then, he had taken no more than three steps until—darkness. Someone grabbed him roughly and rammed a black bag over his head. He heard the screams from Gracie, Tommy and Sparky. Then he felt himself being pushed forwards by rough hands.

It was all over.

16

Shreeve

lfie wasn't sure how long it took, where he was or how many Guards there were. The darkness of the bag shrouded his senses. The drawstrings tightened around his throat as he tried to wrestle his hands up to his face, scared he would suffocate. But rough hands pulled them hard behind his back and pushed him forwards. As he tripped along to god knows where, Alfie strained his ears, he couldn't Tommy, Sparky or Gracie at all. All he could hear was the inside of the bag, which was making small, rude remarks about him. "Felon of the highest order... What sort of scum would do that... Look at the state of yourself... I hope your pleased you worthless scoundrel! You're ugly!" It repeated over and over in a nasty, nasal voice. Alfie couldn't tell where he was or where he was going—what would they do to him? The boy who stole their sword? Alfie shuddered at the thought. But what would they do to Tommy and Sparky? They were outsiders. Lots of things went through Alfie's head very quickly—he could use a spell—but when he came to, he found that his voice didn't work. He tried to shout, but nothing came out of his mouth. Then, as he was pushed roughly up steps he felt the air change. Wherever he was it was cold. He felt freezing air run up his back. Finally he felt himself being forced down into a chair. He felt totally disorientated, he strained his ear for signs that Tommy, Sparky or Gracie were close, but he couldn't hear a thing.

The bag was ripped from his head, he blinked rapidly trying to make his eyes adjust to the new light, what there was of it. He was sitting in a lone chair in the middle of a circular room, with a tall ceiling and a long chandelier supplying some light. Grey stone walls, which seemed to be channeling cold air, surrounded him as he watched his breath freeze in front of him. Around the edges of the room was a strange movement. Spinning black smoke, only just visible out of the corner of his eye, darted around the perimeter wall. They had no shape and no eyes but he could feel them watching him, becoming excited, spinning around the wall faster and faster emitting small moaning noises making the hair on his back stand on edge.

A rough voice spoke from directly behind his chair. "Deternaas."

Instantly the chair Alfie was sitting in came to life. In one fluid motion it sucked his arms into its own wooden ones, Alfie's legs into the chairs and his back into the cold wooden behind until he could not move a muscle. Footsteps approach him from behind and whispered in his ear in a long rasping voice. "Look what the cat's brought in…"

It hissed and spat, dripping with haughty indignation. Alfie, who suddenly caught a whiff of this person started to cough violently—like rotting fish guts. Slowly the disgusting man walked around to face Alfie, who realised his look matched the smell. A long grey jacket reached the floor, it was filthy with mud and stains. He had long mousy greying hair which hung lank against the mans back, thick with grease. His face subsided to the left with his mouth hanging slightly open, a long trail of spittle falling down his coat. Lines covered the mans face, whether wrinkles or scars, it was hard to tell. And he stood as if he was a wolf, ready to pounce.

"Well mister Brown, you don't exactly challenge me in the looks department do you?" He emitted a long rasping laugh, then began to cough violently. "Let's take your pathetic mask off." In one fluid motion the man swiped the air. The mask tore away from his face.

"*AHH!*" Alfie cried as pain burst from every pore of his face. Flashes of light sparkled in front of his eyes as the mask flew across the room.

"Oh," said the man looking disappointed. "It didn't even tear any skin off."

Alfie sat with his head back against the chair. He didn't want to be here. He didn't know who this man was, what he wanted or what he could do to him. Alfie glanced up desperate to get out of the situation.

"*Petivo!*" Alfie said quickly, but nothing happened, not with this hands the way they were.

"Not exactly warming yourself to me are you? I would gag you, but I need you to answer some questions for me. Which you will do." The man was not a happy man—he emitted a cold, dangerous vibe that Alfie would do anything to get away from. He began to pace around the chair. "I don't give a sprats-arse that you have *purple eyes*. I don't care what you are. I don't care what you have achieved. All I want is *answers*. That is what I am paid for. If you don't answer me, I will feed you to *them…*"

The man glanced at them, the moving dark smoke creatures. They emitted another low moan which rippled complete terror through Alfie again.

"So we begin. I am the Second in Command to Councillor Pope, the Defence Cheif of Magicity Council. I am responsible for finding, detaining and questioning felons, spookers, and traitors to the magical race." He took a long breath and wiped the spit from his mouth. "So let us start with why you came back to Magicity?" his voice was long and drawn out, and he had to suck in great lungfulls of air every time he spoke.

Alfie didn't know what to say, should he lie? He didn't want to get fed to the dark smoky things, but could they do that? Alfie had no knowledge of magical rules, could they kill him?

"Tell me," growled the man. The wailing around the side of the wall grew louder. Alfie stared at the ground, his heart hammering into chest.

"I came because I... I was looking for the sword," his voice quivered.

The man crouched in front of him and leaned in. "What sword?"

"The Akashic Sword."

The man growled softly and chuckled. "And why do you require possession of this sword?"

Alfie swallowed. "To kill my Shadow."

"That's a very *neat* excuse. Did Nikolas tell you to say that?"

"No! That is why, honestly. It's true I promise!"

"Un-Inaugurated wizards do not have Shadows!" he said with distain and laughed again, a drip of slime fell from the corner of his mouth. "Wizards are useless creatures until they become Inaugurated," he sniggered, then jumped high into the air, landing inches away from Alfie's face. "Do you know who I am? You think you can lie to me with some pathetic excuse?" Alfie wrinkled his nose at the smell. "You're a thief and a murderer. So at least we have *something* in common."

"I didn't kill anyone," Alfie said desperately. "I told you, it was my Shadow."

The man waved, not interested. He began looking at Alfie out of one eye. "Where's Nikolas Wiseman?"

"I don't know," Alfie said honestly.

"Lair!" cried the man flashing his coat and marching around the chair. "Tell me where Nikolas Wiseman is!"

Alfie quiveringly told him that he absolutely no idea, that the last time he saw Wiseman was Christmas. "Oh nice cosy dinner together was it? I hope you realise what you've got yourself into following *him*!" The man spat, then laughed again. "Where did you meet for this cosy little dinner?"

"His house."

The man stopped. Then leaned over the back of the chair, resting his head on Alfie's shoulder. "And *where...* is Nikolas Wiseman's house?" Alfie swallowed, a bit of dribble fell on his shirt.

"It's hidden, but it's in the countryside somewhere." Alfie lied. The man's beady eyes narrowed. "Honestly," said Alfie. "You really think he would reveal to me where his house was? On a map?" said Alfie desperate to have this man as far away from him as possible.

Alfie faced a barrage of questions, often repeated asking why and how he took the *Magicity Sword* from the *Magicity Stone*. What black magic he used, what inspired him to commit such an awful atrocity and on and on and on for hours.

The questions continued. "Why did you and Nikolas enter

Magicity and steal *Magicity Sword* from the *Magicity Stone?*" said the man for the tenth time.

"I told you I didn't steal it—it just sort of came to me. It's a fake anyway."

The man's eyes flared, and Alfie realised he had said the wrong thing. "WHAT?" he cried moving slowly towards him. "Did you just SAY?"

Alfie was tired and breathing heavily, he hadn't meant to say that. His heart beat heavy again under the stare from the man. "The sword is a fake. Wiseman said so. That's why he gave it back."

"Liar! Liar! LIAR!" The man flew into a mad rage, thunder crackled through the air, almost deafening Alfie who couldn't even shield himself as sparks of static energy thundered about the room. The man jumped to a nearby step as the wailing grew again. He sat down and started biting his fingers. He began muttering under his breath and pointing to imaginary things in front of him. *"Deternaas,"* he muttered. The chair relinquished it's hold on Alfie, the wood sinking back into itself. Alfie rubbed his arms which felt sore and chaffed. Why had he released him?

"If Nikolas goes to all that effort just for you… to risk everything, then something would stop me from killing you. Surely?" Muttered the man softly to himself.

There was no way out and Alfie's gut was telling him to run. He didn't want it to end this way. This man was crazy, his eyes resting on Alfie, then he stood slowly, bones cracking, eyes swimming with confused, befuddled thoughts.

"Yes, *yes*, he will…"

"Wait!" said Alfie, standing from the chair. His legs sore and stiff. The man raised his hands towards Alfie's throat. "Please wait, please…" Alfie pleaded.

Knock, knock.

The man glanced behind him to the large padded metal door as if his sharp grey eyes gave him the ability to see was on the other side. "Enter!" He cried. The door swung open revealing three tall Guards. "Yes?"

"Shreeve," said one of the Guards addressing the man in front of Alfie.

"Yes? What it is?" said Shreeve turning to them. "And what on earth takes three of you to come here to tell me? I am questioning Wiseman's protégée, our hottest new acquisition. You know how important this is! Pope had given me express orders to deal with this purple eyed freak! Oh, and what have you done with his other three little friends? I was looking forward to disposing of them myself…" Shreeve giggled like a child as dribble slopped down his front.

"You will have nothing to do with them," said one Guard curtly.

"I am afraid we are under orders to remove you, Shreeve."

"What?!" Shreeve barked.

The middle Guard stepped forward and repeated. "You are to be removed."

"What the hell are you talking about, I cannot be removed you imbecile." Shreeve was staring at the Guard looking mutinous.

"The boy is innocent," said one.

Shreeve spluttered. "Alfie Brown is about as innocent as my conscience, now get out of my sight! You have no authority to be in here!"

"We have been given express permission. We are to remove you by any means necessary and believe me… I've wanted to do this for a very long time!" And with that, the Guards extended their arms out at Shreeve and three magnificent colours rose into the air from the end of their fingertips. Quick as lightning, red, blue and green collided, creating a ball of swirling fire. It span in mid air then, like a guided missile, flew at Shreeve's chest. Shreeve reacted quickly. Alfie saw him raise his hands and mutter something. The fire flew straight through him, but not entirely without damage—the ends of his coat caught alight. Shreeve tilted his long head, fingers twitching. Then as quick as a gunshot he swiped the air with his long finger nails.

A slicing sound splintered the air like a whip. The three Guards all turned on the spot in synchronicity, a transparent golden shield appeared over them as the claws scratched three dark marks across it.

The Guards stood stock still unmoving. Shreeve was bothered.

"Who *really* are you?" said Shreeve coming closer to Alfie and putting a long scabby hand on his shoulder.

One Guard stepped forward. "Let. The. Boy. Go." He said slow and forcibly.

"Never. Not until Pope himself comes down here to tell me otherwise!"

The Guard sighed, as if content with the answer—but then, quicker than the blink of an eye all three Guards had raised their hands. A bright flash and blast of golden light cracked into Shreeve from all four sides of the room and he collapsed in a moaning heap. Long neon string began to bind Shreeve's body until he resembled a caterpillars cocoon.

"Let's move!" said the middle Guard.

Gracie stepped into the circular chamber followed by Tommy and Sparky, who both looked utterly shell shocked.

"They hid us with magic!" said Tommy as Alfie rushed over to them. "Then broke us out of that horrible cell." Tommy looked terrified but so excited he was fit to burst as Sparky shuddered continually. "They're here to help us."

"Follow our lead," said a Guard voice deep and commanding. "If we ask you do to something, you have to promise to do it. That is the only way we will all make it out alive."

All four agreed.

The Guard nearest the door poked his head round and waved to them. They all moved quickly into a long stone corridor—it looked to be underground, the only light coming from small fire brackets which illuminated rusty metal doors all the way along the corridor.

"Walk fast," said one of the Guards. The corridors were bare and dark, the stone floors were cold and shadows clung to each and every crack in the walls as if would jump out and attack them at any moment.

Just then the Guard in front stopped, twisting his head to the side, hearing something. "Another Guard is coming," he whispered. "Get against this wall."

They did as they were asked and hid in the shadow of the small stone alcoves along the wall. Alfie and Gracie stood huddled together in the first alcove with Tommy and Sparky opposite them crammed against into the dark as best they could, except Sparky's feet were sticking out. All they could do was watch as one Guard stood in the centre of the corridor waiting while the other two were also hiding behind two columns just up the way. Gracie hung onto Alfie's arm—butterfly's in his stomach suddenly came to life. Alfie put his arm around her and she rested her head on his shoulder.

Footsteps from the approaching Guard grew louder.

Then a voice rang aloud. "I assumed I was the only one to be surveying the West Area. Are you on *orders*?"

"Yes," said the more familiar Guard. "There has been an incident, please follow me."

The Guard turned on the spot and walked back towards them with the arrival following. Just as he passed where they were hiding, he stopped, sensing something. But before he could do anything about it the two Guards that were hiding behind the columns crept out of the shadows. Making no noise, they put their hands up to face his back, with a silent swish of their arms, a glowing blue light, gentle like water spun into a snake, coiling up the Guards body until it covered him completely—even his mouth.

"*MMmmm!*" he struggled. "MMm!" The Guard shuddered as he realised what was happening. All three Guards waved their arms, and the captured Guard lifted into the air, and drifted into the empty shadows of the alcove. The tallest Guard waved a hand up to down eliminating all light around the Guard—until he was completely hidden.

"Let's move," he said.

They must have passed a hundred more metal doors. Until at last they reached the tallest, widest stone stairs Alfie had ever seen. They stretched upwards through the splintering rock face for what looked like miles. To the left and right was only the same dark labyrinth of corridors—this was the only way out. They began to climb. But no sooner did they step foot upon them did a noise suddenly hit the air. A screeching alarm pierced their ears. The sound of hundreds of pairs of feet running suddenly echoed ominously above them. Sparky stopped, puffing and panting and they all looked around at each other—they were rumbled.

"Don't run faster!" cried Gracie.

"I can't!" Sparky moaned—one of the Guards grabbed him and hoisted him along by his collar marching ahead.

Alfie's legs burned like acid, a stitch in his side almost threaten to split open it was that painful. They finally emerged at the top of the stairs. Turning left along a light, bright corridor following the Guard in front. It looked like ground level. Natural light spilled in from a large square courtyard in the middle of the building, which you could see across to the other side. But they were in trouble. Alfie glanced back to see five Guards coming down the stairs in front of them. Then more gathered from opposite hallways, there must have been twenty, who all lifted there arms up as one.

"Duck!" cried Alfie over the noise of the alarm. Everyone jumped to the floor as a massive shattering sound split above their heads. The wall to their right exploded showering large stone pieces over their heads. Dust imploding in thick white balls.

"Go, go, go!" shouted a Guard dragging Alfie up and running through the dust as another explosion blasted behind them.

"Turn!" barked the Guard at the front who turned sharp right into the next corridor. This one had large stone statues lining the walls. Alfie could hear the mass of Guards getting closer and closer. Their pounding footsteps rumbling the floor. "In here, QUICK!" The Guard stopped next to one of the statues. He waved his hand and a large iron grate in the floor flew open. Behind the iron grate was a deep dark black hole.

"Jump in now!" he barked. Gracie went first and disappeared, followed by one of the Guards. "All of *you* in NOW!" barked the Guard again as the twenty Guards behind them turned the corner. They raised their hands again. Alfie moved as quickly as ever had, and in one movement dragged Tommy and Sparky by the collar head first into the darkness. A loud explosion rocked the walls behind them as plumes of dust followed them into the darkness.

Alfie felt himself falling, through the darkness as the noise and explosions died away. "*AHH!*" cried Sparky into his ear. Then, he fell flat on his bum, with his hands still grasped round Tommy and Sparky's collars. The ground they had landed on was soft and they could smell earth and wood. Thin rays of sunlight poked through a narrow gap.

"Alfie?" said Tommy's broken voice in the darkness.

"Yeah I'm here..." said Alfie his head spinning. "Come on let's get out." Alfie crawled like a baby through the gap and looked up. Gracie and one of the Guards were standing a little way off and came towards them. "Alfie, are you ok?" she said patting his shoulder down.

"Fine..." he said standing a little dizzy. He watched Tommy and Sparky crawl out of the gap between the roots of a large oak tree and matched his own perplexed expression.

"We're here?" Tommy said looking around with incredulity.

"I know," said Alfie unable to believe it himself.

They were in the Westbury Playing Fields, just a few hundred yards away stood Gracie's house.

After a few seconds there was another short thud and the last two Guards emerged covered in white dust. "Won't they follow us?" said Sparky pointing at the tree.

"No," said one of the Guards who just emerged. "They can't." The roots to the tree suddenly curled and closed the gap they had just crawled through. Well that was a relief, Alfie didn't think he could manage any more running—the stitch in his side burned. And he was still in his school uniform.

"We'd better get inside," said one of the Guards.

"That hand needs seeing to," he pointed at Sparky's cut hand, which had dried blood and dust all over it. The sun was beginning to set casting an orange glow across the deserted park. All sense of time felt like it had been erased from Alfie's head. He had no idea what time or day it was. What on earth would his grandparents be thinking?

"Why are we going to your house?" said Alfie pointing in the direction of the Guard who was marching towards it.

Sparky coughed some dust up. "Won't your parents be annoyed?"

"You'll see," she said, smiling bleakly as she stumbled along. They all stumbled along, wondering how on earth they got out of that. Alfie, most of all. But the question that was burning brightest in his mind was—who are these people that had just saved them?

The three Guards stood over the fire muttering to each other, masks still fastened to their face. Alfie was watching them intently as they whispered to each other. Gracie slumped down on a nearby sofa, with Sparky the other end, head draped over the side and mouth hanging open like an exhausted dog. Tommy and Alfie sat in two, high backed chairs facing the sofa, and just out of range to make out the Guards hushed conversation.

The odd thing was that Gracie didn't seem at all bothered that these men (Alfie presumed they were men anyway) were in her house, nor did she go looking for her parents to tell them what had happened.

Alfie felt the stress of the day pile up on his shoulders leaving a large lumpy feeling in his stomach that made him feel sick with stress. They had miraculously survived the mirror shop owner, the Guards and the horrible man called Shreeve, but for how long could he carry this on? The Dice Duchess, whoever she was, had told him that the Sword, that thing he'd been chasing this whole time—was gone? Taken from the mirror. So how on earth was he supposed to stop the Shadow now? Helpless, Alfie settled into the chair and watched the Guards, the firelight dancing across their navy robes. After a few more minutes of discussion they finally did stop talking.

"Sorry for the delay," said the first Guard stepping forward. "We are not, as you may of guessed, *real* Guards. We all used to be Guards. However… it was stupid of all you to go to Magicity on such a… *whim*. It was foolish and irresponsible and if it wasn't for the message from a well informed insider you'd all be dead!"

The Guard put both hands to his face and twisted the mask off. Jonathan, Gracie's Dad blinked down at them all. Alfie didn't know why he was surprised, this was his house after all. "I am Gracie's father." He said, mainly to Tommy and Sparky who looked blankly at the man. The second Guard undid his coat and draped it across a chair, then slowly twisted off the mask. Underneath were dark handsome features and olive skin.

"Mr Sapiens?" said Tommy wearily.

Mr Sapiens knew Jonathan? He gave them curt nod and joined Jonathan, who ignored him. Alfie's guess was that Jonathan didn't feel that Mr Sapiens did enough to stop them leaving the school.

The third Guard was holding a nearby chair for support, then looked up from the floor. It must be Wiseman, Alfie thought, who else could it be? Yet this person looked a little short to be Wiseman. The Guard unbuttoned and took of the long coat, underneath the Guard was wearing a navy blue jumper. Very slowly, the Guard placed his hands around the mask and twisted. As he did, Alfie gasped…

"Dad?"

"Hello son…"

17

The Chase and the Place

lfie was in shock. He couldn't say anything. His Dad stood awkwardly unsure of where exactly to look. Jonathan tapped Mr Sapiens on the elbow and gradually everyone in the room stood up and trotted out. As Jonathan closed the doors, the clang of them shutting rang through the silence between them. Alfie and his Dad, a few yards apart, but the absence of so many years stretching out like corridors between them until they may as well have been miles apart.

His Dad had the same odd, gaunt face as Alfie and he was quite short, but there, all comparison ended. He was stocky and his face head was round and mostly bald. His eyes were brown, watery and blinked rapidly as he looked around the room. The words of the truth—that *he* was a wizard too—dancing behind his glassy eyes.

Finally he spoke. "I know this might come as bit of a shock to you." He had a soft, soothing voice—but it did little to dispel the raging torrent inside Alfie.

"I haven't seen…" Alfie swallowed hard. "I haven't seen you, in over a year."

"I know champ, I can explain."

"Explain?" said Alfie. "Go on then, explain… explain the last sixteen years!"

* * *

Alfie and his Dad walked agonisingly slowly back to Alfie's house. It was dark now, but orange streetlamp dib-dabbed light along the streets, but doing little to light up the darkness in Alfie's mind. His Dad, now wearing normal clothes—a beige mac, over his navy blue jumper—was sullen and quiet, quite unable to find the words. He, it seemed, was also struggling to comprehend the fact that his only son, was a wizard.

"If…" started his Dad. "If I'd have know, I would have helped, you know that don't you?"

Alfie grunted. Hollow words, he thought. "Why didn't you? Perhaps if you'd have dropped by, like ever, I could have told you."

"I've been very busy… and *I*…"

Alfie chuckled, more to himself. He had always wondered what his Dad did, but never, ever, in a million years would he guess he was involved in magic. "So, it's a magic job is it?"

His Dad sniffed. "Something like that."

"I assume," said Alfie tartly, as they walked up Mulberry Drive. "That you will want to know all about what's been happening the last year or so?" Alfie said, not knowing why he should.

"Yes, of course," said his Dad enthusiastically. "When?"

Alfie sighed. "I've got exams coming up, and Grandma won't let me leave the house until I've revised and… I do have a Shadow after me."

"Ah *yes*," said his Dad. "They told me. Well let's say, on the last day of your exams? At least then you will be free. We can have a celebration drink!"

"Sure," said Alfie flatly, looking around at the darkened street.

287

The end of his exams was a little way off yet—Alfie laughed to himself, he might even be dead by then.

His Dad glanced around the street, then back at him. "Can you do spells?"

Alfie blinked surprised by the question. "Course."

"Well, there is one that I think might work well against a Lynch Shadow, used it myself once."

"What is it?"

His Dad got a small notebook and pen out of his pocket and scribbled something down, then ripped the page out and handed it to Alfie. The scrawling words spelt Comparle-Compesco-Capiri.

"What does it do?" said Alfie.

His Dad looked around, then saw a snail slithering along the side of a garden wall, pointing his hand at it he said the words in a small commanding voice. *Comparle-Compesco-Capiri.*

There was a shot of brightest white light and the snail was suddenly encased in a glassy white box.

"It doesn't hurt it, does it?" said Alfie.

"No of course not," said his Dad, who flicked his hand upwards and the glass box with the snail jumped into the air. As he caught it, the box burst like a bubble and the snail sat on the palm of his hand looking thoroughly confused. "It just encases something with an impenetrable magical substance. Just in case," he smiled.

"Right... *erm*, thanks for that," said Alfie. "I'll erm, see in at the end of my exams then. You can tell me everything then."

"Yes!" said his Dad. "We can discuss your situation and what we can do about it. Don't worry champ, Nikolas Wiseman said he has it at bay for now, and Wiseman isn't the sort of person to let someone down."

Alfie nodded, too weary to think any more. A part of him

wanted to tell his Dad, everything, now, but he had no strength left after the days events. "Bye."

"Bye champ."

Alfie felt like turning back as soon as he got to his front door. He wanted to look back, see his Dad who he always thought was a nobody—someone who ran out on him when he was a baby. With the new information they now shared about each other, it just brought up new questions. But Alfie couldn't wrestle the resentment away. He still seethed that his Dad didn't stay with him, dumping him with his Grandparents. As Alfie opened the front door, he thought, maybe he couldn't have looked after him, maybe it was something to do with magic. He closed the door behind him. Instantly he felt an urge to go back outside and see his Dad. He should apologise for being short with him, and arrange to see him tomorrow, to tell him everything.

Alfie snatched open the door and ran back outside. "Dad?" he said. But no one replied. He looked up the streets around him, he scoured the darkness for any trace, but there was no one to be seen. His Dad had gone.

The next day was Friday, Alfie didn't go to school. He didn't fall asleep until the early hours, even though he was immensely tired. When he did finally falls asleep he dreamt continuously about strange magic trapping him in his bed and woke in a sweat when his alarm clock buzzed. Slamming it off and falling back to sleep, through his doze he heard his Grandma open the bedroom door.

"I am just so worried about him," she said softly. "Coming in at all hours, having arguments with his friends, going off to meet strangers. I just don't understand it Bill."

Grandad put a comforting hand to her shoulder. "We were

the same when we were that age."

A few hours later Alfie woke up—it was too late to go to school now anyway. A cup of cold tea stood on his sideboard with a note underneath.

I've gone to work. Bill's gone to the allotment to help some people with their new patch. Have a shower, and make sure you eat something.

G xx

At eleven-thirty Alfie was reawaken by the downstairs telephone. He crashed down the stairs nearly slipping, whilst wrestling his dressing gown on and wondering who on earth would be rude enough to disturb him, better not be a salesman or they would get a few of Alfie's choicest words.

"Hello?" he said hurriedly, it wasn't a salesman.

"Alfie, it's me Gracie. Listen, I hope you don't mind, Tommy gave me your number, I was hoping you were in, I guessed you weren't at school…"

Alfie softened, little butterflies whizzing into his stomach. "Oh," he stammered. "Hi Gracie… no I'm not, obviously…" said Alfie going red for no reason. "Why aren't you?"

"Same reason you're not. Tired. I was wondering if we could all come round and *talk*."

"Sure," said Alfie, grinning to himself.

"Okay, we'll be over in half and hour."

Alfie put the phone down and ran upstairs, putting his best jeans and t-shirt on and spraying himself with some spray he got for Christmas.

Alfie felt nervous about Gracie arriving at his house. What would she think of it? It was nothing compared to hers, which was huge, like a mansion. Alfie's was a tiny terrace. He tried to tidy up as best he could, hoping she wouldn't ask to see his bedroom, which would take longer than half an hour to clean up—a week wouldn't have been long enough.

Soon enough, they all arrived and trotted into the lounge. Tommy raised his eyebrows at Alfie as Gracie passed. Sparky looked fully refreshed after a good nights kip and lie in.

"So we all took the day off!" Tommy announced.

"Sure did!" said Alfie. "I would challenge anyone to go into school after a day like we had yesterday."

Gracie sat down in Alfie's Grandma's chair by the fire. She must have thought it was cold in the house because she kept her scarf on. Tommy and Sparky resumed their seats on the sofa and Alfie paced around offering drinks. Everyone shook their heads.

"You never usually offer drinks," said Tommy. Alfie went a little red, he knew what he was insinuating and sat down in his Granddads chair.

Gracie puffed her cheeks out and stared round at them. "How you lot can not feel tense is beyond me. I hardly slept a wink last night, thinking about all this."

"Yeah," said Sparky, looking at Alfie. "What did… you and your Dad say? I mean, he's a wizard and you never knew?"

Alfie shook his head softly. "I never knew."

"Gracie's Dad has known your Dad since they were our age, can you believe that?" said Tommy. "You did know that, didn't you?"

Alfie looked at Gracie. "Is that true?" he said and she nodded.

He chuckled. "You've probably seen more of him than I ever have then."

"What did you talk about?" said Gracie quickly.

"Not much," Alfie grunted.

"You were right about the Sword being in the Mirror Shop

though."

Alfie nodded slowly. "I was… but that still doesn't stop the fact that someone already took it!"

Tommy sighed. "It's like one problem after another isn't it! A trail of clues with nothing at the end."

"Yeah," said Gracie. "But seriously Alfie. If someone doesn't find a solution soon, you won't be around that much longer." They all stared at him.

"Do your Grandparents know?" said Sparky.

Alfie sighed and slowly shook his head. "I have to try and find a Sword that's been taken from where it should have been and find the person who has taken it."

"But," said Sparky. "The woman in the mirror said that if you go after the Sword now it will only lead to more trouble… Devils and fire," he shuddered.

"So what!" said Tommy. "It was only some old bag… if Alfie doesn't go after the Sword, he will *DIE*!"

Sparky chewed on Tommy's words, unconvinced, clearly he didn't want to be anywhere near a *devil*, if such a thing existed.

"She's the Dice Duchess," said Gracie importantly. "She knows what's she's talking about." Tommy shrugged.

"How did you lot get out yesterday?" said Alfie remembering, they hadn't even spoke of their capture. "I mean, after they black bagged us."

"We just got chucked in a room, next to yours I think," said Tommy. "They left the bags on though, horrible thing, kept telling me nasty things, anyway then the three Guards came and saved us, then went after you."

"They risked a lot to come and save us Alfie…" said Gracie. "A lot."

He didn't think about that. Suddenly he felt awful that

he hadn't thanked any of them for what they did, what they sacrificed for him. Anything could have happened, it was a reckless idea in the first place—Alfie had felt so excited for working it all out, that he risked everything to return to Magicity. It was... selfish of him.

"What did that man Shreeve do to you?" said Gracie, and Alfie suppressed a shudder when she said his name.

"Just asked questions, mostly about Wiseman and about the Sword, why I was in Magicity etc, etc. I accidentally let it slip that the Sword was a fake though." He grimaced.

Gracie shrugged. "I don't think that matters."

"Oh no," said Tommy suddenly. He stood up, with a panicked expression on his face. "Oh NOOO!" he called.

"What? What is it?" said Alfie. Sparky was cowering against the back of the chair looking round the room as Tommy clamped his hands to his face.

"Tommy! Tell us what's happened," said Gracie loudly.

"I've..." Tommy struggled, tears forming in his eyes. "I've just remembered... I left my school bag *IN THE MIRROR SHOP!*" He wailed at the top of his voice, a pitying cry of hurt.

Gracie looked perplexed. "So what?" she said. "That's the least of your worries, we got out alive didn't we?"

But it suddenly dawned on Alfie why Tommy was so upset. "Oh no," said Alfie clapping his hands to his face.

"Will someone please tell me what has happened?" Gracie called.

"Tommy, I'm *so* sorry," said Alfie.

Sparky tapped Tommy on the shoulders and looked at Gracie. "He had his Gnarlus Paper in that bag..."

Gracie frowned. "How on earth did you have some Gnarlus Paper? Really valuable that is!" Tommy wailed even harder.

293

"Sorry, sorry!" she said.

"And now *IT'S GONE!*" Tommy wailed again collapsing on the sofa in a heap.

It took a whole hour to try and calm Tommy down. In between muffled yelps, mumbling feebly that he was going to use it to get some answers about what happened yesterday and how his life was now over because he was going to fail his exams.

"It's okay mate," said Alfie, who was secretly very annoyed, the Gnarlus Paper would be long gone by now and it could have given them answers. "Best to forget about it now, the fire would have disposed of it," said Alfie as Gracie grimaced, it was her fire spell.

"How am I going to pass my exams NOW!" Tommy called, and Gracie frowned suddenly understanding Tommy's rise to the top of the class in every subject.

Over the coming weeks school became excruciatingly tense — the end of year exams were less than three weeks away. The teachers were on tenterhooks as they organised extra classes (Alfie was invited to all of them). Some of the teachers were not brilliant at coping with the stress at all well. One, Miss Graves, nearly feinted in Geography because her class didn't understand the formation of clouds. The art teacher Miss Cairney ran out the room screaming because the scissors weren't sharp enough and Mr Woodbridge the English teacher started shouting at a pile of textbooks for no apparent reason.

In fact the only teacher dealing with it all with any respect was Mr Taylor-Swift, who had changed dramatically since his 'breakdown', and was the only one who didn't give copious amounts of homework and revision.

Tommy had almost gone the same way as some of the teachers since realizing he had lost his Gnarlus Paper, and all his school text books—his Mum was so thoroughly confused as to why he was so upset about losing his school bag, that she forgot to be angry with him and bought him a new one. Sparky saw it as some sort of divine retribution, *"cheats never prosper..."* he said, causing Tommy to almost pierce him with a paintbrush.

Each new week they turned up the teachers and staff would announce they were not working hard enough, more revision was needed! Sparky was turning halfway into the frightening halloween mask Alfie had used to get into Magicity. His face becoming red and blotchy, his hair frazzled and fly-away. Even Gracie, who was always so calm and in control, looked frantic. She would wave to Alfie across the classroom when they caught each others eye and had promised him before she left his house that she would continue to search for answers with her Dad. When they tried to speak at school however, Christian, was never far away, with Joel sniggering behind them. Alfie still had the same funny feeling in his stomach whenever Gracie looked over, or when they spoke and he still held a fleeting feeling that she might like him too, and as more than a friend—but then the small voice in his head would tell to not be so stupid. She was beautiful and going out with the best looking guy in the school, and Alfie was short and gaunt with long curly hair. His Grandma had been making mutterings about Alfie's hair, that she would like to *'sort it out'*. Alfie knew she was angling to take him to the hairdressers. But poor Alfie was still scarred from when he went a couple of years ago and they cut his hair so badly it resembled a large fish bowl on the top of his head. He was laughed at for weeks in school. He was safe for now however, his Grandma was too preoccupied with getting Alfie to actually revise and had been on ruthless form. She sat near him on the end of his bed knitting while he worked, fetching him sandwiches and cups of tea while he worked. Alfie read about civil wars, algebra, rock formations, times tables, a book about a mockingbird, wood work theory, French words and phrases, chemistry, physics, biology, artists and paintings and a play for drama about blood brothers. Day would turn to night before his Grandma would let him leave, most times Alfie would collapse on his bed and fall asleep. Some of the time, when Tommy and Sparky were both allowed out too, they would meet up. But it was rare. When his Grandma would go to bed, Alfie would lay awake in bed, thinking about his Dad. *His Dad* who was a wizard. Who could do magic. Alfie wondered if that's why he had the powers he did, because his Dad was a wizard. Alfie cursed himself that he didn't get a number, or contact details for his Dad, he desperately wanted to call him and ask him all these questions that bubbled just under the surface of his brain. Did he live in Magicity? Or in the magical world somewhere else? Did he work with magic? Did he have a magic job?

Alfie hid the new spell his Dad gave him in his side table. He committed it to memory first, like the others. His Dad said it would work against the Shadow, but Alfie knew he needed a proper solution, like the Sword. With all the studying and revising he hadn't had time to investigate anything. The loss of the Gnarlus Paper was a kick in the teeth to possible answers and clues.

By late Spring Alfie was almost sick to the back teeth of revising, and not being allowed out, or even time to think. He even debated telling his Grandma *everything*, maybe she would relent with the endless studying. But he knew deep down, it would be too much for her to take. Magic was outside both his grandparents vision of the world. She would call Alfie crazy and call the doctor round with the white coats, most probably.

A few weeks before the exams were due to start Alfie, Tommy and Sparky were sitting on the field. The sun was out but they didn't have chance to enjoy it. Sparky had all his books laid out on the grass and was flitting between History and Maths. Alfie was finishing his sandwich and reading some of Tommy's notes he had grudging made about the book they had read for English.

"Can I have a bite? I'm starving…" said Sparky. "Mum won't let me eat anything at home at the moment because I accidentally broke the fridge and all the food went mouldy." Alfie handed him the rest of the sandwich.

"Bummer," said Tommy.

Suddenly a sweet voice behind them cut across the hubbub, making Alfie's insides go all gooey. "Hello you lot."

Alfie spun round. Gracie looked as if she was sparkling in the sun light, her golden skin twinkling like a million diamonds as she handed out three tickets. "These are for you three."

Alfie suddenly thought madly of Magicity tickets.

"What is it?" said Tommy, huffing.

Gracie flattened her dress, moved one of Sparky's books and sat down, causing him to frown. "They're tickets, for Ashley's Birthday party next week."

Tommy's face suddenly lit up. "Really? Cool, and she wants us to come?"

"Well," said Gracie grimacing. "Not really, you know what she's like, but she said I can give some out to people I want to come."

"Thanks Gracie," said Alfie, reading the ticket and laughing. The card was an ornate white card with pink frilly bits all over and read:

Yay!
You have been invited to Ashley Di Franco's Birthday Party!
Fancy dress—classic film theme.
Bring presents.

From Tuesday to Friday that week Sparky was strangely off school. Alfie and Tommy were concerned, this was not like Sparky, not all at. He was annoying early for school and had hardly missed a day all year. On Friday night Alfie and Tommy decided to go and see him and find out what was wrong with him. Also, they wanted him to come to Ashley's birthday party which was on Saturday night.

"Do you know where he lives?" said Alfie.

"Yeah…" said Tommy. "Been there *once*, over at South Westbury. His Mum's a bit of a *nutter*. Just to warn you."

After a long walk all the way to the end of town, they arrived at a small dishevelled semi-detached house on the corner of a rather rough looking street. As Tommy knocked on the door a large, aggressive dog immediately began to bark. Alfie gave Tommy a concerned look, they didn't like big barky dogs and they couldn't imagine Sparky did either.

A large woman opened the door and scowled down at them. She was a harsh looking women with a tight greasy bun on the top of her head and scary uncaring eyes that peered through bushy eyebrows—but she did look a lot like Sparky.

"Yeah?" she said. "Who are you?"

"Hello Mrs Sparker, we were wondering if Daniel was in?"

said Tommy in his best parents voice. She pushed the door open and walked off. They walked through a cramped hallway filled with old newspapers and bicycles. "He's in the garden…" she said as if they should have known. "Where he belongs!"

Navigating their way into the garden they saw a sizeable, but run down shed at the bottom. Tommy knocked on the shed door.

"Sparky?" he called. "It's us, Alfie and Tommy." There was a short shuffling noise and the door opened.

"Come in," he mumbled. As Alfie went in, he saw a bed in one corner with a small desk covered in school books, and chair next to it with a lamp. Behind the door was a small workstation, with wood carving equipment. As they ducked to go inside, they saw Sparky sitting on the end of his bed—oddly, with a paper bag on his head. Alfie didn't know what to ask first.

"Do you live *in here?*" said Alfie perplexed. Sparky's papery head nodded.

"*Why* mate?" said Tommy.

"Not enough room in the house, anyway I like it. Gets me away from *them*," he said, with toxic anguish.

"Okay, second question…" said Alfie. "Why have you got a bag on your head? I'm guessing that's why you've been away for the last week?" Alfie sort of didn't want to see what was underneath.

Tommy suddenly stepped back towards the door. "It's not contagious is it?"

"It's your bloody fault!" said Sparky, loudly, pointing at Alfie with a gloved hand.

"My fault?" said Alfie. "What did I do?"

Slowly, Sparky pulled the brown bag off his head. Alfie and Tommy gasped, then burst out laughing. Sparky's face was completely green. His skin, all over his body was the brightest green, not a patch was missed.

"How could you?" said Sparky pulling a mirror close and inspecting himself again. "You knew that cheese was magical... I was starving!"

Alfie could hardly reply, he was laughing so hard and holding Tommy for support.

"Is that the cheese that you got him from *ha-ha*... Magicity?" said Tommy through fits of laughter.

"LISTEN!" cried Sparky. "It's our exams in two weeks! How can I take them looking like *THIS*? Oh god! I'm gonna have no qualifications, I'm not going to get a good job, I'm going to be like them..." he pointed at his house. "I'll have to clean toilets for a living or something..."

"Oh shut up!" said Alfie. "It's fine, look I'll ask Gracie, she must know a cure or something. You won't miss your exams."

"I haven't been out the shed in a week..." said Sparky looking crazed.

Tommy, who finished laughing remembered why he was here. "But you have to be better by tomorrow, it's Ashley Di Marco's party! Everyone is going to be there!"

"Oh yeah," said Sparky his voice dripping with sarcasm. "That will be brilliant, I'll wear my best shirt... and in case you hadn't noticed I'm BLOODY GREEN!"

After half an hour trying to calm Sparky down, they all sat round and discussed what they were to do. Alfie and Tommy were pleased with their conclusion—Sparky would come to the party.

It was a calm and sunny evening in Westbury, perfect for a garden birthday party. Alfie, Tommy and Sparky had spent most of the day preparing their costumes. Sparky ventured out of his shed and walked to Tommy's house in a balaclava, gloves, scarf and biggest coat Alfie had ever seen—he looked like a huge ninja.

But now, as they walked across the gravel driveway to Ashley's house and saw the huge mansion they clapped each other on the back—this looked amazing.

Ashley answered the door and for a moment, just stared.

"Hi Ashley..." said Tommy.

"Wow," she managed. After going inside and being guided into the garden they managed to cause quite a stir. There were a lot of people here, most of the school in fact and they all turned to look at them.

Tommy, who was covered in copious amounts of tin foil and cardboard boxes—was the tin man. Alfie who was wearing his lion mask and a yellow boiler suit with homemade fluffy tail was a the lion and Sparky who was dressed in a very extravagant floating black dress, black hat and broomstick—was the wicked witch. They had decided that it was the perfect solution, Sparky was already green, they couldn't change that. So they would go as characters from The Wizard of Oz.

"Ha ha!" cried Nigel running over to them dressed as Superman with a camera. "Those costumes are brilliant!"

After a while the fuss died down, much to Sparky's relief, who had been told quite flatly by Ashley that she specifically said 'no paint.'

When Ashley left Sparky punched them as Alfie and Tommy laughed behind their masks.

The garden was huge, it had a swimming pool, a large marquee tent with drinks and food, a DJ blasting out happy party music across the garden and even a clown stood by a flower bed performing balloon tricks. Everyone they knew was at the party. Alfie spotted Jessica Curdle dressed as a candlestick, Henry Goofham dressed as Charlie Chaplin and weird Aaron dressed in his school clothes. Alfie spotted Christian and Joel standing idly by the conservatory. Christian was dressed smartly as some sort of prince charming and Joel, who Alfie would have loved to see in a frog outfit, stood next to him dressed as a vampire. Alfie thought this was a better choice, as he could suck the life out of any room, Tommy laughed when Alfie told him this. Then Alfie caught sight of Gracie who was carrying drinks outside for her and Christian. She was dressed as Snow White with a long flowing blue, red and white dress with gold lapels. Her hair was tied up, and her lips glowed bright red. When she spotted Alfie, Tommy and Sparky (who she didn't recognise at first), she handed both drinks to Christian and bounded towards them looking happy. "You came!" she said.

"Sure did," said Alfie and she hugged each of them, which was hard because Tommy had a large silver cardboard box for a head and Alfie, a big bushy mane.

"Cool costume," said Alfie. "Snow White, very… *you*." He went a little red and glad he still had the mask on. "Err… oh yes…" he said remembering as Sparky nudged him frantically. "We have a slight issue with Sparky."

"Go on," said Gracie looking serious. Alfie made sure they were out of earshot moving to some nearby bushes, as they received daggers from Christian and Joel.

"Well, you see Sparky's face…" Alfie pointed at Sparky's bright green face. "Well it's not paint. It's… cheese."

"*Cheese?*" she said, looking at him as if he was mad.

"Yeah cheese," said Tommy, then whispering. "Alfie got it from *Magicity*."

302

"Ohh, I *seee…*" said Gracie, then continued to stare blankly. "So?"

Poor Sparky looked frantic. "Is there a cure? Can you do a spell to make it go away?"

"I don't know, maybe…" she said.

Sparky swallowed. "What do you mean *maybe*? What if I can't do my exams because I am still green?"

"Oh come on…" said Gracie. "Stuff like that only lasts a couple of weeks then it wears off when it leaves your system. Just drink plenty, it's better than finding a spell to rectify it. I might end up doing more damage than good!" she laughed.

Sparky cupped his face in his hands. "Look," said Gracie. "If anyone asks, just say the paint was permanent or won't come off and I'll ask my Dad if he knows anything in the mean time."

Sparky whimpered. "And your sure he can do something about it?"

Gracie smiled reassuringly. "If he can't, I don't know anyone that could. I am positive."

After that reassurance Sparky was fine, he socialised and mingled and even made a few jokes about his greenness.

"Here, got you some drinks," said Tommy, handing Alfie and Sparky another glass each.

"Tommy, I don't want anymore. I still haven't finished these," said Alfie, indicating to the two full glasses in his hands. Alfie didn't know, but he was sure his drinks tasted funny. "Have you been putting things in this?"

"Yeah, but *shhh…*" said Tommy, looking a little slanted as his cardboard face slipped over his eyes. Sparky tutted and propped him up. Alfie had taken his lion mask off because no one knew who he was. The amount of unwanted attention Sparky got for his amazing costume was unparalleled.

As day turned slowly into night the party remained in full swing. There had been a dance off in the middle of the garden in which Sarah Ashdown danced off against Nigel, then Tommy made a fool of himself against Jessica Curdle. Christian tried to dance but got laughed off, and Gracie held her face in her hands with embarrassment. Joel tried to talk to Ashley and give her a drink but she blanked him completely causing Alfie and Tommy to laugh hysterically. Joel saw them laughing and skulled off. Nigel came up to Alfie at one point and told him he was the best next door neighbour ever and he was going to write a newspaper about his moment. "What have you been drinking?" said Sparky.

Later on Alfie nearly got locked into a conversation with weird Aaron about donkeys. Then walked off, he'd lost Tommy and Sparky. He walked around the edge of the swimming pool, which was perfectly still, and scoured the garden. The large tent was almost bereft of food now, after a food fight broke out. Tommy got Joel in the eye with a mini apple pie, and Sparky shouted at them all that it was a waste of food. Henry Goofham got hit by a custard tart in the melee and went home crying. Then Alfie saw Tommy, standing behind the marquee tent with Ashley, standing in relative shadow away from the crowd.

"Hey," said a voice. Alfie wheeled around to see Sarah Ashdown.

"Oh, hi Sarah…" said Alfie, voice quavering as he looked around to see if she intended to speak to someone else. She had taken her costume off after the food fight and stood in one of Ashley's old t-shirts.

"Want to take a dip?" she said smiling, glancing towards the still swimming pool.

Alfie swallowed. "Err," he hesitated. "It looks cold."

"Oh come, on you big baby!" she looked at him pleadingly.

Sarah jumped straight in without hesitation, breaking the calm surface. Alfie took off his shoes and yellow lion costume, luckily underneath he had a shirt and shorts on. He climbed in slowly, it was freezing.

"See," she said. "This is fun!" The pool was lit by underwater lights. Sarah paddled towards him. "So," she said flicking her hair back. "Looking forward to the exams?" everything she said sounded seductive.

"Oh yeah, can't wait to get stuck into those exams!"

Sarah laughed. "You're funny!"

"Comes naturally with being short and odd looking."

"Ha-ha!" cried Sarah laughing hard. "You're not odd looking." She smiled.

Alfie felt a funny feeling in his stomach that was usually reserved for Gracie. Sarah smiled and chewed her lip, then splashed him.

It was nice, being in the pool with Sarah—on their own—most people had gone inside. Alfie taught her how to float on the waters surface. She made him hold her up while she got used to it. Alfie wasn't quite sure where to put his hands. After ten minutes she had mastered it and they floated on the surface of the water together, staring up at the clear, starry night sky talking idly about their lives, (Alfie not mentioning anything magical).

"Do you ever think…" she said. "That there is… I dunno, more to life? Somehow, I can't explain it. It's like, sometimes I just think there must be more? Something else."

Alfie smiled to himself. "I know exactly what you mean. I think there are places and things we never thought were possible that we will understand one day."

Sarah sighed. "Do you think so? I would love to find out now. I find it hard to subscribe to the normal way of things. My parents want me to be a doctor. Honestly that's a million miles away from what I want."

"What do you want?" said Alfie.

"Adventure. Quests, searching for hidden treasure, old maps and books, I don't know. It's more of a feeling. A feeling of wanting… something different I suppose. It's hard to explain."

"Well maybe one day, you will." Alfie smiled to himself again.

"Your nice," she said, cocking her head to the side and smiling.

"Thanks, your nice too…" Alfie couldn't help feeling that he'd done rather well for the (second) prettiest girl in the school to be floating next to him alone in the swimming pool telling him he was nice. For a moment, their hands touched and neither did anything.

"Shall we get out?" said Sarah, slowly. "It's getting a bit cold. I'll get us some towels from inside."

They paddled to the edge and got out. It was cold and Alfie shivered. Sarah too, but she limped off inside. Gracie was standing inside the conservatory, Alfie didn't see her watching him. Tommy came up behind him suddenly.

"Werhay!" he called. "Alfie, I think you have pulled the prettiest girl in school!"

"No, no… it's not like that!"

Tommy frowned again. "It looked like that to *meee*. Anyway I thought you liked Gracie?"

Alfie swallowed. He did, but he didn't have a chance with her and she going out with Christian. Anyway he was pretty sure he didn't have a chance with Sarah Ashdown either. "I don't… they, she… its not… Oh I don't know!" he said flustered.

"Anyway, what was going on with you and Ashley behind the marquee?"

Tommy smiled. "We just spoke. It was cool. Anyway, I'll er leave you to it," he said as Sarah returned with some towels as Tommy walked inside, he turned halfway and gave him the thumbs up.

"Here we are," she said shivering again.

After drying and dressing they went back indoors "I'll get us some drinks," said Sarah.

But as Alfie got to the patio doors, Gracie walked outside with a strange look on her face. Sarah walked straight in and only glanced behind before she disappeared into the crowd. Alfie felt his heart sink a little—but then it fluttered wildly as Gracie now cornered him outside, alone.

"You okay?" she said, her voice loaded.

"Fine. Are you okay?" Alfie said softly.

"Fine," she said, then moved a little closer. Now they stood in a large pool of darkness next to the conservatory. "I saw you and Sarah, getting on well. That's good, really good." Gracie looked odd, not like she usually did, not calm or in control, but odd. "You... you have to be careful with girls like *her*."

Alfie didn't know what she meant but nodded anyway, staring straight into Gracie's perfect eyes and perfect face. The dark pool of shadow around him reminding him that he might never Gracie's true beauty ever again.

"I just... I just want you to know that... I..." Gracie stuttered. Her eyes sparkled and flickered to his mouth. "I really..."

"What?" said Alfie softly. Gracie had a tear in the corner of her eye.

"...I want..." she bit her lip. "Y—"

"What's going on out here?" came a sly, nasal voice. Gracie

jumped away from Alfie and turned. Joel was staring at them.

"Nothing, nothing!" said Gracie. "Anyway, what do you want Joel?" she said, obviously she didn't like him much either. Alfie was livid, his blood boiling, Joel must have seen Gracie come out with him and had ruined… *everything*.

And that was that. The moment passed frustratingly away. Gracie gave Alfie a short look then went back indoors. Alfie too, to find Tommy and Sparky, his legs feeling like jelly after that strange encounter. He drifted back in, dazed and immediately saw Joel, now boldly going up to Sarah who stood alone, and engaging her in conversation. Alfie thought steam might explode from his ears. He swallowed hard, no way was Joel going to get away with this. Alfie had a sudden and devilish idea. He raised his hands at the glass in Joel's hand and said. "*Vanearo…*" the glass vanished out of his hand. But the contents in it, went right down Sarah's front. She gasped. Then, she slapped Joel square round the face. *WHACK*! It echoed around the room.

"WERHAYY!" called the crowd, as Sarah stormed off and Joel stood looking thoughroughly confused. Serves him right, Alfie thought.

After Alfie told Tommy and Sparky what happened outside with Gracie, someone nearby was sick everywhere. "Ut-*ohh…*" said Tommy. "She *is not* going to be happy!"

Sure enough, Ashley let out an ear piercing scream. "All OVER THE PERSIAN RUUUUUG!"

They were all evicted and the party ended and all the classic film characters walked home. Alfie didn't see Sarah Ashdown again, nor Gracie—and he left with a tight knot in his stomach.

It was the week of the exams. Everyone was wound up, from

his Grandma waking him up extra early to cram some revision in, to Tommy who was also being nagged in the same way by his mother who had told him that "Fifteen years of education had led to his moment…"

"So no pressure," said Tommy.

Sparky was fretting too, but not as much as he would if he was still green, it had, mostly worn off, only a few patches remained. The teachers were acting as if their lives depended on it the outcome of the next few weeks and even Mr Sapiens looked unusually forlorn.

Alfie felt nervous going back to school on Monday, mainly because he hadn't spoken to Gracie since the party. When he did see her, sitting with Ashley on a school bench, away from Christian for once, she caught Alfie's eye, then looked away pretending she hadn't noticed him. Sarah too, didn't even say hello to Alfie when she walked into class first thing Monday morning. She simply swept in as if nothing had happened, sat next to Jessica and blew a big bubble gum bubble. The teachers in every lesson went round and made sure that each pupil had the right equipment for each exam—pencil, pen, protractors, rulers, rubbers, calculators and everything else.

Their first exam was maths. Alfie had crammed in as much theory as possible before and they all lined up outside the hall in silence. Joel and Christian stood just ahead looking sullen and Gracie and Ashley behind staring into the ground. Henry Goofham was sharpening his pencil and Jessica Curdle was tapping her calculator to make sure it worked.

"In we go. Good luck everyone!" called Mr Ward, as if they were going into battle. This was it, what they had spent the last ten years preparing for. They all walked quietly in to the musty hall, with its echoing wooden floor, small desks and chairs which lined the hall in perfect lines. The large exam clock stood at the front of the hall, with two suited exam invigilators either side, holding large piles of exam papers. They walked round and found their seats which were marked with their name. Alfie was just off to the right, but towards the middle of the hall. Tommy was just a few seats behind him and distractingly Gracie was right within Alfie's line of vision up ahead to his left. Mr Taylor-Swift, Mr Ward and Miss Cairney stood at the front of the hall with the invigilators.

"You may…" said Mr Ward watching the big clock high above them. "Begin!" There was a scuffle of paper as the booklets were opened and the exam started.

The rest of the exams came thick and fast throughout the next two weeks. Alfie started to get very tired and depressed, the routine was unbearable. His Grandma would make him revise for the next days exam straight away when he got home. The one thing keeping him going was the fact that he would see his Dad at the end of it.

English was next, and by the end of it Alfie thought his hand might fall off with all the writing. He had to write a short story, so wrote about a boy, whose shadow detaches itself and comes after him, hell bent on killing him—the boy finds a Sword hidden in a stone and kills the shadow with the help of a wise old wizard—this one had a happy ending. He hoped his did too.

The next day was science. Alfie loathed science, but managed to get through it relatively unscathed. The same day was geography and on the Friday it was drama, and then technology. Which all passed by like a blur. It started becoming extremely taxing, sitting for long silent hours trying to rack his poor memory for the names of cloud formations and wood work theory. Alfie half wondered whether all his memory was taken up with magic and he didn't have as much room as anyone else for all these facts. The only good thing was that when he finished the exam early, he would have some time to think in relative silence, with no one to disturb him.

The weekend was a godsend. His Granddad had managed to convince his Grandma to give Alfie the afternoon off. She was reluctant, but relented. Alfie used the time well, he slept and dreamt. Only two more exams then he was free.

Alfie was standing outside the exam hall with the rest of the year, pens and pencils in his pockets awaiting the last exam of the year—history. There was a buzz around the playground, in just over two and a half hours they would be totally free! Sparky shuffled awkwardly in front of him as Tommy brushed his hair back glancing towards some girls at the front of the line.

"So what questions do you think we'll get?" said Sparky, he didn't look good, half his shirt was hanging out and his school tie was all chewed up.

"How are we supposed to know," said Tommy. "We would know if we had the Gnarlus Paper. Oh that reminds me, after this exam mate, get ready because we're gonna be burning our ties on the field."

"I'm not burning my tie," said Sparky, chewing it.

Alfie turned back and saw Gracie watching him. She looked away quickly. Alfie's stomach went all funny again. He still hadn't spoken to her since the party, Alfie wondered bleakly if he had done anything wrong. One of Nigel's school newsletters flapped across the playground, caught by a short gust of wind.

Exams Begin!

Read the headline. Alfie watched it flap away across the

concrete. But then his gaze was suddenly caught by something at the back of the playground, where the tall wire fence with the forest behind, shook. It was as if someone had just jumped over it.

"In we go," said Mr Taylor-Swift who began ushering everyone inside.

After two hours Alfie's bum started to feel sore. He shifted uncomfortably, tapping his pen on his hand and glancing around. Most the people in the hall had finished—yet the clock showed they still had half an hour to go. He saw Sparky and Gracie both scribbling away frantically and looked down at his own answers which he was quite pleased with. Alfie leaned back in the chair, he would be seeing his Dad tonight. At last, in all the time he had known him, they could actually have a proper conversation, about magic—he might even have some answers for him.

But then, strange things began to happen… the clock at the front of the exam hall changed before his eyes.

11:11.

No one noticed, except one of the invigilators who got his watch out frowning. A creepy feeling started to wash over Alfie and run down his spine. Something had changed in the air around him. The sun outside had gone behind the clouds and the hall darkened. The Desire Stone burned against his chest. Quickly Alfie pulled it out so it was just visible and made sure no one was looking. It hadn't done or read anything since he last went to Magicity. But now, black ink was swirling round under the surface of the glassy purple stone. Strands connecting together until the words—*'Find Found'* appeared.

Find Found? The phrase startled Alfie and he looked from the clock to the stone. Alfie frowned at it, Find Found? Did it mean Richard Found? It must have done. Did it think he would have the answers? Alfie knew, ever since meeting Richard Found, who had the same purple eyes as him, but with the invaluable experience of defeating his Shadow, that he needed to find him again to get the answers he needed. But he had reasoned against it—he had no idea where to start looking for him. Alfie's spine tingled. He felt a cold rush of air brush across his neck as if someone was touching him.

"Alfie... Alfie..." came a long haunting disembodied voice. He shuddered, not daring to turn round. Then something darted across the opposing wall. People started to look up from their papers, disturbed. Then, as quick as a flash Alfie's pen rose up into the air and stabbed him in his outstretched left hand. Alfie yelped and buckled with pain. Suddenly, there was a massive WHOOSH! All the papers in the exam hall flew into the air.

"AHHHH!" everyone screamed, not knowing what was happening as exam papers reined down around them. Alfie clutching his hand, knew what was happening. He saw dark shadow darting around inside the hall as blood and ink curdled out of his left hand.

"Alfie!" It was Gracie, she was out of her seat and charging towards him. "Alfie, it's here! Get out of here!"

Alfie's heart jumped into his chest. He turned and lunged for the back of the room. The papers still falling like confetti. He charged past Tommy and burst through the fire door. As the door slammed shut behind him, he turned into the playground. Now, something worse, a lot worse, faced him. The Shadow was stood already waiting for him, in the middle of the playground. A thick crazy smile spread across its face, glaring purple eyes peering from under a black top hat and baggy miss-matched clothes. But behind him now were hundreds more Shadows. All different shapes and sizes standing stock still, their deep dark eyes watching him gleefully. Time stopped still. Alfie tried to take in the horror that now faced him. Time had seemed to slow to a crawl. All sound had vanished as if they stood in a void. But he could feel the terror rising up inside his stomach—he could feel the power of the dark shapes watching him. He could feel the glee inside his Shadow, it could taste victory.

Without waiting another second, Alfie ran. He saw the Shadow wave his arms and hundreds of shadow people sprinted after him. Alfie turned right into the main corridor and sprinted as hard as he could. Several thoughts occurred to him at once—why had the Wiseman's defences failed again? He was meant to be keeping him safe. What about his Dad? He had saved him from the Guards of Magicity, but where would he be now? Alfie tried to think of somewhere safe. Mr Sapiens office!

"Mr Sapiens!" Alfie started to cry. "Mr Sapiens!" He called in a crazy attempt to be heard. Alfie glanced over his shoulder and fear gripped his insides. He had never seen anything like it. Galloping, sliding, running lop-sided, bouncing and bumping their way towards him were endless silent Shadow people, murderous faces burnt with the task of capturing him. Alfie turned a sharp left at the end of the long corridor. He slammed into the door at the end and burst through into the courtyard. But then he stopped. Up ahead, three shadow people were waiting for him.

Alfie took a deep breath before screaming. "PETIVO!" Time slowed as purple sparks ignited at the end of his finger tips, then the air swelled. A ball of purple swirling light gathered between his hands. Fizzing and popping. Then, all at once, burst towards them like a cannon.

BOOM! The ball exploded into the middle shadow casting them fifty feet into the air. Alfie burst onwards ignoring the large scorch mark on the concrete. The shadow people were now sliding through the door he had just emerged from. Alfie found a stitch forming in his right side. His legs like melting jelly. The spell *Petivo* had completely taken all of his energy. Pushing open the language block door Alfie stumbled into the wall and pressing it instantly with his hand. He waited, glancing through the doors windows at the shadow people getting closer and closer.

"Come *ON!*" He said helplessly. But the door did not materialise. "Mr Sapiens!" Staring around Alfie pressed his hand into the wall again and again. But nothing happened. Now the Shadows were approaching the door. Alfie turned his hand towards it.

"*Consisto.*" There was a rush of air and a small snap! The language block doors sealed. Alfie pressed his outstretched hand to the wall again and again and again, but to no avail.

"Mr Sapiens! Mr Sapiens!?" There was no reply. The Shadows reached the door and started banging against it. With a sickening feeling Alfie watched some of them start to seep through the crack in the door. Alfie backed off. What did he do now? He needed to escape and find someone, Mr Sapiens, Wiseman, or his Dad.

There were two more doors behind him. Alfie tried the door to the right, locked. Then the left, to his great relief it was open. Alfie slipped inside and ran for the window at the back of the room. Grasping at the catch and shoving it hard, he realised with a horrible knot in his stomach, that it wouldn't budge.

"Please, COME ON!" He cried frustrated. Alfie turned, picked up a chair and threw it at the window. It shattered. The Shadows were at the door behind him. Alfie clambered through as fast as he could. Something caught his leg. Alfie looked back, one of the Shadows had caught his foot.

"AH! Get off!" Alfie kicked out. But his foot went through its head. He thought quickly. "Vanearo!" he cried at his shoe and it vanished. Scrambling away he fell backwards out of the window and caught his right arm against the glass shards. He yelped and clutched it as he landed, wincing as small beads of blood started to appear through his torn shirt. Ignoring the pain he ran round the block and back towards the playground. Hoping, just hoping that Mr Sapiens would see him.

Alfie saw the mass of shadows trying to get into the languages block. All turned at the same time and saw him. He was wobbly on his legs now. But on he ran. Feeling his breath grow shorter and shorter. He tried not to panic. Was this the end? Had he failed? As he ran he caught sight of something in the window of the science department to his left. Wiseman's reflection greeted him, Alfie stopped.

"Wiseman?" said Alfie. "Please, you have to help me… I don't know what to do!" But Wiseman started to grin, horrible pointed teeth dripped blood and slime. Alfie backed away as the reflection started to laugh cold and callous. The echo of the shadow people behind him rumbled deafeningly loud. Alfie, using all his willpower, sprinted ahead again. All of a sudden they were so close they were snapping at his heels. In a desperately cry, Alfie jumped over a small fence that ran round the lunch park. He heard several crunches, as some of them collided with it. Alfie tried to put that vision of Wiseman out of his mind, it wasn't real, it couldn't have been. A purple glow greeted the corner of his eye. He didn't notice it at first. But then, as his lungs burned, and side felt as if it was splitting open, he saw it. As he came back round into the playground, which was now empty, he saw... a purple stream of light shooting upwards into the sky, a little way off into the school, near... reception.

It was the hope Alfie needed. He think he knew where this purple light was coming from—the old library! Alfie took one look behind him at the galloping monsters and with all his remaining strength exploded towards reception. Alfie rammed through the doors into the corridor, nearly getting knocked out in the process. The horde of shadow people approaching fast. He sprinted past the hall, and turned left at reception. He stopped before the old corridor. Purple light was spilling out of the old library. Alfie, trotted forwards towards it. Hoping against hope that the answer to his problems was in here.

"Ha, ha, ha..." came a raucous cry from the other end of the old corridor. "Thought it was that easy did you?"

Alfie stopped. The echoing footsteps of the shadow people were approaching fast behind him.

"Who's there?" called Alfie.

His Shadows purple eyes appeared in front of him, seemingly to float in the middle of the corridor. The rest of the Shadow appeared. It's dark body, clothes and hat swirling round until it became whole. Alfie's heart was beating so fast after the chase he thought he might collapse. The shadow people that were chasing him, appeared behind him now and his Shadow waved at them to stay where they were. Alfie was trapped. Yet, the door to the old library was very slightly ajar. If only he could get to it. His Shadow very slowly, started to walk forwards.

"At last..." it laughed, speaking in a posh, well mannered voice. Alfie remembered the last time it could hardly speak, opting just to growl. "As you can see, I've been very busy…"

Alfie knew that if he was to do something, it had to be now. Hundreds of thoughts were racing through his mind, as he stood, wobbling and breathing hard, clutching the stitch in his side. The purple light from the Old Library was spilling out into the hallway, beckoning him inside. He didn't know what to do once he was in there, but he sure as hell knew that it was better than whatever was about to happen here.

At that moment the Desire Stone lit up. Huge rays of bright purple light streamed through the corridor.

"*Ahh!*" cried the Shadow which began to shield it's eyes.

Alfie took his chance. With his heart in his throat he lunged for the old library door. He sailed across the threshold and skidded across rough carpet. The Shadow looked up furious and raised its hands. Alfie, from the floor, raised his hands too.

"Comparle-Compesco-Capiri!" cried Alfie at the top of his voice.

He felt a burning hot sensation run down both arms, his palms seared with pain as a pure silver light ruptured the air. The Shadow suddenly raged, screaming, in absolute uproar—from inside a tight glassy, luminous white, glassy box. Alfie crawled backwards against the carpet. The rest of the shadow people came into view from the corridor. Staring down at him, their murderous faces were intent on his murder. But miraculously, the white light wouldn't allow them. It sparked, and expelled a shard of white light sealing across the doorway. Alfie turned over and saw, past the bookcases, the purple wall glowing. A face swam up into the surface of the purple wall—Richard Found.

There was a cracking noise behind him, Alfie turned again—ripping his eyes away from the hypnotic purple wall.

The Shadow was raging and screaming. Sending red sparks shooting around him inside the silver box. But now, it had done something, the ball had cracked like glass, a tall shatter line stretching across the middle. Alfie didn't have long. But as he turned back to the purple wall, long stretching strands of light were reaching out to him. Begging him forwards, towards the purple wall. Alfie felt his weary legs moving.

There was a momentous shattering sound. The Shadow was out.

Without turning back to look, Alfie looked up at Richard Founds face in the purple wall and ran. He felt the light accepting him, pulling him forwards. And then, instead of smashing into solid wall—Alfie went straight through it. The Shadow roared as Alfie felt himself soaring through purple sky. The roaring fell away like an echo from a lost dream. And then, he felt himself falling, falling very fast.

18

The Deal with Found

As soon as he jumped through that wall, Alfie didn't feel entirely himself. It was as if he had entered a dream world. He had passed through the purple rock as easily as through a thin sheet of water. But now, as he soared high above a snowy kingdom, he felt odd. It was the same feeling as when the clocks would strike *11:11*. That ominous, dangerous feeling, usually right before something bad happened. But how could it? He had just been saved.

Alfie soared through the air like he had been catapulted, but now he was slowing—and yet, he was not falling. Rather, he descended gracefully as a feather. Slowly gliding towards the new world below. The snow flakes collided with his face tickling him, as they swirled through the air. He was gliding down, down to a snowy world below. Huge swathes of Fir trees, showing small patches of green beneath their snowy coats, covered the land below. Snow capped mountains, lay like vast worlds of their own, many miles off in all directions, under a huge grey sky. It was the strangest sensation—time felt completely different—he could have just been soaring towards the ground for days. As he touched down, he noticed even the snow didn't feel quite right, it was soft and bouncy. Up ahead and all around him was a dark, dead looking forest with long, sharp spindly branches reaching down to the ground like long bony arms, surrounded by high, mean prickly bushes. Alfie turned around on the spot and saw he was in the middle of a small, snowy hollow. He stood cold and confused, wearing only his school shirt. Despite feeling dreamy and far away, he still acknowledged the fact that he had just come through the purple wall and escaped his Shadow unscathed, yet again. His heart was still beating six to the dozen and his breath felt short and dry in his throat. He looked around to see if he could see the purple wall. Above the snow fell thick and fast. He couldn't see it—there was no way back. He pulled the Desire Stone out, it might have new instructions on where to go or what to look for. Alfie was disappointed, it continued to read *'Find Found'*. Was Richard Found somewhere in here? Alfie severely doubted it, they had met in London. This place, wherever he was, was as far away from London as you could possibly get.

Alfie knew he had to start walking, to get out of the cold as much as anything. A small knot formed in his stomach. He was scared and felt on the border of panic. He didn't know where he was, or where he was supposed to go. And he was cold, so very cold.

Slowly but surely he moved, drifting through the forest and across the spongy snow. He shivered and held onto himself as he trudged on and on until his feet felt sore and worn. Alfie wished above all things that his friends were with him. He imagined Gracie, Tommy and Sparky next to him—trudging along, Sparky would be moaning and complaining about the walking. Tommy would be trying to engage him in a conversation about magic. Gracie would be thinking about where the sword could be, and thinking of a way out of this place. Alfie sighed, it was selfish of him to want them here with him, they would hate it here as much as he did. He couldn't keep dragging them into his mess. Alfie kept walking, the landscape didn't change, snow, trees, bushes, snow, trees, bushes, snow, trees, bushes. Small cold drafts worked their way inside the rips in his shirt and trousers. Once or twice he thought he saw something, watching from a nearby tree, in amongst the dark snaking thorns. But when he looked closer, there was nothing there.

The rest of the walk was dreamlike, the darkness of night started to set in, even though Alfie had no idea what the time was or how long he had been here for. He passed more trees, hills, and snow—the cold became biting and the wind whipping. The landscape never seemed to change. Snow and sleet started soaring and spinning until all Alfie could see was white. His head began pounding with the cold. He scraped around through the trees desperate to find some shelter. Soon, he found it in a small hollow of a tree. Crawling inside he fell asleep, feeling low and on the border of death—barely able to think, he curled up, pulling earth and twigs over himself, resting his head against the soft bark and slipping away into a deep, dark, cold dream.

It could have been days, months or years. The linear passing of time here did not exist. Whatever this place was—it certainly wasn't like anywhere else he'd ever been. Alfie, with his head pressed against the cold inside of the tree dreamed of someone finding him. A tall man with purple eyes and a kind, chiselled face. He dreamed of being carried along by this man, through the snow, except the man had made a warm invisible blanket to surround him. Then through the thorns and dead forest a giant grey stone building loomed up ahead of them. Stood on flat, soggy land in a tree and bush-less surround. Orange light flickered warm and alluring through the windows in every room. The sky behind the house was a deep, dark green and purple which hovered low on the horizon, before fading into black with twinkling dots spreading slowly across the vast baron sky. He dreamed of being safe, and warm.

Alfie woke, eyes shooting open. He blinked and rubbed them, feeling disorientated. He was in bed. He sat up slowly, this didn't feel like *his* bed. As his eyes blinked away the fogginess he saw that this wasn't his room either. He was lying in a tall, soft four poster with heavy sheets. The room was big, two very large floor to ceiling windows let in streams of bright sunlight. There was a fireplace across the room which was big and open with a lovely warm orange fire flickering away inside the grate. Above was a enormous mirror with dark oak frame. Below that, on the mantelpiece was an antique clock, and although ticking still read *11:11*. Alfie got a funny feeling in his stomach, there it was again—*11:11*. The strange feeling of being outside time still remained, although not as strongly as last night. It was a smart room in all, with three leather sofa's around the fire, a big old bookcase with leather bound books. Two doors; one next to the bed and the other next to the fireplace, opposed the windows. Alfie felt curious and anxious as to what was behind them. Someone must have found him and brought him here.

He peeled the sheets back and stood, he felt ok, considering what had happened, if it was even real. Looking down, he realised he was wearing striped pyjama's. His school clothes, which now resembled tattered rags, sat in a small folded pile on a nearby chair. The floor of the room was wooden and creaked as he moved. Alfie wandered over to the window, keeping his ears open for noises. Outside the window was a soggy, wet lawn from the melted snow. Grass stretched out a long way into the distance, before a thick set and dark, forest. It wasn't a dream, Alfie was in that forest last night. Snow could still be made out in dribs and drabs amongst the trees too. But who on earth had saved him?

He eventually plucked up the courage to open one of the doors and see where he was. But the strangest thing happened. When he opened the first door—the one next to the fireplace—it opened out onto… exactly the same room. Alfie saw himself, peering round a door. He looked behind himself at the door next to the bed and it was slightly ajar. Through the gap however he could see a boy with purple eyes and striped pyjama's looking off to his right. Alfie blinked and gazed and looked from one door to the other, trying to get his head round it. This door he faced, if he walked through it, led out to the other one and straight back into this room. Alfie stepped forwards over the doors threshold. And now stood next to his bed. Alfie went and sat on the end of the bed and stared at those doors for a good ten minutes. It wasn't the fact that they led to each other that scared him—it was the fact that there was now, no obvious way out of here.

His stomach rumbled ominously and he wondered if he would ever eat again. Alfie paced around the room and tried to recall everything that had happened. He was in his exams when the Shadow made an appearance. Luckily in the melee of the exam papers flying into the air he had made an escape—but then he was chased by an army of them around the school. Alfie glanced at his right arm and rolled his sleeve up. There was a short gash where he had caught it on the glass of the window pane when he jumped out of the window. Then, he followed the purple light shining from the old library, but his Shadow beat him to it. Alfie had used the spell his Dad gave him, it had worked, buying him just enough time to get through the purple wall. Alfie suddenly remembered, he was meant to be seeing his Dad after school last night! What if his Dad thought Alfie didn't turn up because he never wanted to see him again? He sighed, he would have to explain to him after—if he ever got out of here, and if, he could find a way of contacting his Dad.

Alfie became bored and hungry, he poked the fire a bit more, opened all the drawers in the room, which were empty, walked through the doors in a large loop many times, then laid on the bed wondering and trying not to panic that he couldn't get out, and why no one was here to tell him what was going on.

"Would you like some tea?" came a smart voice. Alfie jumped and bolted upright, he'd almost drifted off back to sleep again. He gazed as a tall, smart man was standing pouring tea into two cups.

"R-*r*-*r*... Mr *F*-Found?" Alfie stammered, sliding off the bed and standing upright awkwardly. Richard Found glanced up, purple eyes glinting from the fire and waved the teapot in the air. "Err yes, yes please."

Found pushed the cup and saucer across the coffee table. Alfie went over and took it, feeling rather embarrassed standing in pyjama's. "But, you're here?"

Richard Found held up a hand slowly. "I know, I know." He said coolly. "You have nothing to worry about here. You're safe now. I also did you the courtesy of bringing you freshly laundered clothes. I hope they fit."

Alfie glanced round, but couldn't see any clothes. Richard

Found pointed without looking to the end of the bed where a neat pile of clothes appeared out of thin air.

Alfie dressed as quick as he could. He now wore a smart white shirt, waistcoat, trousers, navy jumper and even a thin black tie. It wasn't what Alfie would usually wear (except to a funeral) and wouldn't call it lounge wear exactly, but it would do. Found stood by the window, hands behind his back, wearing the same clothes as Alfie now was, but with a purple tie and a long black jacket. He turned and sat down on the sofa, waving for Alfie to do the same. Alfie sipped his tea, which he felt ran all the way down his throat and into his stomach.

"Well, I didn't quite expect to be seeing you again in such a fashion," said Found eventually.

"I know," said Alfie hurriedly, a hundred questions rising to the fore. "Did you find me in the forest?"

Found chuckled and sipped his tea. "Inside the hollow of a tree."

"I see," said Alfie. "The doors, they open out onto each other, there's no way out?"

"It's a Prism. It's what we use to keep magic-folk prisoners." Alfie swallowed and Found read what Alfie was thinking. "No, you're not a prisoner. Think about it, if you can't get out, then I am sure nothing else can get in. Except me. We're in a magical void. It the safest way. Built it when my own Lynch Shadow was after me. Lived in this room for a while," said Found gazing round at it fondly.

"But… I saw you in London on my Art and Drama trip. How on earth did you, of all people, come to find me?"

"I know, strange how these things happen isn't it? I like to think of it as… oh what's it called, a longish word…" Found tapped his head. "Synchronicity! I thought the same." Found frowned, glancing out of the window, his face heavily chiselled, more so than when Alfie met him in the bookshop. But there was that ever so attractive charm and sereneness about him, that put Alfie completely at ease.

Several thoughts bubbled below the surface of Alfie's mind and he struggled to think which one he should ask first. "I've sort of been searching for you for ages... but I didn't know where on earth to look."

Found laughed coldly. "Good job you didn't try, you wouldn't have found me."

"The Desire Stone, it told me to find you. Then your face appeared in the purple wall in my school, I jumped through it and landed in the forest. If it hadn't have been there, the Shadow would have got me."

Found's purple eyes swam, and sorted through Alfie's words. "I have a confession to make..." he said nodding once and putting his tea down. "After our meeting in the café I decided to do something. Something told me I should for I've never seen anyone else with the same eyes as myself and I also know how hard it is having a Lynch Shadow after you, let alone being a child wizard with no training. So I set certain things in order to make sure you found me again when the time was right. I did my research on you of course. One has to be careful. What I found convinced me that you were worth helping. The purple wall you jumped through is an Akashic Gateway. I didn't know where you lived, so left it all up to the magic and low and behold you found me and you are here."

Alfie took another gulp of tea and felt the sugar replenishing some of his energy. "Did you hear about what happened in Magicity?"

Found smiled. "I think you did surprising well, considering.

I have to go and attend to some business now. When I return, tomorrow, we will talk business—the business of this Shadow," said Found putting his tea down abruptly and standing. "That mirror up there will give you everything you need. Food, drink, just ask it what you want. And, help yourself to the books over there in that corner. I should be back here within a day."

"Okay." said Alfie wondering why there was such a rush for Found to leave. "And thank you, for you know… saving me."

"My pleasure." Found, curiously, decided to climb onto the mantelpiece. Without turning back he disappeared through the surface of the mirror as Alfie just stared blankly after the man who had saved him.

Alfie didn't really know how long he was there for. The clock on the mantelpiece never moved from *11:11*. He sat on the leather sofa thinking about Richard Found, someone he had miraculously bumped into in an old book shop, whom he thought was his Dad, and who had the same eyes as him and the same former problems. Now here Alfie was in his house, eating a cheese burger and chips he'd received by asking a mirror. Alfie was a little nervous at first, but his rumbling stomach forced him into action. He looked into his own pale reflection and asked it for some food. Soon enough, a steaming cheese burger and chips, just how he liked them, were sitting just behind the surface. Alfie reached in a took them, then ate happily, soon ordering a fizzy drink and pudding. He lay on the leather sofa and dozed off as the sun drifted off into the deep afternoon. Alfie didn't feel trapped, being in that room, he felt safe and it didn't bother him that he couldn't get out, as Richard Found had said—nothing can get in. Alfie wondered about what Tommy, Sparky and Gracie and everyone else would be thinking about his disappearance. They didn't know he'd gone through the purple wall. Perhaps, thought Alfie shuddering, they had seen the purple light too, followed it into the purple wall and jumped through. They could be in that forest right now, shivering and cold inside a tree hollow.

After finishing his food the plate vanished, replaced with a steaming wet, scented flannel. Alfie washed his hands and face with it before that too vanished. After a short doze he wandered over to the bookcase and flicked through some of the books. Hoping, that inside would be hundreds of fat, juicy spells that he could add to his list. But he was wildly mistaken, these books had nothing of spells in them, nor did they even allude to their being spells in them. They were titled things like:

Academic Appreciations of Apraxiacz's Zodiacal Influences.
Wernham's Dogma in Yoaman's Dutiful Bounty.
The Six Special Signs of Xander's Law.

Alfie continued to flick through, but had literally no idea what any of it was about, or meant. He sat down again, had a drink of tea that he got from the mirror and had a good hard think about what was going on. He needed to ask Found when he returned about how he got rid of his own Shadow—that was, above all, the most important thing and Alfie's priority. Then it was to find out who set the Shadow on him and why. As Alfie drifted off into sleep, night falling outside the window, the fire and the clock didn't change. The fire burned still brightly, as if burning an everlasting log. Alfie felt warm, cosy and safe—nothing could get him here.

He was woken much later, and quite abruptly. Found stood over him shaking Alfie gently. Alfie startled, woke, wiping dribble from his chin. "Sorry…" said Alfie sitting up straight on the sofa. Outside it was still dark, but Found stood expectant and straight backed.

"I've brought some stuff to go through," he said immediately.

Alfie wiped his mouth, and tried to wake himself from his slumber and said instinctively. "What time is it?"

Found smirked. "There is no time here." Found then directed him to a bundle of papers and books on the coffee table. He sat down and began unrolling them.

"I've been doing some digging and I think we can solve your problem," said Found.

Alfie's heart leapt. "Really? You really think you can help me?"

Found looked up and smiled. "Well of course I can."

Alfie grinned, as Found continued to unroll maps and blueprints and opening large books to specific pages. He pulled out a large mug of tea from the mirror and some cups. "I think you will remember, that when we were in the café in London, I told you… that I once had a Shadow after me?"

"I remember," said Alfie, excitely, he had thought of little else since meeting Found.

"Not everyone has the dishonour of that. That's what makes you unique, being an unqualified wizard—but more so, the fact that you too, have purple eyes. No coincidence then that the weapon of choice against this particular demon happens to be the exact same colour and shade."

Alfie leaned forwards, thinking he understood. "You mean, the real sword is purple?"

Found nodded curtly. "It is indeed. The Akashic Sword is not the only weapon against a Lynch Shadow per say, but for you it is by far the best way. I have already held the Akashic Sword. And I do know you already hold the key to it."

"The key? What key?" said Alfie, looking about himself.

Found continued, slowly and hypnotically. "You have seen the large rock in the centre of Magicity—you pulled the pathetic replica out did you not? Well that rock is merely a cheap copy of what it used to be. They got the position correct, but you cannot duplicate Akashic Stone."

"Akashic Stone?" said Alfie, the name caused something to stir in his subconscious.

"Yes, in that same spot seven-hundred and fifty years ago that rock used to be a full sized Akashic Stone, the same size as the rock now. A rock like that has an energy, and the people build their town around it—unknowing of its full power. The sword, they say, grew out of the top of the stone. People would come by, hearing of the myth and would attempt to pull it out. It would attract hundreds of people, hoping that it would come out to them. And the people build their town bigger and bigger as more would come to try their hand at getting it out—until the town grew into a City. Everyone wanted to try. If they could be the one to get the Sword then obviously; money, fame and power would be theirs—they could control the demons, making them their slaves—and that brings great power. A festival was born—the one you went to and every year some chosen people were allowed to try and pull it out. But never did it come out. So the people grew frustrated, one day this frustration boiled over, people went crazy and sent spells flying at it, one after the other. The Akashic Stone's natural defences tried to repel them, but there were so many crazed wizards that when Guards came and dispersed the crowd, the Akashic Stone was a poor pile of shattered pieces. They'd tried to blast it apart and take the Sword. Of course, it doesn't work like that! A couple of people took a piece of the rock but the rest was cleared away and vanished. Because this was a myth, it soon disappeared into obscurity, only able to be found in certain even more obscure books…"

Alfie motioned to the Desire Stone around his neck. "My…"

"Yes your purple Stone, is a piece of that Akashic Stone and thus, to cut a long story short, is the *key* to finding the Akashic Sword."

Alfie looked down at the pulsing purple stone in awe. He held the key to the Sword all this time round his neck! All this time and now it all slotted into place perfectly.

"So you must have had the Sword and a Desire Stone too?"

"There was a point, when I held the Sword. Not for long, but I did. And used it to, to it's advantage to get done what I needed. You will too. Now, where is that book…" Found flicked between the open books on the table, then tapped one. "This is where I found it…" he said.

Suddenly shapes and sound from the book leapt into the air and formed all around them. A huge transparent glassy, purple statue grew into the middle of the room, but remained like the rest of Magicity Square, a translucent echo of the past.

"Woah," said Alfie, as small figures were milling around the square, dressed in mostly brown, but that could have been mud, as the square was feet deep and covered in it. There were shouts from street traders from stalls and such, which looked like crude wooden tin pot versions of the shops that were still there today, which ran around the outside of the square. Alfie watched people walking past him, in the room and towards the Akashic Stone which stood tall, purple and shining. He could make the Sword out too, standing tall at the very top, glinting in the sun. Then the scene changed, fading into shouts and screams as people looked manic—fighting each other in the square and charging towards the Akashic Stone. Then they were all throwing their arms at it. Loud whizzes and bangs echoed around the room as blinding flashes continued to stream down around them at the Akashic Stone. Some of the spells were rebounded. But soon enough the Stone was obliterated. Guards came charging into the crowd with force, blasting them back. Then a little boy next to Alfie picked up a shard of the Akashic Stone. It twinkled in his hand. He pocketed it and ran off. The Guards stood trying to re-erect the shards and broken pieces, but failed, so large brooms solemnly began to sweep up the mess as Guards, shopkeepers and a very upset Pendragon stood atop the hill watching on in mourning at the loss of the City's greatest treasure. The people, realising what they had done, along with the shocked inhabitants, wept.

The scene died away, the shouts and colours and shapes disappearing, folding back into the forms of the book.

"*The Sword in the Stone*," said Alfie looking down at the Desire Stone around his neck. Found rolled his head, obviously he partly agreed, but didn't want to be abrupt. "So…" said Alfie, desperate to understand how the Desire Stone was a key. "How do I get the Sword then?"

Found held up a long white finger. "We'll get to that in a moment, but first…" he said. "We need to see who is the culprit for this action… it's a very serious crime to set a demon on someone, of course, you are condemning them to a fate worse than death." Alfie shuddered. "To me, this looks like it has all the hallmarks of an attack by the Scarlett Council."

"The Scarlett Council?" said Alfie, the name did not ring a bell.

"My reasons for thinking this are; no wizard would set one on you because your untraceable—you have not been inaugurated as a wizard. However, the Scarlett Council, are a collection of deep-seated old seers. They make and interpret prophesies and act on them for the preservation of the magickal kind—even though most of them are mad."

Found tapped another book and figures in red leaped out of the page and into the room. It was a dark chamber, lit with candles and fire brackets. Men, wearing all red cloaks with the hoods hiding their faces walked in line, slowly forwards.

Alfie pointed at them incredulously. "One of these men attacked me the first time we… in the LeyCorridor!" Alfie turned back and watched, one by one, as they reached the bottom step they removed their hood and took a sip of something red from a golden chalice. It was a creepy sight, and now the shapes moved so Alfie could see the hoods being removed. Slowly, the man's hood came down and Alfie nearly wretched—he had the most disgusting, disfigured face he had ever seen. Bile rose in his throat. His head was charred and black, blotchy and bulging, his eyes red and mouth a mere blackened hole. But then, the next man took his hood down—he didn't have a blackened, charred head. He had a normal head, with white skin and shoulder length black hair—Nikolas Wiseman! He smiled as he took a drink from the cup, his eyes flashing red.

Alfie couldn't speak. He could only point. "*W-w*-Wiseman?" he said.

"*Yeees…*" said Found slowly. "He's a long and established member… everyone knows. He is not trustworthy."

Wiseman had been there through it all, but now Alfie was coming to realise slowly that he'd been duped! It must have been Wiseman who set the Shadow on him… then tried to use him to get the Akashic Sword for himself! The images around him, changed, three men in red robes stood atop a large stone plinth, orange firelight illuminating a huge underground canyon. With many more men in red robes, on the floor cross legged, in deep contemplation. The three men raised their arms and a huge thrashing tentacled beast, rose up into the canyon before them. Alfie could only watch open mouthed, as the men dropped their hands and the beast vanished with a pop.

The illusions around him ceased and silence fell. Alfie struggled for what to say. "It was *him*... all along?"

Found sighed. "You must forgive yourself, he's a clever, tricky man."

There passed a silence, Alfie sat wondering about Wiseman, that man who he thought would be his saviour—actually turned out to be using him—and he had been warned many times. The note with the Desire Stone, whoever that was from. Gracie was unsure of him, and other niggling suggestions. What would Mr Sapiens say? He was a friend of Wiseman's.

Found just stared out of the blackened window as snow began to fall again. "This is a tricky situation..." he said. "Even if you do get the Sword, it doesn't guarantee you victory against the Shadow, and, it's small army... mine didn't have an army." Found seemed to be suggesting that the task ahead was a lot more complex than simply finding the Sword and killing the Shadow. Alfie just wanted this to all be over, he craved a normal life—one without monsters, demons, and even... magic. He would trade it all in right now, for a slice of normality—to get to know his Dad, go to college with Tommy, Sparky and Gracie, even to play football again and help his Granddad on the allotment, he might even get a little part time job this summer. But only if he could get this major Shadow problem out of the way, or he would always be looking over his shoulder.

"What happens, if I fail?" said Alfie. "As in, say the Shadow kills me. Then what?"

"Well..." said Found. "It will take your body, look the spitting image of you, posses unlimited powers, pose a huge danger to both magical and non-magical communities, your friends and relatives will all be in great danger and you'll be confined to a ¬fate worse than death."

Alfie swallowed. "Oh."

Suddenly the weight of what would happen if he failed dawned on him. He couldn't, just couldn't fail. His Grandparents faces flashed across his mind, of their grandson bearing down on them with pointed brown teeth ready to kill them—then Tommy and Sparky looking confused as their best friends turned on them, and Gracie...

"I'll do anything!" Alfie cried. "I'll do anything! If you can tell me how to make this all be over!" said Alfie, cupping his head in his hands trying to block the images out.

"*Anything?*" said Found curiously.

"Anything! I swear!"

Found stood, content for a moment, his posture straight backed, eyes narrowing. "Okay Alfie. I would like to make a deal... I offer you this: I will tell you exactly how to defeat your Shadow by gaining possession of the Akashic Sword. In this contract, your destiny will be tied to mine... therefore, if you fail and die... I die too."

Alfie stared at him for a moment, he didn't want Found to die. But Found must be pretty confident that he could help him, if he was prepared to put his life at risk—and really, what other choice did Alfie have? He stared into Found's purple eyes, the purple eyes. Was it chance, or luck that Alfie should happen across the only man who could help him? This was a golden chance to finally, have his problem over.

"Okay," said Alfie. "I agree to this contract."

Alfie's felt pins and needles start to run up his spine and down his arms. Small sparks of purple light fizzed and whizzed through the air around both of them as Alfie's voice suddenly echoed around the room.

"I'll do *ANYTHING… Anything… Anything… Anything…*" echoed his voice.

Found sat comfortably, smiling and looking content, watching the purple sparks dying away.

"W-w-what was that?" said Alfie.

Found laughed softly. "That was a *magical contract*," he said in a soothing voice. "Your *word* is as good as a sighed contract in magic."

Alfie felt strange, a small chill ran down his back—but there was nothing to be afraid of—Richard Found had just promised him, by magical contract, that he would help Alfie find the Akashic Sword and get rid of his Shadow once and for all. What was bad about that?

Found sprung to life immediately—ordering coffee from the mirror, he settled down and began riffling through papers. Alfie felt the energy which Found now brought to the search energise him too.

Found's knowledge of Magicity was far reaching and in depth. He had maps and blueprints of the town stretching back a thousand years. The first thing Found told Alfie were the different routes in and out of Magicity, known and others that were not so well known.

Alfie reeled off the four ways he had already entered and exited Magicity, counting them on his hand. "LeyLine, magic flying carpet, borrowed tickets, and the hole in wall in the building where they kept us prisoner."

Found decided that they needed a new entrance and exit strategy. "There are a couple of LeyDoors in and around the square," said Found. "One above the magical herb shop, and another in a Spindleclick Station."

"What on earth is a *Spindleclick*?" said Alfie—the name was completely foreign to him.

"It's a train that looks like a snake," said Found. "You must have seen it?"

Alfie nodded, he remembered it vividly.

Found carried on. "The LeyDoors will be useless currently, even though they are secret, the Guards would have sealed." Found shuffled a piece of paper showing something with colourful lines on. Alfie recognised it almost immediately—at first he thought it was a LeyLine map. But upon looking closer, it was a map to the London Underground train system.

Alfie chuckled. "What's that doing there?"

Found's smile curled. "Apparently…" he mused. "There is a way into Magicity on one of the London Underground lines. My friend gave it to me, he's circled the stations between London Bridge and Old Street. You must sit in the last carriage and under the window that has *'MGCTY'* scrawled in graffiti—and some other stuff, can't quite remember the full process."

Found gathered several papers and Alfie was interested to see the multitude of ways that one could get to Magicity. Found showed him a sheet of instructions and a map for how to sail into Magicity. There was a river on the Norfolk Broads that, through some thick reeds, at the precise location, would pass you straight through into Merlin's Lake.

"The only one I truly recommend," said Found leaning

forwards. "Is not on any sheets of paper." He smiled, his purple eyes twinkling as the fire crackled. "It's called the *MirrorWays*. It's highly secretive. Only a handful of people know about it. I, being one of them. There is a place behind all mirrors which allow you passage to any suitable mirror in the world. Undetectable, untraceable and safe. This is your way into Magicity..." said Found glancing up at the Mirror above the fireplace. Now Alfie understood why Found had clambered up their and disappeared through it earlier.

Even though there was no time, according to Found, what felt like hours upon hours went by, of Found hunting through books and pages of notes and Alfie inspecting everything he was given and listening to Found's explanations and possible routes to the Akashic Sword. Alfie didn't get tired, somehow Founds enthusiasm was infectious.

"These are the maps of Magicity. Interestingly..." said Found using a long finger to point out the centre of the map. "These three shops going this way, haven't got an underground basement. Now see the lines on this other map..." Found snatched up another paper with *underground waterways* written at the top. Alfie followed his long finger westwards along a blue line through Magicity Square underneath where the Rock stood. "This is a natural water line. If you follow it all the way out of Magicity it runs straight out into what looks like baron land, but actually..." Found snatched up another book open at the right page. "If we see this book of mythical places, that *baron land* actually leads to a place where they think the mythical Akashic Lake lies." Found was flicking between map and books so fast Alfie struggled to keep up.

"So, what does that mean?"

"It means..." said Found, incredulous that Alfie hadn't realised.

"That the Akashic Stone grew from the Akashic Lake which runs directly beneath that spot."

"I get it," said Alfie. "But you must know all this already because you *had* the Akashic Sword?"

Found eyes darkened. "Briefly," he said coldly. "But that was a long time ago, when the circumstances were different. Your's are much harder. You have half the wizarding world looking for you!" Found waved a hand as if dismissing any quarrels outright—and stood. "This is what you need to do…" Images and shapes, like the ones in the books started to appear in the air. Magicity Square returned again transparent into the room. Then Alfie saw himself standing next to the Rock. Found spun the picture round so they were zoomed in on it.

"When you get to Magicity, head straight for the Rock. You will have some disguise and there won't be many people around. Climb to the top of the Rock and pull the fake Sword out. You have the ability to do that, as we know."

Alfie watched himself run to the top of the Rock and pull the fake Sword out. It acted like a trigger, the whole Rock suddenly melting. The fountain appeared beneath, the water turning purple. "You must drop your Desire Stone into the hand of the Lady…" The image of Alfie did so. "And take the Akashic Sword." As the image of Alfie did so, a thunderbolt stuck the air onto of the sword and the vision disappeared in a flash.

"Simple then really," said Alfie grinning. "But I still have to not get seen by anyone, and not get killed by the Shadow."

"We will come to that," said Found.

"But…" said Alfie. "Something still doesn't make sense. Why did the hand in the fountain point to the mirror shop? And all the clues led to the looking glass?"

"The Desire Stone was in that looking glass. The Lady was

pointing to the Mirror shop, because the key to the Sword lay inside. Except it had been taken already—and it ended up in the hands of someone who wanted to help you."

"*Ahh...*" said Alfie, now it made sense. But then, someone must have got it for him? Wrapped it up in brown paper and delivered it to him on Christmas Day. Someone, who according to the Dice Duchess, looked like a Devil. Perhaps it was Wiseman, he had dark eyes and if he wore his red cloak from the Scarlett Council he would look just like a Devil! And then Alfie would have the key, would find the *real* Akashic Sword, and Wiseman could then take it from him, like he had tried to do before with the fake one! It all made sense. But then, if it was Wiseman, why did he write on the note—*do not trust him?*

Alfie sighed. He didn't need to be thinking about this now, he had to think of defeating his Shadow first.

"Why did I have the ability to pull the fake out again?" said Alfie.

"The fake sword is like a doorway, the Akashic lake beneath will only let the worthy open it."

Found said that Alfie would have to act very quickly once he was in Magicity, for the Shadow must have some way of tracking him. Therefore, he must get the Akashic Sword before the Shadows arrive in Magicity—Found estimated around three minutes before the Shadow and it's army get past Pendragon. He touched another book and Pendragon floated into the room, the wall of mist puffed into the room, Found raised a hand and lines pointed to certain area's of Pendragon, with a description at the end.

"Pendragon could handle one, maybe a few Shadows, but not an army of them... The Shadow's have a negative frequency that parallels the Pendragon's, therefore he is unusually receptive to their attacks." Found waved the vision away, but found another book and tapped that. The huge tentacled beast fell into the room with a thud. Alfie's heart started to throb. Lines and descriptions jumped out of the vision of the beast. Then Alfie's Shadow faded up in front of the beast, frozen to the spot and unmoving—more lines and descriptions arising from it.

"The beast itself is a high ranking Demon. But it's not without it's weak points. For example…" said Found rubbing his eyes and pointing to one description near the mouth. "It needs a constant supply of blood to sustain itself in our physical world. It's major strength is it's ability to handle magic in whatever form it sustains. So is particularly useful at hunting down wizards." Found waved a hand and the beast faded. "The Lynch Shadow and beast can both be killed with the Akashic Sword. The Shadow had weak points, and you should aim for these when attacking with spells and the sword." His Shadow suddenly had a red marker around its mouth. "If Spelling, aim for the mouth, their sustenance is blood and a *Petivo* would weaken it. This is the important bit. There will be a point when the Shadow will begin *swirling*. It does this when it's about to enter and take over your body. You will have a *three second window* to kill it. From the second it starts spinning you count, one-two-three—stab! Wait any longer and it will invade you. This is the only way to kill it…"

* * *

Over the next few days, even though it could have been months, Alfie and Found went over and over the plan. Over meals, which they ate together Alfie would ask Found about certain possibilities, but Found would dismiss it and say there was no point talking about *what if's*. Alfie rather thought there was, seeing as both their lives were in his hand. They went through everything a thousand times, to make sure the plan was watertight. Except, Alfie didn't have a plan B. So far it consisted of—running away. Found insisted that if you have a plan B, it waters down the effectiveness of getting plan A right. Found only gave Alfie one spell, which made Alfie quietly seethe inside. He was about to fight an army of Shadows and all Found gave him was a spell that would make him almost invisible to passer-by's, but not Shadows. He must perform it on himself as soon as he entered Magicity. Apart from that, no attacking spells whatsoever, Found said that the Sword was all he needed and there was no point getting distracted with different spells.

Found finished reciting the plan for the thousandth time and looked up at Alfie. "Tomorrow evening it is then," he said, closing the books that were laid across the table.

"What?" said Alfie. "Tomorrow evening is what?"

"Is when you kill your Shadow." Found smiled. "Get some rest."

"But... *but...*" Before Alfie could complain, or say that it was too early, or that he wasn't quite ready just yet—Found had climbed up the fireplace and went through the mirror.

Alfie sat dumbstruck, tomorrow?

In all truth, Alfie felt very comfortable in this room, with whatever food he desired, comfy bed, and warm fire. He slowly climbed into bed and lay staring up at the ceiling, trying to suppress the thought that tomorrow, he would be charging around Magicity after a Sword. He went through the plan in his head, again and again, then lay on his side fiddling with the Desire Stone. No words swam in it. Alfie stared into the surface, hoping a picture of Gracie might fade up.

Alfie woke early, startled awake from dreams of running.

Found was pouring tea and getting breakfast from the Mirror.

"Big day today…" said Found. "Come and eat, get your strength up." Alfie couldn't eat. He sat down and nibbled at some toast and eggs. "Come on… you need the strength."

Alfie felt a tight knot in the pit of his stomach ever since Found had said that Alfie would be going to Magicity today. Alfie didn't know how Found remained so calm, but sat and watched Alfie eat. Alfie's hands shook as he raised the fork to his mouth and he tried as hard as he could not to think about what he would be doing soon.

He dressed slowly, this would not be his last day on earth or whatever this place was, he simply couldn't think of failure. He put on some different clothes that Found had prepared for him, which were still smart but he felt a lot more mobile in them. Alfie tucked the lion mask under his arm and checked the Desire Stone was still round his neck—for he would be needing that. Found stood hands behind his back, next to the fire, and turned smiling encouragingly.

"You know the plan. You needn't worry. As long as you stick to it—you'll be fine."

"And you're sure that I come back through the same mirror and it will take me back *here*…" said Alfie, and Found nodded. The last part of their plan was slightly vague—Alfie was to hopefully, kill the Shadow and return through the mirror that let him into Magicity, back into this warm, cosy room which Alfie had grown fond of. With its grey stone walls, tall windows with scaling views, high ceiling and comfy double bed. Alfie noted to himself, that if he got into trouble he would run, back through the mirror at the first opportunity—he hadn't told Found this.

The knot grew painful, his hands sweaty and his heart

pounding as he readied himself to climb the mantelpiece and descend into the MirrorWays. Alfie gave the room a swift goodbye glance, then nodded—he was ready. Found gave him a leg up and Alfie perched on the end of the mantelpiece. He touched the surface of the mirror which was cool and silky.

"Walk through…" said Found.

But then, something strange happened. As he looked at Found in the reflection of the mirror to give his thanks before he went through—that he caught a strange sight of Found's face, which had turned… *nasty*—big black eyes and pointed vampirish teeth. But when Alfie turned to look properly, Found returned his curious gaze with friendly purple eyes. Alfie blinked, thinking he was going mad—must have been the stress. Then he moved forwards, crouching low, he moved through the mirrors surface. He felt cool silky silver strands stoke his skin. As he looked up, and gasped, gazing in wonder at the whole of the MirrorWays.

19

A Throw of Faith

Alfie gazed ahead and all around himself. He was perched atop a wide stone plinth. His stomach turned violently as he looked around. Below him was the deepest, darkest drop he had ever seen. It was so black and wide, that upon looking down it appeared to descend to the very depths of the Earth. Huge rock faces loomed up all around him and continued up into the gloomy darkness for what looked like miles. There was no natural light, only that of fire brackets, large and small, which scattered the walls intermittently. Some, were so far off into the distance that they looked like tiny, shining stars. Alfie took a moment to assess the wondrousness and horror of his surroundings. He knew by now that heights were not his strong point, and he felt giddy as he surveyed the MirrorWays in its entirety. He also didn't know what he had expected to find in the MirrorWays.

Alfie stood and backed away from the edge. He knew what to do from here because Found had given him a spell word which activated a path downwards to the walkway below. Found's face flashed before Alfie's mind—in the reflection of the mirror, for that split second, he had looked positively evil. He couldn't be, Alfie thought, he had just given him detailed instructions to defeat his Shadow. Alfie shook the image from his mind. Below, over the edge of the plinth was a long, wide and well lit bridge in the middle of the dark canyon. The bridge was thin and grey—a long slab of smooth concrete with hundreds of mirrors lined along it, hanging in the air. Now Alfie noticed around the canyon, next to each fire bracket, was a mirror. Alfie could see them now, the light reflecting off them, strange smooth patches among the jutting, sharp canyon wall. Each mirror had a small, mantelpiece plinth underneath it.

"*Somar...*" said Alfie. The fire bracket behind him gave a splutter and grew brighter. The plinth rumbled beneath his feet and Alfie leant backwards and clutched a sharp bit of wall. Steadily, the plinth came out of the wall a few feet. Then, stone slabs began to slide out underneath forming a staircase down to the bridge below. The stairs hung in mid air and Alfie felt unsure putting his foot on them.

Carefully, he balanced himself down the stairs as if descending an obstacle course. Now he stood on the bridge the stairs behind him vanished—sliding back up into the plinth and back into the wall. The bridge stretched out in front of him like a train track—the end it disappeared into a black hole in the canyon wall. A tall decorated sign stood reading simply *The WalkWay.*

Alfie was cautious, in case the bridge might disappear beneath his feet at any moment. So he began to move, very gradually. The sound of his footsteps and quickening breath, disconcertingly, the only noise. Found hadn't told him what to do once he was in the MirrorWays. This now, seemed a huge oversight and Alfie kicked himself for not asking—but how should he have known? Alfie assumed Found's lack of advice meant that it was simple, or didn't need explaining—that there would be a sign above, as soon as he entered that read *'Magicity Here'* with a large red arrow. But there wasn't.

Some of the mirrors had signs, and some a brass plaque. The mirrors along the WalkWay bridge looked important, or well used. The wide wooden oak frames were huge and ornamental. The one Alfie was looking for wouldn't be as popular. Alfie tried his hardest as he trudged along, not to look over the sides. But then he heard the strangest, out of sync, noise...

Meow.

He was sure he could hear a cat. Alfie glanced towards the noise. Above him was a cat, walking along in mid-air! But when Alfie looked closer he saw a translucent stone path underneath it. Alfie stopped and watched it hurry along an invisible bridge it seemed to know well, to a mirror in the canyon wall just away from Alfie. It jumped onto the plinth and then straight through the mirror. Then he saw another one, walking casually along behind him. It scuttled past and into a large frame on the right with a large plaque that read *'Magicity Council Offices.'* Another bridge appeared to Alfie gradually through the darkness, the further along he walked. This one too was suspended seemingly in mid air, hanging across the canyon like some miraculous floating barge. On this one where around a hundred cats, all hurrying around. Some were jumping through mirrors as others were jumping out of mirrors and into others. Alfie was perplexed. The further Alfie walked along the WalkWay, the more paths and bridges appeared around him. Connected to the one he was on, they jutted out between the mirrors, and snaked off, upwards or downwards, into the darkness.

There was another WalkWay directly beneath him, travelling the opposite way. He heard a slight commotion, and watched as another man—large and cloaked up to the neck—began to walk briskly along keeping his face hidden. One cat, spotted the man and stopped, eyes trained on him. The cat made a bee line towards him and landed on the walkway directly in front of the man's path. Alfie stopped to watch, transfixed. The cats on the bridge opposite, were all now staring at the man. The cat facing the man began to hiss and spit. The cloaked man looked terrified, and began to plead with it. In a flash the man threw his arms out, several dark spells whizzing towards the cat. The cat jumped, spun and avoided them. In mid-air, it grew, and roared so loud the canyon shook. The man screamed and ran back the opposite way, as the lion chased him and knocked him down, sending him sprawling to the edge. The lion stood over him as the man pleaded. Alfie wondered who the man was and what he had done? Was Alfie allowed to be in here? Or would a lion come after him as well? Grudgingly the man was escorted to a mirror where he disappeared. The lion turned back into a cat to a cacophony of *meows*.

Alfie continued to walk, heart beating a little faster. At the end of the WalkWay the black hole sparked orange firelight on his arrival, illuminating the tight tunnel before him. Alfie stepped off the bridge and into the tunnel.

As he did, Alfie heard a voice.

"Who goes there?"

Alfie swivelled round. A large mirror set away from the rest with a ghostly, enlarged face nearly forced Alfie back off the edge of the WalkWay.

"*Ahh!*" he cried.

"Apologies," said the mirror politely, bowing. The ghostly face smiled and looked pleasant, if not a little spooky. "May I be of assistance? Where be your intended destination?"

Alfie came a little closer to the gold framed mirror now. "I was looking for the mirror into… I think it's called *Merve's Magick Mirrors*, a mirror shop in Magicity."

The mirror laughed. "You must really like mirrors." It giggled. "I'm sick of them. Moaning lot. Anyway, it's down there…" the face nodded his head into the tunnel. "Two lefts and three rights. Look for the third on the left."

"Ok thanks," said Alfie. Alfie walked away and distinctly heard the mirror telling another: *"See it wasn't hard to be polite was it?"*

The tunnel was rough, as if it had been carved out in a rush. Alfie's mind was still half on the man that was attacked by the cats, but he put it out of his mind and took a deep breath. He followed the mirror's instructions and wandered the small airless tunnels that any taller person would have a severely sore head with. He did two left turns and three rights and now finally, stood in front of a long thin blackened Mirror. The frame was cracked black, and the mirror didn't look especially grand. A small sign next to it read: *Merve's Magick Mirror Shop, Magicity, 111:27.*

Alfie took a deep breath. Once he stepped over the threshold he had three minutes until the Shadow would find him. Gently he touched the surface. His hand went though and it felt like water was tickling his skin. Alfie put all of his right leg over the surface and stepped out of the MirrorWays and through the mirror. His heart was beating fast as the cold silky surface enveloped him. As he stepped through, a screen of black overcame his vision. As his eyes adjusted he saw he was standing in a burnt out shell of the mirror shop. There was an acrid smell of charred dust and rising soot. Rain was hitting him on the head from above where the roof was partially destroyed. A dark grey sky loomed above him. Alfie stepped away from the mirror—in fact it was not a mirror, it was the looking glass he had spoke to the Dice Duchess through. It still stood, undamaged. All the other mirrors in the basement of the shop were gone or blackened beyond repair.

Alfie took a deep breath and moved for the exit. The wooden stairs up to the main shop were gone. That was a problem. Now all that remained was a ten feet climb up to get into the shop and Magicity Square. He couldn't climb that, it was too high. Alfie thought hurriedly. If he went back through into the MirrorWays he could find another suitable mirror around Magicity that he could climb through. There must be one, there were hundreds, if not thousands down there. But when Alfie touched the surface of the looking glass expecting it to let his hand through. It stubbornly resisted. His hand hitting the glass with a thud.

Then a more pressing thought occurred to him—if it wouldn't let him back through into the MirrorWays, then where on earth was his escape route? Alfie tried and tried to get back, he pushed against the cold surface, but nothing happened. Found hadn't told him this would happen. That he wouldn't be allowed back! Alfie wheeled around looking for another Mirror, but there were no others down here that were not charred or broken.

The feeling of panic started to rise in his chest. He was trapped here. And the mission ahead suddenly weighed on his shoulders as he stood in a burnt out shell of a shop that he played a part in the destruction of. As rain fell damp and cold on his head. Alfie turned and looked up at the doorway above. This was it. He knew now he had to be brave and follow Found's instructions, however much he wanted to go back—he had to do this for more than just himself.

He found his footing on a shaky charred plank and hoisted

himself up the broken staircase. All above him were old wooden beams and bits of stairs that hung together by the slightest thread or loose rusty nail. Halfway up Alfie heard the wooden plank he was standing on creak. There was no time to jump for the top, he felt himself slip and fall to the ground with a crunch as he landed on a pile of old wood yelping as a splinter sliced the back of his leg.

"Ahh!" he cried, rolling out of the way of the plumes of black smoke and dust.

Alfie stood breathing heavily. This was ridiculous. He was trying to defeat a demon hardly any wizard had done in recorded history, and here he was struggling to get out of a basement. Then the answer came to him. Alfie put a hand in his pocket and pulled out his list of spells. He scanned the list, there was one, he remembered that he had inadvertently taken from Richard Found, in the café the first time they met. It was scribbled in the corner of the note of spells. He'd written it when he was on the bus home from the trip—*Hexplico*. That's what Found had said that fixed his broken mug. Without waiting around or thinking any longer Alfie bent down and picked up what looked a small shard of broken stair. Then placing it beneath his feet he put his hand over it and muttered *"Hexplico!"*

The broken shard of stair grew exponentially. At first the shard grew into a plank, then it sprouted nails, and grew more shards of wood on either end which grew into planks, which did the same, all the way up until a wobbly, but erected staircase now stood directly in front of Alfie's feet.

Jumping up the wobbly stairs, Alfie didn't stop in the burnt out shop front—he continued, sprinting into the Square towards the Rock.

The rain was beating down fast. Someone across the Square looked up at the sound of Alfie sprinting through the thick rain puddles. Alfie stopped, he had forgotten the masking spell! Quickly, Alfie put his hands by his sides like Found had said, stood with a straight back, then said aloud the words: "*Aspectus—apsens—abscondita…*" the effect was instant. It felt like a egg had been cracked on the crown of his head, as a cold wet feeling dribbled down his head, back and shoulders, and all the way down his body to his feet. The person watching him hurried away and now the Square was empty. The only sound was the constant pattering of heavy rain. The Square was a inches thick and as Alfie sprinted as quick as he could across the cobbled floor, his shoes squelched. All the shops around the edge of the square were shut, and not even a light was on inside. It was as if the whole town had left. The tough rain was making it hard to move, Alfie's clothes already soaked through and the raindrops falling like bullets. At the foot of the Rock Alfie took one last look around the Square, his eyes scanning in between the shops where, he couldn't decide if he could see movement, or was it just rain? Alfie swivelled and climbed the stone stairs. It was slippery, small patches of green moss encircled the steps and Alfie tried his hardest not to slip. Breathless and soaking Alfie trudged the remaining few steps to the top. The incline was steep, Alfie had to hold onto the stairs in front of him for support. The fake Sword stuck out proudly from the stone. The fake Sword that Alfie had pulled out only a few months before. The Sword that had caused he and Wiseman to run around Magicity, trying madly to escape the towns people. And now here he was again. But, he knew why this time. Alfie, slowly, took two steps forward, it was very wet and he faced the very real possibility of slipping and falling.

He put his hand out reaching for the hilt that would grant him access to the real Sword below. Then, out of the corner of his eye something, or rather, some-thing's moved.

Outside the bakery Mollinaries, something moved slowly from the darkness. Just enough to show itself. Then more came. Out from every dark place in the Square, and every possible crevice. They moved slowly, as one, keeping to the sides of the Square. Silently staring up at Alfie. Their cold, dead eyes sullen. It was Alfie's worst nightmare. He swallowed hard, ice cold chills running down his spine. His hand outstretched for the Sword, was inches from his fingertips. For a very long moment Alfie stood stock still, unable to move, frozen to the spot. From the alleyways, the cracks and the crevices, they came. Up from the drains, and down through drain pipes. Slowly and surely the army of Shadows rose into the Square, gazing upwards at the boy, atop the Rock.

Alfie's felt a huge anchor drop inside his chest. He wasn't quick enough. Did he have time to pull the fake Sword out and hide before running back to the fountain, dropping in the Desire Stone and taking the Akashic Sword? Alfie rather thought, he didn't have even a fraction of that time. A sick gurgling feeling returned to his stomach, a knot tightening. They knew who he was even with the concealment spell.

Two familiar figures trotted out from a dark alleyway straight ahead and began marching militarily into the Square. It was his Shadow, flanked by Nikolas Wiseman, who smiled contentedly.

"No!" Alfie cried, unable to help himself.

The Shadow stopped and looked up at him, the purple eyes he shared with Alfie peering from beneath the top hat.

"Feeling… *betrayed?*" cried the Shadow, and the Square of

shadows sniggered. "Feeling lost and scared? Without anyone to help little didums?"

Alfie didn't answer, he couldn't. He felt, completely and utterly numb. All the plans he and Found had gone through for it to all be dismantled in a moment. Alfie cursed. Found said he had three minutes to get the Sword before the Shadows would arrive. He had spent most of that time trying to get out of the basement of the mirror shop, and now it looked like he was going to pay a costly price.

"You must be feeling awfully desperate, pinning your hopes on a fake Sword!" the Shadow shouted up at him. "Yes that's right, Nikolas told me everything!"

Alfie swallowed—his Shadow knew about the fake Sword—but did it know about the real one that was right beneath them?

"Oh I *forgot*... have I introduced you?" started the Shadow in a long drawling voice, indicating Wiseman on his left. "This is my *good friend*, Nikolas Wiseman."

Alfie couldn't understand it. All this time Wiseman was playing him. None of it added up, but at the same time, it made perfect sense. "I don't believe it," Alfie said defiantly.

"Working for little old me all along. Does it hurt to know that you have been manipulated and played to where you are now? I have played with you like a cat plays with a mouse before it kills and eats it..." the Shadow licked its lips, purple eyes burning with malicious laughter. Wiseman looked to be enjoying himself too as he laughed along.

"How do you *feeeeel* Alfie? Sad, upset... *angrrrry*?" The audience of shadows roared with laughter. "Such an awful place to be when you don't know who to trust."

Alfie didn't say anything, he couldn't. But he knew that he

ALFIE BROWN: THE BOY WITH PURPLE EYES

needed to act fast. The plan he had made with Found was already out of the window. He needed to pull the fake sword out of the Rock and then bide his time.

"*But enough of this talk!*" called the Shadow to his adoring audience. "It's time for action. Time I killed you!" Alfie moved his feet infinitesimal amounts, sliding them across the slippy stone. "The conditions are perfect, the numerology sound, the stars… in my favour. I will be *all powerful*. We will be all powerful." The crowd roared again.

Alfie swallowed and took a deep breath. He felt the panic in his chest, but suppressed it. The Shadow turned addressing the army of shadows behind him. "And then… my dear compatriots, we DINE!" The crowd roared deafeningly.

Alfie took his moment, and lunged for the fake Sword. He grabbed the stone hilt and yanked. The Sword slid out and Alfie felt the Rock begin to rumble beneath his feet.

The Shadow turned and saw what Alfie had done. Some of the Shadows in the Square recoiled, baulking in surprise. There was a sudden flash of black as ten sparks of black fire reigned in on him from all sides. Alfie didn't have time to avoid them—and braced himself as one hit him hard in the side. There was a black thunderclap, then, he toppled. Alfie felt himself sailing through the air. Alfie saw the world vertically as he soared off the top of the Rock. Heart in his mouth, the wind blasting his ears Alfie soared into the crowd of shadows.

CRUNCH! Went the shadow beneath him breaking Alfie's fall. Dazed, he jumped up and wheeled around trying to get his bearings. The Sword had remained stuck to his right hand and the army of Shadows were doing anything they could to get away from him.

Alfie raised the Sword and spun around. But they looked

terrified, all eyes on the Sword in his hands.

"Don't worry!" called his Shadow standing calm arms behind his back, in the middle of the Square. "My compatriots, that Sword... is a *fake*! It is no more powerful than a lump of concrete!"

Some of the Shadows looked reassured, but others remained where they were. Alfie didn't know what to do. The spell had stung his side, and he clutched it—feeling like he had been stung by a hundred wasps, he gritted his teeth. A loud rumble made the floor shake hard.

The Rock in the middle of the Square melted. The grey stone shrinking away, down back into the ground. Leaving only a large circular fountain with a glassy water surface jumping as rain hit it.

The Shadow began to laugh. "Very good! You succeeded in destroying the prized possession of this town."

Some of the Shadows sniggered, others still looked wary. "Doing my work for me?" the Shadow muttered, looking around the Square, then he bellowed at the Shadows. "You don't believe me that the Sword is a fake?" The Shadow raised a hand at Alfie, who felt the Sword in his hand twitch, then it shot into the air. The Shadow caught it and held it aloft. He even swiped it through his own arm—it passed through as if he were smoke, leaving no damage. "You see how pathetic this is?!" he cried.

The shadow people around the Square smiled.

Wiseman walked forwards and joined the Shadow happily. "I told you." he said aloud. With one flick of his hand, the fake Sword flew into the air. Then in a shower of red, it exploded, casting stone, dust and red sparks down upon them.

The Shadow jumped up and down, clapping. "Oh yes, I liked

that!"

Suddenly anger at Wiseman burned red hot inside Alfie. His stomach felt as if it had ignited. In a flash Alfie raised his arms and without throwing caution, he cried as loud as he could "*PETIVO!*"

The purple flash erupted across the Square, as if this anger had given it increased fuel. The ball expanded in a flash. Then shot at Wiseman, who, with a lazy flick of his hand, rebounded it back. Alfie jumped out of the way as the Spell flew into a gang of Shadows behind him, casting them into the air like bowling pins.

"You betrayed me!" Alfie cried. "You told me all that stuff! How to get the Sword, how to defeat the Shadow! And it all meant nothing did it!?"

Wiseman flicked his eyes up at him. "No, not really..." he couldn't have sounded less bored if he tried. "You are simply a commodity. You will only have great power if you work hard and learn. Whereas, when he kills you and takes your body, it will have almost *unlimited* power. It can draw on the experience of lifetimes it already has. Yes I manipulated you. But you shouldn't have trusted me."

What was he to do now? Alfie stood soaked to the bone, shaking with anger. With no idea of how to get to the fountain which lay just beyond his Shadow and Wiseman. If he could just find a way of getting to it, then he would be able to end all this. But he felt on the border of tears. His side hurt inextricably, the anger and frustration at Wiseman boiled over, there were no words he could express that would let it out. He wanted to scream and shout. He didn't ask for any of this!

The Shadow seemed enthralled by the outburst. "Oh yes, that's what I like to see!" It drooled.

Alfie huffed, looking around for an escape. He envisioned Richard Found walking across the Square, and ridding all of these Shadows for him.

"And now!" cried his Shadow triumphantly. "It's TIME I KILLED YOU!"

There was a dart of movement. One of the shadow people made a bee line for Alfie, who ducked as a dark fist sailed for his head. Alfie scrambled across the soaked stone floor. There was nowhere to hide, nowhere to run, all the exits blocked by shadow people. More came at him. From all around dark figures charged. Five to his right loomed across his vision. Alfie slid on the water surface, raised his hand and shouted *"Petivo!"* the ball grew large again, then exploded, blasting the shadow people through the window of the herb shop with a giant *CRASH!*

Alfie lifted his left hand, and aimed for the ground where a whole line of shadow people were charging.

"Laravatus!" he said. The surface water jumped into the air and formed a huge wave. Alfie did the same behind him, trying to work his way closer to the fountain. A dark fist flashed across his vision, then pain shot across his head. He hit the floor, as light danced in front of his eyes from the blow. Shadow people were on top of him before he could move. But then more were jumping on. Soon, all of them were piling on top. Alfie felt the air leave his lungs. He was being crushed to death beneath a mountain of shadow people. He couldn't even open his mouth to cry. It was unbearable. Alfie could just see patches of light, but these went hazy as he gasped for air. His head spinning, small lights popping in front of him—he couldn't move. He was trapped and about to feel his last breath leave him.

But then, something miraculous happened.

A shining purple light expanded across his vision. There were muffled shouts all around him. Shadow after shadow began jumping off. The purple light was coming from the Desire Stone around his neck. It was shining dazzlingly bright. As they all left him and stood back shielding their eyes, wailing with agony, Alfie still didn't move. He opened his eyes and let clean air back into his lungs which heaved with relief. The Desire Stone was shining brighter and brighter, filling the Square with fluorescent purple light.

As Alfie opened his eyes again, he saw the Shadow and Wiseman looking perturbed, they were looking towards the fountain, which was also lit up. A purple column of light shooting into the sky, illuminating the whole town—purple rain fell from purple clouds and purple sky.

The Shadow, shielding its face, turned to Alfie, looking malicious as the army of shadow people backed off again.

"Give me that Stone!"

Alfie took his time getting up. Every part of him was soaked and sore. A hand began to emerge from the fountain. Then a face, a beautiful sculpted ladies face. She stood so her knees were just above the water surface, a long white flowing dress drifting on an invisible wind, her golden hair kept in place by a chain of small flowers. Her blue eyes looked up, directly at Alfie.

The Shadow took a few steps back as it clapped eyes on the ghostly figure of the Lady. Then he started to move towards Alfie. "I said... GIVE ME THE STONE!" Wiseman began to move with the Shadow, but it waved him back. "This is the deal... you give me that Stone and I won't murder everyone you've ever known, everyone you've ever spoken to, or even looked at."

Alfie shifted his sodden feet. "And if I do?" Alfie recognised the emotion in the identical eyes facing him—fear.

The Shadow was struggling to stand so close. "If you do, well, you have my word I won't harm them."

Alfie stood, wet and cold as rain continued to batter his face—he couldn't, and wouldn't make a deal with the Shadow. The formations of a tiny plan were knitting together fast inside his mind.

"You can go swivel…" said Alfie defiantly.

"Then I will make you GIVE IT ME!" The Shadow wheeled round, hands shooting up and firing black fire. Alfie quicker than he had ever reacted in his life did the same. *"Laravatus!"*

The water rose up into a wave and extinguished the Shadows spell, which went up in a plume of acrid black smoke. It grinned. Alfie steadied himself for another attack, he couldn't last much longer, his legs felt like jelly, his clothes sodden and eyes drooping with the strength. All of a sudden their was a buzzing all around him. A swarm of wasps dive bombed for him and were trying to get at every part of him. Alfie flailed his arms at them hopelessly as the crowd erupted into raucous laughter. Alfie tried to compose himself as best he could.

"Laravatus!" he said quickly. The buzzing stopped abruptly as the wasps turned solid and fell to the floor with tiny clunks. Without stopping to think he aimed and cried: "Consisto!" The Shadows hands struck rigid. Alfie moved his hands up in front of him and pulled them taught, summoning up the reserved of his energy before he screamed at the top of his lungs: *"PETIVO!"*

The energy drained out of him as a swirling purple ball turned flips between his hands. Time glitched, then with an almighty *BANG!* Erupting the Square in brightest purple light, the ball flew at the Shadow. Hands still rigid it lost its balance and hit the floor hard, sprawling back through the puddles sending up a wave of water. The crowd went silent. There was a sudden stillness in the air.

But it didn't last long. A far off rumble shuddered beneath the Square. Stones beneath Alfie's feet dislodged. Uprooting with the force of an earthquake—the ground shuddered violently all around. With an almightily force, the ground shot upwards, tipping Alfie onto his back, his head hit the floor hard as a large pile of stones landed on his leg. Alfie scrambled up in agonising pain, wobbling and limping as the ground continued to rumble. In a black blazing column of smoke the Shadow was back to it's full height, and more. Growing to at least eight feet and looking cantankerous with rage. An orange spark came from nowhere and hit Alfie full in the face. Alfie squirmed with the sudden pain, the orange spark had lit every pore in his face with fire. He fell willingly to the wet floor, splashing water onto it, screaming with agony as the pain did not relent.

"Okay!" Alfie cried. "Okay! I will GIVE IT TO YOU! PLEASEEEE!" Alfie screamed, rolling on the floor clutching at his face, which had swelled. He would do anything to stop the pain, the awful stinging pain.

"You have been *disrespectful* to me," said the Shadow, voice far deeper than before. "You think you can challenge and beat me? You got lucky boy, but this ends *now*. GIVE IT TO ME!" It screamed.

"I will—I *WILL*!" Alfie cried, sobbing into the wet stone floor. It was over, he knew it had to be. The Shadow lifted a hand and the pain ceased. Still clutching his face, Alfie rose, lifted by an invisible hand.

"Take it off and chuck it to me."

Alfie looked at the scene—a smiling army of shadow people, a contented Wiseman. And a monstrous, tall Shadow standing between Alfie and the fountain. His face still prickled with sparks of pain as a soft wind blew past him. Alfie reached for the Desire Stone around his neck and pulled. It came straight off, the silk metal string unclipping automatically. Alfie held the it in his hand. It was still shining bright, but no words swam inside. No clues as to what he was to do next. The lady in the fountain stood still staring blankly ahead.

A tiny plan hatched itself in the confines of his mind—could he do it? Could he risk it?

"Chuck it this way!" bellowed the Shadow—brow furrowed so low the purple eyes were barely visible.

"Fine," said Alfie as his heart beat fast as he made his final decision. "Catch this!"

Alfie acted. In one smooth movement, he pulled his arm behind his head, aimed and launched the Desire Stone into the air. The shining Stone left his hand and sailed into the sky, high above the scene below. The Shadow looked confused, but then realised—the Desire Stone was not being thrown to him. He was right. Alfie wasn't aiming for the Shadow, he was aiming for the fountain.

"NOOOOO!" Cried the Shadow.

Time seemed to slow to an agonising pace. Alfie using all his might to guide the Stone into the fountain. The short lessons with Mr Sapiens returning to him, trying to control the feather with his hand and mind—now Alfie willed the Stone towards the fountain. It looked to be on course. But now, shadow people began running towards it, launching themselves into the air and grasping at it, becoming translucent the closer they were to it.

Some sent spells whizzing through the air at it. Dark flames and electric fizzes shot towards it from all around, but the Desire Stone was doing something miraculous. The Desire Stone, or rather—the shard of Akashic Stone, was repelling them like a magnet—sending them back the other way, or just skimming off the edge of the light and away into the sky.

While the Shadow watched dumbstruck, Alfie reacted again. He took a breath and burst forwards towards the fountain. Sprinting with all his might, using the very reserves of energy he knew he had to find. Raising his left hand at the Shadow he cried: *"Comparle-Compesco-Capiri!"*

A shot of whitest light burst from his hand. The Shadow screamed as it was encased in a tight white glass box. Wiseman turned and cried too, but Alfie was ready for him. With his raised right hand, he cried *"Petivo!"* This time, Alfie concentrated, aiming for his mouth—the purple spell, seemingly accelerated by the surroundings, expelled from his hand and clapped exactly where he had aimed with a deafening thunderclap. There was a CRASH! As Wiseman flew backwards, smashing through the window of the herb shop.

Alfie looked up—the Desire Stone was starting to fall. Alfie raised his arm at it, continuing to run full pelt, and steered it as best he could towards the waters surface. And then with a brilliant, fantastic, miraculous *plop*, the Stone hit the surface. Purple hit purple and light ruptured the air. Both lights combined into one. Igniting the sky into a furious mushroom cloud of indigo. The shadow people all around fell back screaming and wailing trying to shield themselves. Alfie passed through them and reached the edge of the fountain. The lady in the fountain turned towards him—her brilliant eyes sparkled with the most brilliant, dazzling purple Alfie had ever seen. She smiled, then slowly began to sink beneath the surface. Alfie clutched his side, breathing heavily—the sound of the Shadow smashing the white glass box reverberating. The shadow people's wails and screams pulsing in his ears like a deafening nightmare.

But then, her hand cracked the surface, holding, a sword hilt. The Desire Stone firmly encased in the middle of the silver hilt, began to grow. Purple stone slowly grew upwards through the hilt like water, crystallising into long purple shards. The Shadow roared with rage behind them and sent spells whizzing round the glass box. Alfie watched in awe as the Akashic Sword fashioned itself in front of him. From the Desire Stone, the Sword grew. Light pulsed from hilt to tip and the lady angled the hilt towards Alfie to take.

He reached out a trembling hand. His skin felt the cool silky metal hilt and elation coursed through his whole body. Purple spirals shot from the smoothened purple blade and entwined themselves up his arm, sending shivers up his spine. The connection he now felt with the Sword was beyond his comprehension. It was like being reunited with a best friend, a beloved, unmoving, never-ending feeling of togetherness. The Sword raised itself into the air. As shadow people piled backwards into the walls of shops—trying to get as far away as possible, trembling with fear.

A voice echoed inside Alfie's head, it was velvety soft and comforting yet stern."You are worthy. You are worthy. You are worthy."

The lady smiled again and descended back into the water. The purple column of light from the fountain dissolved, until the only purple light came from the Sword. A few seconds of peace fell over the Square, as all went quiet. Unfolding in his mind was the rest of this mission—*end the Shadow.*

The Shadow stopped battering its prison, it looked smaller now and was watching Alfie with the same curious, cautious expression as the rest of them.

One brazen shadow person suddenly started screaming and burst forwards out of the crowd. Alfie just had time to note the black, dead eyes, the ripped clothes and the putrid smell. The Sword lifted and pointed at the oncoming enemy. Then, it all but swung itself—Alfie felt the Sword connecting with his mind—until he could feel what the Sword wanted to do. It was surreal. The shadow person was no more than three feet away, when the Alfie raised the Sword high and... *sliced.* He caught the shadow person across the chest. Causing it to stop and clutch at it. The shadow person looked up into the sky and wailed as a large gash appeared. Then, purple light began pouring out of the wound. Looking in pain, the shadow person started to wail pitifully. It was as if it were a piece of paper—for the shadow person fell, curling, burning and smouldering to the ground in a pile of blazing ash.

Alfie drew the sword closer, feeling its power pulse in his hands. The Sword was angry, charged and ready to blow. It was as if the Sword had a mind of its own. There was a gigantic smash as the Shadow cracked the glass box—in one second flat it had snaked it's way through the minuscule cracks, seeping through them like smoke. The Shadow raised both hands and black fire shot straight for Alfie's face. Instinctively, the Sword raised and Alfie whacked them away like they were baseballs—the spells flew into the crowd and knocked ten shadow people into the next street. Without waiting, the Shadow clicked his fingers and a fierce wind shaped like a dagger exploded out of it. Alfie just had time to see the Shadows uncertain eyes, before feeling the Sword raise again. Carving the spell in half, it sent two halves of the spell crashing through shop windows.

Alfie wielded the Sword around this time and pointed it at the Shadow—then ran forwards. Heart in mouth, Alfie swung at it. The Shadow dodged, dematerialising and materialising the behind him. The Shadow looked at its nails, one hand behind his back grinning and feigning boredom. Then it bowed its head and narrowed its eyes—Alfie was stunned by the smack. He toppled to the floor, face smarting.

"NOW!" screamed the Shadow. Every single shadow person in the Square raised their arms high into the sky. A spinning black force streamed into the Square. A hurricane of black wind descended down—and Alfie felt himself lifted him off his feet. He shot into the air, high above the Square and spun round and round, over and under. Alfie cried and screamed as the world danced before his eyes, his stomach turning flips and summersaults. Sick rose in his throat. The breath caught in his chest. Then... he felt the Sword leave his grip.

The wind spun him round. Then in one violent abrupt finish, the wind stopped. Alfie fell, sailing through the air with all the other debris. With a crack, he fell hard into the second story of a shop. Then he slid down the wall, hitting a wooden sign. The wood splintered and fell hard along with Alfie into the ground below. He was severely winded. Struggling for breath, he lay, his back on fire with pain as light flickered before his vision. He tried to stand as soon as he could, but fell over, head spinning. Vision swimming madly in front of him. The shadow people called and taunted, laughed and cackled. Clutching his side, Alfie ran straight for the only glimmer of purple in front of his hazy vision. The Sword. But a dark shape blocked his path.

The Shadow had stepped in front of him. It's hands twitched into an odd shape. Something that Alfie would never be able to do, unless he broke all his fingers. Three loud bangs hit the air. Three flashes of red thunder and three crippling blows, once in his stomach, once across the legs and the last across the face. Alfie toppled. The back of his head smacking the hard slippery floor.

He sat up, willing himself on. As he lifted a hand to spell, the Shadow flew at him and kicked him down. It stood over him muttering deep, unknowable words. Black liquid began to ooze up from the ground, covering his wrists and feet. Like thick oily snakes, entwining themselves in between Alfie's fingers, around his ankles, across his waist and over his mouth.

"This ends *now*. You put up a good fight..." said the Shadow spitting, almost sounding breathless. "And its good to see the powers I will inherit. But I am afraid with all the trickery that..." The Shadow prepared itself. "You lose." It said simply, then it began uttering dark, deep words which made the air tremble and ground rock. "I WIN!" It cried as the crowd of Shadows roared.

Alfie could do nothing. The Shadow was beginning to swirl violently up in to the air. Alfie could only see spinning, black smoke with flashes of purple. It loomed up into the sky, dark malevolent face pointed and evil. Then it zoomed towards his face and dived for his throat. Alfie struggled hard against the inhuman invasion of his body. There was nothing he could do. This wasn't how it should be. Smoke reached every part of his body. He felt black acrid, pungent ingredients reach the ends of the his fingers, coursing through his heart and brain like poison.

He didn't know how long for, but longer then three seconds. He felt the Shadow invading his very soul. Trying to push him aside. With every second that passed, he felt more malevolent and evil as thoughts sprung into his mind that were not his. Alfie struggled as hard has he could possibly manage. Forcing the Shadow back out. He could see the Sword, next to the fountain, wriggling in the dirt. The Shadows face was still visible in amongst the swirling black smoke above him, its eyes bulging with effort.

Alfie willed his mind to make the Sword come to him. The Sword twitched. An understanding between Sword and Alfie rooted in his mind. Alfie smiled and the Shadow was deterred by it.

'But he can't! I've almost done it, that's impossible'—Alfie heard himself think. Except it wasn't him. It was the Shadow.

"Laravatus…" Alfie said aloud in his head. And the black oily snakes that held both his hands set alight. They recoiled into the ground squirming away. Alfie freed his hands. The swirling increased as the Shadows face contorted with effort.

'I'm almost there! It is almost done!'—Alfie thought. Then shook, that wasn't him—it was the black smoke entering his nose and mouth. He was Alfie Brown… not Shadow. He was *AlfieBrown*. A great surge of energy arose inside him. He was the only one who could end this—Alfie's left hand reached up and grabbed. Fingers closing around the throat of his enemy. Alfie pulled it closer. And he stared into the identical, but terrified purple eyes, struggling against his grip. He saw the contours of his own face and at last he could finish it.

"You *lose*…" said Alfie. Then with his last remaining ounce of energy he aimed his hand at the Akashic Sword and cried "Promoveobardus!"

The Sword launched into the air, sailing point first. It glided true.

"*WAAAAHHHHHHH!*" Screeched the Shadow louder than an earthquake. It's eyes bulged and flickered to the Akashic Sword which had pierced its swirling back, fatally. Alfie swiped his arm through the air, causing the Sword to slice through his Shadow.

Then it wailed. A huge dark mouth opening wide, letting out an exorbitant scream as the Sword's light expanded. Purple light burst from the wound as the Shadow's body began shrivelling like burning paper—the many layers on fire. The long coat, the top hat and the purple eyes all melting. The Shadows face froze, stuck in an expression of realisation that it had lost. And Alfie had won.

Then, it wilted to the floor. Sending billows of acrid black smoke into the air. A vision of a humungous tentacled beast, thrashing around violently in the smoke, collapsed and died. Dissolving away into nothing. The sky blackened with falling ash and it rained down covering the Square in grey smouldering mush.

The purple light ceased. The Sword dropped to Alfie's side. His energy, what was left, was gone. He couldn't stand and his eyes were swaying.

It was done, at last.

The army of shadow people, having witnessed a violent, unhappy death of their leader, scarpered. Faster than lightning, they ran as far away from Alfie as they could. Only Nikolas Wiseman remained face plastered with incredulity.

Alfie slowly stood and felt himself heave. The effort too much.

Faces and bodies began emerging around the Square. Curious, scared and friendly faces, in windows and through cracks in doors. The people of Magicity were coming out, now it was safe, to see who he was. Hundreds of faces stared towards him—not daring to move, or say anything.

Then, high above, there was a whooshing sound. Something in the sky was flying fast towards him. It looked like... a carpet with two people on it—one of which looked like... Nikolas Wiseman.

Suddenly Alfie understood. The carpet descended faster than light. Alfie, with his last ounce of strength, launched the Sword high into the air. The *real* Nikolas Wiseman caught the Sword and plunged it into his own shadow.

Alfie just had time to see the Wiseman's shadow burn in a huge plume of smoke, writhing to the ground. Before he felt himself fall back as the carpet landed. Hands caught him and the last thing he saw before his eyes shut... was his Dad's face. Then the sensation of flying, upwards, away and to peace.

20

The Faerie Plan

Alfie fell in and out of consciousness—one moment they were flying into the sun lit sky, the next, they were sailing through silent twilight, as the carpet surfed the clouds. His eyes opened only a fraction to see a sky full of stars twinkling brighter than a thousand dancing diamonds. His Dad and Wiseman sat cross legged upon the carpet, not speaking as they glided home.

The carpet held onto Alfie with it's tassels and as it descended he felt his stomach roll. Cold, salty air filled his nostrils as they glided low over an unmoving ocean, so quiet it could have been a vast black mirror. They landed softly, and the next second the carpet was tipping him out onto soft sand. All Alfie wanted to do was sleep—he couldn't help it. But, now his Dad was shaking him awake. Alfie stood, with help, wrenching his consciousness back to his body. They stood on tiny expanse of wet sand, minuscule waves lapping the edges of Wiseman's boots. All around was a blue mist that hung stiff, blotting out any horizon.

Alfie's Dad had his hands upon his shoulders, when he spoke his tone was soft, yet anguished. "Alfie, where… where have you *been*?"

"What… do you… mean?" Alfie mumbled.

Wiseman turned. "You've been missing for three days," he said, face hidden by his large hat. "And how on earth did you work out what to do?" Wiseman wasn't pleased, he was stern—as if Alfie had done something terribly wrong.

"Why are you asking… me this… now… here?" said Alfie wobbling.

His Dad and Wiseman exchanged a guilty look. "I've never seen you wearing those clothes before?" said Wiseman his face narrowing like a wolves on it's prey.

His Dad looked Alfie full in the face, brow furrowed. "Where did you get them? Who gave them to you? Who helped you Alfie?"

Alfie wobbled again, he just wanted to lie down and go back to sleep. "Richard Found."

Wiseman let out a hysterical noise and his Dad turned away clutching his head pacing the sand.

Alfie stood feeling more confused by the second. What were they so upset about? Did they not know what he had just done? He had defeated the Shadow! Why were they so upset?

Alfie crawled across the wet sand and lay back on the carpet, which rolled up into him wrapping him up. He turned away from his Dad and Wiseman and fell back to sleep—it was probably all a dream anyway.

Dreams and reality curdled in Alfie's brain for what could have been years. The strange sensation of flying through the night, away from the silent beach, across countryside and over glittering towns, towards a large crumbling manor house which stood as far away from any other humans as possible, hidden by large stone walls, overgrown hedges and magic. The long garden was unkempt and had fountains and statutes littering it haphazardly.

Finally Alfie woke with a violent jolt as consciousness flooded back to him. He didn't open his eyes straight away, but just lay where he was as feeling crept over him once more, he wished it hadn't for aches and pains started throbbing all over his body. For a long moment he yearned to back where had just been—the dreamworld—where he felt weightless, thoughtless, timeless and good. His muscles were sore and tight, his neck stiff and face stung. Suddenly familiar voices drifted across the room towards him.

"This house is special," said Tommy's voice. "And massive, I bet he's loaded. Have you been here before?"

"Once or twice," said Gracie's soft, warm voice that made Alfie's heart flutter. "When I was little."

"I don't like it…" said a scared voice. "Too big."—Sparky.

They were safe. Alfie breathed a huge silent sigh of relief.

Alfie, very slowly opened one eye a fraction. He saw the outlines of his best friends sitting round a stove, which seemed to be supplying the only light in the room. A tall window to the left showed only darkness and from what he could see, the room was small, cramped and filled to the brim with books. Behind his friends in the other corners of the room were large objects covered in greying, dusty cloths. The bed Alfie lay in was small but very comfortable, with a squidgy mattress and heavy silk sheets. He didn't move for a while, but listened to his friends making idle chit chat, thinking he was asleep. Alfie collected his thoughts, replaying what had happened over in his head—yet it all felt like a blur—something quite far away.

Alfie took a deep breath, then sat up blinking away the fogginess. "He's awake!" cried Sparky, they jumped up and rushed towards him.

Tommy said. "At last!"

"Do you have any idea how long we've been waiting for you?" said Gracie coming to kneel by his side.

"Why? How long was I asleep?" he said rubbing his sore eyes.

"About thirteen hours!" said Tommy smirking.

"But we've been waiting for you to reappear for *four days!*" said Gracie, who felt his forehead.

"Oi..." said Alfie. "Gerrof, I'm fine."

He smiled, it was true, he did feel fine, better than fine. "Are we at Whiteholl? Wiseman's house?"

"Yeah, it's awesome here, honestly mate, the magic things he's got working..."

"Alright, alright!" said Gracie, calming Tommy down—Alfie could tell even she had had enough of Tommy's enthusiasm over magic.

"So what happened to you guys?" said Alfie.

"What happened to us?" said Tommy. "Why don't you start by telling us what happened to you?"

Alfie shook his head. "You lot first..." he smiled.

Tommy rolled his eyes and took a deep breath, then exploded: "Well, we were all a little freaked out by the papers in the air thing in the exam hall—and when we saw you run out, well... we knew something was up. So left as soon as we could, you know amid the chaos and we went to find you. When we went into the playground, we saw all these shadow, hundreds of them all vanishing, shooting up into the air in a sort of line of black smoke. There was no one else around—I don't think—honestly if the rest of the school had seen it, they'd have *freaked out!*"

Gracie sighed impatient. "Get on with it…"

"Then we went and found Mr Sapiens in his office which is through a secret magical *LeyDoor*, Gracie got us in. Mr Sapiens was already curious because he heard people say they had seen you running away from something. Then, he contacted Wiseman, told us to wait in his office while he searched for you—but he came back and he looked sort of… frightened. He took us here. It was all a bit of a drama—apparently we weren't safe to be left alone, could have been used as hostages or something!"

"Tommy!" cried Gracie, hurrying him on.

"Ok, ok. When we got here, Wiseman didn't look good, he was on the floor being tended to by that butler man—"

"Theadore," said Sparky tutting.

"It was like he'd just had a fight… Then he told Mr Sapiens that you were in trouble and they started whispering to each other about what to do. Well, they sent us away, up here. Gracie's Dad and your Dad arrived pretty quickly after—and they all kept disappearing, and returning…"

"Looking for you," said Gracie narrowing her dark eyes at him.

"Then, on the third day…" Tommy continued. "With people all coming and going—they all got excited, Wiseman and Jonathan and your Dad, because someone had let them know that you were in Magicity. And we watched you…"

"You watched me?" said Alfie abruptly.

"On the mirror downstairs, it's like a TV but Wiseman had a live feed of Magicity Square. We watched you… couldn't see you at first, then you appeared at the top of the big rock thing—and Wiseman was pacing around with your Dad, they didn't know what to do mate. And when your Shadow turned up… well, they started arguing and all sorts... your Dad snatched up that flying carpet and tried to take off, but Wiseman caught hold and went too. Next time we saw them, they were on the screen!"

"Everyone was... flabbergasted by what you did," said Sparky slowly, adoration in his eyes.

"We've stayed up here mostly, since you got back..." said Gracie. "They're all arguing downstairs, all though for the last couple of hours its been pretty silent."

"Theadore has been bringing us food..." said Sparky happily and Alfie noted all the plates and cups piled up neatly next to the stove. "Wiseman shouted at Theadore this morning."

Alfie frowned, confused. "Why?"

"Because he found your tattered school clothes," said Tommy. "It was really weird. He said they were inside a mirror in the kitchen. They just showed up behind the surface... and he gave it to Wiseman and told him. Wiseman went crazy, started putting up spells all over the house. We could see them all whizzing through the air. Then he told Theadore that he was stupid to have taken it... we thought he was bang out of order... everyone did."

Gracie tutted and said in a diplomatic tone. "We don't know the reasons why... but I am sure he has a valid one."

Sparky, who Alfie gauged was quite fond of Theadore, sniffed.

"So..." said Tommy leaning forwards. "You going to tell us how you did it all then?" Gracie and Sparky inched forwards.

Alfie sat up a little more in bed. "I thought he'd be waiting for me," said Alfie. "The man who saved me, I was at his house for three days—he has purple eyes too, like mine."

"No way..." they chorused.

"Met him in London, on the Art and Drama trip—we sat in a café and he spoke about our eyes and magic. He defeated his

Shadow too. Well, after I learned that, I wanted to find him and ask him how I could do the same… but I couldn't. Then when I ran away from the Shadows in the school, I found the old library with the purple wall in it again… it was shining really bright. The Shadow nearly got me, but I jumped through the wall. And then I was in this like snowy forest, nearly died of cold… but *he* found me. Woke up in this great big room and he said he'd help me. He told me exactly how to get the Sword—and he wasn't wrong! I did get it!" said Alfie exuberant, then coughing as his chest wheezed. "And I thought I would see him again after, at least to say thanks…"

There was a knock on the door and everyone jumped. Theadore entered sideways, carrying a tray of tottering sandwiches, a crisp salad, fresh doughnuts and bright red strawberries. Sparky licked his lips as Theadore placed the tray on top of a pile of books, then looked up and gave a terrific start.

"Alfie!" he cried. "You're awake!" Theadore rushed across to him and shook his hands. "Well done Alfie, well done!"

Alfie thanked him, blushing a little.

"Would you like me to tell them lot downstairs, or would you like me to wait a while?"

Gracie said it was probably best if they waited a tad longer. There was a high pitched gaggle of noise as ten or so Imps flew into the room carrying four mugs, a tray with sugar and milk, which sloshed over the sides as they laughed. Sparky covered his head in his hands looking terrified. Five more came in carrying a huge pot of steaming tea and immediately poured and delivered one mug to each of them. One Imp that Alfie recognised, flittered in front of him. It was the scared one he saw when he came tumbling into Whiteholl accidentally. The

Imp grinned at him and indicated if he would like some sugar or not.

Alfie nodded. "One please…"

The Imp heaved a heavy spoon into his cup, then flew around in a circle stirring, all the while grinning at Alfie.

"That will do." Theadore called and the Imps, still giggling, flew off. "I'm glad your awake Alfie. The en-suite is through the largest pile of books on the left, if you would like to have a wash before you come downstairs just pull the book about Dragon's three times and it should let you in."

Alfie nodded and gingerly got out of bed, his span a little but he felt better than he had in a long time. Gracie spotted the book about Dragon's entitled: '*Why Slaying Dragons Is Necessary To Stop The Spread of Diseased Magick*'. She pulled the spine three times and an outline of a door in amongst the books clunked open. "I won't be long…" he said, as Sparky began tucking into the sandwiches.

It was a small dim bathroom with a sloping ceiling that caused Alfie, who was only small, to crouch. The only light a blue fire in a bracket above a big bath tub on legs. Alfie went to the sink and washed. Looking up into the mirror at his gaunt, purple reflection, he suddenly jumped, his heart skipping a beat. Behind him was a shadow—Alfie spun round raising his hands. But then with a brilliant, dawning realisation—he saw that it was *his*. The shadow now being reflected on the opposite wall… was his very own.

Theadore waited for them outside the bedroom and escorted them along the maze of stone floor, red carpeted corridors with blue fire in brackets and chandeliers floating above their heads. They walked slowly as Alfie hobbled along apologising, his left leg stinging a little. As they turned a corner a vacuum cleaner, which was operating itself, looked at them, blinked and carried on hovering. With a small pop, something large materialised above their heads, it was beating its small scaly wings furiously—it had the face of a wrinkly old man, sour and unhappy, but was the size of a baby and wore fine white clothes and sandals with a daisy chain about its head.

"Go away *Gareth*!" said Theadore in a bored voice. It glowered at them and beat off down the opposite corridor.

Finally, they came to the top of a wide staircase, opening onto a wide hall. It was a well used room, with three staircases at either ends with lots of hidey-holes, alcoves and hidden spaces, shrouded from view by long hanging drapes, with a couple of steps up or down to each one. The fireplace sat in the middle of the room, the humungous mirror Tommy had mentioned sat importantly, atop it. White stone floor reflected dancing orange flames and a large green, oblong rug sat beneath four red leather chesterfields around the fire. A bulky chandelier hung suspended in mid air, with far too much wax. Tall windows stood either side of the fireplace with long, falling red curtains. Even more pictures littered the walls. Alfie drank in the room which to him, felt warm, cozy and immensely satisfying.

Theadore directed Alfie excitedly to a table at the bottom of the stairs, where, laid out neatly were two newspapers.

The first was called: *'The Second Star'*—the headline beneath was bold and popped out into the air as Alfie looked at it.

'SHADOW SLAIN IN SQUARE BY SWORD THEIF'

The picture below it was strange. It was not a photograph but a very good pencil drawing of Alfie leaping through the air with a sword above his head. More text popped up, reading:

Lion-boy takes Magicity Sword and slays Lynch Shadow—Council on High Alert.

Lion-boy? Alfie thought curious.

"We've read them already," said Sparky quickly. "They don't know who you are, no one does, so they call you *lion boy*." he sniggered. "Because you used my mask?" he beamed.

Theadore smiled. "Actually, I think it more because of the courageousness which Alfie showed. I also think Nikolas may have had something to do with them not printing who you really are. He has been busy... Nikolas has friends in high places."

Alfie swapped *The Second Sun* for *The Daily Pendragon* which looked very different to the first, the headline still popped out into the air however.

'Boy Claims Magicity Sword, Slays Shadow Army. The Saviour?'

Unfolding the page, the bottom half was a full sized picture of a lion-faced-boy, hand drawn in pencil, but very real and scary, the fierce eyes seemed to size up the reader like prey.

"I thought perhaps you should like to keep those copies," said Theadore. "For your scrapbook. I can package them up for you?"

"No thanks." Alfie said. He couldn't explain the feeling he had—it should have felt brilliant to be on the front page of two magical newspapers—but all he felt was... numb.

Tommy huffed behind him. "I'll take them," he whispered.

"It's all anyone has been talking about," said Theadore, placing *The Daily Pendragon* back neatly. "It seems there were more sightings of Shadows recently than at any other time—now they are gone, well, people want to know who their saviour is."

"You might want to keep *these* newspapers," said Gracie smirking, she turned to Theadore and speaking in a loud whisper said—"He's never opened a wizard newspaper before." Alfie looked perplexed at her. "Just open the first page..." she said.

Alfie, frowning, opened the first page of *The Daily Pendragon*. Instantly, shapes jumped out of the pages—a huge, bold *'THE SAVIOUR?'* Popped out and hung in mid air next to the headline.

A miniature pencil drawn Magicity Square sprung up from the middle of the page like a pop up book and expanded. The Rock first, then the shops around the outside, they looked down at it as if they were the town planners taking a look a prototype for the Square. A boy with a lions head stood by the Rock, the lions mane being tussled by a soft wind. A voice rang out across the room, clear and sharp like a radio broadcast.

"There were dramatic scenes in the centre of Magicity Square today, as an unknown individual believed to be a wizard and outsider, was seen to be in a showdown with an army of what terrified witnesses claimed to be 'an army of Lynch Shadows'. Witnesses also claim the unnamed, who used a protective masking spell, pulled the ancient Magicity Sword from Rock—this being the second reported theft of the Magicity Sword in six months. Others claim however that it was actually the resurfacing of the legendary Akashic, or Excalibian Sword. The Council denies these reports however, with Councillor of Defence, Rupert Pope refusing to comment immediately. It's claimed that the so called, lion-boy, fought the Lynch Shadow and defeated it—another fact as yet denied by the Council, however Margot Shreeve gave this comment..." A voice that Alfie recognised floated into the room, making him recoil. *"Any notion that an untrained wizard, one not inaugurated by the Council or even registered as such, that enters Magicity undetected, steals the Magicity Sword and defeats an army of reported Lynch Shadows is absolutely preposterous..."*

The drawing of the lion-boy ran up the Rock and pulled the Sword out as tiny sparks of black and white thunder went off all over the miniature Square. Hundreds of Shadows floated into the Square like ghosts. The lion-boy leapt from the top of the Rock and pierced the nearest one which set alight instantly as the rest of the shadows vanished—it wasn't as dramatic as what Alfie remembered, and he certainly didn't leap off the Rock, but he was enthralled at the moving, quirky drawings.

"Later the King of Magicity came out and gave his support of the unknown individual, saying 'he's done the citizens of Magicity a great service'. This just another sign of growing friction between the Council and the King. More on the mysterious lion-boy later on with opinion divided over whether he is good or bad for the City..."

The shapes popped and dissolved, the headline fading and the drawings of the Square slithering back into the folds. A small framed picture of a man sprung up, he looked hang-dog and tired, but retained some very good looks with flyaway blonde hair—Gracie crooned as... *reported by Ulysses Sunday*, scribbled itself beneath the face.

Alfie closed the paper, the picture and the name fell back into the folds.

"Think I might keep them actually..." he mumbled.

There was a sudden babble, down one of the passages under the staircase came three voices—Mr Sapiens, Jonathan and Alfie's Dad came marching into the room talking fast.

"Well I did say..." said Jonathan loudly. "That if we told... Well hello!" said Jonathan immediately changing tone as he noticed Alfie, Tommy, Sparky and Gracie standing at the bottom of the stairs.

Mr Sapiens and Alfie's Dad came in close behind, then seeing Alfie, all three marched towards him, Alfie's Dad reached him first and gave him a rib-breaking hug.

"I am so, so glad your ok!" he said. "Do you feel ok? Sleep well?"

"Yes, yes I'm f-fine!" Alfie just about managed, after having all the air squeezed out of him and noting his Dad's black-bagged, bloodshot eyes.

Mr Sapiens beard had grown long and unkempt, his clothes unusually crumpled and untidy. Jonathan shook Alfie's hand formally and beamed. "Well done Alfie, that was some heroic performance you gave us."

Alfie blushed and thanked them all, then they stood in silence for a few moments, all looking around at each other. They all looked so tired that Alfie got the impression they hadn't slept for days, or washed for there was a feint musty aroma that filled the air. At that moment, a small white rabbit came bounding into the room.

Tommy nudged Alfie in the ribs. "Oh 'ere 'e is at last…" said Mr Sapiens taking a seat. "Now we can proceed!"

The white rabbit started to grow and morph—white fur and body being replaced by a tall thin man, with shoulder length black hair and a cowboy hat. Tommy's mouth had all but dropped to his collar.

"I am not late am I?" said Wiseman defensively.

Alfie could feel the tension in the room already with Mr Sapiens, Wiseman, Jonathan and Alfie's Dad not looking at each other. Wiseman looked towards Alfie and seemed to struggle with something internally, his eyes twitching—then he marched forwards, took Alfie by the shoulders and looked down, a worried expression on his face.

"Alfie, I must ask you to be honest with me… did you, or did you not, make a deal with *Richard Found*?"

The whole room tensed, eyes only on Alfie and Wiseman.

"How did you know?" but Alfie stopped.

Wiseman dropped his head to his chest and Alfie's Dad turned away and sat in a nearby chair. Jonathan looked flabbergasted with his mouth open wider than Tommy's.

Alfie was confused, what were they so upset about? What had he done wrong? He looked towards Tommy, Sparky and Gracie—they looked as confused as he did, but daren't say anything.

"He helped me... without him I'd be *dead*?" said Alfie slowly. No one looked up. "I killed the Shadow, I found the Akashic Sword... isn't that enough?"

When Wiseman spoke, his tone hissed with anger. "The Duchess told you, PLAIN AND SIMPLE, not to go after the Sword! Why didn't you LISTEN to her?"

Alfie was shocked by the furiousness of Wiseman's outburst as it echoed round the hall.

"You were the one who wanted me to GET THE SWORD!" he shouted back. "If I didn't get it, I wouldn't be here now!"

Wiseman threw his hands in the air. "You don't understand!"

"No I don't! Would someone please tell me what I've done wrong? The Duchess told me I couldn't find the Sword, but then Richard Found—he showed me how to get it!"

Wiseman paced in a circle muttering to himself and shaking his head. Alfie spoke slowly, trying to make them understand. "We made a deal, so that if I failed Found would die as well—he was that confident in the plan... he's killed his own Shadow before and he has purple eyes like me!"

Wiseman looked pitifully at Alfie and sighed, shaking his head.

Gracie stepped forward and dared to speak. "What's the problem here?" she said softly. "I don't get it, Alfie made a deal with someone to help him get the Sword. What's the harm in that?" She slunk back under a silent Wiseman stare.

"Alfie…" Wiseman shook his head. "You're so *naïve*."

"Oi!" said Tommy. "Don't speak to Alfie like that, if you all would have been a bit less secretive and told him what was going on from the start, then whatever this bad thing is that your so worried about, wouldn't have happened! He's had to rely on *us* all year… and me and Sparky, we are not wizards, we are just ordinary folk—and look how much Alfie has done, figured it all out by himself. It shouldn't have been like that—you all should have been there for him, like we were!"

Tommy looked fired up as Sparky sunk into the background as far as he could. The silence echoed loud with angry thoughts and prickly tension.

Alfie nodded, how could they be annoyed with him? When they had left him to feed on scraps, rumours and tit-bits?

"Found was right…" said Alfie, his tone poisonous as he turned on Wiseman. "I couldn't trust you. All you've brought me is trouble and danger. It was *you* who set the Shadow on me wasn't it?" There was a loud gasp. "I saw it…" said Alfie, voice rising. "The Shadow was set on me by the *Scarlett Council*, those people in red cloaks? You are in the Scarlett Council. *You* set it on me."

Alfie's mind was racing—he remembered the night the tentacled beast attacked him, right before Alfie was looking out of the window looking for Wiseman, who he had just seen in a bush. He hidden Nigel's memories of that night too, he had all but admitted that.

Wiseman didn't speak straight away, but chewed his lip, when he spoke his voice was defiant. "It's true, I am part of the Scarlett Council."

"WHAT ON EARTH!" Jonathan bellowed, face flashing red.

Wiseman raised a hand. "Hear me out… I did never and would never set a demon on Alfie. In fact I am offended you even think so! Can't trust me? *Ha*! Is THAT WHAT *HE* SAID!" he shouted at the top of his voice.

"Now, now…" said Alfie Dad, standing and taking charge of the situation before it completely blew up. "No one could have known that Richard Found was involved. If we did, we would all have done something about it. Alfie you are not to blame at all, for you were not to know."

Wiseman huffed and puffed, but Alfie's Dad ignored him, his face pleading with Alfie to listen.

"But the fact of the matter is Richard Found is a very dangerous individual."

"Why are you on *his* side?" Alfie said.

"I am not on anyone's side."

"Found helped me," Alfie pleaded. "He saved me, he was there for me… he gave me a plan that worked. That's more than either of you have ever done! Me and Found are the same… he has purple eyes, exactly the same as mine! He killed his Shadow too…" Alfie's Dad was shaking his head. "What?" said Alfie.

Mr Sapiens stepped forward and said gravely. "Found does not have purple eyes."

"And he didn't help you…" said his Dad. "He helped himself."

Wiseman stopped pacing, and said lightly—"He only wanted you for the Sword and now he has more…"

Alfie muttered that was rubbish and that it was Wiseman who really wanted the Sword, he was the one who took the first one from him. Wiseman marched to his fireplace and touched the nose of a stone bear that stood at either side of the mantelpiece. It's mouth opened wide, and he pulled out the Akashic Sword, thrusting it into Alfie's arms.

"If I wanted it to myself, I would've kept it and left you to die in the Square!"

Alfie held the hilt again, the cold, silky metal greeted him as warm tingles rose up his arm. "You were supposed to stop the Shadow attacking me! You said you had it at bay!" Alfie's anger bubbled in his stomach.

"Use your head!" said Wiseman hitting a chair. "I was attacked by the Scarlett Council. They took my shadow, thus the protection stopped... I could do nothing about it!"

Alfie's Dad touched Alfie on the shoulder. "Those three days you were missing, Found had you in a room didn't he? A Prism?" said his Dad, eyes narrowing.

"To keep the Shadow away..." said Alfie as even his Dad looked exasperated.

His Dad rubbed his face. "Why can't you see? It wasn't to keep the Shadow away, it was to keep *us* away!"

"That does sound more plausible Alfie," said Gracie softly.

Alfie turned away from them and stared into the fire, grinding his teeth. Why didn't they understand? "He saved me..." he said softly.

"Oh I can't stand this!" cried Wiseman, who suddenly turned on Alfie's Dad. "How you can just stand there and not tell him Bernard!"

Bernard's eyes bulged in fright, as Wiseman manically cried: "If you think Richard Found is *sooo* brilliant, then why is he the one whose been keeping your mother hostage all these years?!"

Everyone froze. Alfie stared. His breath stuck. He moved his mouth but nothing came out. Utter shock smacked him harder than any spell.

His Dad looked incandescent with rage, he was shaking, eyes narrowed murderously at Wiseman. "Dad?" Alfie muttered, his voice quivering—but his Dad turned his back on them all, shaking with rage. It was as good as an admittance.

It was too much, with everyone all looking at him—Alfie felt the tears well up in his eyes uncontrollably.

Wiseman knew he had done wrong, he looked sheepish and couldn't look up from the ground. Alfie swallowed the lump in his throat, the rage had subsided, now a great tidal wave of grief and regret burst out of nowhere. He turned on the spot and ran as fast as he could.

"Alfie wait!" some of them cried starting after him.

"Leave me alone!" he screamed back—he did not want *them* coming after him. Not now.

Alfie ran up the stairs and along the corridors, as fast as he could. He had to get away from them, away from his Dad and Wiseman. He walked fast as tears streamed down his face, he didn't know where it had come from, the grief and sadness just spilled out of him, as if they had been locked away in some deep well. Alfie kept walking, movement seemed to temporarily numb the pain.

When he was young, he had always wondered about his mother, where she went and why—a thousand explanations in his head, occupying the majority of his thoughts. A thousand times they reunited, a thousand times he would repeat different ways of saying hello. But, after so many years, the thoughts about her became less and less until months would go by and Alfie would realise that he had not thought about her at all. Then he would feel guilty and sad. He had learned not to ask about her—his Grandparents were touchy about it. And his Dad, when he used to turn up on his Birthday would disappear as soon as he mentioned anything to do with her. But now he felt sick to the stomach, because if Wiseman was right, then

Richard Found, the man who he had just stuck up for, the man who saved him—was the man who had his mother hostage!

Alfie recognised the same door to the cramped book room. He went straight through into the bathroom and splashed his face with cold water over and over pushing Wiseman's words out of his head and regaining some form of composure.

Alfie lay down on the bed. After ten minutes he paced the room, and calmed himself down, the grief had quelled, but what felt like a huge open wound had materialised inside—maybe Wiseman lied and said it just to hurt him? Or maybe they were mistaken?

His mother—was *alive*.

He shuddered, he barely knew what she looked like—all he had was one vague memory of a sweet smell of roses… maybe, but that was all.

There was a short knock at the door before it opened and Mr Sapiens walked inside. "He shouldn't 'ave said that. He was not the person to tell you." Mr Sapiens was frowning and looked uncomfortable in such an apparently intense situation.

Alfie stopped pacing. "I thought it was all over… I thought when I woke up, everyone would say well done and I could get on with my life… whatever that is."

"I know, *I know…*" he said softly. "But it seems, there were *higher forces* than ourselves at work here. The rabbit 'ole goes deeper."

"Is it true? What Wiseman said about my mother?"

Mr Sapiens brow furrowed again—he closed the door and sat down on the edge of the bed. "Your father is the one to 'tell you all 'dis… not me. You know, it could look like Nikolas acted selfishly. But I know 'im and 'e isn't like that. Trust me. He is a good guy."

Alfie chuckled. "I suppose it could be argued that he only showed an interest in you because of 'de link spotted between you and Found..."

"Why would he be interested in me because of a potential link with Richard Found?" said Alfie.

"It's not just your mother. There are lots of others Found 'as taken hostage."

Alfie gasped—"Venusias?"

Mr Sapiens nodded gravely. "Maybe 'e thought that you were the link to 'im finding his fiancée again—who knows... searching for the Faerie world can send a man mad."

Alfie blinked, thinking Mr Sapiens had perhaps made a mistake. "What do you mean Faerie world?"

"You mean you don't know what—" he looked dumfounded. "Then I 'ave said *too* much... I am sure it will be explained for all, later, when we continue talking downstairs. *Civilly.*" Mr Sapiens raised his eyebrows in his best accusing teacher face.

Alfie huffed. "I am not going down there, to talk with anyone. So you just tell me right here and now what the Faerie World is."

Mr Sapiens stood and something in the garden fixed his attention. "Perhaps you should ask you father." He pointed. Alfie stood and saw his Dad outside walking slowly around the large garden.

It was chilly outside, Alfie tucked his hands in his pockets as he traipsed across the long wet grass. The garden was huge and unkempt, with a long, high square surrounding wall. From the back of Whitehoil Alfie saw that it was almost as bad as his house, for the state it was in with tottering chimneys, bricks missing, and broken windows. It must have been early as just on the horizon, light blue sky was leaking into the night.

His Dad was sat on a big log. Alfie joined him slowly.

"So that's why you're never around…" said Alfie voice low. "You're searching for her."

His Dad gave a huge sigh and looked into the moonlit sky. "Yes. That's why. Sixteen years and I am no closer than I was then. It's ridiculous to think that you, me and your mother would—if I ever found her—all live together like normal people. But that's what kept me going." It was an uncomfortable thought, them all living together again. "I couldn't just get on with life, knowing that she was still out there… that she was alive. Of course I couldn't really tell anyone, not our *dormant* friends on the outside anyway—told your Grandparents as best I could… and I… think they understood."

"You told Grandma and Granddad that Mum was taken by Richard Found?"

"Yes. I am not sure if they believed me or not, what right minded person would?"

"So, do they know about magic?"

His Dad uttered softly. "I told them… carefully."

"Mr Sapiens said it's something to do with the Faerie world, but he wouldn't tell me what."

His Dad nodded grimly. "She was a wonderful person, she lit up a room. The most beautiful person you could ever meet. Would do anything for anyone. I know that sounds cliché, but she was the embodiment of goodness and joy. And he… he took her." He spat. "And I don't know why."

"Venusias," said Alfie. "Wiseman's fiancée too?"

"Yes. Her too…"

"Was Mum a wizard too? Like you?" Alfie was only just

realising how little he knew.

"No, no, she wasn't. She knew I was obviously… like my parents were before me. Even took her to Magicity a few times—back in the days when it was more lenient… Alfie, I am so sorry you had to find out like this."

"It's not your fault."

"I've been searching for so long that it can… send you a little mad… *I* should have told you the whole things as soon as possible, but somehow it never seemed right. Whenever I visited, you always seemed so happy—how could I pull you aside and explain all *this* to you? I had no idea you would become a wizard!" He spluttered.

"But, you're a wizard right?" said Alfie. "Doesn't that automatically make me one?"

"No, the wizard gene is recessive. Like blue eyes, or blonde hair."

"You must have thought I was… different? When you saw I had purple eyes?"

"Believe me, I intended to stay with you, or at least be near you. But certain things happened and… well, you wouldn't have been safe with me." His Dad puffed again, and Alfie shivered against the cold. "Here…" he said, putting his coat round him, which was very warm.

"Thanks…" said Alfie, grateful. "Oh, and er… I didn't mean what I said, you know back in the hall… *erm*, you did help me out… that spell you gave me worked brilliantly. Used it twice."

His Dad sniggered and Alfie asked him what he was sniggering at.

"I am glad, I am glad that's all. That I could've been of some service. I think I owe you after all these years don't you? Anyway… I was sniggering because I never, ever, in a million years thought that I would be sat here with you talking about magic… isn't it funny how life can work out."

"Yeah…" said Alfie knowingly. "I know what you mean."

"Come on," he said. "Lets get back inside. More answers await."

Alfie walked behind his Dad as they entered the hall again. Mr Sapiens, Jonathan, Gracie, Tommy and Sparky were all sat round the fire looking tired and glum.

Alfie's Dad announced. "We are ready to talk."

"I'll fetch Nikolas…" said Jonathan, marching briskly from the room.

Tommy marched across the room, looking like he'd just been asleep. "You alright mate?" he said, putting an arm round him.

"Course," he smiled.

A minute later Wiseman trotted in slowly behind Jonathan, the tail firmly between his legs. "I want to apologise to everyone for my behaviour. It was uncouth and uncalled for. And I want to…" he took a deep breath and looked up at Alfie. "I want to give my deepest apologies to you and your father. What I said was… unforgivable and not my place. I was totally out of line."

After a few more grumbles from all of them apologising to one another the air felt cleared.

Tommy, Sparky and Gracie stood from the leather chairs by the fire and hung awkwardly. Wiseman waved a hand and a small side table leapt up and waddled towards him, he clicked his fingers. The wooden side table grew, swelling into a large, grade dining table which shuffled around positioning itself. It then gave a short cough and tiny miniature chairs popped into existence, they shuffled to the edge of the table, jumped down to the floor and swelled in size until they were big enough to sit on.

"Please…" said Wiseman gesturing. "Everyone sit." Alfie took the seat in the middle, facing Wiseman. His Dad sat on his right and Tommy leapt across the room to sit on his other side.

"Shall we start? I thought we would begin with this…" His Dad held up a black and white photo. "This proves that Found is not who he told you he was."

His Dad threw the photo into the air, it hung for a moment, then shapes began to lift out of the photo and enlarge into the room. Until all around them, were people—unmoving, grainy and grey.

"Woah," said Tommy. It felt like they were being transported back in time, to a black and white party. Wiseman stood with Alfie's much younger Dad and Jonathan who stood smiling jovially for the picture. "This was the last photo took that night." His Dad stood and walked around the table. "Because, we were blown up later that evening—this place was the headquarters of the White Union. We know who blew us up that evening. I mean, it could have been several groups. But this photo proves it…" They craned their heads to see where Alfie's Dad was pointing. "If you notice here is a man whom looks pretty normal." Alfie's Dad pointed out a plump man in a tight waistcoat laughing jovially. "But, he's not who he appears to be, for if we zoom into…" his Dad twisted his hand in the air, the photo began to zoom into the mirror that hung on the wall next to the laughing man. "And, now… do you recognise him?"

Alfie swallowed. The reflection of the laughing man was different, the reflection was of a tall and thin man with a scary, devilish face—it was Richard Found. But not the Richard Found with the nice face and purple eyes. It was the same Richard Found that Alfie had seen in the mirror when he left the Prism to the MirrorWays. The terrifying, devilish face, black eyes and pointed teeth.

Now Alfie realised what the Duchess had meant when she said: *'He looks like a Devil.'*

"I was there too," said Mr Sapiens, pointing to himself. "There I am, talking to Richard Parsons near the fireplace. Found must 'av blew us up because the White Union was becoming too powerful…" he said. "We were about to challenge for Magicity Government, backed by the King and with very 'high public opinion—we 'ad already done so much good."

"That's why he took Venusias," said Wiseman into his cup. "To try and stop me, and us, doing what we were doing."

Alfie's Dad walked back round the table, and standing just behind Alfie said softly. "He must have showed himself to have purple eyes to… endear himself to you… make you both seem to have some… common connection."

His Dad was right, Alfie knew it and now a huge stone in his stomach plunged into darkness as all at once, he realised he had been duped.

Tommy gasped and looked sideways at him. "That's who you were speaking to in the café on the art and drama trip wasn't it?"

"Yeah… I left the gallery, I was bored," said Alfie. "Then I thought I saw *you Dad*." His Dad was frowning so much his eyes were at risk of not seeing anything. "I saw you walk into this bookshop, and after looking for you in there, I bumped into Found—we both noticed each others purple eyes and he took me for a drink. Told me he had killed a shadow once, then Tommy and Sparky showed up and he vanished."

Mr Sapiens tapped the table. "He can change make you see whatever 'e wants you to see."

396

"I know," said Alfie, pained to admit he was wrong.

"But..." said Jonathan, indicating the picture behind. "A mirror will always give him away."

With a swipe of his hand, Alfie's Dad made the photo disappear, the shapes flowing back to the small fold of paper which flittered back to his hand until the room returning to normal.

"I would never, ever..." started Wiseman speaking softly. "Set a demon on you Alfie. After all we've been through I thought you would have known that?" He had a look of disappointment on his face, like a scorned child. Then Wiseman heaved a huge sigh, grimacing into his cup. "But I do need to come clean on something." All eyes turned to face him. "I was infiltrating the Scarlett Council—which I can tell you, took many years..." he took a sip of dark liquid that appeared in his glass and wrinkled his face. "I already knew that Found had connections to it, he passed a lot of work and information their way. I thought it would lead me to him so I could find everyone and take them home. I was there for many years working a way in slowly. And then last year, while I was at one of their *meetings*, I found out about you. They had orders to target you. I investigated immediately because I'd never heard of an untrained boy wizard being targeted with such a strong and vicious attack!" Wiseman shook his head. "You were... way too young to have a Demon set on you—I remember thinking at the time how pointless it seemed. It didn't make any sense to me."

"What is the Scarlett Council?" said Gracie. "I've never heard of it."

"They are a collection of Seers, kept alive on a cocktail of magic and madness. They spend all their time performing daft rituals, trying to eek out prophesies and read time-slips. They see the same things as the Duchess—she reads *The Paths*. Except they are driven by evil. Not 'de sort of people you want to bump into on a dark night.'"

Alfie knew what Mr Sapiens meant as he and Tommy both shuddered.

"They seem to…" started the Wiseman hunting for the right word. "*Smell* new wizards and like to collect them. Obviously, after saving you and Thomas from the LeyDoor, I was out of the Scarlett Council—I didn't bother going back and I had to take greater precautions. They don't take kindly to being thwarted like that. It was the least I could do though, to save you both. Unfortunately, when I tried to show you Magicity through the LeyDoor, I didn't bank on a Scarlett member finding us."

"Of course!" said Alfie beating Tommy to it. "You *are* the white rabbit. But why were you trying to take us to Magicity?"

"Didn't bank on him being there either!" said Wiseman pointing at Tommy. "I wanted to see you for myself. I planned to bump into you *'by accident'* as your curiosity for the place behind the door burdened you to take a look. When you stepped through I would be there… then I just wanted to get a look at you, to try and understand why the Scarlett Council were planning to send a demon after you."

"But you still let them send the demon?"

"Nothing I could do about that—beyond my control. This had Richard Found all over it. It just took me ages to work it all out!" Wiseman slammed the table.

The mysteries from the last year toppled over each other in his head. Now, some of the blanks began to fill themselves: the Dice Duchess had said that the Desire Stone had been taken by *'the man who looked like the devil'*. Then, at Christmas the Desire Stone was on his bed—which led him to the wall in the

398

old library to Found's place—Found then told him exactly how to get the sword. Because, he couldn't get it himself. Only Alfie could. Found had manipulated him and the situation. And now Alfie had made a *deal* with him—what on earth would Found want in return?

"Richard Found is a Faerie," said Jonathan gravely. "They are so very different to us—they are an older race, they have different magic, and are inspired by the negative forces."

Wiseman nodded hard. "They're cunning, manipulative, clever race and live many, many years longer than we do. They love drama and trickery and will kill their mother if it helps their cause. To get involved with any Faerie is a hundred times worse than any demon." Alfie barely nodded as they spoke softly around him. "The problem is…" said Wiseman. "Richard Found is only half Faerie."

Gracie gasped. "What's the other half of him?"

Mr Sapiens, who was rubbing his head said: "Wizard."

There was a low dull groan from the table, but Alfie, Sparky and Tommy didn't understand. "So? Is that worse?" said Tommy.

"*Much* worse." Wiseman tapped his glass on the table and it refilled. "He can be in our world and theirs. It is an invitation to war…"

Alfie's Dad and Jonathan looked at each other as if finally convinced that Wiseman was mad. "Alfie, that note you found on your doorstep with spells on was in your trouser pockets that Found sent back. This is the right one isn't it?" he said holding it up.

"Yes. But what's that got to do with anything?"

Wiseman fished inside his pocket again and pulled out a piece of parchment. "This is a letter I received from Found many years ago." Then he passed both around the table. "The handwriting is exactly the same."

"But why *war*?" said Jonathan having inspected the letters and spell list. "I mean, I know its obvious that Richard Found did all these things but why does that mean *war*?"

Wiseman rolled his eyes and stood up and began to pace around the table. "He wanted us to know it was him. We've spent years searching for him, but it was impossible to get even close! And now he send us Alfie's things and lets us know it was him—not operating under another name when dealing with Alfie. And now... Alfie is completely and utterly indebted to him. He made a deal with Found in exchange for information on how to get the Akashic Sword and kill his Shadow. The Akashic Sword that you can only get if you have the Desire Stone—the Desire Stone that *he* took from the Dice Duchess. And of course he knew about the Shadow—he was the one who told the Scarlett Council to set it on him! Alfie is now bound by a Faerie magical contract to do whatever Found wants, whenever Found wants. He can use Alfie, his powers and the Sword against *us*—use your brain... with that Sword and Alfie under his control, they can now command the Underworld to join their side and fight for them! They have been waiting for this moment for centuries—a moment when they hold the upper hand over Humanity."

"So, let me get this straight," said Alfie feeling more than a little overwhelmed. "Found did all this... just to make a *deal* with me?"

"Of course..." said Wiseman. "Not even Richard Found could make the Akashic Sword come to him! He *neededAlfie*."

"And it's purple..." said Gracie, looking at the Sword which was propped up on the mantelpiece. "Same colour as your eyes.

Same colour as magic."

Alfie, Tommy, Sparky and looked at Gracie curiously. "What do you mean the same colour as magic?" said Alfie spluttering.

Mr Sapiens spoke in a meaningful voice. "Magic, in it's truest form, is purple."

"There is no mistake here Alfie." Wiseman drained his glass. "The Akashic Stone didn't choose you on a whim, it wasn't an accident. But now, unfortunately Found has a big hold over you and that means the Sword too."

Alfie's Dad looked grave. "You cannot dishonour a Faerie Contract… terrible things happen to someone who does."

Gracie said aloud, as if reading a poem—"If a Faerie offers you a deal or certain death, take certain death."

A silence fell in which Gracie's words echoed around their minds. "But I didn't know he was a Faerie did I?"

Alfie's Dad put a comforting hand on his shoulder. "No, you didn't. And it's nothing to be ashamed of. How on earth were you to know?"

"The Faeries use Richard Found because he can operate perfectly in this world and his own," said Wiseman standing over the fireplace. "The Faeries long term plan has always been to take back the lands that they think are theirs."

"Found is centuries old…" said Alfie's Dad. "Perhaps more. There has never been, to our knowledge another person who is both Faerie and wizard."

"The Faerie world is a very different place." Wiseman stood and looked out of the long window next to the fireplace, a stream of sunlight had just stretched into the dusty hall. Their race is a lot older than ours, so can see why they think we stole their lands—they're very territorial and hate Humanity, they're always looking for ways to wipe us all out."

Alfie's Dad took over. "Their magic is different and dangerous. The people are cunning, wise, wicked and long-lived. They have a particular thirst for blood, treachery, violence and war."

Mr Sapiens leaned forwards. "When a Faerie is close you can tell, because all the clocks turn to 11:11..."

Alfie gasped. "I've see that all year!"

Wiseman nodded sagely, chuckling. "11:11 is an indicator that their world is encroaching upon ours—or ours on theirs. They live in a state of timelessness, you could say, a non-linear, non-cyclical world of their own creation."

"And 'dat, is what makes Found different. He can come into our world at will... they prize him very highly."

Alfie remembered the first time he came to Whitehol for the meeting he had with Wiseman. "But the clocks in your house, when I first came here to Whitehol, they were on 11:11. I remember..."

Wiseman said softly: "Yes, maybe I had found a way of encroaching on their world too... when I am searching."

Then Alfie felt a sick feeling in his stomach—he had been in Richard Found's house, in the Faerie world... what if his mother was in the same building? Alfie couldn't disguise his voice cracking. "I was there wasn't I? I was at Found's house in the Faerie world in that prism room."

His Dad and Wiseman looked at each other and nodded stiffly.

"And erm..." said Jonathan, attempting to move the conversation on. "We believe the wizard government is being leaned on by Found—who himself is under orders from the Faeries."

"In the last few years they have escalated their suppression of the wizarding kind and humanity ten fold. That's why we..." he nodded towards Gracie. "Decided it was time to move away..."

Tommy leaned forward and said—"What if Found had the

whole government under a Faerie Contract, is that possible?"

"Certainly..." said Alfie's Dad. "And probable."

"The purple wall I jumped through in the old library which led to Found's place, was the same purple stone as the Akashic Stone, but led to the Faerie world?"

Mr Sapiens slapped the table. "I caught a glimpse of this myself," he said. "My theory is that Found created that wall to make Alfie willingly trust it—he already trusted the Desire Stone."

Wiseman nodded vigorously and said he agreed.

"It would have made sense..." said Alfie. "That Found created the purple wall, because I did sort of trust it. But what about the Desire Stone? It told me to... *'find Found.'"*

Tommy said earnestly—"Perhaps Found found a way of *hacking* the Desire Stone?"

Mr Sapiens hummed looking into the high roof space. "I am afraid I do not agree, there is no way Found could *'hack* the Desire Stone."

They all sat for a few seconds in silence—and yet Alfie could hear them all thinking audibly. The morning sun streamed in, waking them all to the surroundings—it was very early. As they light hit them Alfie saw just how exhausted everyone looked—a pain of guilt shot through him—that they should stay up for him.

"So what now?" said Alfie rushing ahead.

His Dad rubbed his eyes "The reason we think Found targeted you, is because of your eyes. There has long been the story, or myth, amongst wizards that one day a person with eyes the colour of magic will return, sent by magic to save magic. Found would not intercept you otherwise... he knows who and what you are. That's why he wants you... that's why he's got you."

Alfie swallowed chewing over his Dad's words.

"So what next?" said Alfie, the uncertainty clear in his voice.

Gracie cleared her throat. "You're going to have to do what no wizard has ever done *again*. You're going to have to work out a way of undoing the hold that Richard Found has over you. If I am correct, Found will use you against your own people to kill humanity's magic and we will have no weapon against the Faeries if they decide to declare war against us…"

After the conversation in Whitehall finished, they all went up to their separate bedrooms and slept until well into the afternoon. The next day they all left Wiseman's mansion through a door into Mr Sapiens office in Westbury School. From there Alfie, his Dad, Tommy, Sparky, Gracie and Jonathan walked home—Alfie had the Sword wrapped in a silk cloth in his school bag—the hilt poked out—and Alfie felt it emanating a kind of *proudness* as it bobbed along behind him.

Alfie's Dad and Jonathan walked ahead muttering to each other grimly. Tommy asked if they all had their prom outfits ready. Gracie replied exuberantly that of course she did, what a silly question. Sparky muttered something about he supposed so, but Alfie frowned.

"What, we're still doing that are we?"

Alfie could barely remember what the day was and saw the prom as inconsequential, especially after everything that had happened.

Gracie seemed to read what he was thinking. "You can still do normal things Alfie…" said Gracie, in a sardonic tone. "You have to come. What else are you going to do? Sit and home thinking about stuff."

Alfie made a face and nodded, she was right.

When Alfie returned home, flanked by his Dad, his Grandparents were fine and greeted them with a smile and an offer of tea and cake. Apparently, Alfie's Dad had told his Grandparents that Alfie was staying with him for a little while. Sitting around the kitchen table Alfie desperately wanted to tell them everything that had happened. But when they asked what they had been up to, there was a short pause and his Dad lied—"Oh, not too much."

Alfie smelt his Dad's warning—his Grandparents were not to know. Yet. His Dad left shortly after, but told Alfie once they were alone on the doorstep that they would be in touch soon and handed Alfie a piece of paper with a phone number on. "In case you need to phone me… keep me updated."

And with that he marched up the road, flicked his hands over himself and became invisible.

* * *

Alfie couldn't believe he was being dragged to the school prom. He had far more important things to be thinking about—and yet here he was, somehow convinced that it was a good idea. Alfie and Sparky hobbled together up the long driveway to the hired out room of Westbury Country Manor House, in their itchy shirts, uncomfortable jackets, choking tie and tight shoes. Alfie looked and felt like a penguin.

"Ergh," he said. "I hate this don't you?"

Sparky nodded and smiled, glad that he had someone who felt the same. Alfie and Sparky waited on the front lawn and watched idly as some flash cars came down the driveway like a procession and dropped their beautifully dressed children off. The girls screeched as they saw one another and admired each others flowing dresses—Alfie rather thought they looked like toilet roll holders. Whereas Alfie himself had received a few laughs and sneers on the way in, owing mainly to the fact that he was wearing his Granddad's clothes, which were too big for him. His Granddad had fetched a crutch for him too, one that his Granddad had spare when he fell into a hole on the allotment that *"some silly old bugger left"* and sprained his ankle. His Grandma was very suspicious about how Alfie hurt his leg, but he palmed it off, saying he fell over a loose paving stone.

Alfie leaned on the crutch which helped support his sore leg, wishing the whole thing would be over already. Soon enough Tommy arrived with Ashley DiMarco in a huge flashy car, and walked arm in arm with her across the grass. Alfie and Sparky sniggered as he joined them, leaving Ashley to join the girls.

"Alright prince charming?" said Alfie smirking.

Tommy eyed him suspiciously. Soon enough the entire school arrived. Alfie wished they would hurry for his leg was beginning to ache. The teachers arrived together—Mr Taylor-Clarke in a polka-dot suit, Mr Woodbridge wearing a trilby hat which didn't suit him, Mr Drake and Miss Cairney. Even the bullies: Frank, Bruno, Titan and Curtis turned up, in large scruffy suits and stood rather awkwardly at the side of the crowd punching each other in the arms.

A large black limo with chrome wheels rolled up the gravel driveway. Alfie sneered as Joel got out slowly—Jessica Curdle on his arm, flashing scarlet when she saw everyone watching her and tried to hide behind the car door. Then Christian who helped Gracie out of the car. Alfie's heart skipped a beat—she looked stunningly beautiful, but then Alfie always thought she looked beautiful, no matter what she wore.

The evening started with them taking seats at tables. Alfie sat in the middle of Tommy and Sparky. The starter was a chicken salad, Alfie hated salad. "Your supposed to wait for the speech!" said Sparky, who looked annoyed that Alfie had started to pick out and eat the chicken from his salad.

The Headmaster took to the stage. "I wish that you are all having a brilliant evening, but I have a few words to close the show…" He rambled on for a bit before announcing: "Now let the meal commence!"

A loud applause echoed inside the large hall, then the sound of a hundred knives and forks filled the air. After dinner, music was started by a DJ and there was much dancing.

Alfie sat alone at his table watching everyone go up and dance. He couldn't dance, he could barely walk. That was his excuse anyway. He had enough to think about, the conversation at Whitehall going round and round his head—however all was much clearer now. As the night wore on, several people came up to Alfie and had a quick chat while fanning themselves, getting a quick drink or asking him to *look after their stuff*, before returning to the dance. Then, Alfie spotted someone out of the corner of his eye. Someone he did not want to speak to—Joel Pope. "Oh, of course, you can't dance can you?" he sneered.

Alfie sighed. "No, I can't. *Unfortunately,*" he said with as much sarcasm as he could.

Joel sniggered. "Everyone thinks you're a freak because you ran out of the exam. See a ghost or something?"

Alfie sighed, if only Joel knew. Anyway this was (hopefully) the last time he'd ever see Joel. "If you don't get lost, I will make all your clothes disappear—just like I did to Mr Taylor-Clarke's…" said Alfie, and both of their gazes drifted to the man dancing manically in front of them.

"*Pfft…*" was all Joel could manage as he eyed Alfie guardedly. "What, you can do *magic* now can you Brown?" Joel snorted.

Alfie didn't say anything, but felt a wry smile creep across his mouth. *"Yeah* I can," he whispered. "But *shhh...* keep it to yourself..." he winked.

Joel didn't say anything else, but turned away with a worried expression on his face.

Alfie looked around at everyone having a good time and decided he needed some fresh air. He limped off outside to the patio area and down some stone stairs that led to a long green lawn. The moon was full and bright, beaming a silver blanket across the well kept garden. What would the future hold now? Alfie thought, as he meandered across the soft grass. People seemed to think he was different, even in the magical world, that hurt his brain. Delicate footsteps echoed behind him, coming down the stone stairs.

"Hey," called Gracie. "Mind if I join you?"

Alfie couldn't help his heart all but jumping into his throat as she stood close to him. Even though he had access to magic the whole year, none of it came close to the magic he felt inside looking at Gracie. They stared into each others eyes for a long moment.

"I've split up with Christian."

If his heart wasn't beating fast enough already, it now threatened to burst out of chest. "Oh no... *why?*" Alfie attempted with all his earnest.

"Well, he's not my cup of tea. He looks the part but he's shallow. I can't be in his company for longer than a few hours or I start getting really bored!" She sighed. "Let's lie down and watch the stars!"

Alfie lay down gingerly on the cool grass. Gracie shifted next to him, as she lay down he felt her arm brush his. A tingle of electricity rolled through his chest.

Alfie didn't know how long they lay there on that grass for and he didn't care. They didn't need to say anything, both just looking up into the night sky—silent. Wonderful. Something bright and orange suddenly flashed across their vision.

"A shooting star!" said Gracie.

Alfie turned his head. "Make a wish."

There was a rustling in one of the bushes ahead of them. "What is it?" said Gracie, hugging his arm tightly.

Alfie looked closer. "I don't know, must be a rabbit or a fox or something." But then, he saw it. Whatever it was had a decadent patten all over it, was big and had golden tassels. "It's my flying carpet!" said Alfie amazed as it broke free of the bushes and sailed silently across the lawn towards him—laying down before his feet, the golden tassels appearing to wave at him. "You didn't wish for that did you? If you did it was flipping quick!" said Alfie causing Gracie to splutter aloud.

"Not quite," she said making sure to gaze knowingly towards him.

"Climb on," he said—Gracie didn't need a second invitation. "Where do you want to go?" said Alfie sitting next to her on the carpet as it began to rise of the ground a few inches and glide slowly around the lawn.

Gracie suddenly gasped and pointed. Alfie and Gracie's shadows cast from the moon behind them stretched long across the lawn as they hovered. Alfie's shadow leaned across the shadow carpet. Their two shadow lips met and kissed in the moonlight. Alfie felt his face grow hot and red in the moonlight, even though he hadn't done anything.

"Ah brilliant!" called a loud voice splitting the tension. It was

Tommy who spotted them at the top of the stone stairs and came sprinting across the grass. "Wow! It's the carpet!"

Sparky, who was anxiously waiting at the top of the stairs in case anyone else should see them, came down too. "Some of the teachers are trying to comfort Christian, because he's crying..." said Sparky glancing up at Gracie who sighed—Alfie wasn't sure if it was because Christian was crying or because Tommy and Sparky had joined them and ruined their moment.

The carpet settled down on the grass and they all lay together, gazing upwards. Tommy took a deep breath and gazed above at the starlit sky. "What a year."

Sparky nodded stiffly. "If you would have told me everything we now know at the start of the year, I would have called you all mental!"

"You did many times," said Tommy.

"I know..." said Sparky. "I thought when I moved here that I would keep my head down, get the exams done and leave finally. But meeting you guys has been... well... I've never been very—*adventurous* and I've never really had any proper friends. The last year has been crazy, and strange and scary and weird. But I wouldn't change it for anything!"

They all smiled, Sparky looked emotionally spent and fumbled with the carpet tassels.

Gracie said quietly. "And you'll always have us Alfie. Through everything."

Alfie felt so happy in that moment he could have stopped everything. "Weird isn't it?" said Alfie. "That a shadow can just bugger off and do what it likes!"

They all laughed.

Alfie sat up and looked around at his best friends. "So, where do you want to go?"

* * *

As Alfie and his friends flew screaming into the night sky, someone emerged from the bushes. A tall smartly dressed man with purple eyes pushed through the bush and stood on the lawn, watching the boy leave. As he did, his eyes changed colour from purple to black—his handsome face sharpened: his ears became pointed, his nose longer, his cheekbones more pronounced and his hair long and straggly. Richard Found smiled to himself—the job was all but done.

Did you enjoy reading?

If you enjoyed it then I would be honoured if you shared your thoughts via a review.

They are the lifeblood of an Indie authors career and give some social proof so that others, like you, will be able to find it on Amazon and take the (tiny) gamble to download, read and enjoy it.

I would **really, really, really** appreciate it!

Thank you for supporting my work! :)

About the Author

Jack Simmonds was born in London U.K where he still lives, writes and drinks tea. Lots and lots of tea.

I love to hear from my lovely readers! — You can connect with me at the links below. If you would like to contact me about anything, then please email :)

I look forward to hearing from you.

EMAIL: jack@jacksimmondsbooks.com

Go to my website: jacksimmondsbooks.com for a great free book offer.